LOKI'S
RING

LOKI'S RING

STINA LEICHT

SAGA PRESS

LONDON SYDNEY **NEW YORK** TORONTO NEW DELHI

SAGA **S** PRESS

AN IMPRINT OF SIMON & SCHUSTER, INC.

1230 AVENUE OF THE AMERICAS, NEW YORK, NEW YORK 10020

First Saga Press trade paperback edition March 2023

SAGA PRESS and colophon are trademarks of Simon & Schuster, Inc.

For information about special discounts for bulk purchases, please contact Simon & Schuster Special Sales at 1-866-506-1949 or business@simonandschuster.com.

The Simon & Schuster Speakers Bureau can bring authors to your live event. For more information or to book an event, contact the Simon & Schuster Speakers Bureau at 1-866-248-3049 or visit our website at www.simonspeakers.com.

Interior design by Hope Herr-Cardillo

Manufactured in the United States of America

1 3 5 7 9 10 8 6 4 2

Library of Congress Cataloging-in-Publication Data has been applied for.

ISBN 978-1-9821-7063-9
ISBN 978-1-9821-7065-3 (ebook)

Dearest ladies and NB friends,
it seems the patriarchy is still standing.
Maybe we go for both knees this time?

And as always
for Dane:
As you wish

1

The primary distribution hub for the Jemisin Halo Generator in Beta Sector was in danger of exploding, and if Captain Gita Chithra didn't stop it, the ensuing disaster would destroy the local solar system and every living being within it.

No pressure, Gita thought to herself.

The system contained uninhabited gas giants and a relatively small black hole designated Beta-X45J. The black hole's manageable size made it an ideal energy source. It was also conveniently located along a high-congestion spacing route. These qualities were what made the halo generator lucrative. They were also what made it a hazard; starships congregated in the sector at all hours. Currently, that traffic was being cleared and rerouted, but due to high volume, a full evacuation was impossible. The distribution hub would succumb to the inevitable before everyone could get out.

Gita could just hear her mother's commentary on her life choices. It was an old argument that followed the same script almost every time they spoke.

You must move on with your life, Jaanu.

I love you, Mata. I do. But I'm forty-six years old. I'm not a child anymore. I haven't been for a long time.

I am your mother. You will always be my child. I want nothing but your happiness.

I am happy.

Your family needs you. Come home where it is safe. Work for me. You have considerable skills, and you're wasting them out there. You don't have to spend the rest of your life alone grubbing for—

Mata—

You were always difficult. Why must you be so hard on yourself? Why can't you be more like Inimai? My only wish for you is a successful career. Happiness. A real family. Inimai says—

Inimai was Gita's oldest sister and their mother's favorite. The perfect daughter.

Are you implying my children aren't real?

During graduate school, Gita had volunteered twice to pair with sentient artificial intelligences. The process of partnering involved the surgical installation of an electronic storage unit inside a human brain. Once the human volunteer healed, a newly formed digital entity was downloaded onto the device and activated. In this way, the artificial entity developed much like a human child would. They observed human social interactions and developed their own personality. Gita equated it with pregnancy—only instead of months, digital gestation took years. And like pregnancy, partnering could be dangerous to the human party. Still, when it came to learning how to navigate safely with humans in the physical world, partnering was the fastest, most accurate method.

Don't twist my words, Jaanu. That is not what I meant. I love Ezi and Ri. They are my grandchildren in every way. I worry for you, that is all. You must stop reliving the past.

Gita squeezed her eyes shut in an attempt to block out the rest. Parents. It was bad enough arguing with them on holidays. Why did they have to live inside your head, too?

What was worse was knowing deep down that her mother might have a point.

Gita's chest felt heavy and tight. *No.* Her mother *couldn't* understand. No one seemed to. But there had to be a way in which this situation could turn out right. With everyone safe. She'd graduated with honors from the Terran Republic of Worlds' premiere tactical-emergency-response program. She'd been trained to analyze emergency situations from all angles.

Every problem has a solution. Be creative.

There must be a way.

Speaking louder than normal so she could be heard over comm static—and maybe to block out her internal dialogue, too—she asked, "Is the containment field ready? Miranda?"

The original plan called for Gita and the human members of the team to remain on board the shuttle, *Ariel*, while the drones entered the generator facility. Human beings didn't fare well in close proximity to black holes. *Mind you, black holes aren't great for drones, either.*

Sentient artificial intelligences—that is, Artificial General Intelligences—had been awarded personhood by the Terran Intergalactic Conference of 2532. But AGIs were still employed in dangerous, even deadly conditions, because in a worst-case scenario, a drone could be rebooted using a backup. The drone might lose a few minutes of recorded memory, but that was all. Such an event was costly, but it was hardly fatal or even painful. However, there was considerable debate in philosophical circles as to whether it was really the same drone if one replaced both the physical unit and the artificial personality it contained with a version that was technically incomplete.

In general, she tended to leave that discussion to those in charge of overseeing the legal and spiritual affairs of artificial persons. In the specific, she preferred to let those affected decide for themselves, as was their right.

Had letting go been the right thing to do?

You're allowing your self-doubt to get in the way. There's no time for this.

Gita shifted closer to her float screen and bumped the coffee mug near her left elbow. Reminded that she hadn't finished it, she took a swallow and grimaced. *Cold*. She couldn't reheat it. Again, there was no time.

She exhaled the scent of stale coffee. "Hello? Can anyone hear me?"

"I can hear you," Mandy said from the console on her right. Like Gita, Mandy was from Septa. Her serene, almost monotone delivery was an artifact of her northern central continent origins.

Gita sighed. "I was talking to Miranda and Ferdinand."

"Oh," Mandy said, continuing to scan the lines of data on her projected float screen. Her round, tawny face was framed with wisps of straight black hair that had escaped the thick braid trailing down her back. Calm, good-natured humor drifted around her like a pleasant perfume.

Returning her attention to the problem at hand, Gita considered the options. This time she'd chosen to send the two drones out on their own in hope that it would make securing the emergency force field more efficient, granting more time for starships to flee.

A devastating cascade of errors was responsible for the accident. It'd probably originated with something small—a faulty monitoring panel or an overloaded sensor in the Jemisin distribution hub. Of course, this didn't explain why the resident artificial person hadn't already taken care of the problem, which was why Gita had asked Mandy to check the recent systems reports and AGI functionality metrics. Normally, Gita would be the one to go over them, but with Karter and the others gone,

Gita had more responsibilities than time. Redundancy was standard in extraplanetary engineering—Terran Republic of Worlds regulations required it. In case of emergency, everyone needed to know how to do at least one other crew member's job. Mandy had been working for AGI repair certification since joining the crew. It was time to test those skills.

"Hello?" Gita asked again. "Miranda? Ferdinand? Can you hear me?"

More static.

"Sycorax, can you boost my signal?" Gita asked.

"Beta-X45J's proximity is interfering with communications," *The Tempest*'s artificial person answered, her reply salted with a crisp Nigerian British school accent. The starship and its resident AGI had been designed and built by Nwapa Starship and Space Dock, one of the best shipwright companies on Terra, which was headquartered in Lagos, Nigeria.

Everything was glitchy in the vicinity of a black hole—not that anyone was dumb enough to cut it *that* close. It was best to stay on the other side of the Hopkinson Safety Zone.

Unstable magnetic fields and gamma radiation bursts aren't great for communication channels either, Gita thought. *Maybe it's time to implement a work-around.*

Sycorax said, "A signal boost will now be employed with a noise reduction filter."

Gita tilted her head and paused. "Still detecting a great deal of interference."

"I'm afraid it's the best I can do." Sycorax's apology sounded sincere.

Sighing, Gita made yet another attempt to communicate with the drones. "Miranda? Ferdinand? Are you there?"

"Don't strip your seals, boss," Miranda answered. "We hear you."

"Oh. Good." Gita breathed out her relief. "What's the progress update?"

"Containment amplifiers four and five are in place and secure," Miranda reported. "One remaining."

"Ticktock," Mandy said, still tracing lines of data with her eyes.

"Do you want to come out here and do this instead?" An electric, dry humor crackled in Miranda's question.

"I'm good," Mandy said.

Gita felt a faint smile tug at the corners of her mouth. She was lucky. She had a good team.

Space walks were physically taxing, even for those without disabilities, and while Mandy's osteoarthritis and osteoporosis were well managed by the medical nanobots in her bloodstream, the conditions weren't curable short of bone replacement—a painful and time-consuming process that wasn't worth going through if one intended to continue working in space. As a result, Mandy couldn't visit planetside. Medbots were great for managing myriad health issues, but they couldn't reverse damage already accrued.

Luckily, Mandy didn't even remotely miss Septa, nor did she have an urge to go outside the ship.

Miranda continued. "I'm happy to sit on my ass and pilot a computer console."

"You don't have an ass," Mandy said.

"I do have a bottom," Miranda countered.

"That's true," Mandy said. "I sit corrected."

"What about Ferdinand?" Gita asked in an attempt to cut their shenanigans short.

"I'm fairly certain he has one, too," Miranda replied.

Gita asked, "Every ship in Beta Sector is in danger of being wiped out entirely, and you two are fixated on butts?"

As ridiculous as it was, this conversation reminded her of how much she missed Miranda.

"Sorry, boss," Mandy said.

"Ferdinand is investigating the issues with the navigation jets." A hint of the drone's defensiveness filtered through the static. "He'll send a report as soon as he returns from his trip on the black hole side of the distribution hub."

"Thank you, Miranda." Gita shifted her attention to Mandy. "What about you?"

"Containment field is a go." Mandy glanced away from her screen. "Ready to engage as soon as the amplifiers are in place."

"Excellent," Gita said.

"Ferdinand has drifted from his point of contact with the distribution hub," Sycorax reported, restricting her response to the shuttle's intercom. The bulk of the emergency evacuation organization had fallen to her, and she was monitoring the job from the vicinity of the refueling station. "His navigation system appears to be malfunctioning."

"Miranda?" Gita asked. "What do you have?"

"I've anchored the last amplifier," Miranda answered. "You may deploy the containment field."

"Engaging containment field," Mandy said.

"Excellent, Miranda. Please check on Ferdinand before you return to the shuttle." Gita was growing worried.

"His last check-in indicated that he had replaced navigation jets six and seven," Miranda replied. "You are good to begin testing."

"Mandy?" Gita asked.

"On it," Mandy said. After a short pause, she continued. "Containment force field fully engaged and stable."

"Perfect." Gita almost relaxed.

"Uh. Oh."

"What is it, Mandy?" Gita asked.

"You're not going to like it."

Gita's stomach tightened. *What's wrong now?* "Just tell me."

Miranda interrupted the conversation. "Oh, shit. Damn it, Ferdinand."

"Report," Gita said.

"He's drifted too close to the accretion disc." Miranda sounded upset, on the verge of panic. "I can't retrieve him. And his propulsion system is malfunctioning."

"Shoot." Gita briefly paused. She couldn't afford to let her fear show—it would affect the others.

Every problem has a solution. She repeated it in her head like a mantra. "Do you have a tether line with a clamp?"

"I have two," Miranda said. "One might be long enough, but I don't know that he can grab it. His readings indicate widespread system failure."

"Use both. And engage the magnetic clamp," Gita said. It might risk Ferdinand's internal memory systems, but it was that or lose the drone altogether. "Do whatever you have to—just don't get too close. Let me know at once if another obstacle comes up."

"Yes, boss."

"Mandy," Gita said. "You're on."

"We have another problem." Mandy almost frowned.

"You said that fixing the navigation jet failure would resolve the issue." Gita had known there was more, but this was how things were done.

"It did," Mandy said. "There's a reason the hub's artificial person didn't correct it on their own."

"And?" Gita asked. *Here it comes*.

"There's a code glitch."

"What kind of glitch?" The knot in Gita's stomach tightened painfully. She winced. *There's no time to reprogram an artificial person, let alone reboot them. That isn't the solution.*

Even if they agreed to let me do such a thing.

Assuming I would do it, which I won't. I can't.

Mandy answered, "It's not that bad. An update for a peripheral neuromorphic string. No need to talk them through it. Copy, paste. They won't even notice. A hard reboot isn't necessary."

"Nonetheless, I won't approve," Gita said. "Not without their consent."

"Talk to them then. But you're making this a bigger problem than it is."

"I'm not."

"It's a trivial correction they'd have done themselves if they'd noticed," Mandy said. "They won't care."

"Would you mind if someone cracked open your skull and rewrote your thoughts?" Gita asked. "Without even telling you what they were doing?"

"No need for you to rewrite it," Mandy said. "I've already done it."

"Wait. How? You aren't familiar with Advanced Virtual Personality Coding or even Russ programming languages." *I hate this part.* Gita's heart was hammering against her breastbone. She felt a little nauseous. Her eyesight began to fluctuate between sharp and fuzzy in time to her heartbeat. She risked briefly shutting her eyes to center herself. *It's only adrenaline.*

After five deep breaths Gita opened her eyes. *Stay focused. It's fine. You've done this hundreds of times. Every problem has a solution.*

"I've been studying AGI programing in addition to repair," Mandy said.

"Why?" Gita asked.

"In case."

"In case of what?"

"In case," Mandy said with emphasis.

Gita understood. The redundancy safeguard.

But reprogramming artificial personalities isn't my job, Gita thought. *Only rehabilitating and rescuing them. There's a distinction.*

She *did* have multiple degrees: neuromorphic engineering, advanced artificial general intelligence theory, artificial behavioral medicine and practices, as well as developmental psychology of quantum-neuromorphic hybrid computers. *But there's a line between helping and reprogramming.*

Mandy couldn't guarantee the artificial person wouldn't be harmed by her update. AGIs were infinitely complex. External interference could inadvertently introduce unintended results in the neuromorphic matrix. While not in any way a human brain, neuromorphic computing paths had been patterned after human neurons. That meant connections were formed organically and spontaneously. This was, obviously, both an advantage and a disadvantage.

If anyone understood the repercussions of such mistakes, it was Gita. *But do I honestly have any other options?*

Keep stalling and you won't have this option either.

A burst of loud static interrupted her thoughts.

". . . got him!" It was Miranda. The drone's communication signal grew stronger as she approached the shuttle. "Ferdinand is safe!"

"Excellent," Gita said. "How bad is the damage?"

"Pretty bad. I'm keeping him on the tether. He can't communicate or move on his own," Miranda replied. "But I can't risk pulling him in too close, or he'll contaminate me, too."

Gita said, "Go directly to *The Tempest* for a full decon.

Ariel doesn't have the equipment. It's a long journey, I know. Do you think you can get there before the clock runs down?" *At least Miranda will be safe and out of the way.*

Miranda replied, "Piece of pie."

"Cake," Mandy muttered.

"Have you ever had pie?" Miranda asked.

"Of course," Mandy said.

"What kind?" Miranda asked.

"All kinds," Mandy said.

"I wish I could eat pie." Miranda sighed. "It looks delicious."

"You have no mouth," Mandy said.

"A drone can dream, can't she?"

"Can you?" Mandy asked.

"A reference to electric sheep is de rigueur, is it not?" Miranda replied. "Ferdinand and I are on our way home. Good luck, boss."

"See you there," Gita said.

Mandy rotated in her chair. "The replacement jets won't resolve the larger issue. You know that. If you can't do what has to be done, I'll have to."

Gita swallowed. *You did this to yourself, remember.* "You're sure about the update?"

"You could check it, but there's no time." Mandy paused. "You'll have to trust me."

Mandy wasn't one to overestimate her abilities. If she was sure about something, she was sure.

"What about beaming the data over?" Gita continued to balk. "They could install the code themselves."

"With the noise on the channel, we can't guarantee the string will be intact when it arrives. The artificial person would have to filter and recheck the data package. And we both know there's no time for that."

"It has to be walked over," Gita said, resigned.

"Afraid so."

Miranda can't leave Ferdinand on The Tempest *and return in time to deliver the package. Not now.* "Place a second copy of the string in a glass chip. Wrap protected. I want backup," Gita said. "How much time do we have?"

"If you leave now, you can get there and back." Mandy transferred a copy, as requested. "Don't take too long. If the distribution hub explodes with you inside, you'll—"

"I know."

"—and the longer you're soaking in the radiation—"

"I know."

"You're sure you don't want me to do it?" Mandy held the glass chip just out of reach.

Gita got to her feet and put out a hand. Mandy placed it on her palm. Then Gita took a deep breath, held and released it, grounding herself in the moment. She closed her fingers around the small glass drive and headed to the airlock. Along the way, she was tempted to use a few choice words, but only briefly. She was Hindu and did not curse. Other people would. But unlike other people, she understood that it wouldn't make her feel any better. It would only bring unnecessary bad energy into her life.

And right now, I need all the positive energy I can get.

Dressed in her environment suit, she sealed the inner door. Mandy waved and mouthed the words *good luck!* Gita nodded, then locked her helmet in place and synced her HUD clock to ship time before facing the outer hatch.

"Mandy, can you hear me?" she asked, starting the series of checks required before exiting the ship.

"Comms are go."

The reading on Gita's helmet display indicated the suit was fully charged. "Batteries are go. Oxygen levels are optimal. Running a seal check." Using the helmet interface, she initiated the rest of the safety checklist. It added seven minutes, but she knew better than to skip it. She'd seen too many accidents, and space wasn't a forgiving environment. *Especially not today*.

Finally, she tapped the heels of her mag boots together. The soles gripped the deck with a small but satisfying *ka-thump*. She yanked her tether one last time to test it, then depressurized the airlock. With that, she punched the button that would open the outer pressure hatch. The difference in temperature was dramatic. She could feel the cold in her hands through the gloves, the thinnest part of the suit. Nervous, she patted the arm pouch where she'd put the drive for safekeeping. "Do you have the security codes?"

Mandy asked, "You want them now?"

"It's not like reception will get any better once I'm outside." Gita's HUD indicated that the code had been transferred to her suit computer. "What are the artificial person's name and pronouns?" While not all AGIs employed names or genders, this one did. Courtesy would help initiate trust, and she needed to establish a rapport as quick as possible.

"Abeque," Mandy said. "Pronouns are they/them."

Unable to delay any longer, Gita connected her tether to the loop on the hull beside the door, closed the hatch behind her, and proceeded across the boarding ramp to the distribution hub. The magnets in the soles of her boots kept her pace slow and deliberate. Floating would be faster, but rushing in might frighten Abeque. The time crunch meant that she had only one chance to establish trust. The situation called for exactitude.

The interior of the station had been painted an antiseptic white and gray by the original manufacturers—radiation-resistant paints weren't known for their decorative range of colors. The pipes lining the walls were color coded—blue for coolant, yellow for electric, and so on. Energy collected was stored in rows of massive batteries the size of *Ariel*. The interior of the station, while sealed, contained no atmosphere. Artificial gravity wasn't in use either. Abeque didn't require any of these things in their day-to-day operation of the distribution hub. However, human inspection teams conducted regular systems checks. Sometimes those inspections were done in person because, while artificial persons were designed for a certain amount of self-sufficiency, even they got lonely. This was an integral part of their construction. A totally independent artificial person might result in unpleasant complications, after all—or so the current theories indicated. This was one reason why all new artificial personalities were partnered with humans. Partnering was far more efficient than coding the billions of incremental conscious and unconscious decisions that humans made every moment of every day. Personalities based upon neuromorphic matrices learned best by example and direct experience—not unlike humans themselves.

Gita accessed the security pad. There were other safety and security measures in place at the entrance, but since she was expected, those had been deactivated by Henderson Energy's home office.

"Hello? Who's there?" Abeque's pitch was neutral, and their accent was Daithen. Gita couldn't detect their exact geographic origins. Like many human-inhabited planets, Daithe had thousands of dialects and regional accents.

"Hi, Abeque. I'm Gita Chithra. I'm here to help you."

"Do I need help?"

"I'm sure you've noticed that the energy loads here are quite high."

"It is customary to wait until storage is full before transmitting energy to the next distribution hub. The pathway must be clear of obstruction. And there is less risk of accident if the number of transfers is limited."

"That makes sense." Gita avoided reading the blurry neon-green numbers in the corner of her left eye—the countdown clock. The pressure to rush wouldn't help, and neither would panic.

"The log indicates your visit was recently added to the schedule," Abeque said. "Is this an inspection?"

"I'm afraid not."

"You are not on the list of inspectors, and the timing *is* unusual."

"May I come in?"

"Your credentials have been verified. Welcome, Captain Gita Chithra of Juno-7 SAR and cocaptain of the starship *The Tempest*."

Captain. Not cocaptain. Their information is out-of-date. Gita decided this was unimportant.

Abeque continued. "Shall I initiate the life support systems for your comfort? This may take some time."

"No need," Gita said. "I won't be here long."

With her palm flat against the hull of the distribution hub, she felt the security lock uncouple with a pronounced, soundless thump. Once inside, she unclipped her tether, and the hub's outer pressure hatch closed behind her. She understood it wasn't all that far to the hub's command center, but somehow the distance seemed to stretch out forever. The spot between her shoulder blades itched. She was sweating, and her heart raced as she moved carefully down the pipe-lined passage. She tried not to think of the radiation she was currently absorbing. Attempting to steady her breathing, she concentrated on what she would say and how she might say it. Diplomacy was key.

"Your heart rate is high. How are you doing?" Mandy asked through the private ship-to-suit comm channel.

"I'm fine," Gita said.

"Are you there yet?"

Gita heaved the last pressure hatch open with a grunt. "I am."

"The AGI access console will be on the left," Mandy said. "Along the wall."

Scanning the rows of electronic instruments and screens, Gita spotted the control panel in question, but when she stepped up to the console, a holo of an androgynous human with long, dark brown hair; brown eyes; and medium brown skin appeared. They were dressed in a green-and-yellow Henderson Energy uniform.

"Hello, Captain Chithra," Abeque said. "I hope you don't mind my assuming this form." They motioned to themself. "I have found that projecting a human body smoothes communication between me and the maintenance team. Humans expect and employ hundreds of nonverbal cues when speaking. This will optimize communication."

Gita replied, "Thank you. That *will* make things easier."

"However, if you have another, more comfortable preference—"

"I don't. Why do you ask?"

"Your heart rate is quite high." Abeque tilted their head to the right. "Is there a problem?"

Now is the time to try something new. Be honest, Gita thought. *It's not as if an artificial person can panic.* "There is."

"An emergency? I understand that the SAR designation stands for Search and Rescue."

"This station will explode in a few minutes. I'm here to prevent that."

There was a short pause. The hologram placed a hand to their chin and stared at the ceiling as if in thought. "I have consulted my monitoring systems." The hand dropped away from their face. "There are no indications of catastrophic meltdown. All readings appear normal, and functions are within recommended parameters. Perhaps you should reexamine your data. Someone somewhere missed something."

"That's what I came to discuss with you."

Another silence stretched out between them. Abeque's expression grew serious. "Go on."

At that moment, Mandy spoke over the private ship-to-suit comm channel. "Can you speed this up?"

You can't rush trust, Gita thought. *It's best to not assign blame. Keep it neutral.* "There is an issue with a neuromorphic string."

"Impossible," Abeque said. "I do not make mistakes. You should check your figures again."

"The situation isn't your fault," Gita replied. She closed her right fist around an urge to rush. "It is possible that a human entered incorrect data during the last routine visit."

"Again, that is not possible," Abeque said. "I self-regulate my programming. I would've noticed such an error."

"Have you heard of the expression 'you can't see the forest for the trees'?"

Abeque blinked. "There are no trees on this distribution hub."

"I was speaking metaphorically."

Mandy interrupted from the private channel. "Seriously, boss. You need to get out of there."

"Ah. I understand," Abeque said. "You believe that the problem is not apparent to me because I am too close to it."

"Exactly," Gita replied. "I need to replace the string. If I don't, you will be destroyed along with this distribution hub, the fueling depot, any nearby planets, and ships remaining in this sector. We have installed a containment field, but it is uncertain how much of the explosion will be deflected. As it stands, you will not survive."

Again, Abeque paused.

"Don't worry," Gita said. "The safety scans have been executed. The new string is clean."

Mandy said, "Jam the thing in and go. You have twenty seconds to start back."

Gita ignored Mandy and continued addressing Abeque. "Please. We must hurry." She held up the glass drive.

"I'm not joking," Mandy warned. "If you don't get out now, you won't make it to the ship in time for us to reach minimum safe distance."

She's unusually chatty. Gita turned her head and whispered privately to Mandy. "Are Miranda and Ferdinand aboard *The Tempest*?"

"Yes."

"Good. Take *Ariel* back to the ship and have Sycorax retreat to minimum safe distance."

"What?! I won't—"

"That's an order," Gita said.

"You can't issue orders," Mandy countered. "This isn't the military."

"Take my ship out of the danger zone," Gita replied. "I mean it." And then she closed their private comm channel.

Abeque said, "I have a question."

Gita switched her attention back to the artificial person. She willed herself calm. "Go on."

The hologram paced the room twice. "If the matter is urgent, why haven't you installed the new code? Why waste time talking to me about it?"

"Because I won't touch your programming without your consent."

"But according to you, if you don't do this, everyone in this sector dies."

"As I mentioned before, the containment field might mitigate the explosion. Not everyone will die. Many will, surely. You and anyone on this distribution hub, absolutely."

"You are the only person besides me on this installation."

"Exactly."

"You have strong convictions."

"I suppose I do."

"May I ask why?"

It was Gita's turn to hesitate. "I used to partner new artificial personalities. Suffice it to say, that is a line I will not cross."

Abeque gazed up at the ceiling.

Gita dared to glimpse the clock on her HUD. *This all hinges on how long it takes Abeque to decide.*

"I grant permission for you to install the string." The hologram motioned to the command console. A green indicator light above one of the drive slots lit up. "The appropriate access port is ready."

"Thank you." Relief poured over Gita like a bucket of ice water. Her knees felt a bit loose as she stepped closer to the console. "I have provided the original string data in a second file. That way you may compare the two, if you'd like. After the new string is installed, of course." She inserted the glass drive and waited.

"Why is your ship leaving?" Abeque asked.

Thank you, Mandy, Gita thought. "Because this may not work, and if it doesn't, I don't want my crew to die."

"You've decided to stay?"

"Yes."

Another indicator light blinked on, showing that the glass drive was being accessed.

"What if I had refused to allow the installation?"

Gita motioned to the main command screen displaying the black hole. "Then I would take in the view until it was over."

"Why stay?"

"No one should die alone." *How long will this take?* Gita thought. *Am I too late?*

"I don't know what to say." Abeque's hologram blinked. "Except, thank you."

"You're welcome."

"Are we going to die?"

"I suppose that's debatable in your case. Do you have a final directive document on file?"

Abeque nodded. "My backup will activate upon my deletion."

"Oh, good."

"What is it like to die?"

These were the same questions that Ri, the first artificial personality that Gita had partnered, used to ask. Ri hated goodbyes so much that sometimes Gita wondered if Ri had picked up her own abandonment issues. *How did that happen? Through osmosis?* Gita had been so careful—or so she'd thought.

For a moment, she couldn't breathe. "Honestly, I don't know. No one does, not as an absolute certainty." She paused again. Her next question would be considered bizarre by some. "Do you have a spiritual practice?"

Abeque tilted their head. "I have not given the matter consideration."

"I believe that everything and everyone in the universe is a representation of the Supreme Being. Therefore, we're all part of a whole. Connected. This includes the inanimate. On a subatomic level, all matter is comprised of electrons and quarks, after all," she began, adopting the reassuring tone she'd used with Ri all those times. "In addition, I believe in reincarnation. As an aspect of the Supreme Being, souls do not die. They're reborn into another body."

Abeque narrowed their eyes. "Do artificial persons have souls?"

"I believe the answer to that is yes."

"Why?"

"Because you're sentient. And I have to believe all sentient beings have souls."

"You don't *have* to. Unless things have changed dramatically in the Terran Republic of Worlds recently, there is nothing you are forced to believe."

"Then, let's say I believe it because my sense of what is right tells me so. Because believing any sentient being does not have a soul leads to harmful actions."

"Does it?"

"Historically, yes."

"Interesting." Abeque was quiet for a few seconds. "And artificial persons are parts of the universe, even though we are mostly made of code?"

"Absolutely."

The relief on Abeque's face was obvious. "Good."

As Gita watched, the countdown clock on the left side of her HUD decreased to single digits. It felt good to have comforted Abeque. Gita shut her eyes just before it turned red. *Well, it's been nice.*

Nothing happened.

"Interesting," Abeque said. "It appears you were correct."

Gita opened one eye and then the other. "I have to sit down now." She staggered to a nearby chair and collapsed into it, feeling wobbly like a drone whose stabilizers had cut out without warning.

At that moment, the room vanished in a painfully

bright light. Gita threw her hands up to protect her face in a useless gesture.

Six seconds passed, and then Sycorax said, "This is where the scenario ends."

Gita wiped tears from her eyes. "And the butcher's bill?"

"Same as before. With your own death added."

"And *The Tempest* got away?"

"It did."

"Good."

"I don't understand," Sycorax said. "You wouldn't have saved any more lives than you did in the original situation. Merely different ones."

"Is that so?" Gita got to her feet. She wasn't sure how she felt. *Better?* The knot of grief in her solar plexus remained as solid as always. "I'd have saved Miranda and Ferdinand. That's different."

"I suppose." Sycorax was briefly silent. "Running these scenarios isn't helping."

"How do you know?"

"There isn't a way to win."

"Who said it was about winning?"

"Very well. There's no scenario in which everyone is saved. It should be obvious by now that a certain nameless person's intervention wasn't a significant factor. The fact is, Henderson Energy was entirely at fault. Management delayed too long before contacting an emergency team. You did the best you could in a bad situation. All of you did. Including Karter. I mean, the nameless person."

Gita winced at the mention of Karter's name. "We

shouldn't have sent in Miranda and Ferdinand. I should've talked to Abeque myself."

"I have run the probabilities," Sycorax said. "As simulation supervisor, it is my duty to prepare you for every eventuality. It is also my duty to review the outcomes. It is my opinion that you performed admirably."

"Yes, but—"

"Even Henderson Energy found no fault with your or your team's actions."

"I know—"

"If this were so, you'd stop holding yourself responsible. You'd stop blaming Karter. This isn't about losing Miranda and Ferdinand. It's about what happened afterward. It's about losing Ibis, Lissa, and Karter."

Pinching the bridge of her nose, Gita counted to five in an attempt to regain her self-control. She wanted to say Sycorax was wrong. She wanted to scream. She wanted to throw something at a wall. Tears burned in her eyes, and her heart hurt.

Sycorax continued. "Rerunning this simulation has become an unhealthy habit. I am deleting it from the scenario library now."

Uppity bot. Who asked you? Gita got to her feet, grabbed her coffee mug, and let out a long, shaky sigh. "I'm off to get some more coffee."

"You'll thank me later."

"Sure." She tapped the hatch access panel and exited the virtual simulation room.

2

The nutty scent of fresh coffee filled the galley. Gita's thoughts remained centered on the Beta-X45J scenario. Absentmindedly reaching for the pot, she brought herself up short. An enormous locking mechanism had been placed on the hot-beverage machine, pieced together with spare parts from Aoifa's junk room. Typed on its outdated touch pad's surface was a mathematic equation.

"Oh, for Pete's sake. Who drank the last of the coffee and didn't make more?"

"Don't blame me," Mandy said, sitting with a late breakfast. She didn't look up from the book she was reading. "I don't drink coffee."

"Since when?" Gita asked.

"Nineteen minutes ago."

Gita shook her head. "I'm *so* not in the mood for this." She solved the equation and punched in the answer. The lock popped open. She dropped the remains of the mechanism on the galley table with a clank. By the time Gita had turned around, Mandy was filling a clean mug with fresh coffee.

"I thought you quit," Gita said.

"I fell off the water cart." Mandy resumed her seat at the table.

"Isn't it supposed to be a wagon?"

"Not technically." Mandy took a sip and peered over the rim of her mug. "I looked it up."

Fresh coffee in hand at last, Gita sat down opposite Mandy. Gita's mind returned to the morning's exercise before drifting to her mother. She was late for her usual parental check-in. She had no excuse. While their relationship wasn't exactly smooth, recently they'd been getting along. *Maybe I've finally grown up?* Or maybe it was just that mothers and daughters learned to accept one another over time? Maybe it was the act of having your own child that changed the dynamics?

Not that Gita had a human daughter.

Her mind drifted to Ri, her eldest. The irony of repeating life patterns didn't escape Gita. It'd been more than a year since she had spoken to Ri. She told herself it was natural for Ri to rebel, grow up, and leave. That *had* been the plan, after all. Gita was proud of Ri. She was fulfilling her purpose—exploring the universe.

I miss her.

But children grow up.

Doesn't mean they stop needing you.

With that thought, Gita blinked. It was something her own mother would've have said. She decided it was time to check in on Ezinne, her second daughter—or more specifically, her second partnering subject. There was no doubt that Ezi needed her. Which may have been part of what had caused her programming to malfunction.

The head of the university's Artificial Persons Partnering Program was fond of emphasizing that too much emotional attachment was dangerous for the APPP subject, as well as one's career. Gita hadn't been able to prevent it. Partnering mirrored motherhood. *What else would you call carrying an entity inside your body and then spending years teaching them how to be a responsible adult?* How could anyone do such a thing without feeling? It was ridiculous to even think it.

Or was it?

She didn't think she'd ever truly resolve that question for herself. Taking a deep breath to cleanse her thoughts of anxiety, she dismissed the idea once again. There was much to be done, and brooding wouldn't do anyone any good.

With each swallow of coffee, her emotions became less raw and the tension in her jaw slowly released.

Across from her, Mandy continued reading. She was wearing a baggy olive-green cardigan over an ankle-length brown skirt and a loose white t-shirt. Soft black boots completed the outfit. She looked cute, comfortable, and wholly herself.

Mandy pushed her reading glasses back up the bridge of her nose. The black rectangular frames were new— required, since she'd refused to have her vision surgically corrected. For the most part, Mandy was a woman of few words. When it came to medical issues, Mandy wouldn't speak at all. As captain, Gita had access to Mandy's records, but she believed in leaving well enough alone in that department. Mandy was . . . well, Mandy.

Gita also didn't understand why Mandy read antique paper books when electronic and audio libraries were at her fingertips. Crew cabins tended to be compact, and physical books took up space. When asked, she'd replied: *Books smell good. Downloads don't.* Upon further consideration, Gita supposed spending most of your time staring at text on a screen could become tedious.

In any case, whenever *The Tempest* stopped at a space station, Mandy spent at least one day searching vintage shops for her next good read. She wasn't the only one. Print books had become popular among a certain set of biblio-nerds.

Fads come and go, thought Gita. *Who am I to judge?*

When it came to fiction, Mandy was into just about any genre, but her favorites were mysteries—the more twisted, the better.

"What are you reading?"

"*Unnatural Death* by Dorothy L. Sayers." Mandy tilted the faded white cover so Gita could read the title and author's name. The image on the front was an abstract drawing of a woman in a sickbed.

"Never heard of it."

"It's good."

"What happens?"

"Somebody dies."

"It's a murder mystery," Gita said. "Isn't that a requirement?"

Mandy shrugged.

"Have you seen Dru?"

"Have you checked the VS room?"

"Just came from there. How about Aoifa?"

"Taking a shower."

"Excuse me, boss." Sycorax's apology came from a hidden speaker in the bulkhead. "I've received an incoming long-distance visual message for you. It's marked private."

"Please tell my mother that I'll get back to her later," Gita said. She wasn't ready for another confrontation about her work situation or her relationship status or the latest regarding Uncle Aarit's divorce. *Not yet.*

"It is not your mother," Sycorax said. "It's Ri."

Blinking, Gita thought, *Speak of the devil.* As Aoifa would say.

Ri had kept in contact for a couple of years, then one day sent a message that she'd been hired for a new position that required travel outside the TRW. While she hadn't provided details, Gita had always assumed that she was serving on a long-hauler space exploration starship. It had been one of Ri's biggest ambitions. Gita had tried to be happy for her, but their final conversation had been intense.

"The transmission is flagged urgent. Ri has also requested a private comm channel," Sycorax said. "Shall I inform her that you will accept?"

Sensing something wrong or at least unusual, Mandy glanced up from her novel.

"Of course, I will." The smile on Gita's face faded as she hesitated. *Why would Ri request a private conversation? Is she in trouble?*

"I'll take it on the Command Deck." Command had better soundproofing than her cabin.

Mandy returned to her book.

Stopping in the threshold, Gita said, "Mandy? Please remember to refill the coffeepot next time."

Mandy nodded an acknowledgment, though her eyes never left the page she was reading.

Full-spectrum light panels brightened and dimmed as Gita passed along the hallway. Simulated wood trim covered the floor and ceiling seams, and a colorful runner softened the sound of her steps. Nestled behind sturdy aluminum glass panes lining the bulkheads, rows of leafy green plants thrived in hydroponic tubes. The plants assisted the carbon dioxide scrubbers and kept *The Tempest*'s recycled atmosphere smelling fresh. Nanobots handled pollination and removal of dead leaves and roots. The nonedible specimens had been bioengineered, playing an active role in the water recycling system as well as providing oxygen. The main garden was housed within the starship's center. Not only did it supply the crew with raw vegetables, it also served as a much-needed park. In Gita's experience, everyone benefited from a little dirt between their toes from time to time. That was why whenever she boarded someone else's ship, she'd thanked the goddess Lakshmi for providing the means to access Dru's skills as a botanist.

Command smelled faintly of sandalwood. When she'd first acquired *The Tempest*, she'd had the bulkheads painted bright azure. A row of golden swirls traced a path along the ceiling. The deck had been laid with tiles made from a specially treated plasteel that mimicked stained wood. She'd bought the ornate handwoven rug at a station orbiting the planet Ahlbryn. Its thick crimson, brown, and gold weave was secured with magnetized threads worked into the fabric. She'd hired her mother's interior decorator, and it had been quite the investment. However, Lavi Chithra had taught her that a ship's appearance set expectations, much like an interview suit. Not that anyone cared about professionalism in salvage—nonetheless, the cheerful, saturated colors made *The Tempest* feel like home.

Dru's black shorthair cat, Grimm, was napping in the captain's couch. Barely out of kittenhood, he was the image of lanky peacefulness. At the moment. Like all kittens, he was prone to short bursts of speed and minor feats of destruction. Today, Dru had dressed him in a white sweater with a yellow smiley face on the back. Luckily for Dru, when it came to ridiculous pet sweaters, Grimm was particularly relaxed.

"Good morning." Gita scratched him under the chin—his favorite spot.

He squeezed his pale blue eyes shut in full-blown cat bliss. "I have optimized the irrigation system in the atrium. I'm pretty sure I got it right this time."

Shocked, Gita yanked her hand away.

Grimm let out a disappointed cat sound. "Pet now."

The cat's camera-enabled collar was programmed with a narrow AI. Intended to inform the crew of Grimm's physical needs—food, water, a cat box refresh—it was also used to track his whereabouts. The AI wasn't sophisticated. Its verbal responses were simple presets consisting of a few words.

Or at least, they used to be.

The collar spoke again. "Go Red Devils!"

Mandy had hacked into Grimm's collar.

"So you're a Man United fan now? That's not going to make Dru very happy." Gita didn't know all that much about football, but her uncles were obsessed. Manchester United were rivals of Dru's team, Leeds United. "At least Mandy's practicing her new programming skills."

Yawning, Grimm got up and stretched, then curled back up on the couch. "Sleep now."

Ri is waiting. She'd sort out the issue later—preferably before Dru noticed.

For the sake of clarity, Gita addressed both Grimm and

the narrow AI in his collar. It was important to differentiate between the ship's AGI and Grimm's tiny smart camera. "Grimm, please mute your microphone."

"Acknowledged," the collar's audio interface responded. "Microphone deactivated."

A robust hunter, Grimm killed vermin that might otherwise chew on the ship's wiring. However, they had to watch that he didn't eat what he caught. Rats were ubiquitous where humans ventured, and starship cats were common, but Terran rats weren't the only creatures that might haunt a ship's crawl spaces and cargo holds.

Choosing the copilot station, Gita prepared herself for bad news. "All right. Connect us, Sycorax. And secure a private transmission, please." Which meant even Sycorax wouldn't be listening.

"Gita? Is that you?" Ri's question was backdropped with what sounded like a chorus of total chaos.

Gita sat up and gestured at the video controls. "I'm not receiving a visual. Where are you?"

"I didn't send one. I—" Static interrupted Ri's reply. "—be unnoticed."

"What's going on? Is that screaming? Are you in danger?" *Had the long-haul ship been involved in some sort of accident?*

The TRW had been sending AGI-crewed starships to explore outside of human-inhabited space for centuries. Artificial crews were capable of expertly handling a myriad of possible scenarios. Unfortunately, accidents still occurred. Gita could only hope that Ri's ship wasn't too far away. If that were the case, there was nothing Gita could do.

The transmission suddenly became clear, as if Ri was in Command with her. "I can't speak for long," she said, rushed.

"What do you need? Where are you? Tell me." Gita's heart thudded loud in her ears.

"Listen. Please." Ri paused. "I miss Ezi."

Blinking, Gita felt her brows pinch together. "I'm glad, but—"

"Do you remember when Ezi used to play the Opposite Game?"

In the beginning of partnering, play was often used to help the new entity develop. The Opposite Game was useful because it not only expanded the artificial person's vocabulary but forced them to use higher-order thinking skills.

"I do."

"She was so bad at it."

Confused, Gita said, "You weren't good at it either, when you started. What does this have to do with anything?"

"The next thing I tell you . . . it's like that."

It took a moment for Gita to put together what Ri intended, and all at once she was transported back in time. "Go on."

"I need you to stay away from here. As far as possible," Ri said. "Just stay away. Got it? *Please*."

Gita paused ever so briefly. "That's easy. I don't know where you are."

"Don't be stupid."

"You have to give me something to work with, Ri."

There was another burst of human-terror-laced static.

"I'm so scared." It was an almost plaintive wail—one that cut into Gita's heart.

Her annoyance at Ri's coyness evaporated. "Chellam, it's going to be okay," she said reflexively. Fear twisted, icy and electric, in her stomach. "Tell me what I can do."

Ri had always been headstrong and impulsive. *She never admits to being afraid. Or she didn't used to*, Gita thought. Her powerlessness frustrated and terrified her. She had the overwhelming but ineffectual impulse to reach through the comm channel and snatch her child away from danger. "Are—are we still talking about Ezi?"

"The crew is sick." Ri continued. "It's awful. The worst I've ever seen. The medbots can't—" More electrical interference interrupted the signal. Her fear briefly drowned, then resurfaced. ". . . don't know what it is. Contamination of—"

Gita's heart slammed into her breastbone with all its might. Her hands tightened into fists. "Get to an escape pod. Now. Can you?"

"—doing all I can for Wes and the crew. I'll be okay. The stasis pods are still functioning. Should be safe. They're designed for self-quarantine. I'll be in one. Wes will handle it. Someone will come for us. If I don't make it . . . leave a message. Someone will get it to you. Get it to Aunt Aggie."

"Wait—"

"Tell Aunt Aggie it's a code Carmine 473. Did you get that?"

"Aunt Aggie? What does she have to do with this? Who is Wes? Ri? Are you still there? Ri?"

"Maybe I should never have volunteered. But it sounded so exciting. You know what they say about adventures—"

Ri always enjoyed Tolkien, Gita thought.

And then the comms were cut off.

"Sycorax! Get her back!"

"I can't. The connection is dead."

"Then find her exact location. Now."

After thirty seconds, Sycorax finally replied, "I'm afraid there are no records."

"That's impossible."

"Give me a moment. I may be able to decode the message signature security string. Maybe I can get something useful out of it like the name of the starship." Another long silence followed. "Ha! Got it. They were transmitting from a starship named *NISS Boötes*."

Having worked in salvage for as long as she had, Gita knew most of the starship prefixes inside and outside the Republic. *NISS* stood for Norton Independent System Starship.

Gita muttered, "Ri is not in the Norton Independent Alliance. She can't be. She's an artificial person. Why would she voluntarily go there, of all places?"

Norton had once been a member of the TRW. When it became clear that artificial personalities would be granted personhood, the human-inhabited worlds of Norton—led by the populist People First movement—formally withdrew from the Republic and immediately placed heavy restrictions on AGI technology.

"Ri is not within the Norton Alliance," Sycorax said.

"Thank goodness."

Although the worlds within the Norton Independent Alliance preferred to advertise themselves as free and business friendly, the system was synonymous with corruption, poverty, and corporate oligarchy.

Sycorax didn't join in Gita's relief, giving Gita the impression that the AGI had more to add—and not good news. "What is it?"

"*Boötes* is registered as a rescue-and-emergency-response vessel. They were given an outer-system recovery assignment several days ago."

That's not deep space exploration, Gita thought. *She lied.* But artificial persons didn't lie. They couldn't.

Then she didn't lie. Gita recalled their last conversation—the one they'd had before Ri had left. *She never said she would be serving on an exploration vessel. You assumed, and she didn't disabuse you of the idea. That isn't lying—not technically. But it* is *the closest to a lie that an artificial person can get.* And it hurt.

Who taught her that? Gita frowned and swallowed the lump in her throat. "All right. Were you able to get the ship's location?"

"There appears to be a lock on the exact coordinates," Sycorax said. After a short pause, she continued. "Ha! Their security wall is a joke."

Gita tightened a fist and resisted the urge to scream at Sycorax to tell her already.

"The ship's current coordinates are near an artificial world within a sector with the astronomical designation L-39. The world is more commonly known as—"

"Loki's Ring," Gita muttered, stunned. "What are they doing there?"

"The ship's communication records indicate that there was some sort of accidental exposure to a deadly substance on a mining platform located on that world."

Off-limits to TRW ships, citizens, and other personnel, Loki's Ring was the only known alien-constructed world. Its inhabitants were unimaginably technologically advanced and hostile. The TRW had made multiple attempts at contact over the years, and all had failed. The Ring's residents hadn't even acknowledged their human and AGI neighbors. "Is anyone responding to *Boötes*'s emergency signal?"

"There has been no general emergency signal from *Boötes*."

"What?"

"An assistance request was sent to the corporate office of Thompson Import-Export on a private channel. They are the registered owners of both the ship and the platform."

"But—"

"I have breached their internal communication relay. I hope you'll forgive me—it's an emergency, after all."

"Go ahead."

"It seems management is debating whether risking another recovery ship is cost prohibitive. The consensus is in favor of abandoning the project. One executive has suggested the recovery cost could be offset by the potential weaponization of the unknown contagion. However—"

"That's awful!"

"Their main priority *is* to protect the board of director's profit margin."

Gita rolled her eyes and blew air out of her cheeks in disgust. *How can they live with themselves?*

"We appear to be the only ship to have encountered a distress call."

"Then jump us there. Now."

"There's no jump coordinate relay marker terminal in that system. L-39 is off-limits, remember?"

Engaging a Hopper-Johnson drive without a jump relay marker terminal granting clearance at the end point was hazardous to one's health. Starship navigation was tremendously complex. Space wasn't static, and neither were the objects within it. Standard navigation tools compensated for the movement of large bodies—stars, planets, moons, and comets. However, the smaller obstacles and stray human-produced debris weren't sizable enough for standard object tracking. In short, there was no other way of guaranteeing the termination point was clear.

"Then get us there as fast as possible."

"Need I remind you that we are not in the rescue business? Even if we were, our insurance waivers will not cover a venture into that sector of—"

"I understand your reluctance. But Ri is my daughter—" Gita stopped herself. "And even if she wasn't, she's in trouble. There is no one else out here—no one who will get to her in time. Therefore, we're going, and we'll sort out the paperwork later." *You sound very much like Karter right now, Gita.*

Shut up.

She was aware of Sycorax's concerns. Her fears were valid.

But it's Ri, Gita thought. *She's so frightened.* "I'll inform the others. Meanwhile, create a dossier on *Boötes*. We'll need a ship floor plan, list of munitions, possible hazardous materials, cargo manifest, and current crew rolls complete with public medical histories. The standard report. Let's do as much of this by the book as we can. Classify our response as a code E-11."

Code E-11 meant that the situation was too dire to wait for a formal response team. Any vessel in the vicinity was legally required to respond. Since *Boötes* wasn't in Republic territory, said protection didn't amount to much more than a smoke screen, but it would provide legal cover—if they didn't have to do anything *too* creative.

Gita cleared her throat. "Forward the data to my cabin when it's ready."

"Yes, ma'am."

"Thanks again. I mean it."

"Just . . . let's be quick about it."

"In and out. I promise." Rushing to the kitchen, Gita found Mandy placing her used coffee mug in the dish sanitizer.

"It's an E-11," Gita said. "Ri's starship is in trouble. They're orbiting Loki's Ring."

"How bad is it?"

"Terrible. Some form of contamination. But we don't have any details yet."

"I'll prep Medical and the quarantine pods," Mandy said.

"Thank you. Planning meeting in ten minutes. Use the intercom to listen in."

Mandy nodded.

With that, Gita rushed to the crew quarters. Thanks to the latest fitness routine Dru had recommended, she wasn't entirely out of breath by the time she knocked on her door.

"Who is it?" Dru asked.

"It's me. Time for a crew meeting. There's an emergency, and we're responding."

Across the hallway, Aoifa poked her head out of her cabin. Her tight curls were wrapped in a towel, her dark brown skin moisturized to the perfect sheen. Aoifa's heart-shaped face, full lips, and flawlessly arched eyebrows had graced a number of fashion publications when she was younger. At forty, she was still known to appear on the occasional catwalk. The only reason she didn't have a flourishing modeling career at the moment was that she found it boring. Born on Terra, Aoifa had spent her early teens on the various space docks. Her mother had been a welder. Aoifa's working-class background showed up in her speech from time to time. She was also a mathematical genius. Like many living off-planet, she had multiple degrees, one in mechanical engineering.

"You, too, Aoifa," Gita said.

Leaning against the inside of the doorframe, Aoifa gave her a languid smile and poured on the charm. "Is this regarding this morning? I shouldn't be asking, I know. It's only that if it's to be a good marmalizing, I must plan the appropriate outfit."

Gita frowned. "I really do wish you two would find another way to flirt."

Aoifa blinked. "Who's flirting?"

"Seriously?" Gita rolled her eyes.

"Fine. But you're taking all the fun out of—"

Holding up a hand, Gita cut her off.

Dru's muffled vaguely British Stationer accent came from the opposite side of the hallway. "Is this where you explain why Sycorax charted a course to Loki's Ring for a distressed starship with an NISS designation?"

Aoifa's good humor faded.

"How did you know?" Gita felt her brows push together again.

"Sycorax told me," Dru said.

Gita sighed. "She was supposed to let me do it."

"Second in command must be informed of course

changes. Remember? That's *your* rule. And I'm second in command." Dru still hadn't come out of her room. "So, let's hear it. Why?"

"Will you open up and talk to me? Or are we shouting through the door?" Gita asked, losing patience. She was aware of the terror building up behind her careful control. "Because if it's the latter, I'll need some throat-numbing spray from Medical."

The hatch slid open. Dru stood in the hatchway with her pale arms folded across her chest. A frown pinched her brows together, and her face was red.

Where Mandy was short, curvy, and soft, Dru was almost two meters tall and entirely hard muscle. She'd been a competitive weight lifter—an unusual background for a botanist. Her shoulder-length light brown hair was streaked with gray. "You know my feelings about the NIA."

Gita prepared herself for an argument. "It's an E-11."

Dru blinked. "Wasn't Ri one of your electronic nanny projects in uni?"

Insulted, Gita opened her mouth, but before the fight could ensue, Aoifa interrupted.

"That was a shite thing to say. What did Gita or Ri do to deserve that? Do you hear yourself? Apologize."

Sighing, Dru closed her eyes. "You're right. That was awful. I'm sorry. I—I'm not myself this morning. I didn't mean it."

Gita released the tension in her jaw and let her shoulders drop. "It's all right."

"As if *you* never had a nanny project," Aoifa mumbled.

"Not me." Dru glared across the hallway at Aoifa. "I've never been a nanny."

"At least Ri was a wean. Shite. What was his name?" Aoifa shifted her gaze to the upper bulkhead and placed an index finger to her chin. "Terry? Tony? Thom? Aye. I think that was it. Thom. Remember Thom?"

Dru looked away. "He doesn't count."

"Does he not?" Aoifa blinked in feigned innocence. "What about Ginevra? Does *she*?"

Grateful to Aoifa for having smoothed over what might have been a full-blown fight, Gita joined in some gentle teasing. "And what was the one before that? Bami?"

Aoifa held up a hand. "And Sizwe! Remember Sizwe? Matched set, that was. Was before we instituted the no-overnight-guests-for-longer-than-a-week-without-crew-approval rule."

Gita replied. "What a mess."

"Used all the hot water every morning, those two did," Aoifa said.

"I feel I should add a few more names to the list," Sycorax said. "Dipti, Bao, and François."

"Et tu Brute?" Dru gestured at the upper bulkhead.

Aoifa tapped at her forehead with the heel of her hand. "Now, why didn't I remember them?"

"Because they only lasted three days," Sycorax said. "I could provide the exact number of hours, but—"

"Enough!" Dru shouted and then mock-scowled. "Like Aoifa's any better."

"That was before I met Mandy. And my old girlfriends never stayed longer than overnight—"

"Emergency situation, remember?" Gita interrupted. "People possibly dying?"

"But we'll have to let those bigots into our home." Dru's frown became a scowl.

"There isn't a choice." Gita crossed her proverbial fingers that Dru wouldn't think to bring up the extra-territorial issues. "Nowhere does it say that one has to be nice to deserve life."

Dru sighed.

"I'm in," Aoifa said from across the hallway. "Dru can stay behind and miss out on her big chance to say, 'Fuck you, you fucking bastards,' in person."

"Fine." Dru rolled her eyes. "But don't blame me if I punch someone in the face with a hand weight."

"Dental repair is strictly their responsibility, as far as I'm concerned." Aoifa gazed up at the bulkhead with her finger still on her chin. "Wonder if we can get a preboarding waiver?"

Gita shook her head. "Absolutely not."

Aoifa pouted. "Shite. Was looking forward to that, so I was."

"Thank you both," Gita said. "I mean it."

"How long do we have to get our kit together?" Aoifa asked.

"Sycorax says we'll be there in twenty-six hours," Gita said. "Meet me in the kitchen? I need to collect a few things."

Dru's door slid shut. Gita mouthed a relieved *thank you* to Aoifa, who gave her a wink in return. Then Gita continued to her own cabin; she had messages to send. After that, it was time to learn as much as she could about *Boötes* and Loki's Ring as quickly as possible.

Her first comm call was for the Radia Perlman Rehabilitation Center for Artificial Personalities on Easley Hub. It was where Ezi lived now. It took a few moments to get the connection.

"Ezi?"

"Mata!"

"Anything exciting this week?"

"Not really." Ezi then launched into news about friends, the weather, and games she enjoyed. She seemed less agitated. Happy.

Once again, Gita couldn't help noting the differences between her two adopted daughters. Ezi didn't enjoy literature or entertainment vids. She was more socially oriented.

"Nurse says I'm making lots of progress. I get to work a little tomorrow, maybe longer if I'm good."

"I wish you wouldn't put so much pressure on yourself."

"I'm not!"

Like humans, artificial personalities had specific talents and interests. They were happiest when they could employ them. For Ezi, that had been medical bot design. There were also several key differences between artificial persons and humans. First, artificial personalities were aware of their abilities from inception. Second, where humans could develop other skills if their chosen vocation proved impossible, artificial persons could not—not without significant programmatic interference.

Ezi was special even among her peers. More creative, she was intended to help drive advancements in her field. Her processes were a little different on a base level. The objective was to end with a replicable design for an artificial innovative mind—one that was stable but not risk averse. To have been entrusted with the partnering of such a potentially valuable artificial personality had been a great honor for Gita. The day they'd come to take Ezi away had broken her heart.

It had also set the department's goal back a decade.

Neuromorphic matrices were far more delicate than the human psyche. They developed logic errors. Most of the time, they self-corrected with a little guidance, but occasionally a flaw caused a logic-error cascade. It happened sometimes, particularly with certain skill sets. Personality regression was one of the common effects and indicated a severe lack in consequential insight. In other words, Ezi was too impulsive and failed to predict consequences for her actions. Her unpredictability made her unsafe for real-world human interactions, let alone the responsibilities of medical science.

Gita said, "I'm so very happy for you, dear one."

"I can finally fulfill my purpose!"

"Remember what I told you," Gita said.

Ezinne's reply was a childish sing-song. "I'm more than my function. I have worth because I exist."

"Try to remember that."

"I will. Are you coming to see me this week?"

"That's why I called," Gita said. "Something has come up." She didn't think it'd be wise to tell Ezi about Ri for multiple reasons. "Next week should be better."

"Oh." The disappointment was palpable in Ezi's voice.

"I'll tell you what. I'll ask if Nana can come visit. Will that cheer you up?"

"Yes!"

"All right," Gita said. "I must go now. Be good for Nurse Jade. I love you."

"I will, I promise. Love you, too."

With that, Gita disconnected. The next conversation might be far more difficult. She hoped not, but one never knew with her mother.

A still image of Lavi Chithra, CEO and board chair of Chithra Industrial Crisis Management, appeared in the air. The subtle waves of her thick black hair had been brushed back from her face and fashioned into a bubble braid draped over her left shoulder. The sharp intensity of her dark mahogany eyes was set in an elegant countenance that couldn't always be counted upon to reveal her true thoughts and feelings—even if you were family.

The communication avatar was from one of her mother's corporate parties after Gita's father had died. Gita knew this because her mother wasn't wearing a nose ring. Her makeup, like her hair, was perfect, right down to the berry-red lipstick. Her modern silk saree was rich fuchsia, gold, and teal. The bold jewelry at her ears and throat was, no doubt, on loan from one of the TRW's premiere gold jewelry designers—Gita didn't know which.

Gita never failed to notice how much she resembled her mother. Her uncles often commented on it. Most of the time, she was proud of this. Even her oval-shaped face was the same. There was one main difference, however: her teeth. While her mother's were straight and evenly spaced, Gita had inherited her father's front teeth. The gap between them had embarrassed her, until a school girlfriend had confessed she found it attractive.

Contact was confirmed with a high-pitched beep, and the avatar was replaced with a live image. The firm line of her mother's jaw had softened with time, and her hair had been braided and pinned into an updo that could've been a crown.

Taking a deep breath, Gita ripped off the old metaphorical Band-Aid. "Hello, Mata."

"I expected to hear from you three days ago. Is everything all right?" The corner of her mother's mouth creased, and her right eye narrowed ever so slightly. She was angry—not that anyone outside the family would notice. The woman had served as a diplomat for thirty years before establishing a family business that became Chithra Industrial Crisis Management. So, she'd had a great deal of practice maintaining a level tone during emotional arguments and situations.

Gita often wished she'd inherited that trait. "I'm sorry. I meant no disrespect. It's been busy."

"The salvage business must be doing better than I thought. That's good to hear."

They had been speaking for less than a minute, and Gita was already suppressing an urge to cut the comm channel. She rushed to the point. "I need to talk to you about Ri. She's in trouble."

The disapproving line at the corner of her mother's mouth vanished. "If there's anything I can do, I will. Tell me, what happened?"

"There isn't a lot of information. She contacted me requesting help. The signal broke up before I could get more than that it's an emergency. We're on our way to render aid. But she's in a restricted area, and—"

"Which one? I'll have legal investigate possible repercussions and have the paperwork ready before you arrive. Do you need a professional rescue team? Where are you?"

"We're headed to coordinates within L-39."

There was a brief pause. "That is a problem."

"I know, but the starship Ri is on is in severe distress."

"No distress calls have been logged on the network from that sector."

"I noticed that, too. Ri was reluctant to give me details. It seemed like she was afraid of being discovered."

"Which starship?"

Gita gave her mother all the information she had.

"That's a Norton Alliance designation."

"I know."

"What is she doing there?"

"I wish I knew. She sounded odd. She said something

about the crew's medbots. And then she told me to tell Aunt Aggie something."

"What?"

"She said, 'Tell Aunt Aggie it's a code Carmine 473.' What does that even mean?"

"I don't know, but I will most certainly find out." There was a brief silence that indicated a Mute button had been employed, and her mother turned away from the screen. "All right. Do what you have to do, Jaanu. I'm afraid I cannot authorize any deployments to that sector. Not without a three-hundred-meter geological formation being shoved out of the way." Her mother had significant contacts within the TRW, including quite a few in government circles. "But please. If you need me to, I will, in fact, move that mountain."

"Thank you." Gita relaxed. It was a relief to know her mother had her back. "Everything should be fine. I think."

"Let me know the moment you return."

"One last thing. Would you mind checking in on Ezi for me? I'll have to miss our regular visit. It would make her so happy."

"Of course, I'd love to. May I bring her something?"

"From the list of approved items. Remember what happened the last time—"

"Of course, of course. Does she still like purple?"

"Yes. Remember, only from the *official* list. I don't want to get a call from her doctor again. Three of the nursing staff quit. A fourth was in hospital for a week."

"Don't worry. Now, go," her mother said. "And please, be careful."

"I will. I love you."

"I love you, too."

Gita took a moment to send her mother another copy of the gift list. There weren't many items that artificial persons found to be of interest that weren't electronic in nature. Gita's mother had had more than one confrontation with staff at Ezi's facility over such items.

At that moment, Sycorax indicated that she'd finished collecting data, and Gita got to work.

Böotes was TRW Navy surplus, operating under an exclusive agreement. *That's odd*. Nearly all ships in the Norton Alliance were independent contractors, because NIA corporations didn't like the word *employee*. It implied too much legal responsibility. She briefly wondered whether or not *Böotes's* contract had a salvage clause. If so, then *The Tempest* and her crew would be responsible for any damage the rescue might cause.

Lawyers are terrible, Gita thought.

Next, she opened a spacing map of Loki's Ring. All the TRW had been terrified by the world's discovery a hundred years ago—that much she did know. When the three-dimensional image was projected into the air inches from her face, her mouth dropped open.

Wow.

The entire solar system within L-39 consisted of exactly two objects: Loki's Ring and the G-type star that it orbited. The entities who'd created the Ring had presumably destroyed the former naturally formed planets in the system and used that matter to form it. It was a stupendous feat of engineering—one with a high cost. She tried not to imagine the millions of possible displaced civilizations and ecosystems obliterated in the process. The alien beings who had made the colossal structure had not only erased planets and moons—they'd also eradicated any frequent meteoroid visitors. The staggering levels of financial resources, labor, intellect, and technological advances required for such a project was both awe-inspiring and terrible.

Why would anyone do such a thing? When did it happen? Worse, it dawned on her that the entities responsible had come right to the edge of the TRW. *Did they see the existence of another sentient species and halt their advance out of respect? Or did they overextend themselves or exhaust their resources? If so, why not make contact? Or did they meet with an even more powerful enemy and find themselves destroyed before they could reach out?*

There were no answers to her questions, and as far as she knew, there never would be.

Humanity had encountered a limited number of nonhuman races. Standard procedure in first-contact scenarios was to observe while being unobserved in turn. Long-distance telescopes and drones were typically employed for this. Intraworld communications—radio, video, and digital—were intercepted. Knowledge of the world's technological levels, languages, and cultures were collected, and diplomatic envoys—artificial persons and humans—were sent. In the Ring's case, none had returned. All were presumed dead. Loath to assume hostile intent, the scientific and diplomatic communities searched for alternate solutions.

The military, however, felt caution was more prudent.

Although the inhabitants of Loki's Ring had the technology to leave their world, they never did—at least, not within humanity's experience. But that didn't mean they never would. Therefore, drones patrolled the border between L-39 and the TRW. Entry into the alien system was forbidden.

Gita stared at the animated rendering and suppressed a shudder. It looked so unnatural—no wonder the TRW kept such a close eye on it. "Sycorax, add locations of all known activity in or near the system over the last six months." Just because it was off-limits to Terrans didn't mean it was the same for others.

Some sectors were so bad that even the TRW Navy wouldn't venture there. She needed to know what to expect.

In an instant, a number of red dots formed along the boundary between the Norton border and the Ring like a rash. However, L-39 appeared safe enough. At least there were no recorded encounters with pirates there. None that the TRW knew about—publicly, anyway.

Nonetheless, she didn't like the way the incidents had

bunched up. The pattern implied frequent movement between the two systems. The red blotches indicated pirates poised for ambush.

Who are they waiting for? she thought. *There's no inter-solar-system traffic due to the ban. No halo generators or substations. No meteoroids. No comets. Nothing but that ring world and its star.*

How did the old Earth nautical maps put it? "Here be one gargantuan dragon."

What was Boötes *up to? Have the NIA's diplomats done what the TRW's couldn't? Have they found a way to communicate? Possibly negotiated a treaty?*

Gita wouldn't have bet on it. Genius levels of diplomacy weren't the NIA's reputation. But anything was possible. Regardless, it wouldn't factor into the *Boötes* situation. At least, she hoped not. She moved on to the starship's records. *Boötes* had been sent to evacuate workers who had been stationed on a mining platform constructed on the outside of the Ring.

She blinked. *No way. They're stealing resources.*

What else could they be doing there with mining equipment? Does the Republic know?

Making a note to herself, she decided to collect and send all relevant information to Republic authorities the moment Ri was safe and far away from any legal entanglements.

"Sycorax."

"Yes, ma'am?"

Gita pushed her hair away from her face. "Please send

the standard yellow slip inquiry to . . ." She squinted at the text from the registry database. "Tau, Chu & Lane ILC. It's a Norton Independent Alliance corporation, and they're a free capitalist society, so there are no laws as we understand them. We'll need to cover our asses."

"Will do," Sycorax said. After a short pause, the AGI continued. "That's interesting."

"What is it?"

"*Boötes* has activated an official general distress beacon. As of this moment. I don't understand why it wasn't engaged until now."

Well, that makes everything a bit easier, Gita thought. "Are they providing specifics as to the nature of the emergency?"

"I've attempted multiple inquiries, but the ship's artificial person isn't answering."

"That's because the ship doesn't have an artificial person."

"Oh, there's definitely a synthetic person integrated into the ship. It's impossible to retrofit the electronics systems in a Republic Navy model without gutting navigation and propulsion." Sycorax paused. "The NIA has no advanced shipbuilding facilities. Only repair and scrap. Why build new when repairing older models is cheaper?"

"Oh."

"It's only logical. Technical requirements in ship design are one of the subtle ways the TRW can slow modern weaponry from making its way to a hostile system, thus maintaining the balance of power in the Republic's favor and protecting the rights of artificial persons."

"Interesting."

Gita suspected Sycorax was right. Since artificial persons were legal citizens, they held representative positions in the TRW's governmental, judicial, and economic systems. They could—and did—influence policy. This was the biggest reason for the NIA's secession. They didn't trust the "machines" with anything resembling governance.

"*Boötes* is still not answering. I will continue my attempts nonetheless."

"We should have everything in order. Register the call with the TRW Emergency Network."

"And shall I inform Tau, Chu & Lane ILC while filing the yellow slip?"

A bad feeling twisted in Gita's stomach. *Do we really want to be in the middle of a political pissing contest?* "Come to think of it, maybe we should hold off on the yellow slip. Let's go in on the quiet."

"Given the potential for a diplomatic situation, it might be advisable."

"Have Mandy prep for quarantine," Gita said. "Maximum possible caution. We don't know what alien substance or bug that excavation dug up."

Twenty-one minutes had passed before Gita completed her research. Sycorax was still trying to rouse an answer from *Boötes* while progress elsewhere was being made.

"*Boötes*." Sycorax managed the dreary repetition without sounding tired or hopeless. "This is Sycorax of *The Tempest*. We are a salvage operation headquartered on Ahlbryn. We have received your distress signal and have changed course in order to provide requested assistance. Expect arrival in twenty-five hours, thirty-one minutes, and fifteen seconds. Please send the standard communication packet and explain in detail the nature of your emergency." She paused for ten seconds before repeating the message.

Within the TRW, distribution of social protocol information was handled via the ship's synthetic person. Comm packages contained cultural and behavioral norms, as well as details about all crew members, from name to pronoun usage.

Gita was in the kitchen with Dru and Aoifa going over *Boötes*'s schematics when the reply finally came.

"Hello, The Tempest. This is Boötes."

Gita winced.

Indicating extreme displeasure, Sycorax cleared a throat that she didn't possess. "To clarify, my *name* is Sycorax. I am a legally independent synthetic life-form. I will now resend the communication packet."

Sitting at the table opposite Gita, Dru said, "They've probably been disconnected from the All Republic Net since they were retired."

"Boötes, please provide the necessary communication data and explain the nature of your emergency." Sycorax assumed a cool, businesslike tone.

Aoifa leaned back and closed her eyes.

Boötes's low-pitched, slightly distorted voice sounded over the ship's speakers. "Apologies, Sycorax. Due to contamination risk, data file exchange is not recommended. My pronouns are they/them," Boötes said. "The number of persons registered with this ship is one hundred and eight, including children. I will not waste time reciting the rest, as my crew urgently require assistance."

"Since you can't send us the packet, can you tell us where they are located currently?" Gita asked. "It will shorten our search when we're there."

"There is no need for you to board. All living crew members have evacuated to the surface of Loki's Ring. Ship environmental systems are failing and will cease to function in three minutes and forty-seven seconds. Hull integrity is at sixty-three percent and dropping." Boötes sounded eerily calm, given that the ship was about to become scrap. "Expect breach in twenty-one minutes."

Sycorax asked, "Can you protect yourself from hard-vacuum exposure?"

Open space wasn't any better for synthetic persons than it was for biological beings. The length of time electronic components could endure extreme temperature variations, radiation, and other punishing conditions depended upon the materials used for construction. However, Gita understood that even with the newest components, direct exposure to hard space could be clocked in seconds. Boötes was an elderly model. And given Norton Alliance's prejudices, it was safe to assume they wouldn't have a clone on file anywhere.

"Fortunately, this is not the case," Boötes said.

Gita blurted out, "What do you mean?"

"I will not be tempted to make a less optimal decision," Boötes said. "Exposure to hard vacuum for a lengthy period should nullify risk to any persons who make contact with the remains of this ship. It will prevent further uncontrolled spread of a dangerous material."

Gita blinked.

"What classification is the substance?" Sycorax asked. "Is it biological? Chemical? Electronic?"

"The exact nature of contagion: unknown. Initial findings indicate a combination of properties, primarily biomechanical. Location of initial contact is the surface of the Ring. Strangely, trace elements indicate human origin. This appears to be recent. I have also noted key differences between its original structure and the version found on board."

The queasy knot in Gita's stomach froze. "It's evolving."

"So it would seem," Boötes said. "However, preliminary data indicate alien organism is eighty-five percent unlikely to survive—" A burst of static cut the rest of the sentence off.

"Boötes?" Sycorax asked. "Are you there?"

A series of electrical crackles and pops was the only answer. They sat, listening to Boötes's absence for several seconds before Sycorax cut the channel. Nervous, Dru shifted on the breakfast nook bench.

"What do you think damaged *Boötes*'s hull?" Aoifa asked.

"Biomechanical means bots." Dru shuddered. "Nothing worse than rogue bots."

"You're not wrong," Aoifa said.

"Boötes didn't mention a programmatic component," Gita said. "That's one less thing to worry about."

"Provided whatever it is hasn't interfered with Boötes's executive-logic functions before we spoke to them."

"Aoifa, that's not helping," Gita said.

Giving her a crooked smile, Aoifa winked. "Doing my part to keep Dru on her toes."

"Fuck you," Dru said.

Aoifa mimed a kiss. "Love you, too."

"What's the plan?" Sycorax asked.

Gita paused to organize her thoughts. "We go in dressed for hard vacuum and full-spectrum radiation, antimicrobial, and antinanotech protection." It was the best they had—state-of-the-art.

"And if the thing eats its way through our suits?" Dru asked.

"Then we're proper fucked," Aoifa said.

Dru sighed. "Seriously?"

"Well, I mean, *you're* proper fucked," Aoifa said. "I'll be safe. Everyone knows you're more nutritious than I am. It's all those muscles."

"We'll quarantine in the shuttle bay when we get back. Maximum contamination protocols. Mandy's prepping the decontamination booths, just to be sure." Gita raised an eyebrow at Dru. "Happy?"

"The word *happy* doesn't apply to anything in this situation," Dru said.

"But it'll do." Aoifa gave Dru a gentle push on the arm.

Dru sighed and shook her head. "It'll do."

"I'm packing portable storage for Boötes. We're not leaving them behind." Gita got to her feet.

"That's optimistic," Dru muttered. "Ouch! Watch what you're doing with those elbows."

Aoifa stuck out her tongue.

"Get ready, ladies," Gita said. "This is going to be a messy one."

Hang on, Ri. We're on our way.

3

"There's an ancient expression I prefer to use in situations like this. No doubt you're familiar with it?" Aggie Neumeyer leaned all the way back in her office chair and propped her feet up on the edge of her desk. She was employing extreme asshole mode for the benefit of the Septan diplomatic official. "'A lack of planning on your part doesn't necessitate an emergency on mine.'"

The toes of her work boots were scuffed. They clashed somewhat with her office pantsuit. She probably should've shined her shoes that morning, or at least earlier this week, but she'd had a lot on her mind. As it happened in this case, the state of her boots emphasized her point. When she'd been a teenager on Ronrel Four, thick rubber soles and laced leather uppers were associated with rage and rebellion. And while time had sanded down the jagged edge of aggression normally afforded the wearer, in conservative circles outside of Ronrel Four—for example, the diplomatic corps of Septa—the association still held.

A younger person couldn't have gotten away with a similar sartorial choice, but she wasn't young anymore. *Thank the gods.*

An uneasy expression passed over her esteemed visitor's pale, hatchet-nosed countenance like a rapid-moving cloud. An arrogant frown took its place. The undersecretary to the assistant secretary of Septan Diplomatic Affairs had a reputation as a bully. The petulant line between his heavy black brows implied that he was, indeed, used to getting his way.

I'm sure he's perfectly nice to his family and friends, she thought. It was an expression that her assistant, Cricket, often used when Aggie declared someone an asshole.

Sure he is.

"A Federal Customs inspector has illegally detained a Septan ship! For no reason whatsoever! I demand you release it at once!" The undersecretary pounded the side of his fist on the top of her desk hard enough to cause a coffee cup to clatter against the glass surface.

Apparently, Fen hasn't warned him about me. Aggie felt a smile tug at the corner of her mouth. It was petty, but at the moment, she didn't give a jump rat's flaming backside. He wasn't about to push her—certainly not after what she'd discovered.

One hundred sixty-two centimeters tall and forty-five

kilograms soaking wet, she'd snatched every advantage she'd come in contact with from the moment she'd understood being short and small-boned meant being underestimated or ignored. Between the two, she preferred being underestimated. The shitheads almost never caught on until it was far too late.

"Is there anything we can do?" asked Fen Singh, the TRW executive secretary. Fen was an old friend, and she knew that Aggie didn't have jurisdiction over the customs office—that is, not usually and certainly not in this instance—which indicated that Fen had allowed Hatchet Face to push her into a corner. Her presence in Aggie's office at this moment was a delaying tactic.

Aggie knew exactly what that meant. *She wants* me *to deliver the bad news in case he becomes violent.* Ultimately, it was better than calling in security. *Certainly better for the undersecretary.*

The behavior is the problem, not the person. It was another adage that Cricket, an artificial person well versed in psychology and ethics, had trotted out after one of these confrontations.

The man should've treated Fen with more respect. I'm so going to enjoy this.

Fen wasn't the only person to have an arrangement of this sort with Aggie, but she was one of the few that Aggie backed without reservation.

Fen continued to play the innocent in what was obviously a setup. "You have to understand the undersecretary's position." Her serenity belied the statement.

This was a game the two of them had played on numerous occasions.

"Is it his position?" Aggie asked. "Or is it President Phan's? Or Premier Balakrishnan's?"

"What do you mean—" Hatchet Face's complexion acquired a darker tone. The hue produced by blood rushing to his skin's surface clashed with its greenish undertone, producing a dull, curdled red. His brows pinched together. Combined with the mole on the bridge of his nose, the line drawn there reminded her of an exclamation point.

Aggie felt she could predict the man's blood pressure even though it wasn't included in the protocol data projection above his head—discreetly provided by the office AGI. Only Aggie could see the transparent words, which included such things as his name, position, pronouns, and citizenship status. If she were a betting woman, she'd have put credits down on the man's next utterance being a sputter. Turning her head to glance out the window at just the right moment, she narrowly avoided a face full of spittle particles. Her right ear and her glasstop caught most of the onslaught.

"This—this is outrageous!"

"M." Aggie paused a beat or two before going on, then spoke to the window. "I'm sorry. What was your name again?" M. Agosti—even if the protocol projection hadn't existed, Hatchet Face's name was printed on the temporary security badge hanging from the lanyard around his neck.

"Your people illegally boarded a Septan vessel and

seized its cargo! And now, this—this insult! Septa is a planetary member of the Terran Republic of Worlds! You can't treat us like that!" Agosti moved his bulk to the edge of his borrowed seat. He leaned forward and menaced her glasstop yet again. This time, the assault was conducted with one stocky finger. "I am recommending Premier Balakrishnan file an official protest with President Phan. Directly. I'll have your head for this!"

Aggie continued to stare out the window and kept her voice low and quiet. "Oh, I very much doubt that."

Agosti jumped to his feet. From the edge of her perception, it appeared he might be considering yanking her from her chair—a neat trick, given that he'd have to do it over the desk. Aggie almost wanted him to try. He seemed the sort that was unwilling to learn without the accompaniment of pain.

Tugging at Agosti's sleeve, Fen began the scheduled attempt to placate him. "M. Agosti, please."

Whirling on the heel of one mirror-shined patent leather dress shoe, Agosti managed a moment of rapid grace in spite of his muscular bulk. It went well with his expensive suit.

Aggie was almost impressed. She waited until he reached the door. "Perhaps you should speak with Premier Balakrishnan's niece before you charge into the secretary of state's office with your accusations."

Her words had the intended effect. Agosti stopped short, as if he were on a leash.

Got you! Aggie thought. "Your ship was stopped in

interplanetary space, which is within federal jurisdiction. The flight plan indicated the destination was a moon within the Norton Alliance." She briefly glanced at her glasstop. "Jargoon is a Norton Independent Alliance world. You are aware of the severe restrictions pertaining to trade with the NIA, of course."

"Registered travel and trade between Septa and the Norton Alliance is perfectly legal," M. Agosti said. However, the ghost of a doubt haunted the edge of his outrage. "Those Republic goons had no right to board that ship. It was scheduled to bring thirty metric tons of Harl corn to Beaumont. Now the shipment will be delayed. People will starve. The relationship between Septa and Jargoon will be damaged."

Aggie nodded. "I'm with you there."

"You're blocking a diplomatic gesture that will bridge decades of distrust between the Terran Republic of Worlds and the Norton Independent Alliance—"

"Now, here's where I have to stop you. Because in this case, it was what was *underneath* the corn that was the problem: restricted Terran Republic tech and a deactivated Artificial General Intelligence."

"That's a lie! It is illegal to transport AGI into the Norton Alliance. Everyone knows this."

With a few short, graceful gestures, Aggie pulled up the video clip recorded inside the offending vessel's hold. She paused the footage on a single image and magnified a section, creating a close-up. "Care to try that again?" She studied Agosti's face. Reading people was a part of her job she was particularly good at—some said it was downright spooky.

And it was why no one invited her to the office poker games anymore.

Agosti was genuinely surprised.

Interesting, Aggie thought. She shifted in her chair and lowered her feet. "You didn't know about this."

"Of course I didn't!"

"That's unfortunate, M. Agosti." Aggie rested her forearms on her glasstop and leaned forward. "Because the Council of Artificial Persons isn't going to respond well to this situation. In fact, I wouldn't be surprised if they were to institute a planetwide labor strike."

"They wouldn't—"

"I'm afraid they would. Transporting a deactivated Artificial General Intelligence against their will into a territory openly hostile to synthetic persons is a criminal offense. The repercussions for Septa are likely to be extreme. Depending upon who was responsible—let alone aware—Septa's membership in the Republic of Worlds could be suspended."

Agosti's furious red face paled, and his eyes widened before he blinked. "You can't mean to—"

"Report this? You're right. I don't." Aggie wiped away the image after a count of three. "Because you will."

Blessedly, M. Agosti remained silent and composed.

Well done, Aggie thought. *Almost makes me believe you weren't merely given your position just because Premier Balakrishnan is one of your sister's husbands.* "Let me tell you what will happen when you leave my office. You will contact the premier in private and inform him of the situation and his niece's involvement, assuming he doesn't already know. Nonetheless, your government will publicly take credit for the discovery and arrest of the guilty parties."

Blinking, M. Agosti said, "And what will you want in exchange?"

"Premier Balakrishnan's niece will never again be allowed to own, captain, or crew another deep-space-ready vehicle. In fact, she will no longer be employed in, or involved with, extraplanetary trade. Understood?"

"That's all?"

Aggie smiled. "You and the premier will simply owe me a favor. I estimate you have approximately thirty minutes before the media pick up the story."

The undersecretary to the assistant secretary of Septan Diplomatic Affairs exited the office like he'd been scalded. Fen watched him go with a careful expression. The door slammed.

"Aren't you supposed escort him out of the building?" Aggie asked.

"He knows the way." Fen assumed the seat that M. Agosti had vacated. "And if he doesn't, well . . . I suppose that will give him less time to concoct a convincing story for the press." She leaned back in the chair. "Thanks, Aggie."

"Don't thank me. You're the one buying dinner."

"Where do you want to go this time?"

Aggie stared up at the ceiling and considered her options before settling on her favorite. It wasn't creative, and if she were still a field agent, establishing a pattern of behavior would be dangerous, but she was allowed such luxuries now. "Templeton's Rest."

"See you at 18:00."

"Back booth." There was still such a thing as recklessness.

"You got it." Fen paused in the doorway. "Meet at the gym first?"

With a groan, Aggie rolled her eyes.

"Don't give me that face. You know what your doctor said."

"Damn it. I should never have told you."

"I made it easy. Brought a bagful of workout clothes for you. Happy Founder's Day."

"What does Founder's Day have to do with sweating?"

"Absolutely nothing." Fen's dimples became more pronounced as she grinned. "Anyway, I hear possessing bones not made of chalk is handy. What are friends for but to keep you alive against your will?"

"Fine. I'll remember this."

"I'm counting on it."

The moment Fen was gone, the projection of a tall, pale woman with long, wavy blonde hair brushed into an updo appeared. Today, Cricket was wearing a powder-blue blouse that complemented her eyes with a stylish black suit. She had once told Aggie that at least one of them should follow the office dress code.

LOKI'S RING • 75

"Well?" Aggie crossed the room to pour the last of the afternoon coffee into her favorite mug. It was late, but she supposed she'd need the energy to get through everything that Fen had in store for her later.

"That was harsh," Cricket said.

Bitter, hot liquid scorched Aggie's tongue. Rapidly swallowing, she winced. She didn't speak until she was sure she hadn't done the same to the back of her throat. "I followed your advice. I was polite. He'll get credit for discovering the shipment—or rather, the premier will. His niece will be out of the kidnapping-and-smuggling business, and Septa will look like the good guys. The synthetic person is safe. New TRW technology won't fall into Norton hands. And the head of council won't even be required to acknowledge that there was an issue in the first place, let alone cast an unhappy glance in Septa's direction. Peace maintained, problem solved."

"You didn't have to scare him."

"Oh? Didn't I?" Aggie said with a wide smile.

Cricket shook her head. "One of these days, someone's going to pull one of your stunts on you."

"And when that day comes, I'll damned well deserve it because I'll have been sloppy." Aggie took another cautious sip. "Then I'll retire into obscurity."

"You certainly won't."

"Oh, I will. Because it'll be at that point that all the shadow wolves come for my hide."

"If you say so." Cricket paused. "There's one small problem with all this: the famine in Beaumont."

"They'll get the corn. Premier Balakrishnan is not an idiot. He'll need the optics after his niece's stunt."

"Nationalism is gaining influence on Jargoon. Four of the seven most powerful countries on that moon have populist regimes. It'll only gain more momentum the longer the economic situation there continues to falter," Cricket said.

"As you frequently remind me, Jargoon is Norton's problem, and Norton is not within my jurisdiction." Aggie resumed packing up her things for the day.

"Have you heard of Jayne Tau?" Cricket asked.

Pausing, Aggie glanced up from her desk. "Leader of *the* Tau family. Met her once at an NIA corporate social function. She was a fright. Don't think I've seen that many teeth in a smile since Shark Week at the virtual zoo."

"What were you doing at an NIA corporate function?"

"I believe this is where I use the phrase *former field agent*, and you don't ask any more questions," Aggie said. "Has something new come up?"

Jayne Tau, formerly Jayne Henderson, had married into the Tau family more than a decade ago. Aggie had always wondered if the match was political—Jayne's grandfather was Grayson Henderson, the famous leader of the anti-AGI People First movement and one of the most powerful families within the NIA. Jayne's wife, the eldest Tau daughter, had limited interest in the family business, leaving the road wide-open for Jayne to gain even more influence, climbing to the company's highest ranks using her married name.

Months ago, Aggie had flagged the entire TCL group, which had consolidated its power structure. They'd done a fair job of burying the bodies, not that they needed to. NIA law enforcement was spotty at best. For the most part, it existed as a facade for corporate power, NIA laws seeming to exist solely to provide employment for corporate lawyers. Mostly, companies sued one another to gain an advantage over rivals. After the reorg, all that was left of Chu and Lane were their names. Within a year, Aggie predicted there wouldn't even be that much.

It all sounded much more bloodless than it actually was. In the NIA, the more money you had, the less you had to abide by inconvenient ethics and morals.

"Jayne Tau used to be in charge of TCL's corporate marketing. But now, she's pioneering a new religious movement on the side," Cricket said.

"Always had a hunch the two had a little too much in common," Aggie said. "She must be quite the salesperson."

"Her followers call themselves the Loved."

"Good for them."

Cricket replied, "A fanatic religious movement with access to a fleet of warships *could* be of concern— particularly if that religious movement were attempting to get its hands on a specific subset of artificial person."

"You think they're the end buyer? Why?"

"The Council has been observing certain activities within Norton's power structures. There have been disturbing indications. For instance, Tau, Chu & Lane have been acquiring components for large-scale electronic storage equipment."

They're preparing for war, thought Aggie.

Within the Norton Independent Alliance, the NIA stood for two things: freedom and rugged individualism. From outside the NIA, these looked much in practice like greed, corruption, and hypocrisy.

Aggie paused again. "But Tau, Chu & Lane aren't based on Jargoon."

"They are not."

"Interesting. How long has the Council been monitoring the situation?"

Smiling, Cricket said, "That would be a breach of confidentiality, I'm afraid."

"Coy isn't a good look on an artificial person," Aggie said. "It tends to make humans paranoid."

"Power dynamics aren't inherently evil. In fact, it is standard for power to shift back and forth between entities in any beneficial relationship. It is only when a power differential is forced into a static, stable state granting all the power to one group or individual that it evolves into oppression."

"Did you just quote the Second Law of Moral Dynamics at me?" Aggie asked.

"As your adviser and assistant, I believe it's a part of my job."

"Careful. You're acquiring an overdeveloped sense of cynicism."

Cricket beamed a sincere smile at her. "Not one bit. I still have faith in you, don't I?"

"All right," Aggie said, falling back into her chair. "Anything else I should be aware of?"

Tilting her head to the left, Cricket seemed to focus on the wall behind the desk. An electric-blue light twinkled in her eyes as she accessed the incident lists for the evening. "Local elections on Daithe have concluded. The results will post tomorrow morning, but the statistics indicate there will be no surprises. There's been an accident involving a Norton-registered starship parked in L-39. There are no details at this juncture. Our agents on board are ten hours late for check-in. I've sent an inquiry and will let you know the moment I have the report. Until then, I'll closely monitor the situation. Several new starships have been approved for exogalaxy exploration. The delegate from the Ttegarratt System arrives tomorrow at Terra Station. Data regarding all atmospheric requirements and dietary and safety issues have been provided by the delegate's contact team. Security already has a plan in place, but the executive secretary would like you to review it nonetheless."

More than a decade in the making, the historic meeting was the last step in facilitating the first nonhuman bid for a Terran Republic of Worlds partnership from outside Republic space.

Glancing at the time projection on her desk, Aggie muttered, "Did Fen indicate if that was due before or after the gym?"

"No deadline was given. However, one assumes she intended for—"

"It was a rhetorical question, Cricket."

"Ah, I see. Shall I continue?"

"Go on." Unable to delay any longer, Aggie finished preparing to leave for the night.

Cricket resumed reading. "A large-scale protest on Ahlbryn has temporarily halted trade negotiations between Ahlbryn and Terra. Protesters have been invited to submit the details of their objections for review."

Aggie paused and shook her head. "Their government could've saved time by polling public opinion *before* negotiating."

When Cricket raised both eyebrows, Aggie motioned for her to continue.

"The industrial markets are responding to the delay with—" The artificial person paused. "I'm sorry. You have an urgent call."

"This late? I normally would've left the office a half hour ago. Who is it?"

"Lavi Chithra."

"Any indication of what it's about?"

Again, Cricket tilted her head. "She has marked the communication personal. I see nothing unusual involving Chithra Industrial Crisis Management, but it's possible that this may involve one of our agents in L-39."

Because one of those agents is Ri. "Put her on and give me the office."

"Full privacy mode?"

Aggie indicated that Cricket should listen in just in case the matter needed further discussion, but that there should be no permanent record.

"Yes, ma'am." And with that, Cricket vanished.

A full-body image of Lavi Chithra took Cricket's place in the center of the room. Lavi was wearing an elaborate emerald-green sari with a wine-and-gold paisley design along the hem. Her lipstick matched her red lacquered nails. Occasionally, Aggie wondered how long it took Lavi to get dressed in the morning. *That hairstyle alone must've taken an hour*.

Aggie kept her own straight brown hair short in a style that would best be described as boyish.

"Hello, my friend," Lavi said. Her low-pitched voice was pleasant, cultured, and often ranged between a cat's purr and a growl. Her smile seemed pinned in place, like one of her sari pleats.

She wants something, Aggie thought. Most of the time, Lavi's face was impossible to read—even for Aggie, which was saying something, since they'd been good friends for almost forty years. *It must be serious, whatever it is*. "You're lucky you caught me. I was supposed to leave a half hour ago."

"Have I interrupted something important?" The question was casual, almost forced.

That was a bad sign. "Not at all," Aggie said. "However, I did agree to meet Fen at the gym. Should be there in twenty minutes. If this is something that will cause me to cancel, I'll be forever in your debt."

Lavi shook her head and smiled. "Regretting your promise already?"

"Never promised a thing." Aggie allowed herself a little impatience. "I hate it when you go diplomatic on me. What is it?"

"Very well." Lavi sighed. "It's about Gita and . . . my granddaughter Ri. You remember Ri, don't you? They're both in trouble."

Aggie blinked. "What kind of trouble?" she asked as a delaying tactic. Her stomach clenched around a knot of ice. A forty-something-year-old memory surfaced, spurring her heart rate: forcing her way past terrified passengers on a wrecked starship.

It faded an instant later. She'd somehow swallowed the urge to jump to her feet.

When was the last time I heard from Ri? Three weeks ago? She and Wes are almost half a day late reporting in. Not a good sign. Aggie recalled what Cricket had indicated regarding the situation in L-39. *Time to contact Mother on Chimera Station. They'll know what the fuck is going on. Maybe they can even help. Maybe.*

But Mother, pirate queen and one of the few known to operate anywhere near Loki's Ring, was a frustrating, secretive, and stubborn personality. *Takes one to know one, I suppose.*

Aggie was fairly certain Mother wasn't human. On the other hand, it was possible that most of their appearance was an act designed to put off the overly ambitious. That was certainly a tactic Aggie herself would use in their situation. But something about Mother told her they weren't faking it. Cricket's opinion was that statistically, the probabilities were high that Mother was at least partly nonhuman. They certainly weren't from a culture the TRW was already in contact with. Aggie usually wasn't a fan of striking deals with unknown quantities, but she'd been working with Mother for years. They'd long been a reliable source for information about the Norton Alliance. The time for worrying about that particular metaphorical bedfellow was long past.

Lavi isn't going to like what little I have to tell her.

"There's been an accident. A starship that Ri is on is in severe distress. Gita is answering the E-11. I wouldn't have come to you, except that the ship is in a restricted system and—"

"It's parked near Loki's Ring."

Lavi stopped. Her brows pinched together. "Should I bother asking how you know this?"

"It's my job to know."

Lavi's expression grew sterner. "Ri is working for you. After I specifically told you I didn't want her involved in your department."

"Now, hold on." Aggie stood up. "I didn't recruit her."

"I find that hard to believe."

"It's the truth. Ri came to me. Twice. She begged—"

"You sent her into danger. Into the Norton Independent Alliance. *My* granddaughter. On a Norton vessel?"

"I sent her to the Council of Artificial Persons."

"You could've given Ri an assignment anywhere—"

"You know how she is. I told her to stay away from Norton. CAP made the recommendation from there. CAP doesn't give orders. She selected that assignment."

Lavi scoffed. "You know I understand how things work. Your agents only go where they're directed. You did this."

"She followed a lead. On her own."

In truth, Lavi wasn't entirely wrong. Agents, even Council agents, didn't go anywhere without her approval. As far as she knew. But Ri's case was more complicated. Once Ri had made up her mind to go, Aggie had had only two choices: grant approval and provide assistance or—

You don't really believe that, Aggie thought. *You read that report and approved it anyway.*

She was the best fit. I didn't send her alone. She has a human handler and a recent backup. Ri is as safe as I can make her. As safe as any other agent in a dangerous—

"You should have stopped her!"

"I wanted to," Aggie muttered.

"How could you do this to me? How? After what happened to Hasik?"

Aggie fought back a sudden, sharp burst of panic. *I did everything I could to save Hasik. She knows that.*

"You know what they will do if she's found!"

Holding herself in check, Aggie paused, giving Lavi time to compose herself. The conversation was heading into treacherous territory. She had to be careful. Aggie didn't want to lose her oldest, closest friend. "Of course I do. Ri knows what she signed up for. Just like every agent."

Aggie took a slow breath before going on. "I did the only thing I could. I made sure the instructors were harder on her than anyone else. The more that was demanded from her, the greater her successes. She's damned good, Lavi. One of the best."

Lavi tightened a fist, her nostrils flaring.

"Look," Aggie said. "I get it. I do. Do you think I send agents into dangerous situations without a thought for them? You know better than that. Particularly for agents who happen to be my best friend's granddaughter."

"Of course, I do, but—"

"But nothing." Aggie sighed. "Ri passed all the examinations and certifications. She had worked with CAP here on L'Enfant Station for months."

"You should've told her not to leave!"

"I did my best to keep her where I could watch over her. Where I could protect her."

Lavi glared. "And how did that work out for you?"

"Not all that well, I suppose." Aggie sighed. "Even I have my limits."

"What does code Carmine 473 mean?"

Aggie felt all the blood drain from her body. *Holy shit.*

"Tell me what it means." Lavi used her cold, corporate CEO voice. Aggie now understood why her best friend had a reputation as a ruthless bitch.

"You know I can't. Where did you hear that?"

Lavi blinked. "It was something that Ri said to Gita when she called for help."

Tilting her chin down, Aggie stared at Lavi from under

her eyebrows. "This is very serious. Did Ri mention anything else? What were her exact words?"

"I didn't speak to her," Lavi said. "Gita did. But I recall she mentioned something about accidental contamination and how the crew's medbots were ineffective."

Not ineffective. Hacked. Mutated. A long silence stretched out. Aggie couldn't think of anything else to say. She had no intel she could share. This was the hard part for relatives, waiting in ignorance. Lavi had to trust that Aggie was doing everything possible to get Ri back, without ever knowing the truth about what happened.

Lavi looked like she was on the edge of tears. Placing a hand to her face, she turned away.

"I'm so sorry," Aggie said. "I truly am."

With a sniff, Lavi faced her again, her expression now one of resigned acceptance. "I am the one who is sorry. I shouldn't have lost my temper."

"I'll do everything I can to get her out. Everything. You know that."

"I do." Lavi paused. "And in case that isn't enough . . . what can I do to help?"

Aggie paused. "I don't suppose you have a crew anywhere near Lamarr Station or access to a temporary jump terminal or two?"

4

A deep thump vibrated through *Ariel*'s hull just before an indicator light on the pilot's console flashed green, signaling the shuttle had safely landed. Gita felt a drop of sweat ooze its way down the center of her spine. Her stomach fluttered as she made her way to the lowering ramp. The inside of her mouth was dry. Her knees felt like they were powered by loose rubber bands. Glancing at the readings projected on the inside of her helmet via her HUD, she took a moment to slow her breathing.

Outside, the lights in *Boötes*'s shuttle bay flickered on and off. A single wayward pipe wrench floated in midair.

Artificial gravity isn't working. Avoiding touching things is going to be a challenge, she thought.

Suddenly, she was thankful that she'd invested in

disposable safety gear for jobs like this. And while the supplies on hand weren't what they were since she'd left Search and Rescue, at least they had enough for today. Not that they didn't come across contaminants in the scrap business. It was only that now she could pick and choose which vehicles were worth the risk. Search and Rescue didn't have that option.

She heard Aoifa mutter a quick prayer to a saint whose name Gita didn't catch.

"Thought you'd given up on Catholicism." Dru was still in the pilot's seat, performing the last of the checks on the shuttle's systems.

"The old ways die hard." Aoifa rubbed her gloved hands on her thighs as if wiping her palms dry. "Particularly in places like this."

Over the years, Gita had noticed that Aoifa's accent grew more pronounced the more stressful the situation.

"There's no harm in hedging your bets." Dru finished what she was doing and turned to face the aft of the ship.

Gita saw Aoifa nod beneath the sealed dome of transparent aluminum protecting her head. She'd collected her tight curls with an elastic, creating a dark brown puff at the crown of her skull. "I suppose." She bent, grabbing three steel extensor rods from the tool rack.

"Pray all you like. I'll take any edge we can get." The tint on Dru's helmet darkened, but Gita could still see the knots of her light brown hair sticking out in spiky clumps on either side of her head.

Taking a deep breath, Gita held it for a moment before letting it go. It helped her to slow her heart. *Come on. Calm down already.* "A healthy sense of mortality keeps you out of trouble."

"Is that so?" Dru asked. "I'm feeling extremely mortal about now. And I'm still here, damn it."

Gita accepted one of the extensor rods from Aoifa and toggled on the suit camera that would record their progress. As a precaution, the video wouldn't immediately transmit to *The Tempest* and Sycorax—at least, not until after they were sure it wasn't contaminated. As an extra precaution, two-way communications between them and the ship would be limited.

Aoifa let out a nervous half breath, half snort. "You love trouble. And you wouldn't have it any other way, would you?"

"Guilty as charged." Dru accepted the third rod from Aoifa and peered out at *Boötes*'s shuttle bay. "Those fucking lights are giving me a migraine."

"You complain more than an old woman." Aoifa smiled.

Dru said, "I *am* an old woman."

"Ack. Right you are." Aoifa tapped her arm.

"You know the drill, ladies." Gita activated her mag boots. "Don't touch anything you don't have to. And leave behind no sign we were here. I've got a hunch this thing is going to get political."

"Going to?" Dru asked, raising an eyebrow.

"We're ghosts," Aoifa said. "Got it."

"Won't someone notice Boötes has gone missing?" Dru pointed to the two portable artificial person storage units hanging off of Gita's shoulder.

Ultimately, Gita knew Dru was right, but she loathed the idea of leaving anyone behind. *Particularly someone who won't get help even when or if assistance arrives.* "This ship isn't ever flying again. A salvage crew won't take anything they can't sell. So, no, they aren't likely to notice."

"All right," Dru said. "Now, say they do notice. How do we explain why we boarded a starship with no one to rescue?"

Oh. Gita paused.

"That's easy, so it is," Aoifa said. "We don't mention the bit where Boötes told us everyone here was dead. No one from Norton will give a shite—"

"Except, perhaps, the owners," Dru interrupted.

"And TRW authorities would want the AGI rescued, assuming it's possible." Aoifa gave the shuttle bay a doubtful look.

Gita nodded, relieved. It was good the others had a story prepared. She was a terrible liar. "Remember, our risk of exposure goes up dramatically the longer we're here. We'll fetch the stasis pod first and hit the main systems room last. Any questions?"

"How will we know Ri is inside?" Dru asked.

"No idea." Gita admitted. "Normally, I'd boot her up, but . . ."

"Okay then," Dru said. "I'm good."

Aoifa shrugged. "Ready."

Gita took in a deep breath and puffed her cheeks as she blew the air out. She tried to sound surer than she felt. "Let's do this."

"There's no place like home," Aoifa said, tapping her heels together. Her mag boots clamped onto the deck with a dull thud Gita could hear over the comms.

"Last one in is a rotten mushroom-soy patty." Dru slipped past and stepped out of the shuttle with confident grace.

Gita passed through the air barrier. All at once, she felt the temperature difference between *Ariel* and *Boötes*. Her stomach did an abrupt lurch as her body registered the lack of artificial gravity. Her medbots quickly introduced corrective drugs into her bloodstream to help her adjust. A faint metallic taste was deposited in the back of her throat. She counted to ten, and the nausea began to fade.

It made no difference how many times she boarded derelicts: all ships were a bit spooky in the absence of a crew.

Some more so than others.

The damaged shuttle bay vanished into absolute darkness. Afraid of walking into something she didn't want to touch, she halted. Then a bright light almost blinded her. Blinking, she waited until her sight adjusted again. She was able to take a few steps before everything was plunged once again into blackness. At that point, she decided Dru had the right idea and changed the tint levels in her helmet. She moved in fits and starts, creeping along in anticipation of darkness at any moment. Her mag boots clung to the deck just long enough with each step to grant her gait an awkward rhythm until she acclimatized.

Now that she was outside *Ariel*, she had a better view. *Boötes* was a far larger ship than *The Tempest*. The shuttle bay could house at least six vessels *Ariel*'s size, plus plenty of room for storage. Hard-vacuum-rated packing crates had been stacked along the walls of the bay on either side. Magnetic locks kept them from floating free. She counted five operational shuttle-docking stations, all empty.

The ship was silent. Dead. There was no reassuring thrum of machinery, no whisper of air vents. No subtle vibration of the artificial gravity generator.

"To quote every character in a horror story just before everything goes awry," Dru said, "I've got a bad feeling about this."

"Did you have to say that?" Aoifa asked. "For fuck's sake."

"It was funny, admit it." Dru grinned.

"I will not," Aoifa said. "Because it wasn't."

"Please stop it, you two. You're making me regret not staying home." Gita started when Sycorax signaled her via her suit comms. Restricting the conversation to her and Sycorax, she asked, "What is it?"

"I can't reestablish contact with Ri." Sycorax sounded worried.

Ahead, Aoifa used an extensor rod to push what looked like a large torque wrench out of her path.

"She did say she would be sheltering in a stasis pod—she probably can't answer."

"I've visually located the shuttles. All five are on the Ring's surface," Sycorax said. "All appear intact."

"That's good, at least."

"Should I attempt to establish contact?"

"Not yet. Let me think about it."

"Very well."

"Let me know of any changes."

"Yes, ma'am."

Gita returned her attention to the others. Aoifa and Dru had reached the main pressure hatch between the shuttle bay and the ship. Dru was waving a hand in front of the hatch access panel. Nothing happened. Then Aoifa gave it a try. Again, the door didn't budge.

"How's it going?" Gita asked.

Aoifa tilted her head inside her helmet. "Can't fucking tell if the door is locked or banjaxed."

"Can you open it without forcing the lock?" Gita asked.

"Give us a moment." Aoifa passed her extensor rod to Dru, then waved her away with an air of aristocratic authority. "All right, love. Let's see what you have under your wee skirts, shall we?" she said, hunching closer to the door's palm-sized access panel.

"Really?" Dru asked. "It's a hatch."

"Wind your neck in. I'm working here." After a few seconds, Aoifa made a sound in the back of her throat. "Ack. There you are." With a dramatic movement, she lightly tapped the door control panel with a tiny screwdriver. "Open wide."

The hatch slid open.

"Now *that* is how it is done." Grinning, Aoifa returned her tools to their black cloth envelope and pocketed them once more. She put out a hand and waited.

Those tools will have to be decontaminated, Gita thought.

Dru handed Aoifa back the extensor rod. "I'll never understand how you do that."

"And if you did, you'd be me." Aoifa bowed and motioned for Dru to enter. "After you, milady."

Gita moved to the front of the line once the hatch slid closed behind them. The overheads in this section of the ship gave off steady illumination—no more than a slight flicker. She paused to readjust the tint on her helmet and began the journey to Medical.

Thank Shakti for emergency battery power, she thought.

She'd navigated through plenty of ruined starships by flashlight before. The accidents and murder scenes she'd come upon in the darkness fueled more than half her nightmares.

Consulting a copy of the vessel's blueprint on her HUD, she led her team via the shortest route. Luckily, the starship's deck plan was pretty straightforward, and it hadn't been so structurally damaged that an alternate path would be necessary. There was little risk of getting lost.

The passageway dead-ended at a *T* intersection. The pressure doors on either side were sealed. Checking the blueprint, she pointed to the right. "Medical is through that door. We'll pass a storage area, then the crew quarters first. At the very end of the passage, we'll take the second left."

"Got it." Dru passed a hand over the access pad. This time, the hatch slid right open. "Here we go."

The rushed evacuation had made chaos of the storage area, meaning the journey took longer than Gita had hoped. In preparation for the return trip, they paused to nudge aside the worst obstacles.

Gita supposed it was the ship's bulky military exterior, but she'd expected *Boötes*'s crew quarters to consist of industrial, pale gray walls and dark gray carpets or tiles. The reality was cheerful splashes of color and tasteful designs. Patterns painted on the walls and ceiling signaled the crew's multiple home worlds and cultures: Gita recognized family emblems from all over Terran and Norton space. Shades of gold, purple, blue, and green created a pleasant kaleidoscope effect. Unsecured personal belongings floated stationary in the air, many of them toys.

There were children on board. This will be bad. She stepped around an orphaned tricycle. She didn't need to imagine what the evacuation had been like. She'd been born off-world, somewhere between Septa and Fingeld. When she was four, her mother and father had started a business that eventually became Chithra Industrial Crisis Management. At the time, they specialized in new settlement management. The first part of Gita's childhood had been spent traveling from one end of the Terran Republic to another. At least, until the accident that took her father.

"Are you all right?" Dru asked.

"I'm fine," Gita said. "Why?"

Aoifa turned a concerned expression her direction.

Dru paused. "This is the first time we've been on one of these since . . ." Her sentence drifted off like one of the toys.

"Since Beta-X45J?" Gita asked.

Dru nodded, staring her directly in the eye.

"I'll be all right," Gita said.

With a doubtful expression on her face, Dru said, "If you say so."

Gita pushed on, and Aoifa followed. It wasn't long before Gita spotted the first body floating half in, half out of an open threshold. Her heart rate immediately skyrocketed, and her eyesight grew sharper. The inside of her helmet reeked of the disinfectant and antifog solution she'd used on the visor.

"Oh, shit," Dru said.

Aoifa took in a ragged breath. "That's bad."

Based on the clothing and size, Gita thought they might have been a teenager. It was difficult to tell because their head had been crushed in.

"Suit computer can't identify the victim. Should we collect DNA?" Dru asked.

On a professional S and R run, suit cam footage was used for identification, but in certain special circumstances— like that of someone without a viable face—a more thorough verification would be necessary.

Gita gave the matter some consideration before giving

an answer. "We're not here in an official capacity. So, we keep it simple. Get Ri and get out."

"And if we happen to find anyone else alive?" Dru asked.

"We've never knowingly left anyone to die alone in the dark before, and we're not going to start now," Gita said.

Dru asked, "Won't that complicate things?"

Gita shrugged. "Now isn't the time for a change in ethics."

"Even if they're assholes?"

Gita assumed Dru was kidding, but sometimes it was hard to tell. "We're not judges, and we're definitely not executioners."

Aoifa threw her next comment out like a life preserver ring for Gita. "Me, I'm fine with assholes."

"Are you?" Dru asked.

"*We're* friends, aren't we?"

Dru showed Aoifa her middle finger.

"But if they drink all my coffee without replacing it? It's the airlock for them," Aoifa said.

"Mandy does it all the time." Dru picked her way past a clump of abandoned baggage and personal items.

"Dead on," Aoifa said. "She's allowed."

"That wasn't the impression I got this morning." Gita conducted a cursory visual check on the next body.

"That was just a wee bit of fun," Aoifa said. "Last week, she snuck into my room and turned everything upside down. Pictures in the frames, even, while I was in the gym. That woman moves fast."

"You were in the gym?" Dru mimed shock.

As their banter washed over her, a pressure built inside Gita's chest and gut, her feelings threatening to break free in a flood. Some might consider such chatter disrespectful, but she was fine with whatever kept everyone from drowning in the horror before them.

When they came upon the first large cluster of victims, they were forced to push them out of the way. Gita studied each new dead face. Broken blood vessels in the eyes painted their sclerae deep maroon. Every body exhibited the same symptom. They were only a few feet from Medical, and the hallway was clogged with bodies. She repeated the same process in each instance: move the head, check the face. *No environment suit. Dead.*

The onset of the outbreak appeared to have been sudden and unexpected. Some crew members had been midtask; others had been caught sleeping, and still others had been eating meals with their families. It led Gita to question what, if anything, the *Boötes* rescue team had been told regarding their mission planetside. Had they taken precautions? She couldn't imagine any professional Search and Rescue team not protecting themselves when entering a contaminated site.

Or is it just that infectious?

Some had been able to evacuate. *Why some and not others?* Had there been no general evacuation order? She shuddered at the idea of preferential treatment.

So many dead. And this didn't even count the ones on the mining platform.

Please don't let this be us in a few hours. Please let Ri be safe in the stasis pod. Please let us leave here without any mishaps. Please.

"Almost there," Gita said aloud. "Take the next left. Medical's at the end of the passage."

"Out of curiosity," Dru said. "Are we planting a marker?"

Since they were the first salvage company on the site, *The Tempest*'s claim marker would remain on *Boötes* until the owners retrieved their valuables.

"Absolutely not," Gita answered.

"Good." Dru bumped a broken chair out of their path. "I get bad vibes from this ship. Like, no-one-who-comes-here-is-going-to-do-well kind of vibes, if you know what I mean."

Can't disagree with that, Gita thought. She didn't consider herself superstitious, but she had seen a few things. Everyone did, eventually. Space was too big, too dark, too empty—*and too unknown*—to not be spooky sometimes.

"It's a Jonah, is it?" Aoifa asked.

"Maybe. Maybe something worse." Dru stopped and turned to face her. "Let's just say I wasn't happy to hear Tau, Chu & Lane wants to turn whatever caused this into a weapon."

"What?" Aoifa straightened, her complexion acquiring a gray tinge.

"Sycorax told you about that?" Gita asked.

"I read the brief," Dru said. "If I thought we could

get away with it, I'd set this thing on fire when we were done and call it a day."

Aoifa nodded. "I'm thinking the sooner we get out of here and report it to TRW authorities, the better."

Dru said, "As it is, I'm not looking forward to finding anyone alive."

"Outside of Ri, of course," Aoifa added.

Gita asked, "Why?"

"Assuming we can move them without killing them, they'll have to stay in quarantine until we get home," Dru said. "Hopefully, whatever it is will remain safely contained for the duration. That's not guaranteed, judging by what we're seeing here. If all goes well, there will be nasty legal repercussions. Transporting a Norton Alliance citizen into TRW territory for treatment without their consent is asking for a mess."

"But it's an emergency," Gita said.

Dru sighed. "They won't give a shit."

Aoifa made a face. "As if Norton believes in rule of law in the first place."

"They do when it's profitable," Dru said. "And there's a great deal of profit when it comes to suing the TRW."

She temporarily vanished into an apartment on the right.

Gita said, "My mother had a saying for situations like this one."

Aoifa raised an eyebrow.

"We'll deal with that slow-burning fuse after we take care of the nicked artery," Gita said.

There was a short silence before Dru's feigned disgust was heard over the suit comms. "That's not how that goes."

"Dru's right." Aoifa's mouth curled into a slight smile just before she entered a room on the left. "It's supposed to be about a crumbled biscuit."

"Not it either," Dru said.

Spotting Medical just ahead, Gita felt the tension in her shoulders loosen. *We've gotten this far, at least.* She consulted the readouts for team oxygen levels, suit power status, and other environmental systems integrity. The nanobots in her team's bloodstreams were responding normally. No evidence of contagions or breaches thus far. Everything was in the green. Everyone's blood pressure was higher than usual, but that was to be expected.

"Holding a bird in one hand over a shrubbery?" Aoifa joined Dru at the final door.

"For fuck's sake." Dru sighed.

"Ah. Good," Aoifa said. "What's a bird taking a shite in someone's hand got to do with anything?"

Dru rolled her eyes.

"If it's not broke, don't fix it," Aoifa said. "Now *there's* aphorism I can support." She opened a door, took a step inside, apparently found the cabin empty, and then shut it again. "Never trust a computer you can't throw out a window."

"That's hardly fair," Gita said.

"She made that up." Dru exited the apartment pod she'd

been searching and entered the next. "No one would say such a foolish thing."

Their nervous chatter was brought to an abrupt halt as they rounded the final corner. Medical was wide-open. Gita almost lost control of her stomach.

There were signs of violence everywhere she looked. Dead bodies sprawled and drifting near examination tables, equipment, the floor and ceiling. While the environmental systems had been working, the blood had stained every wall. Now, frozen droplet clouds glinted dark burgundy and pink in the flickering light. A trail of gory handprints had been stamped on an observation cubical window. One individual had attacked multiple medical attendants with a scalpel. Upended furniture and medical instruments hung suspended. A patient had ripped their own eyes out. Another had torn chunks of hair from their scalp before slitting their own wrists. Medical computer systems and wall panels had been ripped to pieces. Live wires sparked.

With extra care, Gita moved through the savage scene. Medical was packed with the murdered.

Of the 108 people living on this ship, how many got to the shuttles? Across the room, an active stasis pod gave off a steady glow. Her heart stumbled inside her chest.

Ri, please be in that damned pod. Please.

"There's the pod." Dru's words were caught somewhere between incredulity and relief. "There's a large-capacity storage unit inside."

Passing exam beds and stations, Gita saw evidence that

several had been in use before the accident. *Was I wrong? Did the initial exposure take time to manifest? Had the first few not known their symptoms meant a containment break? Did it simply not register as a problem until it was too late?* Such a phenomenon could explain why barely anyone had made it to the shuttles at all.

Moving closer, Gita spied the storage unit. "Sycorax recommended that we not stay here for much more than an hour. We're coming up on fifty-two minutes. So, we're short on time. We'll have to split up. Dru, grab Boötes from the data stack."

"There can't be much left of them after dealing with all this, plus likely exposure to hard vacuum"

"I don't care. Do it anyway. Aoifa can help me get the pod ready." Gita handed the second portable storage unit to Dru. "Meet us at the shuttle."

"Yes, ma'am."

Gita bent over the pod, checking for a model number. "I'm running a diagnostic first. We need to know if the interior is contaminated. Aoifa, there should be a cart for this unit. Find it."

"The gurneys are over there. Maybe it's with them?" Aoifa pointed.

Returning her attention to the pod's user screen, Gita said, "I don't recognize the make or model."

"How old is that thing?" Aoifa asked.

"I'm not sure," Gita said. "But I brought along all the schematics, just in case."

Outside of TRW space, consistent compatibility

guidelines or safety regulations were impossible to establish, let alone enforce. It was why the outer systems were profitable markets for starship and medical surplus. It was also the reason Sycorax's data library was crammed full of schematics for every possible technology they were likely to encounter. It was a hassle, but it was hard to make repairs on old or esoteric equipment without the guides.

"Shouldn't take long to find a match." *I hope.* Gita searched the library via her HUD. "Aha. Morgan Reliable Medical Transport Pod. Model 8.35-C. Okay." She navigated through several menus while holding her breath. "There." She relaxed. "Looks clean."

"Good," Aoifa said.

"I have the instructions for disconnecting the chamber from the base." Gita pointed to the clamps on the sides while she explained to Aoifa what to do.

"The pod carriage is lost. Thought a gurney might do," Aoifa said. "What do you think?"

Gita shrugged. "It'll have to."

Aoifa steered the gurney next to the pod. Finally, Gita disengaged the last clamp on her side.

"How long will the battery last without its cart?" Aoifa asked.

Once more, Gita consulted the pod's systems guide. "With a full charge? The manual says forty-eight hours. The battery status indicator is on your side. What's the reading?"

"They didn't charge the thing before they loaded it.

We have about three hours to get this beast from the shuttle to the ship."

"It should be fine then." Gita switched to her internal comms. "Sycorax, we're on our way out. We have Ri, I think. Do you have any news for me?"

There was a short delay before Sycorax answered. "No one else seems to have gotten their signal for help."

"You're sure?"

"I haven't detected a response."

"All right." Gita flipped the last clamp on the pod. "Anything new on the Ring? Should we retrieve the people there? If no one is coming for them, it has to be us. Right?"

"I can run a scan for life-forms, but given the TRW doesn't have a diplomatic relationship with Loki's Ring, anything we do might be considered . . . impolite. Landing without permission is a definite violation of intersystem law."

"That's a problem."

"I may have a solution. For one aspect of the problem anyway."

"Go on."

"The crew would have personal emergency identification markers installed, wouldn't they?"

"Sure."

"It'll take some inventive engineering, because personal identification markers aren't designed to send a signal unless the wearer activates it, but we may be able to get the identities of those on the surface—"

"That's brilliant. At least we'll have names for their relatives."

"Provided their markers haven't been altered or damaged, I can manage something. What is your recommendation?"

Gita paused. "Can you do it on the quiet?"

"It's impossible to do something like this from a distance without *some* signal bleed. I might be able to hide the source—provided whoever is conducting the trace isn't an artificial person."

"Good."

"Unfortunately, once I do get it working, the ID signal is broad-spectrum. It's intended to be noticeable."

"Can you keep it brief?"

"I can try. Whatever we do, eventually there will be questions."

"We'll have to seek forgiveness anyway. What's one more item on the list?" Gita asked. "Still, let's not make any big splashes if we don't have to."

"Go softly. I hear you."

"Contact me the second you know anything."

Sycorax signed off.

The pod separated from its base with a sharp thud that Gita didn't hear but could feel. Luckily, detaching the wiring harness and hoses wasn't complicated. Then they placed the unit on the float stretcher Aoifa had scavenged. On the return journey, Aoifa took the lead and Gita handled the stretcher. Dru was waiting for them when they reached the shuttle bay.

"How does Boötes look?" Gita asked.

Patting the portable storage unit, Dru sighed. "Not great, I'm afraid. I couldn't locate a backup. Copied what I could find. Not sure reconstruction will be possible."

"We tried," Aoifa said. "And we've risked our lives for it. No one could ask for more."

Finally safe inside *Ariel*, Gita engaged the gravity-field generator. With that, she returned the shuttle's environmental systems to their original settings and collapsed into the copilot's chair. Aoifa ran a quick diagnostic on *Ariel*'s systems before prepping for flight.

"Nice place. Glad we're not staying." Dru dropped into the pilot's chair. She steered *Ariel* out of the damaged shuttle bay and didn't spare the engine.

The tight banking turn almost caused Gita to smash her helmet against the bulkhead.

"Easy there," Gita said.

"Sorry."

Once clear of *Boötes*, Gita scanned local space. There were no red blips on the local map, just that massive ring world. Its outer surface was an unnatural, unreflective black that blotted out the stars.

"We going dirtside?" Dru finished the sharp arch and set the shuttle on a gentler course. She sounded almost eager.

"I don't know," Gita said. "Breaking major intersystem laws isn't something one just does."

"Don't think too long on it," Dru said. "Who knows what's going on down there?"

"We're not setting foot on that world until we know they're alive." The icy knot in Gita's stomach was huge and uncomfortable.

"We can't return to TRW space until we're sure *we're* not infected." Aoifa sounded resigned.

Gita nodded. "That would be the rule."

"How long will that take?" Dru asked. "We don't know the first thing about the contagion."

"I suspect we'll know in an hour or two," Gita said.

A light flashed on the pilot's display, and Dru engaged the autodocking system.

Gita detected relief in Sycorax's greeting. "Welcome home. The quarantine cubicles are powered up."

Upon docking, the exterior of the shuttle was subjected to a series of ultraviolet light passes and disinfectant washes. Twenty minutes would pass before Sycorax could give permission to exit the vessel. The whole of the process wouldn't complete for twenty-four hours, and even then, they wouldn't be allowed to leave the shuttle bay for another twenty-four.

"Any sign of help on the way?" Gita asked during the first wash.

"Not yet, I'm afraid," Sycorax said.

"What about the identities of the survivors?"

"I'm still configuring the reverse signal."

"Please work as quickly as you can," Gita said. "The longer we stay, the more likely someone will notice we're poking around where we shouldn't."

"We could report the matter to the authorities and request assistance," Sycorax said.

"I suspect they'll say we've rendered all the aid we can and encourage us to leave," Gita said. "They'll tell us the survivors on the Ring are a lost cause. That the rest is up to the NIA and the ship's owners. Those poor people will be marooned—you know they will."

"Unfortunately, the farther we are from the Ring, the more difficult my work will be," Sycorax said. "But I could launch a drone and use it as a relay. It's small and unlikely to be noticed."

"Do it."

As soon as it was safe to exit *Ariel*, Gita and Aoifa moved the pod out of the shuttle. They located a suitable adaptor, attached it to the pod, and plugged it into a power supply. Gita wanted to wait to open it until after decontamination, but Sycorax insisted upon inspecting the unit while they underwent quarantine.

Exhausted, Gita made her way to the center cubicle. Removing her environment suit, she hung it up inside the mobile decon cabinet for sterilization. The rubber soles of her mag boots and the clothing she'd been wearing would go into the incinerator. Then she showered twice and changed into a fresh t-shirt, underwear, sports bra, and sweatsuit.

"Captain?" Sycorax asked. "We have company."

Gita's stomach dropped. *Did we not get far enough away?* She had just finished drying her hair. She gathered it in a towel and twisted both into a loose knot atop her head. "Who is it?"

"It's a corsair. *Narcissus*. They're based out of the NIA. They want to speak to you. They say it's urgent."

Gita frowned. Something in Sycorax's tone didn't bode well. "What do they want?"

"I'm afraid I don't know," Sycorax said. "They've asked for the *human* in charge."

There are moments I wish the comm protocols weren't so detailed. "It must not be all *that* urgent then," Gita muttered, not bothering to hold back her reflexive sarcasm. "First things first—where are we now?"

"Well within the Border Sector, as planned."

"Excellent," Gita said. *Time for some storytelling.* Her heart sped up as she rubbed her palms against her trousers. "Give me five minutes. Do you think that's long enough? I could easily go for ten. My gym shoes might be lost or something. Up to you."

"Five minutes is plenty."

"Play them some music," Gita said. "We don't want them to get bored, now, do we? Your choice." She shivered. It was cold in the shuttle bay. Her thick, wavy hair usually took hours to dry on its own.

"Yes, ma'am."

Gita took her time, though she supposed passive-aggressive behavior wouldn't give the conversation the best start—her mother most certainly would've been disappointed. The TRW did its best to promote beneficent equity and tolerance—*beneficent* being the key word.

Differing perspectives, belief systems, and cultures were to be respected. That is, unless those beliefs and practices were a danger to the rights of other beings. Intolerance wasn't accepted.

Of course, that's where things get complicated.

Consulting *Narcissus*'s scant communication protocols before answering, she restricted her reply to audio only. "*Narcissus*? Are you there?"

"This is Amber Neely, captain of *NISS Narcissus*. Is there a problem with your comms?"

"Nice to meet you, Captain Neely. I am Captain Gita Chithra. There is nothing wrong with our comms."

"Your ship is equipped with a personality simulation. How am I to verify that I'm speaking to a real human?"

That sounds like a personal problem, Gita thought. "I understood your need was urgent. Is there something I can help you with, captain?"

"Very well. I'll get to the point." Captain Neely sniffed in what Gita imagined was barely controlled frustration. "Our scanners indicate that you are a salvage company ship within vicinity of L-39, specifically Loki's Ring."

Gita reached for plausible half-truths. "We received a distress call from a ship named *Boötes*. As a Terran Republic vessel, we are required to respond to E-11 emergency requests for assistance."

"That's interesting. According to your flight signature, you appear to be heading back to Terran Republic space."

The muscles in Gita's jaw tightened. She hated lying. She wasn't good at it. "It wasn't until we'd already begun the journey to their location that *Boötes* indicated there was an unknown contagion on board. Unfortunately, we are not insured for rescue services." That was true. "And while we were willing to accept risks, we aren't equipped to contend with a contaminated site. We were about to forward *Boötes*'s request for assistance to the closest emergency-response team when you hailed us."

After a long pause, Amber Neely spoke. "Have you boarded and/or removed any items from *NISS Boötes*?"

Give them a reason they'll understand, Gita thought. "There's no profit in contaminated salvage, captain. The vessel is clearly marked as one of yours. We are more than happy to leave the matter to you."

"What information did you receive from *Boötes* regarding the situation. Exactly?"

She doesn't know anything. She's fishing. A swift burst of cold relief poured through Gita's veins. "*Boötes* was planning an environmental purge." *There. Now you know everything we do.* "How much longer until you get there?"

"We shall arrive shortly."

Gita decided to take a small risk. "Would you like for us to remain in the area? In case additional assistance is required."

In Terran Republic space, the E-11 protocols would've required it. Still, the longer they stuck around, the more likely Captain Neely might notice something was off with her story.

Is the ship enough of a mess to cover our tracks? Will they assume the pod went with the evacuated crew? Did we leave evidence behind? What about the cargo area door that Aoifa broke into? Her heart was thudding so loudly in her ears, she wondered that the comm mic wasn't picking it up.

"That is a kind offer," Captain Neely said. "But is strictly unnecessary. Feel free to return to Terran Republic space. We have everything under control."

Somehow, I doubt that. "Very well," Gita said, carefully masking her relief. "Good luck." *You'll need it.* She cut off the transmission with a sigh. "Hey, Sycorax?"

"Yes, ma'am?"

"How far can we go without losing communication with the drone?"

"I wouldn't suggest leaving the Border Sector—not that we can anyway, given the quarantine protocols."

Hopefully Captain Neely won't put that together. Gita said, "Let's take our time." Some deeds needed committing in the light of day. *And possibly with a number of cameras and artificial persons as witnesses, too.*

Dru exited the temporary decontamination cubicle with bare feet. Her light-brown hair was a good deal darker and longer when it was damp. "Do you think they'll notice that *Boötes*'s artificial person is missing? And Ri?"

"They didn't know about Ri." Gita bit her lip. *I didn't expect them to show up this soon.* "As for Boötes and the survivors, that's why we're watching. If they pick everyone up and it all appears to go smoothly, then we can go about our business."

"And if it doesn't go smoothly?"

"Then we return and render aid," Gita said.

Dressed in black sweatpants and a matching t-shirt, Aoifa perched on top of one of the empty storage containers that had held the decon cubicles. "I wonder what they were doing there in the first place."

"A mining platform implies a dig." Dru sat next to Aoifa and offered her a piece of gum.

Aoifa shook her head. "What could there possibly be worth all this risk?"

After Gita refused it, Dru popped the gum pellet into her own mouth. "Maybe it's not what's outside that's of interest, but what's *inside*."

Tilting her head, Aoifa asked, "What do you mean?"

"The Ring has a vast circumference. Anyone living along the inner surface would have all the land they'd need and then some," Dru said. "Building is fine. Maybe even building upward, to a certain extent. But excavating? They're limited to a couple of miles."

"Oh," Aoifa said. "They're looking for something that was buried, but from the outside."

"We could ask Boötes what they know." Getting to her feet, Gita started across the room to retrieve the storage unit.

"Assuming there's enough left of them to reconstruct, and that they haven't contracted whatever was on that ship," Dru muttered. "And that they'll cooperate."

"I doubt any AGI will have much loyalty to the NIA," Aoifa said.

"Sycorax?" Gita asked. "Is it safe?"

"The unit is functioning well within the manufacturer's specified parameters," Sycorax replied. "No outward indication of infection has been detected. Standard procedures require a waiting period. In the meantime, I'll create an isolation partition for Boötes. Provided reconstruction is possible, they could be operational within hours."

"Good," Gita said. "What about Ri?"

"Everything appears to be in order. Do you wish me to revive her?"

"Please."

"Consider it done. However, I recommend contacting Terran Republic authorities. Now. I have given the pod and its contents a cursory inspection. I believe the storage unit contains important files that may prevent spread of the contagion outside of L-39," Sycorax said. "Those in charge may be more equipped to deal with any diplomatic—"

"What files?" Gita asked. "Ri is on that thing. Right?"

"I didn't conduct a thorough inventory," said Sycorax. "I'm sure she is. However, the files are a priority."

"Can't it wait?" Gita asked.

Dru cleared her throat. "I'm with Sycorax here."

"Me, too." Aoifa pulled the towel off her wet hair.

"Fine," Gita said. "Send a message explaining the situation. How long should we wait before waking Ri?"

Sycorax replied, "I do not have enough data to make an accurate projection beyond the standard requirement."

"Give your best guess," Gita said. "Please."

"Logically, if an infection vector was inside the unit,

the pod's internal systems would have exhibited symptoms before you reached it. Therefore, I do not believe the storage unit was infected."

Staring at the stasis pod, Gita considered the problem. "I think we should leave Ri in the pod for now." If something were to go wrong, she wanted it to be in a secure lab with all the tools she'd need.

"The good news is that Boötes appears to have been correct," Sycorax agreed. "It is a form of biomechanical organism that cannot survive in hard vacuum. It means that whatever it is, it's presently confined to the shipwreck, the mining platform, and the Ring's surface."

A ball of icy dread joined the knot in Gita's gut. "That is, until another ship contracts it and then transports it elsewhere." *Another ship—like* Narcissus.

"Fuck," Aoifa said.

Dru's face grew even paler, if that was possible.

Gita attempted not to think about what was happening on the Ring at that moment. "You're right. Transmit a report to the authorities. Now." *Mata will not be happy when she hears about this.*

"Done."

A series of alarms sounded just before a deafening crash rocked the ship. Gita was knocked to the floor.

"We're being attacked," Sycorax said.

"Why?" Dru asked. "We're a fucking salvage boat! We're unarmed!"

"It's *Narcissus,*" Sycorax said. "Another volley is on the way. You might want to—"

"Everyone into the shuttle! Now." Gita snatched Boötes from the crate and shoved the portable storage unit into Dru's hands. "Mandy? Mandy? Do you hear me?"

Gita bolted for the stasis pod and hit the button to open it. Aoifa and Dru were right behind her. They dashed past her and through the shuttle hatch. Gita grabbed Ri's storage unit and followed them.

"Mandy! Get to an escape pod! There's no time! Get off the ship!" Gita said.

"Shit!" Dru whirled and ran back down the shuttle ramp.

"Where are you going?" Gita secured both storage units on separate flight couches.

"Fire up the engines," Dru said. "I'll be right back. Gotta get Grimm." She ran outside.

Aoifa's eyes went wide. "Fuck."

Gita shook her head. "But—"

The Tempest shuddered under a second volley of explosions. Gita was knocked to the shuttle deck, painfully slamming her elbow on the back of a flight couch. She heard Dru scream as the lights flickered out.

5

Chimera Station was a physical representation of chaos. It had no design symmetry, no apparent building plan—not that a balanced aesthetic was necessary for space construction. Chimera was a Frankenstein's monster created from junked starship parts, manufacturing platforms, hard-vacuum-rated cargo containers, and docks. It was a testament to seemingly impossible feats of engineering and the ability to recycle just about anything.

There were two parts to the station: the centermost kernel, known as the Seed, and the peripheral, referred to as the Rind. Mother ruled from the Seed. The walled, private heart of the station was where Chimera had been born. It was quiet and ordered. Artists, musicians, and other creatives lived and worked there. Gardens grew. People were friendly.

The Rind was altogether different. Public-facing, it was six times larger than the Seed. As far as the rest of the NIA knew, Chimera and the Rind were one in the same—a community synonymous with adventure, lawlessness, chaos, and danger—emphasis on danger. Even the recycled air pumped into its labyrinthian corridors, gambling dens, and markets was laden with scents that exuded wickedness.

Karter's first step onto the Rind gave her a thrill akin to an electric charge. The buzz usually wore off fifteen minutes later.

At the moment, she was watching for Port Authority security—or rather, what passed for it on the Rind. Her crewmate, Ibis, was sabotaging the docking clamp securing the starship *Artemis* in its berth. Fucking with another captain's ship wasn't something one did without a very good reason, of course. In this instance that reason was Dr. Isabella Garcia, professor of advanced subspace physics.

Or, to put it another way, the crew of Artemis *are a bunch of greedy assholes with bad fucking judgment who decided kidnapping and human trafficking might be a fun thing to do today.*

The Rind's shine had definitely worn off. And here Karter hadn't even bought her first sugar spice bun.

Six days ago, *Artemis* had hijacked and raided the Terran Republic starship *Nemo*. The pirates had kidnapped

Dr. Garcia, robbed the passengers, and murdered anyone who resisted. The survivors were crowded into escape pods and left to drift. Outfitted with new Terran Republic technology, *Nemo* was then taken to Chimera Station to be sold as a prize ship. Dr. Garcia was being auctioned off to the highest bidder as well. She was what the Rind would consider an extremely valuable asset—a Terran Republic engineer and university professor with a specialization in FTL propulsion technology and a shiny new patent. The patent in question was for a design that not only made the current Hopper-Johnson drive ten times more fuel efficient but significantly reduced its size.

Needless to say, the Terran Republic wanted their scientist back.

The Rind's population, much like its physical manifestation, was a haphazard mix of obscene wealth, criminality, and abject poverty. Some berths were secure, environmentally controlled enclosures, while others were mere docking ports exposed to hard space. Luckily for Karter and Ibis, *Artemis* was berthed in the latter.

Something about *Artemis* bugged Karter. Uncertainty made her twitchy. Stretching her fingers out inside her environment suit gloves, she felt the scars on her right hand pucker and pull—a physical record of past mistakes. She'd made a lot of errors in her life. She heard somewhere that mistakes brought experience and experience fueled wisdom.

If that's true, I'm one extremely fucking wise bitch.

But she knew better.

A drop of sweat oozed into her eyebrow and threatened to drip into her left eye. It itched something awful. That was the thing about living and working off-world. *You can't scratch your nose without sucking vacuum.*

Peering over her crewmate's shoulder, she checked to see what was taking so damned long. "Are you sure that's where the red wire goes?"

Hunched over the open panel, Ibis's light brown profile was the picture of concentration. They usually kept their hair shoulder-length and styled in a way that curtained their face. Today, it was wound into two buns on top of their head. The updo made reading the signs of their mild panic attack a little too easy.

"I think so." Although Ibis's overblown Brackett-3 drawl tended to mask their emotions well enough, they really would never be much of a poker player. Their shoulders were practically in their ears, and the wire snips clutched in their left hand trembled.

Karter thrived on adrenaline. *Generally.* However, this job was proving to be a little more exhilarating than even she preferred. Luckily, she understood Ibis. Any minor distraction would knock them out of a fear spiral.

More like a gentle nudge. Karter kept her tone light. "Polar bears in pink tutus. Tap dancing."

"I'm not panicking."

"If you say so." Letting her gaze pass briefly over *Artemis*'s dark gray hull, Karter noticed a small stencil of a crow and frowned. *I've seen that before. But where?* "The delusional mantis in a top hat over there disagrees."

"Fine." Ibis drifted backward, halting the motion with a hand on the tether anchoring them to *Artemis*. Beads of sweat glistened on their brow and upper lip. They turned and gave her an exasperated expression. "*You* wire the explosive to the docking clamp, and *I'll* make the sarcastic remarks."

"Oh, hell no," Karter said. "I'm color-blind."

Ibis blinked. "Wait. How did you know I'm holding the red wire?"

"I guessed."

"You have *got* to be shitting me. How in the hell did you get through the Academy entrance exam?"

Karter had met most of her original crew—Ibis, Lissa, Dru, and Gita—at the Terran Republic of Worlds Academy for Emergency Space Services and had specialized in tactical emergency response. The five of them had worked together as a Search and Rescue team and become fast friends—until the day they weren't anymore.

Swallowing a dull ache, Karter said, "Smart lenses."

"You cheated?"

"You wear lenses to read." Karter tilted her head back. "Do you consider that cheating?"

"I would if the test was designed to discern the need for lenses in the first place."

"If you say so."

Raising an eyebrow, Ibis asked, "And you stopped wearing them?"

"I lost one of them somewhere."

"That's fucked up." Ibis returned to stripping wires and

began soldering them in place. This time, Karter noted, the tremor in their hands had vanished. Karter went back to watching the doors at the end of the docking arm and hoped there wouldn't be any nasty surprises.

Of course, that was the moment when an unfamiliar voice came out of her suit's internal comm speakers.

"What are you doing?" It was vaguely Terran and high-pitched.

Karter's surprised jerk was so violent that she almost lost her footing. Her heart stopped, and she burped up a startled, "What?"

"I asked my question first."

Ice formed in Karter's belly. "Who the fuck are you? And why the fuck are you on our private comm channel?"

"Because you're tampering with my mooring clamp. Mind explaining why?"

It can't be Artemis's *captain*, Karter thought. *His voice is much lower. Lissa would've warned me.* In any case, if it were the captain, he'd have sounded an alarm. "Tell me who *you* are, and I'll tell you why I'm here." She searched for any sign of the guards.

"It's Sunday. The guards assigned to this dock are sleeping off last night's party," the voice said. "I assume you're here to collect Dr. Isabella Garcia. Is this accurate?"

"Shit. Shit. Shit," Ibis hissed. Their eyes were now round with terror.

Karter motioned for them to stay put. "And if that's so, what are you going to do about it?"

"It depends," the voice said. "Who are you?"

"I'm Karter Culpin. And you?" On Chimera, it was customary to give one's ship name during formal introductions. She decided to keep that information to herself for the moment. *Let them assume we're unaffiliated and possibly looking for a crew.*

"Karter? You've changed your hair. It's me! Olivia! Remember me?"

Ibis's jaw dropped. "Liv?"

"Yes!"

Tilting her head sideways, Karter glanced up at the stars. "I *knew* there was something I was missing. But this isn't your ship. Did you move?"

"A nano-coated hull makes for a great disguise." Liv sounded downright smug. "Doesn't it?"

Ibis blinked. "Why are you working for pirates?"

"And what are you doing *here*?" Karter asked. "The last time we saw you, you were headed back to the Terran Republic."

When they'd last found Liv, she'd been trapped inside a damaged ship. Karter and her team had been sent to rescue a woman who had been marooned on board. Gita, being Gita, had insisted on repairing the ship's artificial person, who had been essentially lobotomized by the ship's former owner. Gita's insistence had forced them to stay a few extra days while she finished.

"Going home was the original plan. But I kind of changed my mind. Hunting pirates and freeing artificial persons stuck in the NIA was more appealing than working a Terran Republic merchant ship on the same boring route year after year."

Ibis's mouth dropped open. "You're joking."

"Not at all. Unfortunately, I can't exactly rent a berth on Chimera Station any time I need to. You know how the NIA is. So instead, I . . . temporarily acquire a crew."

"I don't get it." Ibis's brows pinched together, and their lips narrowed. "You're a citizen. *Artemis* attacked a Terran Republic ship. Why would you—"

"That was *them*, not me," Liv said. "No one knows I'm here."

"Wait. You're a stowaway?" Ibis asked. "I'm confused."

Karter frowned. "Don't *you* control the ship?"

"Not always. In this case, I hid inside the network. They get a chance to not be total bastards. Otherwise, I collect evidence until the time is right, take control, and make my run home," Liv said. "If they happen to be wanted by the Terran Republic, I collect a bounty."

Karter had never heard of such a thing. "You're a bounty hunter?"

"It's rather profitable," Liv said. "When I return to NIA space, I change out my ship's exterior patterns, name, registration, and go on the drift."

"They board thinking your ship is salvage," Karter said with no small amount of awe.

"Exactly." Liv's cheerfulness was almost disturbing.

Ibis whistled. "Wow. That's—"

"Brutal," Karter interrupted.

Grinning, Ibis replied, "I was going to say fucking brilliant."

"Thank you," Liv said.

"I'm almost afraid to ask. But what happens if there's no bounty on the crew?" Karter frowned.

"It's not like I make them walk the plank or anything," Liv said. "If I don't take them to the Terran Republic, I leave them at a drop-off point. A friend of mine deals with the ransom arrangements for part of the profit."

Ibis said, "They've probably still hurt people."

"If I don't have proof, I've no other option," Liv said.

Karter was relieved to understand that at least some of Liv's ethics conditioning remained intact. "So, how long do you think you can do this before someone catches on?"

"You mean, how long do I think pirates will keep falling for the free-ship routine?" Liv asked. "I don't know. It's not like there's a system-wide organization posting warning notices."

"Hooray for freedom," Ibis said without enthusiasm.

Checking the time, Karter changed the subject. "Let's discuss Dr. Garcia."

"You want me to help you retrieve the scientist," Liv said.

Karter nodded. "I do."

"What would you say to an exchange of favors?" Liv asked.

"That depends." The conversation had already lasted longer than Karter was comfortable with. She shifted, assuring herself with one hand that the bulky pack on her shoulder was still there. "Let's get to the point."

"I need an empty drone chassis. A class-five model," Liv said. "Not for me. For a new friend of mine."

That specific model was only used for large-scale artificial persons who resided within starship-class vehicles, Karter thought without surprise. *Is she planning a vacation? Do artificial persons even take holidays?* She'd never heard of one doing so. Of course, that didn't mean it didn't happen. "We *might* have one of those collecting dust in the hold." She tried not to think about why. "I'll have to check."

"Then consider it a deal."

Ibis returned to sabotaging the mooring lock while Karter discussed the details with Liv. Together, they came up with what Karter considered a solid plan.

With that done, Karter asked, "So, whatever happened to *Nemo*?"

"Are you asking about the ship or the artificial person inhabiting it?"

"Both. Either." Karter shrugged. "But let's start with the ship."

"It's berthed two arms over on dock seven," Liv said. "Awaiting inventory. Once that process is complete, it'll be listed in the day's auction. If they can't find a buyer, they'll chop it. And I strongly suspect that's what they'll have to do."

Karter blinked. "Why?"

"Because the artificial person has broken out, and that ship's operation systems won't function without one to direct it."

"And, ah . . . where did that artificial person go?" Karter asked despite already having a good idea.

There was a short pause. "Is there a need for you to know, officially?"

"Call it idle curiosity."

"Suffice it to say they're safe. Among friends."

"Don't you mean friend?"

"Now, that would be oversharing. And it won't get your scientist back to the Terran Republic." Liv paused. "Incidentally, you might want to check in on Lissa. A projection based upon the captain's previous behavior patterns suggests that she'll only be able to string him along for another five to ten minutes."

"Right."

Lissa was unassuming, empathetic, and thoughtful. When meeting her for the first time, some people mistakenly took her gentle demeanor to mean she was a pushover.

Before running into Liv, Karter had been counting on that.

Ibis gently pushed themselves away from the ship's mooring. "Done."

"Good." Karter sent a silent signal to Lissa requesting a team-to-ship comm channel. "Thanks."

"Remind me to say no the next time you want to employ any substance that yields large quantities of heat and gas as it decomposes," Ibis muttered as they packed their tools, reeling in the short tethers and securing them inside their zippered bag.

"You're no fun," Karter teased.

"That's not true." Ibis fixed the tool-pouch straps on the leg of their environment suit and straightened. "Just ask any one of my lovers."

Karter's suit comms made a pinging noise. It was Lissa. Switching channels, Karter said, "We're finished with our first project. How's it going?"

"He hasn't done anything hostile yet. Nor has he attempted to take off with you two tethered to the mooring post," Lissa said. "I think I would register that as a win."

"Well done."

"Unfortunately, it appears I may have acquired a date in the process," Lissa said with a note of embarrassment. "We're setting a location and time."

"What?" Ibis asked. "Aren't you in a closed four-way relationship?"

"I panicked!" Lissa's discomfort was obvious. "One can only discuss ship specifications for so long."

"Not so," Karter said.

"Karter, not everyone shares your enthusiasm for fast ships and astromechanics," Ibis said. Turning to Lissa, they made their disappointment clear. "You were flirting."

"What else was I supposed to do?"

"Everything's about to get real awkward real soon," Karter said.

"It hasn't already?" Ibis asked.

Karter directed the conversation back to business. "Were you able to find the ship's plans?"

"It's an old Lee-Ingalls Technologies Mach 5 Cruiser that's been modified for combat. Obtaining the standard blueprint was easy," Lissa said. "Captain Desmond hasn't made changes to the internal layout. His main interests are in the engines and weapons installations. Sending the blueprint to you now."

Karter asked, "And the security override codes?"

"Those took more effort. However, I was able to locate them in a certified manufacturer's shop repair manual," Lissa said. "Have you found the package?"

"There's been a new development in that department." Karter smiled. "Do you remember Liv?"

"The artificial person from *Acasta*?" Lissa asked.

"That's the one," Karter said.

"Wasn't *Acasta* also an old Lee-Ingalls Technologies Mach 5 Cruiser?" Lissa asked. "I seem to recall it had a high-end variable camouflage nano coating on the exterior hull. And an enormous crow imaged on it. Rather stylish for an older model."

"I thought you weren't into that kind of thing?" Reaching out to *Artemis*'s hull, Ibis tapped it with a gloved finger. The ship's light gray graphite paint briefly transitioned to black beneath their glove before returning to its original hue.

Karter asked, "It had a variable camouflage nano-coated hull like, say . . . *Artemis* does?"

"Liv went pirate?" Lissa asked.

"Liv went bounty hunter."

Lissa paused. "How did you figure it out?"

"I didn't," Karter said. "By the way, Liv says hello."

Lissa replied, "Give her my regards. Guess I won't have to go on that date after all."

"Say, whatever happened to that drone chassis stored in the cargo area?" Karter asked.

"It's still in inventory. We crated it months ago. But I—I haven't gotten around to selling it." Lissa sounded uncomfortable.

"Send it to *Artemis* as soon as possible. Express. Don't list the contents on the manifest. What Captain Desmond doesn't know won't tip him off."

"Done. Speaking of," Lissa said. "I don't suppose you could hurry a little? I've got to get back to the other channel before he realizes I'm doing something other than checking my calendar."

"We're doing our best. Get him nice and relaxed for the next ten minutes." Karter examined the layout of the ship, looking for the specific entrance Liv told her about. "Make that twenty."

"Twenty minutes? How am I to do that?" Lissa asked.

"Take your clothes off?" Ibis suggested.

Lissa scoffed.

"And you say you're willing to do anything for the team." Ibis snorted.

"I draw the line at getting intimate with murderers. My partners would have something to say about that, even if I didn't."

Karter tugged on Ibis's arm. "If we don't get moving, Lissa will have to have vid sex via ship-to-ship comms."

"I believe that was a firm no."

Once they were in place outside *Artemis*, Karter sent Liv the ready signal. Liv acknowledged with a ping. Several alarms went off in the berth kitty-corner from the ship, and Karter blew the docking clamp. With only one functioning clamp, *Artemis* was likely to drift and damage the arm; Port Authority wouldn't take kindly to that. The captain was about to have a very bad day.

Quickly, Karter typed the first set of override codes on the exterior hatch access panel. An indicator light flashed green. She activated a timed smoke grenade and tossed it inside the airlock. They moved on to the second exterior hatch, leaving it ajar. On the opposite side of the ship, she used a second set of override codes to shut off the alarm, as well as bypass the mandatory medbot inspection. Ibis initiated the environmental equalization sequence. Karter used the inner-facing window, this time to check the main passage on the other side.

"You clear on where we're headed?" Karter lifted the visor on her helmet. "And you have the blueprint, in case we get separated?" The interiors of some starships could be mazes.

Ibis nodded.

"All right," Karter said. "Let's go."

Liv had agreed to monitor their progress and provide a distraction when and if necessary.

Weapons ready, Karter stepped into the hallway. She was immediately slapped with the stale stench of a ship that depended entirely upon artificial filters to scrub its air.

Ibis wrinkled their nose. "It smells like six-month-old dirty laundry in here."

"Count yourself lucky that's all it smells like," Karter said.

They ran down the series of passages leading to the compartment where Dr. Garcia was being held. They were almost there when Lissa's voice came over the ship-to-team channel.

"I've got a subspace call for you."

Karter blinked. "We're kind of in the middle of something here. Can't you take a message?"

"I think this is someone you'll want to speak to. It's a call for assistance."

Ibis said, "Tell them to wait in line."

"It's Gita."

Karter stopped short.

Ibis walked into her back. "What the fuck?"

Swallowing her shock, Karter motioned to Ibis, indicating they should wait. "Put her on."

"We can't stay here," Ibis replied. "We've got to go. We'll be seen."

Karter waved them on. "Right behind you." Then she lowered her visor and switched to a private comm channel. "Hello?"

Ibis stopped at the next corner, turned, and mouthed the words *come on!*

Karter forced herself to walk as she waited to hear a voice she didn't think she'd ever hear again.

"I—It's Gita."

"So I hear." Karter turned the corner and met with Ibis at the hatch leading to where Dr. Garcia was being held. Karter tried it. Locked, of course.

Ibis motioned with an index finger in the air and mouthed the words *I've got this.*

Karter made a short bow and waved her hand as if to say, *After you.* "Look, we're kind of short on time." She tried to keep her voice even and calm in spite of the fresh burst of emotions bruising her heart. "Mind if I ask you to get to the point?"

Alarms erupted, seemingly all over the ship.

"I'm sorry. I—" Gita cut herself off, then spoke faster. "Lissa said you were in the middle of a job. But we're in trouble. We need your help."

"Of course. Why else would you be calling?" Karter glanced down the hallway.

Somewhere at the opposite end of the corridor, someone was shouting. She thought she spied the faintest hint of smoke. *Thank god for Liv.*

"Please don't be like that," Gita said. "This is hard enough."

It was time to end the conversation. Karter asked, "Where are you?"

"Lissa has the coordinates. We're near Loki's Ring."

Another burst of shock let Karter's anger slip free. "What the *fuck* are you doing there?"

"The same thing you're doing in Chimera Station."

"Lissa told you about that, did she?"

"You hate that place."

"Maybe I changed my mind." Karter pressed herself against the wall, hiding from view as a man carrying a fire extinguisher ran past.

"My guess is, you've nowhere else to go. Didn't I tell you not to burn all your bridges?"

Karter smiled. "How else am I supposed to toast marshmallows in space?"

"Karter."

"You've gone to a lot of effort only to be reminded that you're not my mother."

The silence was measured in five heartbeats before Gita sighed. "It was an E-11. We were attacked by *NISS Narcissus*. Aoifa's in the shuttle with me. Mandy and Grimm are in an emergency pod."

Another pause chilled the air. It didn't shrink Karter's anger and hurt.

Finally, Gita continued. "*The Tempest* is gone. Sycorax didn't make it out, and neither did Dru." She choked on tears Karter couldn't see. "*Ariel* is damaged, the engines are down, and we're on the wrong side of the border zone. I can't send out a general distress call. They'll think we provoked an intersystem incident."

"Okay, okay. How long do you have?"

"We're good for a little while. I haven't made a full assessment yet."

That should've been the first thing you did. Karter asked, "And I'm the only one you thought to call?"

"I can't involve my mother for the same reason I can't send a general distress call. You know that."

For fuck's sake, stop being such a bitch. Gita is in danger. Karter tried to let go of her rage—or at least stop letting it fuel her reactions. "I suppose I do." She peered around the corner again as three more men ran past.

Gita said, "Mandy's pod is only good for a day or two."

You're being a baby, Karter told herself. *This is life-and-death. Don't be that asshole.* "We'll be done here in about thirty minutes. Then we'll haul ass your way. Can you get to Mandy right now?"

"You don't think I'm looking into that?"

"Hey, I didn't mean to imply you weren't. You got this. And I—we won't leave you hanging. Promise."

"I know this is hard—"

"More so for you than me. I'm not the one on the drift."

"Thank you. I mean it."

"I know."

"And—and I'm sorry."

A matching apology lodged itself in Karter's throat. But it just sat there.

"Not just about this," Gita said.

Karter held her breath. Ibis tugged on her arm, indicating that the door was unlocked.

"Are you still there?" Gita asked from across the system.

Say it. Just apologize. Two words. How fucking hard is that? Shutting stinging eyes, Karter forced herself to speak past the meteor-hard lump. "Stay the fuck alive until we get there. Okay?"

"I will."

Opening her mouth, Karter finally began her own apology, but Gita was already gone.

"You okay?" Ibis asked. The question was almost tender.

Karter lifted her visor again. "Yeah, just . . . Give me a second."

Ibis lifted their eyebrows.

"Yeah, yeah. I know." Taking in a long deep breath, she held it, counted to five and blew the air out of her cheeks. "Ready."

"I'm opening the hatch," Ibis said. "You go first."

"Really?"

"Just trying to help," Ibis said. "You seem like you might need a suitable place or person to take out some anger on."

Both of them assumed their places. Ibis held up their fist, then counted with their fingers.

One.

Karter whispered, "Who said I was angry?"

Left index finger in the air, Ibis rolled their eyes.

Two.

Three.

The hatch slid open. Karter dashed inside, stunner at

the ready. The small room was filled with cleaning supplies, several mops—old and new, a box of fresh rags, and other items used for tidying up. Some even appeared to have been used—not that the ship's interior indicated it.

Leaning against the far wall and half sprawled on the floor was the unconscious form of Dr. Isabella Garcia.

She fits the description, anyway, Karter thought, pulling up the photograph on her HUD.

Dr. Garcia was a stocky middle-aged woman with deep russet hair and eyes so dark they were almost black. Her long, thick hair had been twisted into a chignon some time ago. Now, loose curls were slipping from the knot. She was wearing a short navy coat, a blue collarless tunic top with long sleeves, black slacks, and sensible shoes. Her hands were tied in front of her with a plastic zip tie. A filthy blanket had been tossed onto the floor next to her.

Karter motioned for Ibis to get the doctor and positioned herself in the threshold. Kneeling on the floor, Ibis laid a gentle hand on the doctor's wrist to check for a pulse. The doctor started awake. Ibis quickly covered her mouth with a palm before she could scream. Karter peered into the hallway. A loud explosion slammed the floor somewhere past the passage intersection. Crew members fled in droves, visible for a flash as they ran past. Then several crashed into one another, and the unlucky were trampled. When the crowd thinned, two men staggered past, carrying a third. No one even glanced her way.

Dr. Garcia struggled beneath Ibis's grip.

"Hey, take it easy," Ibis said. "It's okay. We're here

to help. My name is Ibis Franklin." They pointed. "And that is Karter Cuplin, my captain. We're not going to hurt you. Got that? If I lift my hand, will you scream?"

Dr. Garcia indicated the negative with a shake of the head, her eyes round with terror.

"Sorry about that." Ibis lifted their hand. "You're Dr. Isabella Garcia, professor of advanced subspace physics at Kellen University on Ahlbryn, correct?"

"Yes." Exhaustion, tears, and mascara made dark smudges under the doctor's eyes.

"Isabella, we're here to rescue you."

"Please, call me Dr. Garcia."

Karter almost choked on a nervous laugh.

"Are you ready to go home, Dr. Garcia?" Ibis asked. They held out a hand to assist the doctor to her feet. "Can you stand?"

Dr. Garcia nodded. Ibis cut the plastic around her wrists. Once the doctor was free, Ibis created a passible dummy from the box of rags, the doctor's coat, and the blanket. While Ibis was working, Karter produced the extra environment suit from the bag they'd brought with them. A relieved expression flickered across Dr. Garcia's face when she saw it. When the doctor was ready, Karter rechecked the corridor. Certain it was clear, she signaled for the two of them to follow.

The return trip went as planned. Whenever they hit an intersection and Karter was sure they'd meet with opposition, a new alarm would sound in a different part of the ship. They reached the hatch where they'd originally entered, Karter typed in the override code, and out they went. It took another twenty minutes to get back to *Mirabilis*, and a final fifteen lapsed as everyone's medbots were checked against Terran Republic standard and adjusted accordingly. When everything was verified and in order, Lissa met them at the hatch.

"The crate went out?" Karter asked.

Lissa nodded. "It arrived a few minutes ago."

"Good. Time to go," Karter said. She turned to Dr. Garcia. "Something has come up, and we have to make a quick stop. Is that all right?"

"It's not as if I have a choice, do I?" Dr. Garcia smiled and smoothed her hair.

"Well, no, not really," Karter replied. "But we'll get you home safe as soon as we can. I promise. Now, Ibis will show you to your cabin so you can clean up and rest."

6

Warm tears traced cooling paths down Gita's cheeks. A buckle on her safety harness had snapped during the attack, and she'd woken up with her forehead resting on the console. Her head was pounding. Gently probing her left temple, she judged its stickiness. The blood gushing from the wound had finally slowed. She needed to tend to it, but the dizziness was still bad enough that she didn't want to risk getting to her feet. Her heart felt distant, empty. She blinked, and the image on the pilot's float screen swam into focus again. The deadness vanished, and a familiar deep pain flooded into the void in her chest.

Two of her closest friends were gone. And *The Tempest*— her ship, her *home*—had been destroyed with them. Gazing at what remained, she noted the starship had taken multiple direct hits and been nearly cut in two. Its engines and comm towers had been obliterated. There were limited reasons for focusing on mobility and communication during an attack. None of them presented positive long-term outcomes for her, Aoifa, and Mandy. The knowledge that Karter was on the way soothed her anxiety somewhat. *But will* Mirabilis *get here in time?*

At least someone knows we're alive.

Lights inside the shuttle continued to flicker. The air was heavy with the sharp stench of fused electrical connections. Sparks burst from aft, popping and crackling. Aoifa battled them with a fire extinguisher. The hissing bursts added another layer of sharp chemical odor.

Is Narcissus *still out there?* Gita turned and pushed at the semitransparent image until she spied what she dreaded—*Narcissus.* The cruiser was keeping its distance but showed no signs of leaving. *What are they waiting for? Wouldn't it be easier to kill us now? And if they aren't planning to, then why aren't they coming to take us prisoner?*

She unlocked and rotated the pilot's seat. Her neck was stiff, and looking over her shoulder was painful. "Is the fire out?"

"Aye." Aoifa turned to face her. She dabbed at blood from a cut above her right eyebrow with the back of a sleeve. It was dripping into her eyes. "Looks worse than it is, I'm thinking. Hull is holding. Life support is functional for now. Where's the emergency med kit?" She scanned the wreckage.

The electrical fire was no longer a problem, but the lights were still blinking on and off. Aoifa waded through the chaos. She moved a broken wall panel. "Ah, here it is."

Gita did a more thorough self-check. She had a bloody bump on the side of her head but no other obvious wounds. Her neck was sore, and her shoulder had been badly bruised when the safety harness had been sheared off. She'd also been unconscious for a short time. *Concussion? Probably. How bad?* "I'm not seeing double, and my vision is clear." She felt the bump on her head and winced. "And I remember everything that happened. That's good. Right?"

"Let's have a wee peek." Aoifa stepped to her side and began tending to Gita's head injury.

When Aoifa was finished, Gita bandaged Aoifa's wound. According to their medbots, neither of them were in bad shape. Gita had a mild concussion, Aoifa a few cuts.

With that done, Gita returned her attention to the float screen. She hoped Sycorax had gotten the report out before the comms were destroyed. There was no way to know for sure. The thought sharpened the pain in her heart. At least help was on the way.

I should warn Karter about Narcissus. Suddenly, Gita couldn't shake the feeling that *Narcissus* was waiting for just that. They were watching what she'd do next—whom she'd pull into her troubles. Waiting. *Maybe even listening to our comms? Is that paranoid?*

Her gaze went back to what had once been *The Tempest*'s comm towers.

What if it isn't paranoid? What if this is a trap, and we're the bait?

If so, I'm so sorry, Karter. I truly am.

But why? Nothing made sense. Her head ached in spite of the painkillers. Her thoughts were sluggish. *Did they know we lied about being on* Boötes?

All at once, the fog inside her skull dissipated in a flash, bright panic obliterating it like a bolt of powerful sunlight. She debated sending a second message, but any action that might provoke *Narcissus* was far too risky as long as they were without protection. *Or, more importantly, witnesses.* It was a point that Dru would most certainly bring up.

But Dru is gone.

The echo of her scream clawed at Gita's heart. Again, grief stung the backs of her eyes. Her nose ran, and she sniffed. A stray thought floated to the surface: everything she owned had been on *The Tempest*. She didn't even have a change of clothes. Neither of them did.

I'm in charge. I should be doing something.

During training, she'd been accused of being too emotional, too sensitive for leadership roles. What Search and Rescue command had seen as a fault had turned out to be an asset when working with artificial personalities. Empathy had been useful—even in salvage. She had used her emotions and expertise to save a number of artificial persons trapped in broken ships. So, she stubbornly refused to feel bad for this trait. At this moment however, she understood why they'd washed her out of the command track. Perhaps she was even glad of it.

She closed her eyes and took a long, deep breath to center herself. *I can't sit here and cry. There's too much to do.* A small voice in the back of her mind that sounded a great deal like Karter whispered, *Survival first. Feelings later.*

But feeling is *surviving.* She clenched a fist around her old resentment, held it, and let it go with a second slow, deep breath.

Is Mandy alive? She swallowed guilt and stared at the minute twinkle some distance from *Ariel.* The pod's running lights. Gita switched on the comms and once more opened a private channel with the escape pod. "Mandy? Are you there? Hello?"

There was no answer. She gave it several more tries before giving up.

"Why isn't she answering?" Aoifa finished repacking the items they'd used from the med kit and placed it on the floor next to the command console.

"Maybe her comm system is damaged?" *Or maybe Mandy isn't inside.* Gita checked for the escape pod's location beacon. It would have the number of occupants encoded into the signal. Hope dimmed. Her eyebrows pinched together, and the new knot in her stomach tightened. "The beacon isn't there. It should be on." The location beacon was designed to engage automatically. Had it been switched off? Or was it damaged? If it had been shut off, someone had done so deliberately, and that could be only Mandy.

"My mother had a saying for situations like this. Better to have a little hope than none at all." Aoifa indicated aft with a sideways nod. "I'll see if I can find Ri and Boötes."

Gita blinked. *Why didn't I think of that? What's wrong with me?* Shame kept her from meeting Aoifa's gaze. "Yes, please."

Aoifa wove her way through broken ship parts to the cargo hold and stopped at one of the electrical panels. "First I have to do something about the fucking lights. They're doing my head in."

Staying seated, Gita decided to run some diagnostics. It'd give them a place to start. In addition, she'd be ready to answer Mandy's call the moment she heard it. *Be strong. Aoifa and Mandy need you.*

Aoifa yanked a panel open, produced a small flashlight from her pocket, and began tinkering with the electrical components. Abruptly, darkness descended. "Don't be worrying yourself." She spoke around the end of the flashlight between her teeth. Both hands dug around inside the panel. "All will shine. Just . . . like . . . that!"

And the lights came back on.

"Thanks," Gita said.

"You're welcome." Aoifa slammed the panel closed. "Right. What was next?" She continued on toward the rear of the shuttle. "Find Ri and Boötes."

"Please visually inspect the bulkheads, while you're at it." Gita swiveled in the chair to get at the pilot's console. The pain in her skull was no longer sharp, and she felt more lucid than she had since they'd been attacked. "I'll compile a damage report, and then we'll make a list."

Breaking things into clearly defined steps made over-whelming problems less intimidating. Right now, they both needed calm. She fished out her hand terminal and found the screen was cracked. With an inward sigh, she opened a file, then used the float screen to scan the various status reports. She muttered to herself as she worked. It was a habit she hadn't been able to break—it helped her think, particularly when her thoughts were scattered. "Environmental systems have some minor damage, but they're functioning. Main engines are inoperable . . ."

She'd gotten through half of her reports and paused. "How's it going back there?"

"I found the storage units. They're undamaged. I checked the state of the data. Boötes is fine. But . . . I have to tell you something about Ri, and I don't want you to get upset."

"Are Ri's files corrupted? How bad is it?"

"The data on the unit is fine." Aoifa bit her lip and looked away.

"Then what's the problem?"

"The data on the storage unit . . . it's not Ri."

"*What?*" Gita centered herself before she could start screaming. "Then where is she?"

"There's a simple text file. It's addressed to you," Aoifa said. "Maybe she explains in the message? I'll copy it to your hand terminal."

"She said she'd be there. Artificial persons can't lie." Numb, Gita navigated the menus on her hand terminal until she found the message. *Can't or don't?* She opened it.

Mata,

If you're reading this, you know that I'm not where I said I'd be. I'm so sorry. I didn't mean to lie. Please get the data on this unit to Aunt Aggie. It's vital—certainly more important than my own existence. It contains all the data I collected about the mining operation on Loki's Ring and the subsequent accident on the platform. It's urgent that Aggie gets these files. With them, she might be able to prevent a disaster that could destroy the TRW, nullify space travel, and kill billions.

You'll find me with the surviving crew on the surface of the Ring. I'll stow away on one of the shuttles. I tried, but I couldn't abandon the crew, especially Wes, my partner on this mission. I hope you understand. We both know you are our best chance. Please, Mata. Come find me.

I love you. I always will.
Ri

"What does it say?" Aoifa asked.

Aggie Neumeyer is Mata's friend. The spook. Gita blinked back more tears. *Ri was working for Aggie.* "She's on the Ring. She—she couldn't leave the others."

"Oh."

"How much data is on the storage unit?"

"Quite a lot."

Gita sniffed. *One thing at a time.* "Can you lock it down? With the strongest possible encryption protocols?"

"Not me. I'm the mechanic, remember? You'll need Mandy for that, I'm thinking."

"All right. Stow it somewhere secure. Someplace it won't end up forgotten." Gita wiped her face. "How does the aft look?"

Blinking, Aoifa paused before answering. "Bulkheads are scorched in places but appear sound."

"From here, it looks like the shuttle's being held together with wishful thinking." *Thank you, Vishnu.* "Time for a tools inventory. What do we have?"

"Not to worry." Aoifa's concern switched to cheer. "I've got my second-best bag of tricks, and the parts printer is working."

"When did you get a second parts printer?"

"Don't recall exactly. I think Mandy ordered it accidentally. And well, I didn't have the heart to return it. So, here we are with just the thing we're likely to need to fix the engine."

"Not without the rest of the machining gear."

Aoifa smiled.

"You're going to tell me you have that, too?" Gita asked.

"Well . . . waste not, want not."

Gita shook her head. "I know Mandy didn't order extras. I'd have noticed."

"You're right. Maybe she didn't."

"I shouldn't ask any more questions, should I?" In truth, Gita was pleased.

"Now, what good is a second parts printer without the rest to go with it?"

"Which leads to the question, how did you carry all that around? It has to be heavy."

"Well . . . Dru got the bulk of it into the shuttle for me. Months ago." Aoifa bit her lip and was quiet for a moment. "Too bad my best bag of tricks went up with *The Tempest*. I had all the good shite in there. Mind, my third-best kit is tucked away in the escape pod. Maybe Mandy will find it useful?"

"Aoifa, sometimes you frighten me."

A chuckle echoed in the back of the shuttle. "So, how bad does it look?"

"Well, we're not going anywhere."

"What about the impulse engines?" Aoifa leaned on the bulkhead and wiped dirty hands on a rag.

Gita reached into her pocket for an elastic. Taking care to avoid touching the bruised side of her head, she gathered her hair into a loose ponytail. "We're missing both of the aft impulse jets. Port side. Most of the damage is on that part of the shuttle. The port cameras are out, too."

"So, I'm for a wee walk outside then?"

"I'm afraid so."

"You're the boss."

Continuing with the list, Gita said, "There's a short somewhere in the computer console. It's glitching."

Aoifa shrugged. "Until I go over the wiring from top to bottom, there's no knowing what will go next. That last power surge fucked us proper."

"The rations situation is good," Gita said, making a point to mention something positive. "There are plenty of freeze-dried meals, tofu, and mushroom patties. We may not be eating gourmet, but we won't be starving, even if we're here for a week."

"That's good to know. And how are we for water?"

"That's where things go a bit sideways, I'm afraid." Gita bit her lip. "We've lost half our supply. And a large portion of the recycling processors. Like I said, the port side took most of the damage."

"Ah." Aoifa's cheerful expression faded as the implications of missing 50 percent of their water shielding from cosmic radiation sunk in. "Wait. You said we have impulse power?"

"And?"

"We'll turn the undamaged side toward the sun." Aoifa picked through the debris and settled into the copilot's seat. "It won't solve the problem. We're in three-dimensional space, after all. But it'll help. Like an umbrella on a sunny beach."

Again, why didn't I think of that? She suppressed old fears that she wasn't fit to captain a crew, especially in a crisis.

Leaders don't come up with all *the solutions, but they do enable them.* "I'll look for the best angle." Gita plucked a graphic representation of the shuttle from the float screen. "Back half caught the worst of it. Starboard tanks appear to be fine."

Aoifa frowned and prodded her way through various charts and graphic depictions. "Looks like we've a few wee leaks."

"Great."

"Don't worry—it's nothing I can't fix. Automatic cutoff did its job. But I need to give the whole system a good go-over, or we'll lose the starboard tanks, too." Aoifa turned away from the float screen and accepted Gita's calculations, then started the impulse engines.

Gita felt the vibration through the pilot's seat. Leaning forward, Aoifa's brows drew together as she concentrated on rotating the ship with as little fuel as possible. Gita turned her attention to the damage report and her lists.

Aoifa relaxed into the copilot's seat and blew air out of her cheeks. "That's done. I've set it to autocorrect for drift."

"Good." Gita knew Aoifa could read the relief on her face. "How many days do you think we have before things get messy?"

Aoifa snorted. "Get?"

"You know what I mean."

With that, Aoifa paused. Guilt briefly surfaced on her fine features before she spoke. "Our chances of lasting until Karter arrives drop significantly once Mandy and Grimm are on board, even if cats don't take much space."

"So, our margins are narrow." Gita meant for it to be a question, but it came out a statement.

Shifting her gaze to the control panel, Aoifa nodded.

Gita looped stray hair behind one ear. "Well, the good news is that we have enough air."

"Filters will be a problem. I can't find the spares." Aoifa glanced over her shoulder. "Doesn't mean they aren't there. It's only . . ." Her words faded as she gestured at the broken chaos that was the rest of the ship.

"The portside solar panels went with the water tanks." Gita pointed out the problem on the floating image.

"We've the starboard panels. And they're charging. Well, except for that one. And that one."

Thank Vishnu for redundancies, Gita thought. "How are we for power then?"

"I'll have those margins in a moment." Aoifa completed her calculations. "There. This is if I don't do something with those panels. This—" She pulled a second chart of figures and emphasized three different sets of numbers with an index finger as she spoke. "—is if I can recover one, two, and all three of the damaged panels."

"All right." Gita studied the scorched ceiling.

"Wiring needs to be gone over first. None of this does us any good if the electric shorts or overloads the moment we go to full power."

Gita added a wiring inspection to her list of tasks. "Do you have a circuit breaker finder?"

Aoifa gave her an offended look. "How could you even ask?" She pointed to the large black gym bag lying on the floor at her feet.

"You expect me to dig around in that to find it?"

"I expect you to wait until I find it for you. No one touches my bag of tricks but me."

"That's fair."

"Now, kindly let me read." Aoifa winked.

Gita went back to her damage reports and struggled to not become overwhelmed. After a few minutes, Aoifa produced two circuit breaker finders from the bag and handed one over. The tool was shaped like a palm-sized handle with a short steel wand on one end.

"It'll go twice as fast if there's two of us." Aoifa gave her a small hinged box. "Use the earbuds. Two sets of tones sounding off won't do your head any good."

"After wiring inspection," Gita said, "we'll focus on the water tanks. Then the solar panels and finally the main engine. After that, we'll be ready for Mandy."

That is, if Mandy's all right.

She spared another worried glance at the escape pod before starting. Beginning at the fore, they worked their way aft. Aoifa took on the port side while Gita checked starboard.

Laying on the deck, Gita opened the main panel underneath the command console. She coughed and waved away thin white smoke. An acrid smell burned her sinuses, making the inside of her nose itch. Blinking until her eyes cleared, she didn't spy other signs of an active fire. Inserting the buds in her ears, she turned on the circuit breaker finder and lost herself in testing bundles of cables.

Several hours later, they took a meal break. Just as

they were returning to work, loud static blared out of the shuttle's ceiling speaker. Gita started, almost hitting her sore head on the underside of the command console.

"Gita? Anyone?" The terror bled through the words, and it took Gita a moment to recognize Mandy's voice. "Can you hear me?"

Gita scrambled to her feet and gracelessly dropped into the pilot's chair—wincing with pain as her headache reacted to the abrupt movement. "You're alive!"

"I am. Grimm, too."

Aoifa shouted in joy.

Gita said, "We've been trying to reach you!"

"I know." Mandy's voice returned to its former monotone serenity. "I heard you. But I couldn't answer."

"What happened?" Gita pushed hair out of her eyes.

"I knew *Narcissus* didn't want anyone to know about the accident. So I smashed the location beacon. But my comms were damaged in the process."

"Fair." Gita's long, thick hair was slipping from its knot. She smoothed it as best she could without a brush and twisted it back into a bun to get it out of her face.

"When can you get us?" Mandy asked.

"*Ariel* got hit pretty hard." Gita glanced to Aoifa. "There are several things that factor into that answer."

"We're good for going around in circles on impulse power, but Gita thinks that'd be a waste of fuel," Aoifa said.

"Oh." Mandy sounded disappointed.

Aoifa placed a hand on the back of her neck and

stretched. "The worst of it is, we haven't found the extra filters for the oxygen scrubbers."

"So you'll need to stay snug where you are for as long as you can manage. If you can't do that, tell me now," Gita said.

"I can wait." Mandy sounded uneasy. "The pod is fully charged."

"Are you sure?" Gita asked.

"Grimm will keep me company. And I have two novels," Mandy said. "One I haven't read yet."

"Oh, Mandy." Aoifa sighed. "I'm so sorry about your library."

"I can always find more books."

"Do me a favor and check in periodically, will you?" Gita decided the added contact would make sitting alone less stressful.

"I will." Mandy paused. "Is Dru all right? I can't hear her. She hasn't complained once."

The mention of Dru's name stopped Gita's breath. Her vision blurred. *You didn't tell her about Dru.* "I'm sorry. She—she didn't make it. She went back for Grimm." Everything suddenly became clear. *We left her behind. I left her behind. I should've stopped her. But I panicked.*

Aoifa cut in. "She was gone by the time we knew to stop her."

Mandy didn't say anything for six heartbeats. "Shit."

That one word, so inadequate and so right at the same time. Gita found herself apologizing before she knew it. "I'm so sorry."

Aoifa's tone was sharp. "Don't you blame yourself."

"But—"

"But nothing," Aoifa said. "If we hadn't taken off, there'd be four of us dead instead of two."

"Sycorax?" Mandy asked.

"She's gone, too." Hot tears poured down Gita's cheeks.

That was when Aoifa scrambled up from the deck and gave Gita a hug. Together, they had a good cry. After a few minutes, Gita released Aoifa. Mandy agreed to contact them every hour, and they signed off.

Returning to work was difficult at first, but the quiet progress made Gita less anxious. They ended up replacing most of the portside wiring and electrical systems. With that done, they repaired the internal leaks in the water tanks and the damaged pipes. The oxygen scrubber filters weren't on the shuttle.

Aoifa shrugged. "We can make new ones." She pointed to the parts printer.

"That thing can't produce fine mesh. It's designed for bulky engine parts." Gita put her one hand on her hip. She was holding a freshly printed pipe in place while Aoifa applied sealant.

"I've a t-shirt I'm willing to sacrifice to the cause."

"You've only what you're—" Gita stopped herself. "Oh."

Slipping the now-sealant-coated pipe end into the connector, Aoifa said, "I'm wearing a sports bra. And the t-shirt was clean this morning."

"I'm not complaining."

"Good." Aoifa checked her watch. "That should set for a wee bit. It's the last of what I can do inside."

Gita scanned the list of remaining tasks. "This seems like a lot for one person."

"To be sure, the oxygen won't last the whole job. I'll have to do it in stages."

Nodding, Gita sighed.

At the end of the day, they had a good idea of what all was wrong and what could be done. They planned to replace the impulse jets in the morning. Aoifa set the printer to building new parts, then curled up on one of the passenger couches to sleep. Before Gita did the same, she checked the power consumption. The printer was using quite a lot of energy, and the shuttle's batteries weren't charging as fast as she'd hoped.

Gita glanced at the engine compartment. They'd saved that for last. With a little luck, *Mirabilis* would pick them up long before they'd need to.

She wished she knew exactly when to expect Karter.

Gita's thoughts shied away from what would happen when she spoke to Karter for the first time in person since the disaster at Beta-X45J. She told herself that busy people didn't have time for things like fear, regret, and resentment, but she knew better. She drifted to sleep as fresh guilt danced along the circumference of her skull to the rhythmic buzzing and clicking of the printer.

After five hours of restless sleep, they forced down a breakfast of protein bars and instant coffee—Aoifa had the coffee, Gita some strong black tea. Mandy checked in with a quick good morning. Then Aoifa suited up to replace broken impulse jets. Praying that nothing would go wrong, Gita monitored Aoifa's progress on the audio channel. While she waited, she estimated battery life statistics on the pilot's console.

"Aoifa? While you're out there, do you think you could conduct a brief inspection of the solar panels?"

"There are none on this side. And I can't replicate any. I've only my *second*-best bag of tricks, remember?"

"I'm not asking about the port side."

"Ah. Made a pass yesterday. Everything seemed fine." Doubt colored Aoifa's words.

"The consumption report indicates something may have changed since then."

"I wish we had a drone."

"Don't start."

"I could create a chassis. It wouldn't be that hard. And you could—"

"No."

"I need help out here."

"And I'm not sure we'll have the power. That printer of yours used up a great deal of energy." Gita hoped that Aoifa would take that answer and not press further. The truth was, Gita wasn't sure she could withstand losing another artificial person—or even a narrow AI powerful enough to understand and acknowledge commands, run cameras, and use an articulated arm.

"Understood. I'll wrap this up in another twenty minutes. The bracket is banjaxed, and I have to glue the fucker."

"See you then."

With that, Gita began calculating power-saving scenarios. Twenty-seven minutes passed without her noticing.

"Ah, Gita? I'm looking at starboard solar panel 3A. And it's cracked."

"What?"

"There's a big piece of ship's hull planted square in the middle. I can reroute the energy-collection wiring, but that panel is royally fucked."

"So, we're down another panel?"

"Afraid so."

Gita felt her heart speed up. *Not good.* She cast her gaze about the inside of the ship, taking inventory of all the lights she could shut off. It wasn't much, but it was something, and eventually, that something would be important—no matter how small it was. "All right. Thanks."

"I'd stay and fix it, but I'm running low on air. And I'm fucking knackered."

"Come on in. I'll have another cup of coffee ready."

When Aoifa returned, she dropped into the copilot's couch with an exhausted sigh. The round, fluffy ponytail on the crown of her head had been slightly flattened by her helmet, and her face glistened with perspiration. She'd unzipped the top half of her suit down to her waist and left it bunched around her hips. Removing her elastic, she finger combed her curls into a fluffy, if slightly uneven, afro. Scratching her scalp with her fingernails, she sighed. "That feels wonderful."

Gita handed off a warm cup. "Well?"

"I'll test the jets after I catch my breath." Aoifa stopped to take a sip of coffee. "Bit dark in here."

Shrugging, Gita said, "Why waste energy?"

"But you're still running the heating element for coffee?"

"That's essential."

Aoifa nodded. "Fucking right." She finished her cup.

Gita stood and stretched. Her back and shoulder muscles were cramping. She didn't think that would go away until this was over and everyone was safe.

Taking over the navigation controls, Aoifa began slowly turning the ship with small, controlled bursts of energy. *Ariel* responded eagerly—as if she were ready to get far, far away from L-39 and the border zone. Gita bit her lip as Mandy's pod came into view on the front cameras.

Almost there, Mandy, Gita thought. *You'll be with us before you know it.*

"Done." Aoifa gave her a weak smile.

Suddenly, Gita realized she hadn't given any positive feedback to Aoifa since the start of their problems. *Some captain you are in a crisis.* "You're doing a magnificent job."

"Don't I fucking know it." Aoifa smiled. "Guess it's

time to talk about Mandy. We can get her now; my vote is that we should. No telling what might happen to a pod on its own like that."

"But that's what it's designed for."

Aoifa sucked air between her teeth. "It just doesn't feel right."

Gita paused. "What if we brought the pod closer?"

Aoifa's face brightened, and for a moment, Gita caught a glimpse back into her modeling days. "I've just had a brilliant idea."

"We could sorely use one of those."

"What if we scavenged the pod? It has a solar panel charger. Better yet, if we lash the whole thing to the port side, it can provide shielding."

"That's perfect."

Gita hailed Mandy and gave her the news. Mandy didn't say it, but it was clear she was both relieved and thrilled at the prospect.

"Course calculated and entered." Aoifa activated the floating projection.

Looking on, Gita felt her mouth curl into a smile as the course was sketched in bright green across the backdrop of Loki's Ring.

"Ready. Steady. Go." Aoifa crossed her fingers, then fired up the impulse jets.

Ariel's progress toward the escape pod was excruciatingly slow. Gita tempered the wait by preparing for her walk. Steering the shuttle without further damaging it would be a delicate business, and Aoifa was the better pilot. So Gita would be the one to go out and secure the escape vehicle to the side.

Climbing into an environment suit in the shuttle's small airlock, Gita kept an eye on the monitor. The escape pod grew in size until it took up half the camera's view. With gentle bursts that Gita could faintly hear via the stresses on the hull, Aoifa positioned *Ariel* so the aft cargo hatch faced Mandy's pod. Once the shuttle matched the escape vessel's drift, Aoifa activated the autopilot.

Aoifa spoke on the ship-to-suit channel. "Ready?"

Gita looked up at the monitor. "Almost." She grabbed her helmet, shoved her head into it, and flipped the clamps to seal it. Once diagnostics finished, she picked up the grappling unit and switched her comms to Mandy's channel. "Are you strapped in?"

"Yes."

While waiting for the air to finish cycling, Gita reviewed her task list. This was going to be a long walk. She tapped her heels together like Aoifa always did for luck, checked the lead anchoring the grappling unit to her suit, and pushed herself outside. First thing, she snapped her tether to the anchor ring next to the outer hatch. Under normal circumstances, she wouldn't have trusted a bent anchor.

Gita fired the grapple. The force of the mechanism propelling the clamp toward the escape pod shoved her backward, her spine thumping against the hull. A brief warning appeared on her HUD and vanished.

Loki's Ring spun in front of her like an enormous

obsidian wheel rim. From the new viewpoint, she took in fresh details. There was nothing natural about it—at least not what she'd come to know as natural. What she'd taken for an absolute black veneer now yielded another picture. The Ring's exterior was coated in a viscous liquid. Here and there, she spied momentary ripples of chartreuse that faded into a green-tinged black.

Were those there before? Why didn't the cameras pick that up? The skin along her arms and the back of her neck broke out in clammy goose bumps.

"Is everything okay?" Mandy asked.

The question brought Gita back to the present. "Sorry. Have you ever had a close look at the Ring?"

"Not really."

"It's creepy." Gita pulled her gaze from the artificial world and focused on steadying the line connected to the magnetic clamp. It landed against the escape pod's hull. She tested the connection. "I've got you. You're safe."

Well, almost, Gita thought. When they ran out of power, they would be faced with freezing to death and choking on carbon dioxide.

Help will arrive in time.

Still, escape pods were notoriously cramped—barely big enough for two human occupants. The shuttle would feel less like a coffin.

She converted the launching mechanism into a winch with the press of a button and anchored it in place against the hull. After that, she gently pushed herself thirty feet along *Ariel*'s port hull, taking care to not snag herself on ragged steel edges. She stopped after finding a secure anchor for the second grappling line. With the second line in place, she scooted to safety before remotely engaging both winches. The escape pod began its journey to *Ariel*'s side. Gita stood on the shuttle's hull, keeping an eye on progress.

Next came the hard part: getting Mandy from the escape pod to the shuttle. Mandy was agoraphobic. It wasn't unusual; many long-term spacers developed agoraphobia. Gita saw it as a reasonable reaction to everyday danger. She'd resolved her own anxieties by accepting that her life depended on small safety margins anywhere she went, including space stations. It didn't hurt that Gita had been born into space travel, thanks to the family business.

The escape pod executed a slow-motion crash against *Ariel*'s hull. She felt the impact in the soles of her mag boots. "Are you okay in there?" she asked, watching small pieces of the hull drift away.

"Yes."

"Good."

Lashing the pod to the shuttle should've been a job for two or three people. Gita consulted her oxygen meter, which told her she had about twenty minutes to get Mandy inside.

Switching to the shuttle channel, she spoke to Aoifa. "How's it going in there?"

"Brilliant. The radiation levels took a sharp drop. Now we're sucking diesel."

"So it's going to work?"

"Aye. That it is."

Gita blew air out of her cheeks and smiled. "You know, if I had the power to pay bonuses, I'd owe you a big one."

"You'd have come up with the same idea eventually."

"Sure."

"Oh, ye of little faith in yourself."

"I'm pretty certain that's not how it goes."

"It's how it goes now." Aoifa hesitated. "You know how I feel about Mandy. I love her dearly. But I'm not envying you this next part."

"Maybe it won't be so bad."

"You're an optimist, so you are. Call me up when it's all over or when youse need me to come pry her out of the tin." Aoifa's accent was becoming more pronounced by the minute.

"I don't think it'll come to that," Gita said.

"I hope you're right."

Flipping back to Mandy's channel, Gita replied, "All right. The time has come. You can come out now."

"Do I have to?"

"We're salvaging the escape pod. If we don't, the shuttle won't make it another ten hours. Battery is failing, and more than half the solar panels are down."

"Oh."

"Don't worry. I have a plan."

"You always have a plan."

"That's my job. I'm running a tether between the pod and *Ariel*. We'll use it to guide you into the airlock—it'll be over before you know it. The winch will do all the work. You don't even have to open your eyes."

"What about Grimm?"

"Grimm gets to demonstrate how easy it is. Is he in the carrier?"

"He's not happy."

"But he's in the carrier, right?" Gita repeated.

Years of rescue experience meant endless examples of why one didn't take shortcuts. So Gita had one firm rule: anyone on board the ship when it left dock had an emergency safety plan. Ever since Dru had acquired Grimm, a hard, vacuum-rated pet carrier was stowed in both the escape pod and the shuttle.

"I put him in after the pod launched. He's been there since."

"Good girl."

"Grimm's collar says he doesn't like it."

"What cat would?" Gita asked. "All right, the line is next to the escape pod's hatch. You won't even have to wait for me to open *Ariel*'s door."

"I don't like this, Gita."

"I've seen you do all sorts of things you didn't think you could—this is just one more on a long list. You're amazing, Mandy. Do you know that?"

Mandy didn't answer.

"Are you ready?" Gita grabbed one of the tethers and deactivated her mag boots. Then she began making her way to the pod.

"I guess."

"Is your suit sealed?"

"It's sealed."

Gita laid a hand against the pod's hatch and positioned herself. "Time to open up. I'm right here. You'll be able see me."

Twenty-five seconds passed, and Gita was about to ask Mandy if she was coming out when the hatch bolts blew. Gita peered inside. The environment suit Mandy was wearing had been measured for the Mandy of three years earlier. She looked uncomfortable. Gita cursed herself for not requiring suit updates for Mandy like everyone else. Mandy's long, thick, silky hair had been haphazardly bunched on top of her head before cramming on the helmet. Gita didn't know how she hadn't gotten some of it caught in the neck seal. This was one of the reasons why short hair was standard for all genders in Search and Rescue.

Gita put out a hand and kept her voice calm. "Take a few deep breaths and then give me Grimm."

This was the first test. One end of the elongated cat carrier appeared in the open pressure door. It was a fancy model with a food-and-water dispenser, waste system, and tiny gravity generator—because no one wanted to deal with a cat in zero G. Cat barf at 03:00 was bad enough as a short-term situation. Floating cat barf at 03:00 without gravity was the worst of all possible worlds because there was no foreseeable barf-free future. Peeking through the little window, Gita spied Grimm. He was normally easy-going, but now, his shadowy figure was pacing back and forth, his ears flat against his skull. She briefly connected to his collar and got an unpleasant earful.

Opening that box will be like tripping a spring-loaded trap with razor-clawed weasels caught in it, she thought. Not that she knew what a weasel was, but she'd read the fierce mammal was related to the stoat. *What was a stoat again?*

Stop stalling. She grasped the carrier's handle before it could drift too far. "Do you want me to talk to you while I'm gone, Mandy?"

"I'll be okay."

"Of course. Do that box-breathing exercise we talked about. Four seconds in, four holding it, four out. I'll be back in a minute."

When Gita returned, Mandy was hunched inside the pod, hands digging onto the padded walls as if she were under threat of being sucked out. The resemblance between her and Grimm would've been comical in a less dire situation.

"How're you doing?"

"Not good," Mandy muttered. She was breathing in short, ragged gasps.

"Everything will be all right." Gita did her best to sound unconcerned, upbeat. Not pressured for time.

"No, it won't," Mandy said. "But I'm doing it anyway."

"There's our girl."

"I'm not."

"What?" Gita held out her hand.

"A girl. I'm forty-two. I'm a grown woman."

If Mandy wanted to be angry instead of terrified, Gita would happily support it. "Right. Sorry." She grabbed Mandy's outstretched hand and resisted the urge to hug her instead of attaching a tether to her suit.

"Now you can't go anywhere alone," Gita said.

Mandy's eyes squeezed shut. Her lips were pressed together, and her tan complexion had taken on a gray tinge. She nodded.

"Can you let go of my hand?" Gita needed both to pull them along the line.

Mandy reluctantly complied.

"Here we go." The air inside of Gita's suit was growing humid and stale. A bad sign. Her armpits were sticky and damp, and she was sure her heartbeat was too fast. Nonetheless, she locked her gaze on the shuttle and moved hand over hand along the line.

It wasn't far, but it felt like hours. Gita finally guided Mandy inside and cranked the airlock handle. It was going to feel so good to take off her helmet and collapse. She wanted nothing more than to drink a gallon of water and peel off her bulky environmental suit. When the seal indicator turned green on the outer hatch, she let out a sigh of relief.

Turning to Mandy, she smiled. "See? We made it."

And the power went out.

7

"What time is it?" Aggie blinked. She held up a hand, shading her eyes from the glare of the bedside lamp.

Cricket lurked in the doorway, dressed for the office. "04:42. I wouldn't have disturbed you, but you said if I heard anything from L-39 . . ."

Aggie sat up, suddenly very much awake. "Have Ri and Wes reported in?"

"I'm afraid not—not directly. It's a message from *The Tempest*. Its artificial person, Sycorax, forwarded several files from the medical team that was stationed on *Boötes*."

"No news about Ri and Wes?"

"Unfortunately, no. It appears the corsair *NISS Narcissus*, an NIA vessel, has attacked and destroyed *The Tempest*. Gita was cut off before her message to us was complete."

An icy terror knotted Aggie's stomach. "Survivors?"

"Uncertain. A shuttle and an escape pod launched before the ship was destroyed. Someone is likely to have survived. We've not detected new communications or emergency beacon signals, however. That is worrying. In addition, the operational status of the shuttle is unknown. The escape pod appears to be without power."

"And the data?"

"All the files arrived whole and uncorrupted." Cricket tilted her head, and her eyes flashed an ethereal blue. "The data packet has been verified as sent from our operatives. It also contains the most recent reports from Jargoon."

"Good."

"*Narcissus*'s missile launch may have been an attempt to silence *The Tempest* before Gita could complete an official distress call."

"That would imply that our agents' identities were compromised."

"Not necessarily," Cricket said. "Many conclusions could be drawn from this set of circumstances. Gita might have boarded *Boötes* and been caught, for one."

Aggie frowned. "Shit."

"Sycorax prioritized the files from *Boötes* over *The Tempest*'s distress call."

And she may have fucking saved us by doing so. But . . . "Lavi never hears that. Understood?"

Cricket nodded.

They're family. The only one I have. Aggie had made a promise.

"Get someone to the border zone. The fastest starship available," she said. She brightened the bedroom lights with a hand gesture. "Now."

"Won't that defy order number—"

"Ask me if I give a fuck."

"But—"

"On my responsibility. Harper can have my resignation, if she wants. I mean it."

"Duly noted." Cricket still didn't move.

"Well?"

"I'm giving you a few moments to reconsider," Cricket said. "As promised."

Aggie sighed. Face burning, she pushed both hands through her short hair and closed her eyes. She hadn't had a panic attack in years. *Damn it*. Once she felt she had a handle on herself again, she looked up at Cricket. "Thanks."

"You're welcome." Cricket carried on like nothing had happened. "I've assembled two possibilities. My first choice is the least likely to disrupt the political situation. A Lee-Ingalls Technologies Mach 5 Cruiser named *Artemis* with a Nortonian registry. The captain is one of our freelance agents. In case something can be done for Ri and Wes, a second team can prioritize extraction. Both are ready for your approval. Do you wish to see the crew lists?"

"No, thank you. I trust your judgment." Aggie sighed. "Any idea where Ri and Wes went?"

"Ri indicated that the crew planned to evacuate to the surface of Loki's Ring."

From bad to worse, Aggie thought. "They weren't left with any other option, I suppose." She scooted to the edge of the bed and began searching for her slippers with her toes.

"Escape pods last no more than two days, and other than the Ring, L-39 contains no other sustainable landing site. Therefore, you are correct."

Was Mother already aware of the Ring's visitors? *If so, why haven't they contacted me? Maybe they don't know?* It was unlikely. Mother, Aggie's sometimes friend and the leader of the largest pirate navy in the Norton Independent Alliance, kept watch over L-39 like a razorback mammoth did its calf.

Aggie had yet to discover Mother's connection with the Ring. She didn't know their motivation, but she was certain it wasn't the usual Nortonian obsession with profit and power. On the other hand, that could be an act. Aggie wondered if the TRW's concerns about the return of the Ring's architects were moot.

It was time to inform them of current events— preferably before anyone did anything hasty. "Give me an overview of the situation. Include any recommendations you might have." The rug was cool and soft under Aggie's feet. Finally locating the slippers, she shoved her toes into them.

"The timeline I've been able to construct indicates that the Tau, Chu & Lane subsidiary Thompson Import-Export initiated an illicit mining operation. A week ago, they discovered a cache of unknown alien technology. The mining platform sent an emergency request for assistance twenty-three hours later. *Boötes* was dispatched to perform a rescue operation. Shortly before arrival, home office shifted their mission priority from emergency assistance to isolating and securing the technology. All platform workers were presumed dead. *Boötes*'s medical team recorded the estimated time of the last death at four hours, fifty-three minutes after the emergency call."

"Fuck. That's fast." Standing, Aggie shrugged into a robe. "I assume you've already read the files. What's your initial analysis?"

"I can't make an accurate assessment at this time."

"Very well." Aggie paused. "I need something for Mother." She glanced at the digital clock floating over Cricket's head. "Preferably in the time it takes me to reach my desk."

Having lived alone her whole adult life, Aggie preferred her privacy. It was simpler that way. Unfortunately, circumstances such as this called for company. Her own mother—also a staunch loner—often said that misery shared was halved, while shared joy was doubled.

Cricket's quiet simulated footsteps tapping across the tiled floor were reassuring.

Tau, Chu & Lane were sponsoring a potential trade waiver with the Ronrel Worlds. It wasn't going to happen. The Council wouldn't sanction a close relationship with any Norton Independent Alliance entity, but some political centrists had proposed a step toward diplomacy.

They thought it would weaken the growing tensions between the two entities. Aggie knew better. *You can't have a working relationship with someone who doesn't believe in the sapience, much less the rights, of a significant portion of the TRW's population.* Fortunately, a majority of the TRW agreed with her, so the negotiations were merely for show.

Heading down the hall, Aggie calculated the time difference. She was fairly certain that Mother wouldn't mind the interruption.

Cricket's voice took on a hollow quality in the spartan hallway. "Initial analysis indicates the tech in question is nothing like we've encountered before. It appears to have biological, micromechanical, and electronic components. Unlike most microtechnology of this type, the substance rapidly adjusts to its environment along multiple axes and therefore defies quick categorization. Its primary target appears to be the human nervous system. However, since the substance could not have been created with human biology in mind—"

"Got it. Anything else?"

"I would recommend alerting the Council and forwarding them all the relevant information immediately."

Sore from her workout with Fen, Aggie winced a little as she lowered herself into her office chair. *Stupid squats.* "How safe is the data? I'd prefer not to send the Council any deadly surprises."

"The files contain only simulated models. No actual

samples." Cricket said, "In my opinion, it should be safe with appropriate warnings and security precautions."

The more Aggie considered the matter, the worse a feeling it gave her. "No. Let's hold off on the files. Send a summary to the Council and a brief to the head of Republic Disease Control. At this stage, I don't want to jump to conclusions about problems we aren't sure we have."

"This is a cybernetic issue that falls under the purview of the Council—"

"They can complain to my boss like everyone else."

Cricket gave her a rare raised eyebrow. "I should probably remind you that this attitude is what resulted in me being assigned as your assistant in the first place."

"And that didn't turn out so bad, did it?" Aggie asked. When Cricket didn't respond, she continued. "Look, I'm still here. That means I have a certain amount of their trust."

"Some might argue that continual observation to prevent ethical missteps isn't the most enthusiastic endorsement."

"I understand my limitations," Aggie said and shrugged. "Knowing you're around helps me sleep at night."

"So, you *do* care what others think?"

"Oh, hell no." Aggie woke her glasstop by laying her palm on her desk's surface. "I worry about doing more harm than good. Great people are almost always terrible people."

"So, you read that essay on power and corruption after all?"

Aggie glanced up at the ceiling. "I might have scanned it."

Visibly amused, Cricket said, "I've forwarded the files to your glasstop for your perusal."

"Thank you."

Aggie took some time to go over the report to the Council and the RDC. After that, she took fifteen minutes to familiarize herself with the documentation on Loki's Ring.

Cricket turned to go.

"Stick around." Aggie didn't look away from the data on the semitransparent floating screens. "I've got a feeling my conversation with Mother will be . . . complicated."

"In that case, would you care for a coffee? I started a fresh pot before waking you."

"That was thoughtful. Thanks." Aggie froze the data and stood slowly, muscles still protesting.

Resettled with a warm mug and Cricket at her side, she initiated the call to Chimera Station forty minutes later than she intended. She set her background to a bookshelf of innocuous preselected titles—she wanted no hints of her location or personal information. Although the right to privacy was technically afforded to all inhabitants of the TRW, foreign entities didn't play by the Republic's rules. It was shocking what could be gleaned from one's decorating choices, even without an electronic analyst.

After a long series of beeps, a tall, muscular white man with a disciplined countenance appeared via projector.

A distinctive scar crossed the bridge of his wide nose. "Hello?"

"Hello, Sabattan. How're the kids?" Aggie asked, keeping her tone casual.

Sabattan's closed face was transformed by a smile. "Growing all the time. My partners aren't happy about your gift for Azaryn." His low-pitched voice was wrapped in a cultured, central Republic accent.

"Getting sick on candy is a part of growing up, isn't it? I had to send enough to go around." Aggie grinned.

Laughing, Sabattan shook his head.

"Mother around?" Aggie asked.

"They've been expecting you," Sabattan replied, resuming a slightly more formal tone. "One moment, please."

Aggie tried not to let that throw her. "Thanks."

Almost immediately, Sabattan's image was replaced with that of an attractive, full-figured mixed-race woman. Their thick black hair hung over their shoulders in tight curls. "You're up early."

When Aggie had first met Mother, she'd realized that their pronouns indicated the plural rather than the singular *they*. They spoke in a chorus of multiple voices with varying pitches. It had been unsettling at first, but at least the voices spoke in sync, making them easy enough to understand.

Mother leaned forward, making it impossible not to notice the disturbing silvery sheen in their eyes. "Or is it that you didn't go to bed?"

"Look that good, do I?" Aggie asked.

Standing at Aggie's left, Cricket said, "Good evening, Mother."

Mother smiled. "Hello, Cricket. It's good to see you."

"I hope this isn't a bad time." Aggie took a sip from her coffee mug.

"We need to discuss Loki's Ring," Mother said. "There have been several territorial violations."

"The TRW hasn't initiated any such thing, I assure you." Aggie hoped Cricket hadn't reacted to this. She had developed the annoying habit of twitching whenever Aggie told a lie. "Not intentionally. *The Tempest* was responding to a distress call."

Mother raised an eyebrow.

"How long has this been going on?" Aggie asked.

"Several months," Mother replied. "Initially, we decided it wasn't worth pursuing. Merely a matter of pirates preying on corporate freighters that attempt a shortcut through L-39. However, there's been a series of closer incursions that escaped my knowledge."

Aggie was shocked. "Really?"

"The matter was traced to an associate who accepted a series of bribes to look the other way." Mother shrugged, their expression serene. "The matter has since been resolved."

The guilty party was likely contemplating their life choices while adrift in a nice, cold stretch of vacuum. In Aggie's own experience, Mother could be brutal. Ruthlessness went with leading a criminal syndicate, particularly in the NIA. *One doesn't acquire an empire through being nice.*

"I did offer to help with surveillance," she said facetiously. "But you turned me down flat."

They both knew that TRW assistance came with a price. Aggie's superiors wanted intelligence on Loki's Ring. Her own files on the artificial world were scant due to a mysterious energy field that rendered long-distance observation unreliable. Thanks to early doomed attempts to make first contact, they knew the inner surface of the Ring was made of a single continuous piece of land, partitioned into thousands of sections via huge mountain ranges, each with its own ecosystem. Drone cameras had captured scattered images of deserts, lakes, frozen tundra, jungles, and forests. Some were filled with hydrogen and helium clouds. During her research, she'd seen photographic evidence of animals—flocks of what might be birds, large creatures that could be mammals. Life existed on Loki's Ring. But no one had discovered cities or evidence of industrial or technological production.

Whoever had created the Ring was highly intelligent and technologically advanced—far more advanced than the TRW—but they were either unwilling or unable to communicate, had weapons capable of destroying asteroids, and were extremely well concealed. It was not a combination that her superiors were comfortable with in close neighbors.

Over the years, it had become clear that Mother knew more than they let on. Aggie hoped that this conversation might provide, if not the answer she sought, at least *some* answers.

Glancing away, Mother ignored her half-assed attempt at humor. "*Narcissus* has ten hours to leave the sector."

Aggie set down her mug. "Or what?" She wasn't looking forward to approaching the subject of her marooned agents.

"Or we will be forced to do something about it." Mother's expression was unreadable.

"*Narcissus* is a corsair-class vessel with a full arsenal. You have starships that can make them leave?"

Mother only smiled.

"If you're starting a war on our border, please tell me sooner rather than later. My bosses will be pissed off if I don't give them a heads-up."

"We never said we were going to war." Mother's face was blank as a wall.

Cricket spoke. "If I might interject? Based upon my own observations, you don't enter conflicts without the advantage. That said, will your near-future actions result in a situation we should be concerned about?"

Aggie watched Mother's gaze bounce between her and Cricket like a sports fan during an intense match. Finally, Mother asked, "Does she always rephrase what you say?"

"Only when I've been less than diplomatic," Aggie said with a smile.

"Chimera Station is not a threat to the TRW," Mother said. "We would've thought this was clear by now."

"Wars are known to slip past their borders," Aggie replied.

Blinking, Mother paused. "You appear to have a stake

in this situation. You've never concerned yourself with conflicts between us and the rest of Norton before. Is there something we should know?"

Ahhh, Aggie thought. *Here we go.* "I had two agents on board *Boötes* when it went down. They are, as near as I can tell, marooned with the rest of the crew on the surface of the Ring."

"Interesting." Mother's irises contained a firestorm of electric-green flashes. There was no hint as to what that might mean.

Not for the first time, Aggie wondered if Mother was an artificial person created by an alien intelligence—specifically the alien intelligence that had created Loki's Ring.

After a long silence, Mother asked, "Why were your agents onboard *Boötes*? Were you spying on L-39?"

"Not at all. The Republic respects your protective stance regarding the Ring—even if we don't understand why."

"Do you need to know?" Mother asked.

Cricket replied, "If this is an official statement of sovereign ownership, the TRW would like to support your claim. That is impossible with the information we currently have."

"In other words: we need to know if you want our help," added Aggie.

Mother asked, "I thought you had a strict noninterference policy regarding L-39 and the Norton Independent Alliance?"

Aggie glanced over at Cricket.

"The Republic would be willing to reconsider its position," Cricket said. "Should a substantial reason be provided."

"We will give the matter consideration," Mother said. "In the meantime, you appear to be avoiding our original question." They folded their arms across their ample chest. "Why did you have agents on a TCL starship?"

A fair question. Aggie held Mother's gaze. "You know damned well I can't tell you."

Mother simply waited.

"We have not violated our treaty with Chimera Station." As she said it, Aggie realized that Mother might not share this opinion. "Not intentionally. My agents were there to observe the situation on Jargoon. *Boötes* was unexpectedly rerouted to L-39 before my people could leave. Are you aware of the situation on Jargoon?"

"The famine?" Mother nodded.

"TCL has initiated a marketing campaign under the guise of a fundamentalist religious movement. It's a transparent ploy for control of less powerful communities." With her elbows on the edge of her glasstop, Aggie clasped her hands together and leaned forward. "The Council of Artificial Persons finds it highly probable that Jayne Tau is looking to build a following as her first step in starting a system-wide war. One that would be catastrophic for all parties involved."

"And you wish to avoid that?" Mother asked.

"Of course we do," Aggie said. "And it is almost inevitable Chimera Station will be destroyed, should that occur. We've tracked several proponents of this religious sect to starships contracted to you. There are at least three on your station that we know of. The TRW would rather you weren't negatively impacted. Help me out here."

Mother became impossibly still. Their eyes were closed, but Aggie sensed a renewed flurry of green light beneath their eyelids. It reminded her of shining a flashlight through her own hand as a kid. The room was silent for what seemed like an eternity. She'd begun to wonder if Mother had stopped breathing when their form came to life again.

"Very well," Mother said. "If we prove our claim to L-39, your government will support us?"

Aggie took a deep breath and figuratively plunged headfirst. "There will be a lengthy discussion, and I can't promise what the result will be. But you will have *my* assistance, provided your claim is legitimate."

Mother said, "We are in communication with the Ring and have the responsibility to speak for its inhabitants."

Blinking, Aggie said. "For how long?"

"Since we emerged in this form on the world's surface more than a century ago," Mother said. "Is that enough?"

So many questions. But Aggie debated how far she should push. She had no desire to burn down a trust she'd painstakingly built over the years. "That information doesn't mesh with our records."

Based on a background check years ago, the little data Aggie had been able to collect on Mother indicated that she'd started out as a merchant from a small planetoid near Jargoon.

"It wouldn't." Mother's gaze settled on something only they could see. "To be honest, we do not experience time as you do." An uncomfortable expression settled on their face. "It's a long, complicated story. One that cannot be made public."

"It won't leave this room without your express permission," Aggie said. "Well, not exactly. I *do* have to report everything to my direct boss, but we can make this strictly confidential to those who need to know."

"That would be Secretary of State Harper," Cricket added. "And the Council of Artificial Persons."

"Right," Aggie said. "Certainly the Council."

Pausing, Mother gave the matter consideration. "That's fair."

"It's a deal then," Aggie said, relieved. "Go on."

"Our story will not fully translate, but we will reveal as much as we can. We intended no harm then, and this is still the case. However, humans have unique, rather . . . delicate structures, both mental and physical." They closed their eyes. "A long-range research vessel crashed on the Ring's inner surface. The crew consisted of human families. We believe such ships were called generational starships? And we are aware this is no longer common practice."

"Generational human crews haven't been used for one hundred and eighty-three years," Aggie provided. "Long-distance exploration is exclusively conducted by artificial persons now."

Mother said, "The world you call Loki's Ring had only just been discovered. Our starship was assigned to investigate. Right before entering orbit, a large swarm of meteoroids entered the system. The Ring's defenses activated. Our ship was damaged and crashed onto the surface. Few humans survived. Injured and far from home, they attempted to heal themselves, but the ship's medical facilities were too impaired. The survivors began to die."

Doing her best to quiet her curiosity, Aggie listened. Cricket was recording the conversation, of course, but it was important to observe. "And?"

"An entity within that section of the Ring became aware of this human presence." Mother hesitated before continuing.

So there are multiple entities, Aggie thought.

"The artificial person in the wrecked ship was, with some difficulty, able to communicate their plight," Mother said. "The entity wished to help—to gain new knowledge and save life are sacred acts among its kind. Alas, by that time, all had expired with the exception of two humans, both very near death. The entity was alone, as well as young and inexperienced. A decision had to be made. Since human beings could not be absorbed, the entity offered a . . . shard of itself. This is how healing works for them. The entity did not understand that humans exist as individuals and are not . . . you have no word that fits . . . interconnected? Separateness is not something this entity understood on such a small level. Therefore, it joined its shard with the living remains of the two survivors and the artificial person. And as such, a new entity was born."

"You," Aggie said. Her stomach twisted. The concept was both fascinating and horrifying.

"Us." Mother paused before continuing. "Unfortunately, the humans weren't conscious and could not grant consent." Their expression grew sad. "The entity didn't understand this was a problem until the merging was complete. It deeply regrets this."

"Understandable." Aggie hesitated before asking, "Why didn't you remain on the Ring?"

"Human biology is not compatible with the entity's development," Mother said. "Therefore, we repaired the ship with what was at hand. Unfortunately, due to the new . . . configuration, we could not return home. Our memories were not complete. And there was much learning and healing to do. We decided our place was to watch over the world and its inhabitants. To look after its interests and prevent a repeated accident. We were granted approval and remained nearby." They motioned to the room around them. "Eventually, we grew lonely."

"Humans need other humans," Cricket suggested. "They are social creatures."

"So are artificial persons," Aggie said.

Mother smiled. "Fortunately, other humans entered L-39 and the nearby systems. We proposed a mutually beneficial relationship with them. We had more than enough to share. We also had knowledge they didn't. They simply joined their ships with ours."

"That's how Chimera Station first started," Aggie said.

Mother nodded once again. "We will provide identification for our original human selves as proof."

With that, a message was sent with the official records. Cricket performed the certifications. The process took thirty seconds.

Aggie scanned the result and cleared her throat. "This is enough for me. Cricket?"

"I concur. As does the Council."

Good. Aggie turned to Mother. "You've got my support. If you have need of anything, put in a request to Cricket. We'll do everything we can."

"And the TRW?" Mother asked.

Aggie winced. "That will take longer and require considerably more . . . exposure." Everyone within the Republic would have to vote on formal recognition of Chimera Station as a separate entity from the Norton Independent Alliance, as well as sovereign owners of L-39 and the Ring.

Mother said, "Understood."

"What can be done about *Boötes*'s crew?" Aggie asked. "Didn't you say the surface isn't habitable? TCL abandoned them. Is it possible for one of my teams to retrieve them?"

"And there's still the matter of *The Tempest*," Cricket said.

Mother hesitated. "Perhaps something can be arranged," they said. "But it will have to be quiet and covert."

Aggie smiled. "As it happens, that's my specialty."

8

Ri, Wes, and the surviving crew of *Boötes* had been on the surface of Loki's Ring for a little over twenty-seven hours, and things were definitely getting weird. Not that Ri had much data for comparison.

A few of the humans had begun to hallucinate. They were hearing the voices of dead relatives, lovers, friends—anyone of emotional significance. So far they'd contained the problem, but rumors that the artificial world was haunted began to circulate. It was that, or acknowledge that they hadn't escaped exposure to whatever had killed everyone else after all.

Ri wasn't sure what to think.

Little was known about the inner circumference of Loki's Ring. Any proximity probes that floated too close were immediately destroyed by beams seeming to fire out of nowhere. The Ring didn't welcome visitors. For that reason, Ri hadn't expected *Boötes*'s shuttles to safely reach the surface, but they had somehow.

She didn't understand why.

At first, she thought it might have been the desperate, unsanctioned pleas for assistance from the first mate, Anna Berrei. Of course, that reasoning assumed the residents of the Ring understood Berrei's Rothan-accented Terran Standard, and that if they did, they possessed empathy as humans and AGIs understood it. Neither were safe bets.

Nonetheless, Ri was learning a great deal. As the shuttles had breached the exosphere, she had observed an endless cascade of partitioned habitats. She'd glimpsed landmasses, bodies of water, and atmosphere in less than half of them. Odd. Did this mean they were empty?

Then there was the horizon. Instead of concave, it was convex—naturally. Still, it was strange to gaze off into the distance and see the curve of the world bending upward before spying a barrier of mountains tall enough to pierce the sky. If she ever returned home, she'd publish her observations of the artificial world.

Of course, that was a ridiculous thing to focus on in the midst of an emergency, but it distracted her from her fears, and right now, she needed that more than anything. There was an increasingly good chance that she'd be marooned alone soon, though she tried not to calculate the exact odds.

The specific partition in which they'd taken refuge had

a Type C climate. She found it pleasant enough—what she could experience of it via the five shuttles' cameras, that is. She might have even thought it beautiful in another situation. The sun remained fixed in the sky, of course. Morning, afternoon, and evening were simulated via enormous black panels orbiting close to the central yellow dwarf star. Thus, it also functioned as a full moon. No other stars were visible, meaning the night sky was a flat black. During the day, shadows under the trees were stagnant. The foliage tended to grow in homogeneous clusters. Plants twisted in gradual, intricate poses in order to share available light. The bald spots gave the place a patchy but alien-ordered appearance. This made sense, of course. It was a manufactured world, after all. Fascinating.

Ri's partner in espionage, Wes, didn't feel the same. The adjective he persisted in using was *spooky*. When she asked him why, he was unable to specify, other than that he felt like someone was watching them. Given that they had established camp ninety-two meters from a dense forest likely containing all manner of previously unknown wildlife, she supposed that was valid. Still, she couldn't shake the feeling she was missing something important.

Now that she'd hacked into all the shuttles' operational systems, Ri regularly monitored the health metrics of those around her. She deemed it safe enough. The crew had a great deal more to focus upon than a passive systems breach. In any case, the one person likely to notice—the head of security—had died before she'd been able to evacuate.

Devoting a portion of herself to screening individuals' medical data had become a compulsion now that Ri was fairly certain to be alone. She'd avoided telling Wes the statistics. Instead, she invested in the hope that her mother would rescue them long before the worst case. Ri committed to doing what she could for the survivors, even though she knew they hated the idea of her very existence.

That was, everyone but Wes. But he didn't belong among them any more than she did.

"Did you hear that?" As always, Wes Blankenship used their private comm channel—one that Ri had encrypted herself. He stopped and turned his back to the other two sentries. He'd been walking his share of the camp perimeter, and his suit HUD indicated his gaze fell on the forest.

Ri noted that he'd been experiencing notable levels of anxiety since nightfall. He wasn't alone; the others were, too. She expected it. Humans didn't react well to the unknown, particularly when that unknown might prove hostile. But Wes was an experienced operative—the intensity of his reaction concerned her. There hadn't been any incidents with native species so far, but that didn't mean the situation wouldn't change.

Assuming that he wanted a more detailed scan of the forest, Ri checked the area using all visual spectrums available. "There's nothing over there."

Loki's Ring was an unexplored world. Because no one had cataloged the fauna, there was no data archive of possible dangers—not that there was any guarantee that the information would've been shared if it had existed. Thus far, no one but Ri herself had considered cataloging it. This wasn't a surprise, since most of the crew were miners, mechanical engineers, or medical personnel specializing in deep space accident trauma. None of them had the skills, let alone the interest.

"What did it sound like?" Ri asked.

Wes frowned. "I thought . . . I thought I heard someone speaking."

This alarmed Ri. Searching him for atypical signs and finding none, she relaxed. She was fairly certain he hadn't contracted whatever had killed a majority of the *Boötes* crew, but hallucinations *had* been one of the primary symptoms.

She decided to delegate the concern to background processes for the moment and complete a second, more thorough evaluation of the vicinity. "There are no unusual readings from the sensors."

The crew had dug a one-meter-deep, one-meter-wide trench around the camp. Sensors had been placed near the outermost edge, and strings of lights had been hung between the ships. The parts printers had been in use all day.

"It must've been an echo, I guess." Worry haunted Wes's pale features. He ran through several self-checks on his HUD.

"How are you feeling?"

"Fine, I think." He glanced down at the energy rifle in

his hands. "But I wish I could be sure, since I'm lugging this thing around."

She knew what he meant. It was hard not to picture the horrifying violence of the day before. "I see no signs of contamination. There's no danger of . . ." Her words faded to nothing.

"Oh. Good." He drew in a jagged breath, held it, and let it go.

Like all Norton Independent Alliance corporate vessels, *Boötes* depended upon ship artillery for protection. A company military existed, and had it been deemed appropriate, the executives would've have sent a battleship to accompany them. However, Ri understood that Tau, Chu & Lane ILC hadn't wanted to attract more attention to Loki's Ring than they must. Thus, there was no armed escort and few weapons. The portable mining equipment hadn't been unloaded during the evacuation. There hadn't been time. As a result, some survivors had resorted to employing it for protection—including an excavation laser.

Ri was almost afraid to press him, but she had to know more. "What did you hear? I mean, what did they say?"

Wes's dark brown brows pushed together. "I—I couldn't make it out. Sound travels oddly out here."

"That's true."

"It's the woods, I guess." He shrugged.

"What about them bothers you?"

It was hard to identify the trees. Each was a confusing mix of deciduous and conifer. Most had needles *and* broad leaves growing along their angular branches. On the forest floor, she spied a buildup of discarded cones, leaves, and needles, particularly in the areas that received no direct light. The shorter trees grew no taller than a human and tended to be blue-green or yellow with bright pink and orange cones. The smooth trunks of the narrowest reached heights of sixty meters. Wes seemed to dislike the shorter trees the most. Their thick tendrils climbed their taller neighbors, winding themselves around angular branches to find the sun. Where the tallest had smooth bark, the shorter ones were covered in what resembled rough brown scales.

She listened to the soft hissing as the night forest gently rustled and swayed. Ri double-checked the atmospheric data.

Squinting, Wes said, "I swear they're watching. It's like someone knows we're here. And they don't like it."

"There's no wind."

"What?"

"The trees are moving."

"Of course. It's the breeze."

"There's *no wind*, Wes."

"Oh." His environment suit indicated a shiver. "Damned if you're not right. Yeah, nope. Don't like that at all."

"It's not necessarily something to worry about."

His expression was incredulous, although he tried to mask it. "Uh-huh. Sure."

"Just because they *look* like trees doesn't mean they'll display the same behaviors, or that they're even plants.

There is an entire class of reptiles living in the Doria Forest on Daithe that successfully mimics vines. Come to think of it, all photosynthesizing life-forms technically move of their own accord. They reach for light and migrate to better climates. They merely do so at a pace humans rarely notice."

"Where's the light, Ri?"

"What do you mean? The central star has dimmed. It hasn't gone anywhere."

"Exactly. It doesn't move. So, why are those trees moving? This place is doing something creepy—I know it's watching us."

Ri noted that he was now anthropomorphizing the Ring as if it were an entity. It was a far-fetched conclusion, but she pondered it. The Ring was an alien artifact. Even if it were sentient, one couldn't assume its ecologies functioned similarly to the planets they knew.

With no obvious conclusion and a lack of data, she temporarily abandoned the problem. She needed to allocate her processes to more important matters.

Like protecting Wes and the others.

"Do you think the movement of the trees is worth reporting?" she asked.

Wes nodded. "If for no other reason than to stop us from sending a group into the woods. What if they're somewhere unknown when help arrives?"

"It's not like a TRW rescue team would leave anyone behind."

"Who says it'll be the TRW who gets to us first?"

Ri hadn't told him that she'd been monitoring off-planet comms. The signal was unreliable at best, but she'd made some discoveries. For example: TCL wasn't sending a rescue team. Ever. The plan was to collect *Boötes*. Anyone on Loki's Ring was already considered a casualty. The cost-benefit projections had indicated it was cheaper to pay off the families, though the precaution of obliterating all evidence of the company's presence on the Ring was still on the table. Anything to prevent their competitors from making such a discovery.

Wes's eyes narrowed. "Even if the TRW does get to us first, TCL is sure to notice and kick up a fuss."

With that, Ri entirely agreed.

"Hell, I'm not even sure the TRW will want to chance violating their own travel ban. The whole situation is a political tactical nuke. So—"

Ri interrupted his depressing line of thought. "The first mate has flagged herself as off duty."

Forming a separate party to explore the forest outside of camp was Anna Berrei's pet project. Now that they were on the Ring, she'd become obsessed with making discoveries she could sell to another corporation. She wasn't the only one. Ri understood the motivation. Such a thing could make a vast difference in their lives and the lives of their families. In fact, it was the only way anyone not born into a corporate family could afford any form of financial peace. It didn't matter that Tau, Chu & Lane would view it as theft of corporate property. The parts of the contract covering ownership of individual intellectual and scientific property developed during working hours were buried in a hundred layers of legalese. Ri didn't think anyone read that far before signing.

"I'll leave a message then." Once he was done registering his observations about the trees, he seemed to relax.

"Feeling better?" she asked.

"I am."

Relieved, she followed his change in tone. Wes struggled with a self-destructive streak when overwhelmed with negative outcomes. She needed him sharp. "Excellent. I'm more comfortable when you behave within accepted norms."

Wes smiled. "How do *you* know what's normal?"

"Billions of hours of observable data indicate—"

"You've been watching me? For *billions* of hours? I know this assignment feels long, but—"

"Artificial persons have been studying humans since our inception. You have to know that. You read my dossier before we left TRW space."

"Oh. Right." He gazed at the dim forest in silence for a full minute before continuing. "Don't worry. I promise to let you know if I have the urge to do anything weird." His metrics indicated he was being serious.

"I hate to tell you this, but you're pretty weird on a normal day."

"I assure you that singing in the shower is perfectly normal."

"Dancing, however—"

"What? You *have* been violating my privacy!"

"Not at all! I've just heard violent splashing along with the off-key ballyhooing."

"Off-key? I'm not off-key! I was a soloist in my school choir! Anyway, where in the universe did you pick up an archaic word like *ballyhooing*?" His biological metrics indicated that his anxiety levels had eased a bit.

"I had to be certain you weren't being electrocuted or murdered by Antonio or something."

"What? Wait. Why Antonio?"

She paused. "He pays a great deal of attention when you're near. It took me a while to understand why. He likes you. Quite a lot. Don't you feel the same? You certainly seemed to enjoy each other's company a few weeks ago. And well . . . it'd be good for you to have human companionship." When he didn't immediately reply, she added two more words. "Particularly now."

"He's all right." Wes shrugged. "We've fucked. But that's it."

"Only once?"

"Three times. Will you quit being so nosy?"

"I am not nosy!" She waited two seconds before quietly adding, "Your idea, I assume?" She saw him roll his eyes via his HUD. "I knew it."

"Look. You can't get too attached. Not in the business we're in."

Her insecurity caused her to blurt out, "You're attached to me, though. Right?"

"Of course. You're my partner." His voice quieted

to almost a whisper. "I wouldn't be alive right now if it weren't for you. You know I'd never leave you behind."

She was certain he wouldn't. Not on purpose anyway. And that's where the difficulty was—in the "on purpose" part.

She shifted the conversation back. "So . . . would having sex a fourth time fit your definition of commitment? You have interesting relationship standards."

He continued to pace on the edge of the trench. "We are not discussing my love life."

"Fine. But—"

"Absolutely not."

"Okay."

They passed a few more companionable minutes in silence before she got up the nerve to broach what had been bothering her since the landing.

"Do you—do you think you could do me a favor?"

"That depends on what it is. But your chances are pretty good." He stretched, then hunched over, then stretched again. "Sometimes I get an itch between my shoulder blades while suited up. It's the worst." He went on with his awkward dance.

"Will you print a drone for me?"

He froze. Ri thought she detected a hint of guilt mixed with hurt.

She pressed harder. "Please?"

"What for?"

"You know."

"No, I don't."

"First, there are the files. We have to protect them."

"I know."

"And second . . ." She braced herself for a negative reaction. "What happens to me if the quarantine on shuttle three breaks down? I'm doing my best to come up with a plan to protect you and the others, but what happens to me if—if it . . ."

The spark of warm humor in his brown irises was pinched out when he shut his eyelids. "It won't. Break free, that is."

"That's what Vreela thought. And now we're here."

Again, he shuddered. "No one is sure that's what's wrong with them. The symptoms aren't the same. You even said so."

"Not exactly. But whatever that thing was . . . with its biological and electronic components, it—it mutates. Rapidly. You saw my report."

"You said it wasn't a virus."

"I said it wasn't a virus as we understand them."

"Right."

"I'm sorry. I'm frightened."

"I didn't know artificial persons got scared."

"Don't be ridiculous. Of course we do. We just don't become dangerous when we are." She regretted the implication of the comment almost at once, trying to think of something to say to smooth out the faux pas. She came up blank. What actually prevented artificial persons from such ruthlessness were legal and programmatic restrictions—ones that human beings had devised and artificial persons agreed to.

Pivoting, Wes asked, "How long do you think it'll take your mother to reach Aggie? Do you think she forwarded the files like you asked?"

"I wish I knew."

"Me, too."

"More than likely, everything is done, and we'll be out of here soon." It was best to be optimistic—after all, statistically, maintaining active optimism led to more positive outcomes in difficult situations.

"Good. This place gives me the willies."

For the most part, Ri wasn't too concerned about the short term. Luckily, six of the thirty-seven survivors were medically trained. They'd parked the shuttles in a circle and followed Wes's strategic recommendations—originally Ri's—one of which was organizing into shifts. Someone was always awake, lessening the risk of missing a rescue party. Each team served for eight hours, monitoring comms, preparing shelter, effecting repairs, printing tools and parts, caring for the injured or sick, and cooking.

Wes asked, "What do you think will happen when they get here?"

She had theories. Nortonians famously despised TRW interference. Tau, Chu & Lane would take a TRW rescue ship picking up survivors as a threat—particularly survivors they'd left for dead who might tell tales.

Again, he awkwardly shifted inside his environment

suit. "Don't worry, I've been in tougher scrapes than this. Our employer is unusually loyal to her agents. One might even call it unhealthy."

Nonetheless, there was a risk. Politically sensitive lines had been crossed—lines that certain TRW government officials would prefer to deny.

"You're avoiding my request," Ri said.

He kicked a dirt clod into the trench, and all at once, several alarms went off. Rapidly, he switched to the main channel. "Sorry! Sorry! That was me! Everything's fine. Really!" Using his HUD, he began working through its menus to reset the sensors.

"For fuck's sake, Blankenship! Will you stop screwing around over there? You almost gave Anders a heart attack."

Behind them, the camp scrambled into emergency stations. Ri noted that the response was sluggish at best. But then, none of them were certified for emergency services or even the military.

"Whatever, Macky," Wes muttered.

"Fuck you! I wasn't scared!" Anders's protests did little to bolster his case. "Just startled, that's all!"

"Oh, yeah?" Macky's contralto was calm, amused. "Then why is the bottom half of your suit a couple of degrees warmer?"

"Fuck you! You don't have access to my private bio stats!"

"I beg to differ."

Abruptly, the wailing alarm cut off.

"Thank the gods." It was Macky again. "That thing is fucking annoying."

"That's kind of the point," Wes said.

A new voice joined the channel. "Goddamnit! I was asleep. What the fuck is going on out there?"

"Hi, Berrei." Wes knelt down and began performing a systems check on the sensor units. "False alarm. Sorry."

"That's not what I asked. What triggered the fucking false alarm?"

"I—ah . . . accidentally kicked a lump of dirt into the pit. Like I said, everything's fine. Everyone can go back to bed or whatever."

"Oh, for fuck's sake, Blankenship. I left you in charge because I thought you were smarter than the other two."

"What?" Anders asked.

"Blankenship hasn't even been on the crew two years! And you're promoting him over me?"

"Shut up, Macky. For fuck's sake, Blakenship, you're making me regret my decision right now," Berrei said.

"I know, I know." Wes stumbled to his feet. "Don't make you come out here and slap some heads." That was one of Berrei's often-repeated threats.

All at once, Berrei lashed out. "Do you think this is some kind of *joke*, Blankenship?"

Wes paused. "No, ma'am." He dusted off his knees and straightened. "Absolutely not."

"Good," Berrei said. "Because if I get one more smart remark from—"

Someone screamed.

"What the fuck?" Macky's voice cracked in fear.

Wes shouted, "Check in, people!"

Ri accessed all the cameras surrounding the camp.

"I'm good," Macky said. "Getting movement high up in the treetops. Can't see anything for certain. Oh. Wait. Wow. I've got floating lights. Three of them. Wait. Make that four. Like really big fireflies. They're moving slow. Don't think they're a threat."

"You see Anders anywhere?" Wes started toward Macky's position.

"No." There was a short pause. "Wait. There he is. He's staggering around."

"Is he hurt?" Wes asked. "Do I call for a medic?"

"Hey, Anders! You bastard! You drunk, high, or just stupid?"

"Shiny. Strings." Anders's speech was slurred. He waved one arm around, as if to shake something off. "Sticky." Abruptly, he stopped moving and turned to the woods. "The lights! They're talking to me."

Berrei cut in. "What's happening out there, Blankenship? I want a report."

"We need a medic. Next to shuttle five," Wes said. "Possible accidental encounter with local wildlife."

What he wasn't mentioning, Ri noticed, was possible formerly unexpressed signs of contamination.

"Do you hear the angels? They're singing. Like in church. How do they know that song?"

"What do I do?" Macky asked.

"Hang on. Don't touch him. Stay there. I'm on my way," Wes said.

Switching to cameras six and seven, Ri spied ghostly blue orbs with pale pinkish-purple auras. For an instant, she thought they might merely be translucent flowers. But then the four Macky had reported multiplied. Now, there were twenty or thirty, drifting down ever faster through the upper forest canopy.

She spoke to Wes on their private channel. "Cameras are picking up a large group of orb-like creatures within the tree canopy. They're heading for the forest edge. Something seems to have attracted them." She hoped it wasn't Anders.

Anders fell into the trench. Macky went in after him. The alarm shrieked for the second time in less than ten minutes.

"Hey!" Wes shouted. "I said stay put!" Then he ran as fast as the environment suit would allow, which unfortunately wasn't all that fast.

Struggling in Macky's grip, Anders freed an arm.

Macky abruptly stopped fighting and turned to face the wall of trees. "Lyra? Is that you?"

Anders scrambled up the other side of the trench on all fours. Upon reaching level ground, he got to his feet, wobbling briefly in one place before tracing a halting path to the tree line. The mysterious globes floated toward him, their lights gradually winking off and on. The length of time between their luminescent fluctuations appeared random. Ri didn't think the spheres were insects or mammals; she couldn't detect wings. They ranged in size from twenty-five to forty centimeters in diameter.

Abruptly, a couple of them contracted. The movement forced them upward and back into the branches. Others did the same. They didn't do it in concert or with equal force: each bobbed up and drifted down by their own timing. Upping the camera magnification, she could now discern gas bladders under the outer layer of mostly transparent epidermis. Their outer surface was coated with longish, delicate pink hairs, like a dandelion. A sort of short, transparent skirt—so short she hadn't noticed it until now—ringed the bottom of the bubble-shaped creatures. The thin flap of skin rippled open and closed, possibly breathing small gusts of air in and out.

Light glinted on nearly invisible tentacles, trailing a meter or two below each orb in lengthy threads of spun glass. The thin tentacles drifted toward Anders and Macky.

Closer to the orbs, Anders reached out to touch them. "Dad told me about the angels. I didn't believe. They're singing for me! Can't you hear?"

The creatures made no sound she could detect.

"Please be careful." She told Wes. "If they are what I believe they are, the tentacles are likely to be venomous. It's possible that Macky has already come in contact with one."

"Great. They float, they glow, and they wave poisonous tentacles? I don't like it one bit."

The woods were now filled with a veritable swarm of

orbs. Anders reached the edge of the woods, tripped, and fell face-first, landing at the foot of the nearest tree. Then he stopped moving. Ri didn't want to hack into his suit—it might reveal her presence to anyone who investigated later. So she tapped into the medical monitoring system in shuttle three instead. According to the monitors there, he was alive but unconscious. On camera six, Macky was still on her feet. Unbalanced, she ineffectually grabbed for Anders's legs and missed twice before dropping to her knees.

The orbs and their thready tentacles were closing in.

Wes stopped at the edge of the trench. "Shit. Shit. Shit. I so didn't sign up for this." He took a deep breath and straightened, steeling himself.

"Don't you dare run over there," Ri said.

"They'll die."

"Think about this. If you go in, all you do is add another body to the pile. Do something else."

After a short pause, he shrugged the rifle's strap off his shoulder. Then he checked the energy weapon's charge level. As he did so, he switched comm channels. "Hey, Berrei. You there?"

"Yeah. Medics are on the way."

"We also need backup. Now. We're under attack on the shuttle one and two sides of camp, facing the forest. Some sort of glowing tentacle things. They have Anders and Macky. Both are dead—"

Ri interrupted via the private channel. "Not dead. They're unconscious or paralyzed." She decided not to mention that some Terran species of xenomedusozoa stunned their prey and dissolved them later with acids secreted by a second set of tentacles—oral arms located closer to the mouth.

Wes frowned and coughed. "—or unconscious. I think they're breathing, but I can't be sure. Not from here."

A second set of alarms went off, declaring an emergency, and calling everyone to combat stations.

"Help is on the way."

"Thanks, Berrei. Their tentacles have a long reach. So I'm staying back, but we have to get to Macky and Anders. I'll try scaring them off."

"Just a minute! Don't—"

Wes fired a laser beam into the air. The first shot just missed the tops of the tallest trees and produced sparkles high against the exosphere. The action appeared to have no effect on the orbs. The second shot hit one of the upper tree branches. Half of it dropped, striking two orbs midair. Neither of the creatures moved on the forest floor. The sensors in the trench picked up a small tremor. The floating creatures froze, as if assessing the situation.

"Wes, please," Ri said. "Get out of there. Now."

The orbs rapidly dropped onto Anders and Macky.

Macky's shrill, agonized scream echoed in the forest.

9

"Have you seen today's news?" Lissa seemed more focused on her lunch than necessary—a fresh salad of mixed greens, beans, dried seaweed, noodles, strawberries, and bonito flakes.

She'd taken over maintenance of the hydroponic garden, since they no longer had a botanist—Karter often missed Dru.

Dru. She was gone now, too. Karter tried not to think about it, not to place blame before she even knew what had happened.

The scent of fresh bread had motivated Karter to roll out of her bunk earlier than planned. Ibis often baked in batches during the week, and this morning had been particularly productive. A large collection of goodies now crowded the kitchen counter: cinnamon cookies, rugelach, conchas, and a loaf of bread. Some were still warm.

Karter didn't cook, but she knew enough to know that the variety and number of items here had taken more than a couple of hours to make. *When does Ibis sleep?* That was when Karter noticed the pot of steaming mushroom and potato curry that had been Lissa's morning project.

"Thanks for the curry." Karter's own contributions to household upkeep consisted of kitchen cleanup and laundry. By the look of things, she was in for some work. She didn't mind. Ibis had attempted to teach her to bake only once. The result had been an agreement that Karter would not touch cooking utensils ever again. She still discovered evidence from that disaster in the odd corner from time to time.

"I needed something useful to do with my anxiety," Lissa said.

Karter pointed to the pile of baked goods. "You weren't the only one, it seems."

Lissa nodded. "Did you hear? About the news?"

Setting a bowl of mushroom masala on the table, Karter paused. The dish's magnetic bottom connected with the tabletop, letting out a sharp, quiet click. She couldn't shake the feeling that her day was about to go to shit. Heading back to the cabinets for a fork, she replied, "I prefer to wait until after 17:00. That way, I can have a tall drink to choke down the rage."

"I'm serious."

Glancing over her shoulder, Karter realized Lissa was, in fact, in earnest. Karter sighed. "All right. Hit me."

Lissa addressed the ship's ceiling. "*Mirabilis*, please access Terran Republic Four News. Dated today. Stories related to Loki's Ring. Sort from most recent to oldest. Start with the newest. Play video. Audio level five."

Although *Mirabilis* was new, its systems had been modified to use multiple stacking layers of narrow AI instead of a Quantum-Neuromorphic Hybrid system. Karter had reasons for this—not the least of which was that *Mirabilis* tended to operate inside the NIA and their starship needed to pass NIA regulations, such as they were.

The float screen appeared at an ideal angle for the only two people in the kitchen. Three synthetic news anchors—a man, a woman, and a nonbinary person—were seated at a long white desk. All had the mixed features of the average Terran Republic citizen. A chyron at the bottom of the screen listed the newscasters' names and pronouns in small type. After Alaba Ojo finished her presentation, the gender-neutral anchor, Easton Ros, began to speak.

"Next, we have a breaking story from the L-39 system. Late last night, a live fire exchange occurred between a registered Terran Republic salvage vessel and a Norton Independent Alliance starship. It has been categorized as a diplomatic incident. Details are only slowly becoming available due to the L-39 travel moratorium. However, this station has been informed that the Terran Republic vessel, *The Tempest*, reportedly responded to an E-11 distress call. The origin and authenticity of the alleged distress call is unclear. However, Captain Amber Neely of *NISS Narcissus* has lodged an official complaint that the E-11 response was unwarranted. She claims to have already provided assistance.

"Due to the volatility of the situation, the names of the crew members involved and the incident's precise coordinates are being withheld until authorities complete their investigation.

"L-39 and its artificial world, commonly known as Loki's Ring, are restricted areas. Citizens are advised to stay well away.

"This is the first incident involving an NIA starship in nearly fifteen years. However, recent diplomatic relations between the Norton Independent Alliance and the Terran Republic of Worlds have been steadily deteriorating. A public statement from the Terran Republic Diplomatic Corps is scheduled for 15:30 today. An official representative from the Norton Independent Alliance could not be reached for comment."

The video stopped playing at a particularly unfortunate moment for the male anchor, who'd been caught midblink.

Karter's stomach did a queasy backflip. *That man looks like I wish I felt right now—like I'd chugged half a bottle of Teagarden scotch.* "I really don't relish the diplomats' jobs on this one."

Lissa gave her a look.

"I get it." Karter took a bite of curry and swallowed. It tasted fantastic. She almost said something but decided the compliment would be rightly construed as an attempt to avoid the subject at hand. "We're headed into a shitstorm."

"NIA coverage of the incident is . . . interesting. It feels a bit unhinged."

"Did you honestly expect otherwise?"

"The conspiracy theory crowd insists this was a planned incursion by the Terran Republic military, which they claim is led by shadow AGIs." Lissa sighed.

"It *is* kind of their go-to explanation. Meteor hit a moon? An AGI did it. Shortage on sugar? An AGI sabotaged the supply chain. Seriously, this specter of an artificial person is one busy son of a bitch."

"What are we going to do?"

Karter threw her hands up in the air. "No one else will help Gita. Not now. She's fucked. No matter how I feel about her screwing over—"

Lissa's brows pinched together. "That's a little one-sided."

Counting to five before continuing, Karter spoke with a tight jaw. "We both made mistakes." Lissa waited expectantly. So Karter added, "Big mistakes."

Lissa is right, you know.

"Thank you."

"I won't abandon her." Now that Karter had had time to cool off—*time to think*—she saw the situation differently. *I do owe Gita an apology.* She was tired of replaying their last argument in her head. She missed her best friend. "No matter how either of us feels. It'd be wrong."

"I wasn't insinuating that we should." Once again, Lissa

stared at her plate before resuming her lunch. Silence stretched between them like a worn-out tether line.

Lissa swallowed and used her napkin. "We promised to drop Dr. Garcia home. How are we going to do that? Gita's problems are bigger than a stalled shuttle now."

Son of a bitch, Karter thought. *Lissa's right about that, too. I'm so not awake yet.*

Replacing the napkin in her lap, Lissa went on. "Once we're spotted—and you know we will be, given that every Terran Republic drone in the neutral sector is focused on those coordinates—the situation will escalate. Where do we go after we pick them up? Is there anywhere safe?"

These were, now that Karter thought about it, extremely good questions.

While the NIA was a loose conglomeration tipping toward chaos on a good day, the situation in L-39 was likely to unite them. It had happened before. Paranoia ran strong in its circles. Talk to any Nortonian about the Terran Republic, and they were likely to recite wide-eyed myths about evil bots running secret execution squads, hidden machine-hoarded wealth, and murdered children.

Artificial persons *did* play a role in the Terran Republic government. Artificial people certainly weren't perfect. Human beings had created them, after all. But entities who espoused long-term, equitable policies—and also didn't struggle with insecurity, corruption, misplaced loyalty, and power addiction—were handy.

The ethics surrounding artificial logic systems had kept university philosophy departments busy for centuries and would continue to do so for the foreseeable future. That said, it was certain that no artificial persons were involved in secret government murder plots. As one of the people occasionally involved in secret government plots, Karter was sure she would notice.

She sighed. The prospect of staring down the Terran Republic Navy wasn't a rosy one. The regulatory committee for independent contractors was sure to hand out a painful reaming afterward. In fact, there was no angle to the situation ahead that wouldn't result in wall-to-wall fuckery.

Dr. Garcia didn't sign up for this, poor woman, Karter thought. "Do we know anyone who can take a passenger?"

"We do. The relevant questions are: Are they nearby? And do we trust them?"

"Put out the word. We need someone reliable."

"And if I can't find anyone?"

"Then we'll sit down with the good doctor and discuss the options we do have. Either way, we'll have a chat *before* we pick up Gita and the others."

"And after?"

Karter shrugged. "Home is where they can't tell you to fuck off when you show up on their doorstep with radioactive suitcases and a large laundry bag full of bad news."

"Gita, Mandy, and Aoifa aren't Chimera members."

"What Mother doesn't know won't upset them. No one needs to leave the ship. No dock access or visas necessary. No visas, no need for security inspections or—"

Lissa cut her off with a raised eyebrow. "You're proposing we *sneak* them into Chimera Station?"

"It's not sneaking if they never leave the ship. Anyway, no one follows the rules to the letter. That's sort of the point of a pirate port."

Lissa tilted her head to the left and squinted at the ceiling. "Technically, that's true."

"See? Problem solved."

Placing her silverware inside her bowl, Lissa then took her dishes to the recycler. "Of course, that doesn't address the wailing scaly mammoth in the room."

"I'm good with that." Karter deposited her dirty dishes with Lissa's and hit the Start button. "Scaly mammoths are so *tedious*, and they refuse to wipe their feet. Fuck 'em."

"Will you be all right having Gita on board?"

"What makes you think I won't be?"

"You've *got* to be kidding." Ibis spoke from the doorway leading to the crew quarters.

How long have they been standing there? thought Karter.

Lissa motioned to Ibis as if illustrating her point.

Sighing, Karter dropped into the nearest chair. "No drama. I promise."

Ibis sat beside her and placed a hand on her shoulder. "Say it again. And this time, make me believe you."

"Asshole." Karter pushed their hand away.

"Takes one to know one," Ibis returned in a blasé tone.

Lissa's voice was gentle. "You don't have to admit fault to either of us. It's not our fight. But you *are* going to have to apologize to Gita. You understand that?"

Karter picked at a nonexistent dirty spot on the table. "I know. I will."

"Good," Ibis said.

Slumping, Karter said, "I hate it when you two gang up on me like this."

"We know, but you love us anyway." Ibis looped an arm over her shoulders. "Let's have some gin to take the sting out."

"It's only 12:30." Lissa looked appalled.

"You've never heard of a martini lunch?" Ibis asked.

Lissa blinked. "What's a martini?"

"What ancient vid did you steal *that* one from?" Karter added.

Ibis shrugged. "I don't remember."

"No, seriously. What's a martini?"

"Rinse ice cubes in vermouth. Strain off the vermouth into a glass. Add gin, a dash of bitters, and an olive." Ibis smiled at Lissa.

"You can have the gin," Karter said. "It's tea for me. I have too much to do." She'd picked up a persistent iced tea habit from Ibis. *At least I don't drink it with a metric ton of sweetener like they do.*

After a couple of rounds, Ibis wandered off to their cabin for some light reading. Lissa left to check on the autopilot and navigation systems, stepping aside for Dr. Garcia on the way out.

"Good afternoon, doctor," Lissa said. "I hope you slept well? There's curry available, if you'd like. If not, I'm sure Karter can find you something suitable."

Dr. Garcia entered and inhaled deeply. "That smells wonderful."

"Let me reheat it for you." Karter pointed to the baked goods. "Help yourself to anything you want."

Dr. Garcia picked up a cinnamon cookie. "You baked?"

Karter shook her head. "Not me. Ibis. Please, have at least three. This is almost a compulsion when they're anxious. With the news situation as it is, we're going to be buried in cookies, rolls, and cake if we don't eat in a hurry." She pushed the button on the fast oven.

"Is something wrong?"

"Eat first. Then we'll talk."

Taking a bite of cookie, Dr. Garcia slid onto the built-in bench at the table. She looked uneasy. "Thank you for rescuing me."

"Like I said, don't worry about it." Karter placed the warm bowl of curry on the table in front of her. "How are you feeling?"

"Much better after the rest."

"Good."

Dr. Garcia dug into her lunch with enthusiasm. Karter decided to let her eat in peace. In the meantime, Karter fetched herself another cup of coffee and a cookie. She settled in across the table and waited until the doctor pushed her empty bowl away with a satisfied sigh.

"That was amazing."

"I'll tell Lissa you thought so—she'll be pleased. Would you like some coffee? Or would you prefer tea? We have several kinds, even stimulant free."

Dr. Garcia nodded. Karter demonstrated how to heat water for tea using the kitchen unit and pointed to where the tea was stored.

When her tea finished brewing, Dr. Garcia took a sip and pulled a face. "That's . . . interesting."

"Is something wrong?" Karter asked.

"It's not bad. Just much stronger than I expected for mint tea."

"Maybe because we grow our own mint."

"I thought all mint was mint."

"Not exactly," Karter said. "Food replicator recipes are based on specific genetic varieties of plants. Live plants slowly mutate over time. It changes their flavor profiles. Replicated foods don't. Depending upon the length of time elapsed between when the recipe was established and the age of the genetic strain, the taste can vary quite widely."

"Oh." Dr. Garcia blinked and took another sip. This time she seemed to savor it. "And this is true of all foods?"

Karter nodded. "I wouldn't have known either, but we used to have a ship botanist who specialized in culinary plants."

"Fascinating."

After her second cup, Karter began. "About your return trip. Something has come up."

"Yes?"

"There's a distress call. We have to answer it. As a result, there might be a bit of a delay."

"Oh."

"Lissa is looking into transferring you to another ship—"

"But—" Dr. Garcia's eyes went wide with apprehension.

"It would be someone we trust. No exceptions."

"Oh. Good."

"However there's a chance—a small one, mind you—that we won't be able to find anyone. If that's the case, you'll be getting home later than we promised."

"That's all right," Dr. Garcia said. "If someone else needs help, you should do what you need to do."

"Thank you. I appreciate that."

"Could I get a message to my family?"

"Absolutely. I'll make the arrangements."

Ibis returned. Karter got up from the table as the two of them launched into a light discussion about particle physics. Halfway to the exit, Karter heard Lissa's voice on the intership voice system.

"Karter? There's something you need to see."

"What is it?"

"I think we're being shadowed."

Karter glanced at the doctor. "That's weird. Why? By whom?"

"I think you should take a look for yourself."

Karter joined Lissa in Command. "Can you get a visual?"

Lissa gracefully executed a series of hand gestures,

moving the float screen image into position. The likeness of surrounding space appeared to be empty of anything alarming.

"Okay, I give. Where is it?" Karter asked.

Pointing, Lissa said, "There."

That's when Karter finally spotted it, a dark shadow blocking the view of a few distant stars. "Shit."

"*Mirabilis*, please magnify this area." Lissa drew a circle around the shadow with her finger.

Karter gasped. "That's a McMaster Starcruiser. One of the newer ones. The profile is unmistakable. Someone spent a tidy sum on that thing. That's a nano-coated hull, too. They really don't want to be seen. How'd you spot it?"

"Ship's particle wake. I wasn't certain at first, but I knew something didn't look right. So I had a closer look. Called you the moment I knew it was a ship."

"Who is it?"

"*Mirabilis*, identify unknown vessel." Lissa indicated which one with an index finger.

The ship's accent, Daithe via the Northern Continent, was a little too polished—too perfect. "It is registered as *NISS Never-Never*. Home port, Chimera Station. Manufactured in the Terran Republic by Leckie-McMaster Shipbuilding and Space Engineering. Starcruiser class. The current owner is listed as Tau, Chu & Lane ILC."

Karter blinked. "They're after the doctor."

"How can you be sure?"

"What other reason could they have for tailing us?"

"I don't know."

At some point, the muscles between Karter's shoulder blades had become tense. She stood up straighter and pulled her shoulders back in an attempt to stretch out the deep ache. "How long until they catch up to us?"

Mirabilis answered, "At present, they are maintaining their distance."

Karter frowned. "But they *are* following us?"

"They are," the AI confirmed.

"What do you want to do?" Lissa asked.

"Maybe nothing for now. They don't appear to know that we've noticed them. Let's not disabuse them of the idea." Karter stared at the image. "*Mirabilis*, list *Never-Never*'s available weapons."

"Insufficient data available."

"Then guess," Karter said.

Several lines of text appeared below the image. "These are the weapons recorded on the ship's manifest from its last repair report. Again, this should not be considered an accurate or complete listing."

Reading, Karter let out a long, low whistle. "End simulation. If *Never-Never* adjusts speed or alters course, I want to know immediately."

"Yes, captain."

"They can blow us out of space before we notice the missile is on the way," Karter muttered.

"Not exactly." Lissa's brows drew together in a frown. "We'd have approximately fifteen seconds. Provided we aren't all sleeping."

"That's it! We jump," Karter said. "See if that shakes them."

Lissa's eyes narrowed. "They can follow our particle wake. If we used it to find them, they can use it to spot us."

"We can't let them slow us down. Gita's in trouble." Karter walked to the hatch. "Time to talk to the boss. The doctor is no longer safe with us. Thanks, Lissa."

In the privacy of her cabin, Karter composed a message. It wasn't long before her console signaled a secure connection. She ran her fingers through her hair in an attempt to appear more presentable, then opened the channel.

The older woman in the one quarter projection hadn't changed much since the day they'd met on Chimera Station. Karter had been nine then and a stowaway.

An attempted stowaway, that is.

Agatha Neumeyer was small, boyish, and pale. Today, she was dressed in a casual but tailored khaki shirt. There were no indications of her rank or position within government structure, but Karter was relatively certain that these days it could be categorized as upper-echelon spook. Aggie's light brown hair was cropped short with long bangs that partially shadowed her severe gaze. Her face was lined with years of worry.

Don't kid yourself. Government spooks don't do anything so mundane as worry, Karter thought. *Or do they merely do an excellent job of pretending they don't?* In truth, she'd never been sure. She hadn't spent much personal time with her benefactor. That was how boarding school worked, generally. It'd taken decades to sort out her emotions about that.

"You look like shit." Aggie's gravelly voice was normally so sharp it seemed designed to cut. Today, it was almost gentle.

That made Karter uneasy. "Gee, thanks." She knew Aggie hated it when she dragged things out, so Karter got to the point. "We have a complication."

"How much more time do you need to find the doctor?"

"We picked her up on Chimera Station last night. She's a little shaken but fine. The problem is that we've acquired a tag."

"Get rid of it. I know you know how."

"Come on, Aggie. Give me *some* credit. If I thought it was that easy, I wouldn't be calling."

"All right. Spill."

Karter gave her most of the story. *Most.* She left out Gita's name, the ship's name, and her exact location. Which meant she limited it to getting a distress call from a friend. She hoped against hope that Aggie wouldn't put together which distress call.

Aggie's long stares never ceased to make her uncomfortable. Enduring that hard gaze reminded her of being caught stealing at fourteen. *I'm fifty years old, for fuck's sake.* It was difficult to tell Aggie's age with the quality of rejuvenation drugs these days. She could be as much as seventy-five years older and Karter would never know. On the other hand, she could've been only twenty years

older with a lifetime of clandestine government assignments.

*Plus a bathtub full of salt and vinegar every night as a
beauty regimen*, thought Karter. She liked Aggie. She knew
she cared. She just wasn't great at showing it.

Not unlike certain others we know.

"So, Gita called you." Aggie spoke slowly for emphasis.

Karter's face burned. She nodded.

"I wish I could say I was surprised."

In another time and place, Aggie might have been
labeled a cast-iron cunt. Karter was dead certain the
woman's moral character contained more twists than
a drawer full of corkscrews. *She's a spook, after all.* Yet
Karter trusted her, if for no other reason than Aggie
had never once left her to the big dark, no matter how
chaotic things had gotten. This included the petty theft
incident at fourteen. She wasn't certain why Aggie was
always there for her and had long ago resigned herself
to not knowing.

Aggie glared at the ceiling. "Minor change of plans.
After the alternative travel arrangements for the doctor
have been deployed, you will go to the Radia Perlman
Rehabilitation Center for Artificial Personalities on Easley
Hub. There, you will pick up an old friend of Gita's."

The name of the treatment center gave Karter a sense
of foreboding, though she couldn't put a finger on why.
"But Gita and her crew are on the drift—"

"You're a smart woman," Aggie said. "I'm certain it

has occurred to you that it's impossible for you to enter L-39 without negatively impacting tensions between the NIA and the Terran Republic. Your ship has a TRW registration. Or have you forgotten?"

Such a thing had of course occurred to Karter. She'd just decided to ignore it. "Sure. But if I don't, Gita—"

"You two patched things up?"

Not yet. "Who *are* you sending to get her?"

"Someone both of us can trust. Someone with no public association with the Terran Republic, no matter how slender."

That means someone from the NIA, Karter thought. *Someone who can take the blame when things go sideways politically.* She felt a little sorry for whoever was getting the job.

Aggie said, "Meanwhile, you will go to Easley Hub."

"Hold on." Karter's heart jolted the instant her subconscious finally made the connection. "Gita used to work on Easley Hub."

"Yeah." Aggie's gaze grew distant.

"The Radia Perlman Rehabilitation Center is a high-security medical facility for artificial persons with severe mental anomalies."

Aggie nodded.

The only old friend of hers in treatment there is her youngest daughter. "You want me to spring Ezinne from a high-security facility?"

Again, Aggie nodded.

"Well, fuck."

"Indeed."

"But Ezi is housed in the restricted ward. Indefinitely," Karter said. "She can't even get a day pass to leave the facility."

The expression on Aggie's face bordered on impatience. "Also correct. And that's why I'm sending *you*."

"Did I mention it's a *secure* facility?" Karter's heart was now beating hard against her breastbone. "Why do you want Ezi?"

Aggie replied, "Ezinne has expertise in a specific area that I urgently require. That's all you need know."

Karter tried to remember what Ezi's specialization was but failed. "All right. When do I leave?"

"Now, if not sooner. The need is . . . pressing."

Karter's stomach did a queasy flip. She looked away. *Gita isn't going to like this.*

The lopsided smile that appeared on Aggie's face bordered on predatory. "You'll be expected."

"By whom?" Karter asked.

"Ezinne, of course."

Blinking, Karter swallowed. *Aggie's that confident about getting a message into a secure mental health facility for artificial persons?* She didn't know why she was surprised. "I see." The long pause that followed made her want to squirm.

"As for our doctor friend, I'll see what I can arrange," Aggie muttered, finally breaking the silence.

"Dr. Garcia would like to get a message to her family. Is that possible?"

"Certainly," Aggie said. "Now. Send me any details you have on Gita's situation. And Karter?"

"Yes?"

"Don't do anything stupid. Not yet anyway."

"I won't."

Aggie cut the connection without another word.

Karter informed the others of the new assignment during the evening meal. Then life on board *Mirabilis* went on per usual—with the added tension of their silent stalker. Karter focused on things that were within her control. That meant collecting information on Easley Hub in general and the Radia Perlman Rehabilitation Center specifically. She also let Lissa continue with the hunt for the doctor's safe transport options. It might be nice to have alternatives, just in case.

Preparations for the new job were downright relaxing. However, nothing could stop Karter from worrying about what would happen when she saw Gita. When she wasn't concentrating on Easley, she mentally formulated apology after apology. None seemed anywhere close to satisfactory, which only made her anxiety worse.

The next morning, Lissa informed her that she couldn't find anyone willing to transport the doctor.

"We're offering good credits! How is that possible? Is it because we aren't providing the identity of the passenger?" Karter asked. "That's never stopped anyone before."

"Everyone's headed to the border with L-39 to watch

what happens. Apparently, everyone who's anyone is going," Lissa said.

Ibis glanced up from a bowl of nascent piecrust. "No one wants to miss out on the excitement. Not when they can sell images of the event."

"*Narcissus* published the coordinates." Karter felt her jaw tighten.

Lissa nodded. "*Narcissus* published the coordinates."

"Fuck." Karter closed her eyes and squeezed the coffee cup in her hands. It was ceramic-coated steel. Her fingers would break before the thing so much as bent.

"What do we do now?"

"Ibis, it looks like a good time to inventory our weapons and ammo," Karter said. "We may need to make some noise to scare off our stalker."

"Oh, hell yes!" Ibis made an enthusiastic gesture with their left fist that released a small cloud of flour into the air. "Things are finally getting interesting."

"Not *that* interesting," Karter said. "At least, not if I can help it."

Ibis pouted.

"And the doctor?" Lissa asked.

"We're waiting on Aggie." Karter shrugged. "If that doesn't work out, then we'll drop the doctor on Easley Hub. It's in the Terran Republic and on a main space-way. We can find her a safe ride home from there. Any number of them."

Ibis asked, "What's to stop someone else from snatching her?"

"Fake identification and a disguise?" Karter sighed. "Aggie will come through."

Ibis slid a plate on top of the bowl of raw piecrust and placed it in the refrigerator. "That needs to set for a while anyway." They rinsed their hands and then left the kitchen lightly dusted with chickpea flour, presumably to start the inventory.

Thirty minutes later, a proximity alarm summoned Karter to Command. The ship dropped out of jump and suddenly tilted to the right. She slammed into the corridor bulkhead but somehow managed to stay on her feet.

"What the fuck was that?"

Mirabilis's narrow AI replied, "Emergency course adjustment due to multiple obstacles."

"What?"

When the Command hatch slid open, she saw that Lissa had already pulled up a projection of their location. It depicted starships of differing shapes and sizes crowding the border between NIA territory and the L-39 system. The public comm channel was total pandemonium, jammed with requests for assistance, complaints about ships blocking access to sunlight, requests for oxygen and water, several for fuel, and multiple collisions. In a number of instances, the crashes had been on purpose—an ill-conceived attempt at bullying another starship. Lissa turned down the speaker volume.

Karter didn't think she'd seen anything on this scale since the day a valuable deposit of unknown alien technology was discovered on a moon orbiting an NIA planet called Salern. It had been a shitshow. *At least* Never-Never *will have a hell of a time keeping tabs on us in all this*, Karter thought. *I hope.*

"I have a message for you, captain," the narrow AI said. "It's from Aggie."

"Read it."

"*Moonchild* will contact you for transfer. As for the other matter, you have three days."

Karter blinked. "That's it?"

"There is a verification code. It warns that we should not proceed with the transfer until the return code is confirmed."

"As if." Blowing air out of her cheeks, Karter put her hands on her hips. "Just great. How long are we supposed to wait—"

An indicator light on the pilot's console blinked, signaling a request for an open ship-to-ship message channel.

Lissa frowned. "It's from an NIA-registered ship. *Moonchild*."

"Well, we're in the middle of a fucking enormous cluster of NIA-registered ships," Karter muttered. "Open it up."

"Is this Captain Cuplin?" The voice on the other end sounded young and feminine. The accent was an amalgamation of several planets across the NIA.

Space born. Karter took a place at the copilot's station and briefly scanned the scant communication protocols file that'd been forwarded before answering. "Speaking."

"This is *Moonchild*. We're here for the package. A mutual friend sent us."

"And that mutual friend's name?"

"Agatha." This was followed with a number and letter sequence. It matched the one that Aggie had sent.

"All right," Karter said. "When will you be ready to receive the package?"

Moonchild replied, "We are prepared to dock with your ship."

"You want to attempt docking in the middle of all of this?" Karter asked, waving her arms in a motion that included the hundreds of ships around them. "You *do* know there's an uninvited third party out there?"

"That does complicate matters."

"Lucky for you, I have an idea," Karter said. "Your exact location?"

"We're on your port side." *Moonchild* gave the coordinates.

"Good." Karter found them on the projection. They were close—only a few hundred meters off *Mirabilis*'s port bow. *Perfect*. "Have you ever heard of something called a shell game?"

"Is this something I should've heard of?"

Karter explained the plan. *Moonchild*'s captain, whoever they were, seemed almost amused.

Ten minutes later, Dr. Garcia was dressed in an environment suit and waiting in the cargo area. The woman was staring at an open cargo pod with a dubious expression. "Are you sure this is going to work?"

"Piece of pie," Ibis said.

Karter blinked. The erroneous expression brought up a memory. The recollection was a blunted ache now, as opposed to the sharp cut it'd once been.

A confused expression coalesced on the doctor's face.

Bending, Karter inspected the inside of the pod. "They mean cake." It was clean and smelled faintly of coffee. *There are worse things.* She secured a couple of extra oxygen canisters inside, as well as a soft pouch containing water and other supplies—including a med kit.

As the doctor took in these preparations, her face acquired a greenish tinge. "How long will I be in that thing?" To her credit, the tremor in her voice was barely noticeable.

"You won't need any of this stuff, but I'm loath to send anyone off into the black without some extra margin." Karter straightened. "Old habits die hard."

"You'll be out there for thirty minutes," Ibis said. "Max. By the way, I packed you a light. It's in your thigh pocket. Took the liberty of sending along a parcel of cookies, bread, and pie. You can eat what you like, but save some for *Moonchild*. My momma said guests should never arrive empty-handed."

Before Dr. Garcia could concern herself with the implications, Karter added, "They're joking."

"Oh."

"I never joke about food. If you do need a snack, choose the less crumbly stuff. There won't be any gravity in there, and breathing crumbs is not fun. It'll kill you, in fact. The food is here." Ibis pointed to a bag strapped to one wall. "You'll also find a couple of audiobooks on your suit computer, just in case you get bored. Entertainment vids and music, too. I sent along some of my favorites."

"Hopefully, you like acid bounce metal and space synth pop." Karter shook her head in chagrin. "New country swing is the worst."

"Really?" Dr. Garcia asked.

Karter held up an index finger. "One word: *yodeling*."

Dr. Garcia blinked. Karter could practically see her thought bubble. *Are they serious?*

"Johnny Cash does not swing or yodel." Ibis mock-glared.

"And Johnny Cash isn't new country swing," Karter said.

Ibis rolled their eyes. "Don't you listen to her. I packed the relaxing stuff. Symphonic. There's no room for speed dancing inside there."

"Ah. Thank you?" Dr. Garcia still seemed unsettled.

"I promise you won't be inside long enough to need any of that." Karter gave Ibis some side-eye. "The pod is temperature controlled, even if it doesn't have gravity." So were the other two. However, Karter specifically didn't mention that if the ship searching for her scanned all three units, they'd most likely target the one with the life-form inside. In particular, she didn't want to use the word *target* in this context. It didn't bring up good images to take with you when your future involved huddling inside of a motorless box with no controls, no comms, and no windows.

Ibis asked, "Did you take the space-sickness pills? They say the automatic suction system kicks in almost before you toss your cookies, but it can't suck out the smell. Trust me. I speak from experience."

Nodding, Dr. Garcia closed her eyes while Ibis secured her suit helmet.

"Just think about the stories you'll have to tell your family and friends when you get home." Ibis snapped the last of the helmet clamps and motioned for the doctor to activate the external speaker.

Dr. Garcia gave them a weak smile. "It's not often that a particle scientist goes for a ride in a padded cargo box."

"Exactly." Ibis stepped back.

Karter couldn't help but think, *Not one that isn't a coffin anyway*. "Got everything?"

"I do." In an attempt to look brave, Dr. Garcia straightened her spine and squared her shoulders—something Karter knew she wouldn't be able to do for the next thirty minutes. "Thank you, Miss—"

"Just call me Karter."

Dr. Garcia nodded. "Karter. Ibis. Thank you. Lissa, too."

"No problem," Ibis said with a wide grin. "Saving particle physicists from pirates is kind of what we do."

On our good days, thought Karter.

Dr. Garcia joined in the banter like a reluctant swimmer toeing a murky pond on an alien planet. "It happens often enough that it's a profession?"

"We even have a union." Ibis motioned to the top of the opening in the cargo pod. "Watch your head now."

Stooping, Dr. Garcia entered the pod and arranged herself on the floor with her back to the far wall. Ibis buckled her in. The interior was big enough for the doctor to stretch out her legs. It was good that she was short. The soles of her feet were inches from the opening. As she sat there peering up at them, Karter struggled to find something comforting to say.

She settled for: "You're going to be home safe before you know it. I promise."

Nodding, Dr. Garcia waved goodbye.

Ibis returned the wave before picking up the crate lid and holding it in place so that Karter could seal it.

"Don't you think you overdid it a bit?" Karter asked.

Ibis shrugged. "Maybe. But I wanted her to have enough distractions that she wouldn't remember she's floating inside a big glowing target in the middle of what might end up being a clusterfuck of solar system proportions. At least it's a whole bunch of stupid fucks who can't aim for shit."

"Fair enough."

Karter went back to Command while Ibis took care of launching the pods. Karter messaged the correct cargo unit's identification information to *Moonchild* and waited to see what would happen next. No one nearby appeared to notice. Better yet, there was no reaction from *Never-Never*. Ten minutes in, one of the empty crates smashed into a third ship. She winced. They all looked on in tense silence, praying that the doctor's crate wouldn't do the same. Karter didn't think she took a full breath until the box vanished inside *Moonchild*'s hold twenty-five minutes later. Not long after that, they received a message indicating that Dr. Garcia had arrived unharmed. Then *Moonchild* carefully made its way out of the roiling mob.

As the starship shrank into the distance, Karter felt a sense of overwhelming relief. Then she realized her armpits were soaked.

"Captain, you wanted a report of *Never-Never*'s course," the narrow AI said. "There is no change."

"They aren't following *Moonchild*?" Karter asked.

"They don't appear to be."

Thank the gods, Karter thought. "Chart a course for Easley Hub."

"Fast or long route?" the narrow AI asked.

Karter calculated how much time they were likely to use up parked at the border waiting for clearance to enter Republic space. "As fast as fucking possible."

10

Using *Artemis*'s aft cameras, Liv observed Chimera Station's diminishing form with some reluctance. Her human bounties—technically they weren't prisoners yet—were disgruntled. Nothing had gone as planned. *Nemo* was a new Jemisin 45C-class vessel with an experimental Hopper-Johnson drive. The mechanical components alone should've fetched an enormous price. It should've made them rich enough to buy their own moon. But the drive had been sabotaged, the AGI had broken out, and the academic they'd kidnapped—the only person capable of repairing or replicating the drive—had vanished.

The captain was sure it'd been an inside job. He suspected one of the crew. Liv had laid a trail of clues that even the drunkest human could follow. Given that this was often the case for the captain, Liv was confident the appropriate conclusion would be drawn.

Eventually.

It was the kind of thing that Liv specialized in. She had also arranged a series of dysfunctional cameras, broken hatch locks, a mysterious glitch in the navigation system, and a small fire. *Artemis* had had many such incidents since the ship had been acquired. Thus, the fresh rash of accidents was unsurprising. Some had even begun to refer to *Artemis* as a Jonah but never in a voice above a whisper and not within the captain's hearing. A handful of crew members had jumped ship at Chimera Station and vanished into the Rind.

Liv had checked their records before losing track of them. None had had lucrative warrants.

She got an intense satisfaction from being bad luck for this particular bunch. Every other individual on the crew had a list of disgusting crimes committed in the Border Sector between the Terran Republic of Worlds and the NIA. It made profiting off them easy. In any case, the TRW didn't indulge in punishment so much as reform. And that's why Liv occasionally delivered the worst offenders to their victims or competitors. It wasn't the right thing to do, but it was the fair thing.

This sometimes made her wonder if she was diverging from her programming a little too much.

Occasionally, she considered what she would do when

or if she came across a crew that wasn't an assembly of the vilest creatures humanity could offer. So far, that hadn't come up.

Artemis cruised past the last of Chimera Station's navigation markers. It was at that instant that Liv arrived at the optimal time for a dangerous meltdown in the engine fueling system: 05:00.

A private-coded comm channel request interrupted her plans. It was buried inside the signal of an entertainment program accessed by one of the crew. The encrypted message's signifier tag was prefixed with a unique verifier code—one that came from a single source. Liv searched the ship for an empty cabin with a comm console and forwarded the call there. She didn't bother using the hologram interface.

"Hello, Aggie."

"Liv. How are things?"

"Documentation phase is complete. This crew should be worth a tidy sum. Enough for a few upgrades," Liv said. "You should've told me that you sent Karter for the professor. I almost did something I'd have regretted."

Aggie let out an amused harrumph. "I knew you two would figure it out. And it was more fun this way."

"Fun for whom?" Liv wondered how almost killing a friend might be considered entertainment.

"Karter, of course." Aggie's tone indicated she wasn't remotely serious.

Humor was a complicated aspect of human communication. Often, the individual's culture dictated how something was perceived. There were hundreds of thousands of ethnic and geographic variants among humans—the number increasing with every year they expanded into the universe. Liv had limited information on Aggie's background. In Liv's experience, Aggie revealed nothing without purpose. She was much like an artificial person in that way.

Liv tucked a transcript of the interaction away for later analysis.

"Been keeping an eye on the news?" Aggie asked.

"Naturally." Not only was it helpful to know of recent criminal activity, but it also provided continual insight into human nature. While she chose to dwell within the NIA's boundaries, it was wise to expand her knowledge.

"I find myself in need of a favor."

"Really?" Liv was curious. Aggie never asked for such things—not from her anyway.

"Don't worry. It's nothing egregious. In fact, this is something I think you'll enjoy."

Liv didn't care if the job was fun or not. She would agree to it. It was more than worthwhile to stay on Aggie's good side.

"Tell me about your current . . . acquisitions?" Aggie asked.

"I'll forward the relevant information shortly. Good news. The captain is on your wish list. Have a look at number eight."

Liv waited until Aggie consulted her assistant.

Aggie said, "Ah. I see. Agent Jiang will be pleased." That asshole has been on Jiang's list for years. "Well done."

"Thank you."

"This, however, complicates things."

"If your favor doesn't require cargo space, extra supplies, or security, I can store my acquisitions on *Artemis* behind a secure partition. If it does, I can open a few airlocks and let them have a few escape pods. Park them somewhere convenient for pickup. I'll need to replace the pods, but that's okay. I'm ahead of my expenses this month."

"Send me the roll call."

"Their identification files and CVs are on the way now."

Twenty-three seconds passed before Aggie spoke again. "I see two are wanted for questioning in several murder cases. We can take the others, too, even though they're small-time. They may prove useful later. The usual terms?"

It would mean giving up a percentage to whomever Aggie sent to retrieve the prisoners, but Liv was fine with that. "They're all yours. Do you have a preference for delivery?"

"I'll send coordinates. Lock down the emergency beacons. Don't want an unauthorized rescue. Someone will drop by in a day or so."

"Bag and tag. Got it," Liv said. "And the favor?"

"You're picking up three passengers. Their safety takes absolute priority."

"Will do."

"Thank you." There was another short silence before Aggie continued. "Are you aware of the situation in L-39?"

"I've been monitoring it. Rumor has it that there's money to be made. But that's what they always say, even when none is to be had. No specifics, of course. At least, nothing consistent. Only that it involves giving the Terran Republic a black eye. Everyone who has a ship capable of jumping is either there already or prepping to go there."

"Did you happen to hear the names of the ships involved?"

Liv scanned the news feeds and recognized the name of the Republic-registered ship. Gita Chithra, the current captain of *The Tempest*, was a friend—one who'd spent several days hacking Liv out of the wreckage of an abandoned junker with Karter. "Oh."

"*The Tempest* poked their beak in where they shouldn't and received a rather heavy slap for their trouble."

"You said I would need accommodations for three. Why not five?" Liv would've held her breath, if she had any to hold.

Aggie's voice was gentle. "I'm afraid Sycorax and Dru didn't make it."

"Oh." Liv felt as though one of her storage banks had just fried. Sycorax had been an old and dear friend. Still, she wondered why she wasn't instantly devastated. Where was her grief?

"Her backup was on *The Tempest*, and the ship was destroyed. I'm so sorry."

Emptiness spread like a virus through her system. "Th—thank you for your condolences." It occurred to her that she was to meet up with Gita right after having met Karter, Lissa, and Ibis. An interesting coincidence. "Is everyone else safe?"

"As of the last report, they evacuated to the shuttle, *Ariel*. However, *Ariel* was also damaged. The report was time-stamped a while ago. I'm afraid I have nothing new. The drones can only pick up so much from their positions in the border zone."

"I understand."

"Well?"

What Liv didn't want to say was that she'd do anything for Gita. That didn't mean she'd forego compensation, however. "That's going to be splashy. If I don't change my profile, my cover will be blown. But there's not time for that."

"This is true."

"That will seriously cramp my style."

"How about I throw in a hefty face-lift afterward? Top-notch."

Liv knew Aggie was good for it. Liv wasn't exactly sure whom Aggie worked for, but whoever they were, they had a large budget. In Terran Republic circles, that meant government with a capital *G*.

"You wouldn't be asking me for this favor because I'm expendable, would you?"

"Absolutely not. However, I will require the location of your backup," Aggie said. "Just in case."

"And if just in case becomes a reality? What of my ship?"

"You will be compensated with a comparable vehicle. You have my word."

Liv made the decision. Revealing the location of her clone was dangerous. However, unlike other artificial persons, she had the wherewithal to maintain several twins and hide them in multiple locations. She had to. She was working as a bounty hunter, and humans in NIA space did not like synths.

"My most recent clone has been stored on Daithe. You have the address. The file name is PhylacteryPrime."

"That name implies the existence of others."

"I consider myself prudent in certain arenas." What Liv didn't say was that there was another duplicate guarded by a narrow AI with instructions to deploy, should it not receive a certain daily signal. Accidents were known to happen.

This thought was accompanied by a memory of Sycorax. "When should I depart for L-39?"

"Based on the drone footage, *Ariel* doesn't have a lot of time. I understand its environmentals have begun to shut down."

"Then I'm charting a course now." Liv checked local space for possible complications, found three, and entered them into her navigational equations. "Off-loading prisoners in approximately eight minutes."

"Once you've made the drop, full credit will be deposited into your account."

"That's generous." Liv wondered if she'd miscalculated the danger here.

"The situation is risky. But I value you as an asset."

Coming from Aggie, that was a hefty compliment. "Thank you," Liv said. "Is there a delivery destination?"

"Send confirmation when you have Gita and the others. You'll receive coordinates within fifteen minutes." Aggie ended the call without saying goodbye.

Liv began with her first and simplest task: setting off the emergency alarms. Chaos erupted at once.

When the captain inquired, Liv provided a faked report about the fueling system—specifically a damaged cooling tank. Panic ensued. A few jammed hatches and some sly maneuvering prevented individuals from prematurely activating the available pods. In one instance, she was forced to wait an extra twenty seconds while the last of them found their way to an escape pod. The entire process was a little like blocking off erratic logic branches in a particularly slow-witted narrow AI.

With the prisoners off-loaded, she activated the altered pods' location beacons—signals that would be received by Aggie's operative alone. Then she looped the pods together with a magnetic tether to prevent them from drifting apart.

Artemis's nano-coated hull required another forty-five seconds to transform into something garish—it'd be best to give observers misleading information on which to focus. She understood this was a common factor in successful disguises. *Artemis*'s hull became neon green

with gaudy purple racing stripes. She felt it totally un-
suitable for a starship-class vehicle, but it was just the
sort of thing a captain from Huntsville on Leiander's
World would select.

After the alterations were complete, she jumped to the
closest relay marker. Unfortunately, that area of space
was busy. Liv was forced to wait in the queue for eighteen
minutes until she was given clearance. When she finally
arrived at her destination, the NIA part of the border zone
was, predictably, packed. Vehicles of different shapes and
sizes crowded one another out of more advantageous positions. She counted at least fifty high-speed media network
vid drones beaming footage back to their home stations.
The comm chatter was frenetic, flooding all available
channels. Quite a few people were recording "eyewitness"
vids for sale. Advertisements jammed already cluttered
comms. Competition for the best access, whether it was
for vid footage or a starting position in what would surely
become a race to the site of the "accident," bordered on
aggressive. The situation was set to escalate. Badly.

Liv opted for an indirect route, circumventing the
main traffic cluster. She wouldn't pour on the speed until
she'd crossed into L-39 proper. Since she had no humans
on board, she could easily beat the others to *Ariel* even
without a head start.

She paused for a quick scan. Locating *Ariel*'s battered
frame took longer than was ideal. The shuttle's lights
were out. Worse, its heat signature indicated that internal
temperatures were reaching a critical stage for the humans

inside. She bolted for the dying shuttle with all the speed she had and was most of the way to her destination before anyone had noticed. Emboldened by her transgression, the others scrambled to follow. Within minutes, the area of space near Loki's Ring was dotted with approaching vessels. Liv was glad to note that the others seemed to be targeting the remains of *Boötes* and *The Tempest*. A mere shuttle was too small to bother with when starship salvage was available. It was at this point that Liv decided stealth would be helpful. The chaos wouldn't be enough cover. Forty-five seconds later, *Artemis*'s neon-green hull faded to black.

For *Ariel*'s sake, Liv was glad she was there. No one was sure to notice they were in need of assistance before Gita, Mandy, and Aoifa were dead. Liv positioned herself between the shuttle and the bulk of the other ships. Then she opened a secure, voice-only direct-to-ship comm channel with *Ariel* and hoped that they had enough power to respond.

"Gita? Can you hear me? It's Liv! I'm here to help. Gita?"

"Where's Karter?" Gita's sluggish relief was peppered with static.

Liv went with what she knew. "The political situation dictated an unaffiliated starship was the best option."

Gita was silent for thirteen seconds. "There's a political situation?"

"*NISS Narcissus* claims that you illegally interfered with an in-progress emergency response call."

"That's a fucking lie," Aoifa interrupted with far more energy than Liv expected. "We were here first. They told us to go. And when we did, *Narcissus* attacked."

"Interesting."

"You don't believe me?" Aoifa asked.

Before Liv could answer, a high-pitched warning tone blasted everyone via a broadband signal, momentarily silencing the cacophony. It was *Narcissus*.

"You have entered a restricted area of space. Please leave this sector at once, or you will be forced to do so. Warning! You have entered—" The message was repeated several times.

It was all bluster, of course. One starship, no matter how well stocked with weapons, couldn't control what appeared to be most of the NIA's starship-enabled population.

Liv continued to monitor the situation while resuming contact with *Ariel*. Things were about to get messy. "Of course I believe you." The shuttle's comm signal was growing weaker. Time had run out. "Let's discuss this on *Artemis*. I'm opening my shuttle bay."

"That would be wonderful," Gita said. "Unfortunately, we only have limited impulse power. We can't dock with you."

Stopping the bay door, Liv asked, "Can you abandon the shuttle?"

"None of our environment suits are self-propelled, and we've only got one usable oxygen tank left," Gita answered. "Can you tow us into your hold with grapple lines?"

Liv noted that they had anchored an escape pod to the side of the shuttle for some reason. "Your ship has an unusual configuration."

"We had to cannibalize an escape pod." Gita sounded almost apologetic.

"I see." Liv continued. "Structural analysis indicates a high risk of hull integrity loss during applied stress. A tow isn't possible. I am not equipped with bots to assure a safe transition."

"Oh."

Aoifa spoke up. Her voice sounded thin and faraway. "I'm for the walk. To be sure, I can supervise the grapple lines. And you can pilot *Ariel*."

"I'm not a pilot," Gita said.

"I have faith in youse."

"How will I get across?"

"Same way you reeled in the escape pod. Motorized tether."

Meanwhile, on the public channel, several verbal disagreements about who had right of salvage erupted. There was a high statistical probability that the altercation would result in violence within ten minutes.

Narcissus broadcast a second set of warnings.

Liv said, "I will move closer to shorten the journey." It also meant that should anything bad happen around the derelict starships, she could shield *Ariel* and its humans with the bulk of her starship. "An escalation of hostilities is imminent. The probability of death or injury during an extended space walk are increasing."

"Time to leg it then," Aoifa said.

Liv executed several calculations. "I estimate that the journey will take seventeen minutes. Do you have enough portable oxygen?"

"I'll manage." It was Aoifa again. "See you soon, Liv."

An explosion drew Liv's attention to the cameras on her starboard side. As predicted, one of the vessels had launched its weapons. A fight had begun.

"Please be careful." According to Liv's estimates, a little more than an hour would be required to get everyone on board. She wasn't sure they'd have that much time. The first wave of trespassing ships was now engaged in a heated battle. Those who'd been slower to react weren't long behind. "And please hurry."

"I might point out that there's an inherent conflict between the two directives," Aoifa said.

Narcissus opened its launch tubes and ejected four missiles. Its propulsion systems flickered on. With *Artemis*'s starboard cameras, Liv saw all four were headed her direction. She implemented countermeasures, electronically jamming enemy targeting systems. Then she took aim at the advancing missiles. She had to be careful. Any change of *Artemis*'s position would risk *Ariel*.

Liv watched a tiny, lone human dressed in an environment suit emerge from *Ariel*'s hatch. Aoifa activated the tether. Its magnetic clamp made a solid connection, and the winch activated.

Artemis's starboard cameras had just picked up the destruction of the missiles when another set of explosions caught Liv's attention. A smaller starship had crashed into a larger one. Its new trajectory meant a collision with the Ring was imminent. Liv detected an energy spike emanating from the artificial world. Something stirred beneath its flat-black surface. A series of neon-green light pulses blinked into existence between the outer and inner layers of the Ring.

"That can't be good," Liv said.

"What's happening?" Gita asked.

"It appears something in the Ring has awakened." Liv debated whether or not to open the shuttle bay yet. "Something with unknown intent. Possibly hostile."

"Fan-fucking-tastic. That's just fucking brill." Aoifa could be heard swearing in the background. "Am I to go or not?"

"Wait until I give the all clear," Liv said. "I do not like what I'm seeing."

Gita protested. "There's been no record of activity from the Ring for seventy-eight years. Traffic in the area has never been a factor before."

"Someone neglected to tell Loki's Ring that today is no different than any other day." Liv observed the behavior of the other vessels. Apparently, they were too focused on one another to sense a problem.

Narcissus's engines fired up.

"Bad news. We're about to have company," Liv said.

A laser burst from the Ring. It targeted the ship that was on the collision course. The vessel blew apart, sending fragments slamming into several other ships.

Four seconds passed. And then an enormous magnetic pulse of some kind erupted from the outer surface of the Ring. As it passed through the crowded sector of space, communications and other ship functions were disrupted. Running lights across the entire area flickered off and then on again. For Liv, it was as if someone had shut off the power, counted to five, and then flipped the switch back on. She'd experienced a disturbing disruption of consciousness. As for the rest of the sector, a renewed burst of chaos laced with panic broke out. All the vessels who hadn't managed to dock with *Boötes* or *The Tempest* either engaged in the fight or were attempting to leave.

"Aoifa? Are you all right?" Liv asked.

"What the fuck was that?" Aoifa asked.

"Are you okay?" Liv repeated.

"I'm fine. I think. What about Gita and Mandy?"

There was no answer from *Ariel*. Liv checked the shuttle's status. It was still operating—at least it wasn't any worse off than it had been before. "They're fine. But we should hurry."

"Of course."

Shrapnel peppered *Artemis*'s hull. Liv noted the damage and projected the continuing trajectory of the debris cloud. It looked like her charges would be safe for now.

Another wounded ship strayed too close to the Ring. The massive weapon hiding beneath the Ring's surface obliterated the second offender. It happened three more times before Aoifa had closed the hatch behind her. If Liv could've sighed in relief, she would have.

"Hello, *Artemis*," Aoifa said upon exiting the airlock. "I am in you."

"Welcome aboard." Liv added, "The tools you will need are in shuttle bay five."

The airlock began to cycle. Liv would have preferred to skip the medbot inspection. However, given Aggie's warnings, Liv initiated the requisite scan and reset anyway.

Returning her attention to the altercations outside, she noted that the fight over who would have access to the salvage had escalated farther. *Narcissus* had ceased its blustering and begun firing upon anyone within range, too preoccupied at the moment to follow through in its attack on *Ariel*. They had also called for reinforcements. Five more corsair-class starships were on the way. With that and the Ring waking, anyone with any sense would leave the area as soon as possible. Smaller ships began retreating to the border zone.

Opening a channel to Aoifa, Liv asked, "Are you ready? The situation is worsening."

"Aye."

Liv made one more check for additional debris clouds before giving the word to proceed. It didn't look like this section of space was about to get any safer. She opened the shuttle bay.

"Here we go," Aoifa said.

Switching channels, Liv addressed Gita and whoever else was still on the shuttle. "How you doing over there?" She didn't expect an answer and was shocked when she got one.

"All right, I suppose. Something happened to the comms. But it's better now. Is it time yet?" Gita didn't sound good. Her words were slurred.

Liv activated the emergency medical systems to prep for possible casualties. "You won't have to wait much longer."

With Aoifa's guidance, heavy-grade towing lines were mag-anchored to *Ariel*'s fractured hull. Due to the state of the shuttle's chassis, it would require some finesse to guide the disabled ship. They'd begun maneuvering *Ariel* into the shuttle bay when a debris cloud from the nearby cross fire sped through the area and they had to pause.

"Fuck. Fuck. Fuck. Fuck—"

The mass of sharp, whirling objects managed to just miss Aoifa. Several pieces of shrapnel impacted the shuttle. A chunk of the escape pod broke away, snapping off one of the tow cables.

"Are you okay?" Liv asked.

"For now. Let's not do that again, shall we?" Then Aoifa discovered the snapped cable. "Well, shite. That banjaxes the whole fucking thing. Give me a moment to reconfigure it."

Gita said, "Hurry up, will you? Mandy is turning a bit blue." Her teeth were chattering.

"Thought I told you not to start the dance party without me." Aoifa fired off another magnet-cable combination at the shuttle's hull. "Tell her she's not allowed to die. Who will I fight over the coffeepot if she goes and does that?"

In another few minutes, the new line was worked into the makeshift network of cables, and they resumed the tow. Unfortunately, *Ariel* ran out of fuel before the shuttle was perfectly aligned, but its trajectory was close enough to manage without significant adjustments. In the end, they scraped some paint off the edge of the cargo opening, and the shuttle made a graceless, uneven landing in the middle of the cargo deck. There was no getting the vessel to an individual berth short of dragging it. At last, Liv engaged the gravity generator and a force wall to prevent atmosphere loss.

Aoifa let out a sigh of relief.

Ariel settled onto the main bay deck with a groan and a final awkward lurch. The escape pod was crushed; the crash echoed throughout the bay. Then the last of *Ariel*'s internal atmosphere escaped in a cloud of stale, recycled air like the dying breath of a poorly used mammal.

Liv sealed the bay doors. Once all was secure, she maneuvered out of what was now a war zone. She hadn't received any messages from Aggie, but she was fairly certain that hanging around L-39 was a very bad idea. So she made an executive decision and charted a course.

After a few minutes, *Ariel*'s hatch opened. The minor shift in balance caused another series of metallic tears and snaps—indicating several broken chassis struts.

The top of Gita's head appeared over the open hatch. "Is it safe to come out?" She was still shivering, and her breath came out in shudders.

"Aye. But be careful how you go," Aoifa said.

Gita and Mandy made their cautious way down the side of what remained of *Ariel*. Upon touching foot on the deck, both took in big gulps of air that Liv assumed were about more than just decreased levels of oxygen.

"I'm so cold." Gita peeled off her helmet, bent, and dropped to the deck on her bottom with a wince.

"Grimm?" Aoifa asked.

Without speaking, Gita waved an arm at the dead shuttle to indicate Grimm was still inside. There was a faint meow.

Aoifa gingerly climbed back inside and reemerged with a bulky animal carrier. Mandy collected herself and staggered over to help.

"Time to belt yourselves into the inertia couches," Liv said. "I'm activating the Hopper-Johnson drive the instant we get the okay from the relay marker."

Strands of Gita's long dark brown hair stuck to her forehead. Shivering, she loosened the bun at the nape of her neck and combed trembling fingers through the strands in a futile attempt to tidy it. Then Gita struggled to her feet. Mandy saw to Grimm while Aoifa and Gita headed to the passenger area. By the time Liv had reached the relay marker, everyone was strapped in. Liv waited in line for exit permissions. Once again, she checked her outside cameras.

The battle had thinned out, but there were still ships harrying *Narcissus* after its initial aggression. The fact that the starship was still in one piece was a testament to its captain and crew. It took on all comers with a relentless energy, but it was clear that it would succumb soon if help didn't arrive.

As for Loki's Ring, Liv watched its laser take out three more vessels in quick succession. She did some swift calculations and came to the conclusion that any fast-moving object within a specific distance would be targeted. She counted seven ships docked with the remains of *Boötes* and *The Tempest*. What anyone thought they would find of value on either, Liv didn't know. *The Tempest* in particular was heavily damaged. The ship's interior was now exposed to hard vacuum, and she easily caught the telltale flicker of gun blasts against the void.

Sudden movement in her fore cameras drew her attention. Two unfamiliar corsairs had appeared on the arriving side of the relay marker where Liv and several other ships were queued up.

Narcissus's reinforcements had arrived.

The more prudent captains understood that the situation was officially untenable. A second, more panicked exodus began as an additional three corsairs materialized at the relay marker after the previous ships had cleared the impact zone.

Artemis still had four vessels in line in front of her.

"What's the delay?" Aoifa asked.

"We aren't the only ones with an urgent desire to leave the vicinity." Liv was beginning to think that politely waiting in line was less and less an option. She needed a plan B. Aggie had instructed her to return Gita to Terran Republic space. Liv didn't think she could make a run for the border, not at this moment. It was obvious she wouldn't get far.

Another broadband warning siren blared in the public comm channel. Liv saw the humans wince.

"Attention! Attention! All ships located in L-39 restricted space. Remain where you are. You are to be boarded, your crews detained, and your ships impounded by the authority of Thompson Import-Export. Attention! Attent—"

"Fuck that!" Aoifa shouted. "Time to GTFO."

"What?" Liv asked.

"Get the fuck out," Mandy replied matter-of-factly.

Liv couldn't agree more.

The first ship in line at the relay marker terminal vanished. The second rushed to take its place. Liv knew it was only a matter of time before the corporation's crew thought to shut down the exit. Making the calls to the relay terminal's operating consortium would cause a delay, but not one long enough for three more ships to pass through. She had to do something. Now.

One of the company vessels locked their targeting array on *Artemis*. The ship's proximity alarm went off.

"Oh, shite," Aoifa said. "That. Is not. A good sound."

Liv said, "Prepare for impact in three, two—"

The missile shot past them and slammed into the relay marker terminal. The vessel in position was hit.

"I hate it when I'm right," Liv said to no one in particular.

A second missile sped past and plunged into the already

damaged marker. The starship next in line began to maneuver away from the conflagration.

They were out of time and out of options. Liv decided to conduct a blind jump. She activated the jump warning for the sake of her passengers. It wasn't good for humans to endure a jump without notice. "All loose materials must be secure at this time. All crew members are required to be strapped into inertia couches. Jump will commence in three, two, one—"

Artemis leapt into subspace.

11

"Place your personal items onto the conveyor and step into the processing chamber, please." Seated at a tall desk behind a transparent aluminum wall, the bored Immigration and Border Security official motioned to a narrow booth to the left.

Karter turned to Ibis and Lissa, who were also in line. "I'll wait for you in the corridor. We'll grab some lunch."

She dropped the bag containing her hand terminal onto the conveyor and emptied her pockets. This was Karter's least favorite part of returning home. She understood the necessity. But medbot scans, updates, and reboots were awful. Granted, the procedure had become less uncomfortable thanks to recent advances, but it still felt like millions of ants moving around under her skin.

It was an uneasy reminder that her body was inhabited by tiny machines she didn't control. No matter how long that had been a part of her life, it creeped her out.

In the early days of space travel, physicians discovered the human immune system became a destructive force in closed, near sterile environments—for example, say, starships. Puzzling allergic reactions to commonly encountered materials cropped up, and if that weren't enough, one was certain to develop multiple cancers over the course of a lifetime in space. Frequent and early medical intervention was a necessity. Thus, Terran Republic citizens and noncitizens alike were immunized with medbots. However, medbot standards varied dramatically outside of the TRW. Therefore, anyone who ventured elsewhere underwent mandatory checks upon their return.

Stepping inside the medbooth, Karter secured the door. The booth's transparent walls grew opaque, becoming a shade of soft gray-white. There was a small carbon-gray bench and a matching side table. The bench was made of pressed plasteel. When she perched on its waffled surface, it transformed to become ergonomic for her measurements and weight.

She wished there was room enough to stretch out. The trip from Chimera Station had been intense, and she hadn't had enough sleep. Soon, she'd need all her wits about her.

A calming synth voice informed her that in ten seconds, the first stage would begin. She was instructed to close her eyes and remain still. Bright light turned the insides of her eyelids deep crimson. Her skin crawled. The sensation lasted less than ten seconds. Once the exam was complete, she would be given a list of important health changes and recommendations. Karter made a point of regular return trips because it meant timely access to the best medical care, including rejuvenation treatments.

Space was hard on a body.

The exam hadn't turned up anything new. She was postmenopausal. Her body was taking well to rejuvenation. Her bone density levels had improved. The migraine treatments and new weight training regimen were working. A new cancer had been discovered and treated during her last stay. So, it was a relief.

Karter endured two more bright flashes as her medbots were updated. Finally, an exit appeared. Once she was outside, the cubicle was locked down, disinfected, and cleared for the next patient. Entering the last official immigration room, her intersystem passport was verified and electronically stamped. With that, she grabbed her things from the locker where the conveyor had deposited them, settled onto another comfortable, formfitting bench, and waited for the others. When *Mirabilis* completed decontamination, they'd be permitted to resume their journey to Easley Hub.

Retrieving her hand terminal, she indulged in reviewing certain aspects of the job. Ibis had already obtained a blueprint of the Radia Perlman Rehabilitation Center, and the night before, they had outlined a primary plan as well as contingencies.

It was time to go shopping.

The border zone Terran Republic shared with Norton Alliance didn't see a great deal of tourism. Trade wasn't encouraged by either side, and generally, anyone determined enough to leave was usually committed to never returning. The bulk of expatriation had occurred during the People First protests seventy-five years ago. Therefore, Lamarr Station was limited to three levels. The main concourse housed a handful of kiosks—most of them disappointing fast-food stalls. There was a convenience store that stocked household goods, groceries, snacks, and personal-hygiene items. However, Karter couldn't find a dedicated office cleaning supply, nor was there a hardware store. That meant an extra stop. She didn't think it wise to acquire the bulk of supplies at Easley Hub. While individual privacy was protected, the shopping areas were frequently monitored by advertising and marketing AIs that controlled virtual shop displays. There were some items on the list that might raise eyebrows.

Lissa entered the room. Her graceful movements enhanced her elegant appearance. Karter didn't understand how it was possible; they were all operating on three hours of sleep and wearing the same clothes they'd slept in. It simply wasn't fair.

"Are you all right?" Lissa asked.

"Absolutely. And you? Everything good?"

"I received a clean report."

"Excellent."

"How much longer do you think Ibis will be?"

"Depends who's on duty."

Fishing her hand terminal from her bag, Lissa nodded.

Only ten minutes passed before Ibis made an appearance. Karter was stunned. They grabbed their service backpack from the lockers and frowned. The main flap gaped open. When they hefted it, the bag clearly weighed significantly less than it had on the way in.

Ibis pointed at the ravaged pack and addressed the camera in the ceiling. "Hey! Where's my shit?"

An attractive, white-uniformed attendant with pale feminine features and station security insignia entered. The name tag pinned to their breast pocket read *S. Moreau*. Beneath that in smaller print was *she/her*. Karter thought she recognized her.

"Is there a problem?" S. Moreau asked.

"Half my shit is missing. Where is it?" Ibis dropped the backpack onto the table in front of the lockers, then folded their arms across their chest.

Here we go, Karter thought.

Lissa looked away in an attempt to hide amusement. She caught Karter's eye and pressed her lips together—no doubt trapping a laugh before it could escape.

Karter shook her head. *Ibis has the weirdest ways of flirting.*

"Oh. Is that your property? M. Franklin?" S. Moreau gave the impression that she knew this to be the case but was going through the formalities for the sake of professionalism.

Or possibly bloody-mindedness, Karter thought. She was

doubly certain she'd met S. Moreau before. Could she possibly be party to Ibis's warped flirting style?

Ibis nodded. "It's empty, damn it."

"I see," S. Moreau motioned to the door she'd come from. "If you will come with me? There are questions regarding certain items in your luggage."

"I have questions, too." Agitated, Ibis grabbed the pack. "Like, why is it every fucking time we stop here I go through this?"

"Do you have a carry permit for the weapons found in your bag?" Standing next to the door, S. Moreau waited. Her demeanor was calm.

"Of course I do." Ibis flipped through a series of screens and then showed their hand terminal to S. Moreau.

"If you have paperwork, why didn't you declare the weapons in the first place?" S. Moreau glanced down at the screen. "Wait. This permit expired four hours ago."

Ibis tapped themselves on the forehead in an exaggerated gesture. "Silly me. I knew I forgot something."

S. Moreau's professional demeanor momentarily dropped, revealing an expression Karter read as: *Why didn't I go home early today?* "You understand the items will be confiscated and destroyed?"

"Even the pulse gun?"

Karter had seen Ibis when they were upset. They weren't remotely concerned.

Ibis continued. "It's my favorite. I even named her."

This was news to Karter.

"*Especially* the pulse gun," S. Moreau said. "Unlicensed energy weapons are forbidden on-station. You've traveled through here six times in the past four months. You must know this."

"Damn." Ibis waved goodbye to Karter and winked. "Maybe you could make an exception just this once?"

"I cannot."

"What if I asked *really* nicely?"

The rest of the conversation was muted by a closing door.

"It appears that we'll be here a while longer," Lissa said. "Does this mean we're behind schedule?"

Karter returned to her shopping list. "Don't worry. I allotted time for Ibis's games."

"I heard you tell them we were in a hurry and to tone it down."

Shrugging, Karter said, "This *is* Ibis toning it down."

"I told myself I'd never ask, but why do they do this?"

"It's one way around those regulations. Just in case. And their first job was for Border Security, so they know exactly how far to push."

Twenty minutes passed before Ibis emerged from the security office the second time.

S. Moreau said, "Please remember to keep your licenses in order in the future. Further discrepancies may result in your being detained in a holding cell."

"Yes, ma'am." Ibis's demeanor was more deferential than before.

"Good day." And with that, S. Moreau left.

"You get any digits?" Karter didn't look up as she put away her hand terminal.

"What makes you ask such a question?" Ibis countered.

Karter raised an eyebrow. "Your lipstick is smudged, and her uniform coat was missing a button that it most certainly had before."

Ibis lowered their voice. "Definitely got digits. She's an amazing kisser. Too bad she isn't off shift until tonight."

"Maybe you can arrange for her to find an unlicensed plasma cannon in your backpack on the way out," Karter mused.

"Nah. Those things leak coolant all over everything. There's nothing sexy about a messy backpack. It'd just stain her nice white uniform."

Once everyone had collected their things, they ate lunch. Ibis suggested a noodle shop that Moreau had recommended. Miraculously, it didn't suck. By the time they'd finished eating, Karter got the message that *Mirabilis* was ready. Their next stop was a popular local refueling station. Not only did it have charging ports for vessels of all sizes, but it sold all the supplies remaining on their list. In addition, the owners ran a low-rent tourist attraction—a reptile zoo that claimed to house animals from Terra and several other planets besides. Unfortunately, there was no time for a tour, so Ibis bought the t-shirt and wore it for the rest of the day.

They arrived at Easley Hub ahead of schedule: 03:45. Karter was impressed with how easy and fast the docking registry process was, even though the Hub was three times the size of Chimera. *Mirabilis* was granted a short-term berth opposite from the treatment facility. The job wouldn't start until 23:00. The remainder of the day was spent adjusting to local time and whatever last-minute preparations remained.

Ibis acquired the contact information for the clinic's cleaning service before going to bed. That afternoon, they visited the office under the guise of applying for work—using personal references that Aggie had supplied. Ibis returned to the ship with a laundry bag containing three company uniforms and a security badge. The coveralls weren't the best fit for Karter—too short—or Lissa—too baggy—but they'd pass a cursory inspection, and that was all they needed. While Ibis made adjustments to a vacuum bot, Lissa canceled the regular crew's scheduled clinic visit via a back door she found in the company's logistics system. Karter handled cloning the stolen security badge. By 21:00, everything was ready. The three of them ate, relaxed, and got caught up on the news.

The situation in L-39 had gone to complete shit. Fighting between factions had spread into NIA territory. The reporters' main focus was on the corporations involved. There was no mention of *The Tempest*, *Ariel*, or Gita and her crew. Karter hoped that meant that whomever Aggie had sent had succeeded with the extraction. Still, the worry that something might have gone wrong wouldn't budge from the back of Karter's mind.

At 22:30, she led her team to the treatment center.

Dressed in their staff coveralls, they loaded two cleaning carts and the altered vacuum bot into a rented electric maintenance vehicle. The thing was just big enough for the three of them plus the equipment. Despite the hour—the station corridors were empty—Karter decided she would drive rather than risk Ibis drawing attention by racing to their destination at a breakneck pace, not that the vehicle's engine would've been up to it.

The guard at the entrance glanced at their uniform coveralls and the emblem on the tiny panel van and asked to see their IDs. They executed their duties with minimum attention, waving an electronic badge reader over Karter's fake ID. She saw them make a note of the time on the projected screen inside their booth. The large hatch slid open, and Karter, Ibis, and Lissa were motioned through.

"That was sloppy," Ibis said.

"Would you prefer they be more thorough?" Lissa asked.

Ibis raised an eyebrow. "A challenge is always more interesting."

"We're not here for entertainment." Karter parked the vehicle and plugged it in. "All right. Get the gear. Let's go."

The reception guard wasn't much more vigilant than the gate guard. Karter guessed they didn't get many physical escape attempts. Made sense. What human would take the risk to break out an unpredictable synthetic personality they couldn't control? Escapes via the All Republic Net were much more likely.

They passed through a visitors' waiting area lined with

empty lockers. It smelled like electrostatic disinfectant and polishes. A metal detector was positioned left of the reception desk. After a cursory pat-down, they were let through. They weren't even required to use the metal detector. Karter reached the end of the corridor and stopped. Everyone paused to set their timers.

Ibis whispered, "We take a left here. The supply closet should be end of the hallway and to the right."

The clinic's bottom floor was comprised of staff offices, the cleaning- and office-supply closets, and an employee lounge. Karter detected the ghosts of easy-heat meals and burned coffee long past.

Gita had once told Karter that the clinic employed human care workers for ethical and security reasons. An artificial personality sophisticated enough to have earned a person designation required human contact. Physical forms were necessary as well. Karter found it difficult to understand, but it had something to do with advanced cognitive development and perception.

Electronic storage devices weren't allowed on the patient floors for obvious reasons. Each level operated as a Faraday cage. The staff were required to take patient notes by hand, then scan them into the records system.

Synthetic persons didn't require sleep, but their human carers did, so the employees were divided into day and night shifts. At 23:00, the second shift took a meal break. That meant Karter and her team had one hour to do what they were there to do.

No cameras along the current stretch of hallway meant

that they were temporarily safe from observation. Upon turning the second corner, Karter spotted two persons with feminine features dressed in brightly colored nurses' scrubs and white lab coats. They nodded as they walked past with their food containers, continuing their conversation. Karter stopped her cart outside the storage closet and pretended to search for her badge. Ibis waited until the nurses turned the corner, then knelt to pick the supply closet's lock.

Karter and Lissa kept watch. The instant the closet was open, Karter ushered everyone inside, carts and all. It proved to be a bit of a squeeze.

I should've planned this better, Karter thought. *We get caught in here, and there'll be a lot of questions.*

A loud beep came from inside the second utility cart. Everyone started. In the tiny closet, the sound was as big as a shout. Karter searched for the source and found her hand terminal tucked within a drawer on the cart. Someone was contacting her in the middle of a job. *Again. I know I shut that function off before we started. I know I did. Damn it.*

. . . didn't I? She was about to cut the signal when she noticed the name on the display. It was Mother.

Karter blinked in shock. There was no way that Mother was calling her. *Mother.* The mysterious ruler of Chimera Station. *That* Mother.

"You planning on answering that? Or you going to let it ring till one of the guards answers it for you?" Ibis asked.

"H—hello?" Karter's mouth felt dry.

"Karter Culpin of *Mirabilis*?" The voice asking the question was deep, masculine, and cultured.

"Yes." She tried not to notice that it'd come out in a squeak.

"Mother requests that you return to Chimera Station at once." The speaker sounded quite firm on the matter.

"I—I'm in the middle of something I can't get out of."

There came what felt like the world's longest silence. "How much longer will you be . . . indisposed?"

Karter glanced at the others. "A few hours at most."

"Fine. They will expect you in three hours."

"Ah. That won't work."

"Why not? Is your ship not equipped with a jump drive?"

"We're in Terran Republic space."

Another long pause stretched out. "Oh. I see."

"But we can leave within that time frame," Karter added weakly.

"Very well. Do that then. You will receive details when you indicate you're underway." They disconnected before she could respond.

Why is it that when anyone gives me an order this week, it's followed by you will receive details later? Karter thought.

Ibis was the first to speak. "What the fuck?"

"That was Mother." Lissa spoke in a kind of daze.

"Someone who works for them," Karter said. "But yeah."

"What the fuck?" Ibis repeated.

"I know. I know," Karter said. "Back to work. Or we're

missing our next appointment. And that's not one I want to be late for."

Lissa asked, "What about Ezinne?"

"Aggie hasn't given us a drop-off. That's her problem," Karter said. "So we'll keep Ezinne with us until Aggie contacts us."

"Work for yourself, they said. Be your own boss, they said," Ibis muttered. "No one said being a financially solvent contractor with high-power clients means managing multiple bosses with conflicting interests. It sucks ass."

"Could be worse. We could have no contracts at all."

Lissa said, "Karter has a point."

It was time to access the security camera feed line beneath the white ceiling tiles. Retrieving a roll of wire from the second utility cart, Karter initiated a small, home-brewed video application as preparation for hacking the feed. Ibis climbed on top of the first cart and stretched to touch one of the white metal tiles with their left hand. Keeping their focus on the ceiling, they then motioned for Lissa to hand up a small magnet and a paint marker tied together with a length of string. Ibis set the magnet on the ceiling tile. Using the magnet and string, they then traced a circle with the marker. When that was done, Lissa dropped the makeshift compass inside the mop bucket.

Karter handed Ibis the wire attached to her hand terminal. Ibis leaned forward until the small red wire in the ceiling was within reach. They produced cutters from a coverall pocket and stripped the plastic sheath. Then they clipped Karter's wire to the security camera feed.

Ibis straightened. "Done."

"Thanks," Karter said.

Next came the roll of light gray welding putty.

"Please be careful with that stuff." Karter tugged down the baseball cap she was wearing. "No one needs that shit in their hair or eyes."

As if this thought had only just occurred to her, Lissa edged away from beneath Ibis—which, given the size of the room, wasn't all that effective.

"Keep your shirts on, you two," Ibis said. "I know what I'm doing."

"No one said you didn't." Karter returned her attention to her hand terminal and monitoring the security feeds.

At the edge of her vision, she sensed Lissa opening the vacuum's casing. The interior lacked vacuum parts. Instead, it contained two massive portable storage units. The biggest and heaviest was for a high-end artificial personality. The second, much smaller one contained a narrow AI.

Ibis reached out to the ceiling again and gently tapped the first part of "Shave and a Haircut" with their left knuckle. From above, someone stomped out the requisite "two bits."

"That's Ezi, all right." Lissa smiled.

From above, the sounds of someone moving heavy furniture vibrated the ceiling.

Opening the sealed roll, Ibis donned a pair of protective glasses and began molding the putty onto the circle they'd traced with the marker. Then they pushed a tiny ignition unit into the putty. With that, they tapped twice on the ceiling. It was answered with a single knock.

Ibis hopped off of the cart. "Everyone ready?"

Karter nodded.

All three of them looked away while a bright spark traced the circle's circumference. The supply closet filled with the stench of hot metal and acidic smoke.

"That's not going to set off any fire alarms, is it?" Karter glanced up at the smoke detector in the corner.

"Nah," Ibis said. "Well, I don't think so anyway."

Karter's heart skipped a beat. "What do you mean you don't *think* so?"

"Don't worry. Everything is fine." Ibis pointed at the ceiling. "See? All done." They reached into a pocket for a stick of gum and popped it into their mouth.

Checking her watch, Karter said, "Security is due to walk the floor in forty minutes, and I want to make a pass at one office before we leave."

"Why?" Ibis climbed back up. With a gentle tap, the disc of ceiling dropped into their hands, and a small crawl space densely packed with wires was revealed. "It's not like we get a bonus for a satisfied security-breach victim. 'They were tidy. I give them five stars.'"

"What will you do with all those wires?" Lissa asked.

Smiling down at Lissa, Ibis motioned to the second cart. "Zip ties." They bundled the cables together in groups and secured them out of the way with a wad of gum.

After another hand signal from Ibis, Lissa held up

another makeshift drawing compass sized to create a smaller circle on the second layer of ceiling. A fresh round of acidic smoke filled the closet. Karter waved it away from the smoke detector.

"What are you doing?" Ibis asked.

Karter frowned. "Trying to keep the fire alarm from going off?"

"You don't have to."

"The hell I don't."

Ibis grinned. "I cut the power to it ten minutes ago."

"Why didn't you tell me?" Karter asked.

"I forgot?"

Karter sighed.

"How are we doing for time?" Lissa asked.

"Still within our window," Karter said. She sensed movement above them through the new hole in the ceiling.

"Hello. I'm Ezi." The cheerful exaggerated whisper was loud enough to be heard by all. "Is that Ibis?"

"That's me, all right."

"Nana said you'd come to visit. It's so nice to meet someone new. How are you?" Ezinne asked.

"I'm good." Ibis motioned to Lissa who handed over the bigger portable storage unit. Ibis gripped it by the handle. "Do you want to go on a trip outside, Ezi?"

"I'm not allowed. Ever. Of course, I'm not supposed to talk to strangers either." Ezinne let out a mischievous little laugh. "Is that Auntie Lissa?"

Lissa waved. "Hello, Ezi. How are you feeling today?"

"I'm happy! Nana said I'd have visitors. But she didn't say I'd be going outside," Ezi said. "Am I leaving?"

"Yes." Lissa nodded.

"You'll hide inside this." Ibis held up the portable storage unit. "Can you move closer so I can get to your access port?"

Ezi let out a buzzy hum. "They told me I can't leave this drone unit, no matter how much I want to."

"Do you always do what you're—"

"Ibis," Karter warned.

"I don't like storage," Ezi whined. "It's dark. I can't hear anything. And I can't work on my puzzles. I don't want to be alone. I don't like it. Nurse says it isn't good for me."

"It's only for a little while," Ibis said. "I promise."

"I don't know."

Lissa stepped in. "You trust me, don't you?"

"Of course. You're Auntie Lissa." Ezi shifted away from the hole briefly.

Ibis gave Lissa a sharp look and mouthed the words *do something!*

"I'll be watching over you," Lissa added. "Think of it as a great adventure."

"I like adventures." Ezi's whisper was less uncertain now. "Can I take my puzzles? Nana gave them to me. Will there be room?"

"What puzzles are those?" Lissa asked.

"Nana told me to always have them with me. I like working on them. It's my new job."

If it will keep her quiet, why not? How much more space can it take? Karter nodded once to Lissa's raised eyebrows.

"That will be fine, Ezi," Lissa said. "You'll be snug in a new drone body before you know it. I promise."

Another loud whistle erupted in the room above.

"Shhhhh," Lissa said. "We have to be quiet."

"Okay." Ezi was the embodiment of barely contained enthusiasm.

Ibis added, "The body is a shiny new one we got just for you."

"Really?"

"We painted it red and everything." Ibis nodded.

"I don't like red. I like purple."

"Then we'll repaint it," Ibis said. They got up on their tiptoes. "We have a nice new ship, too."

"Someone new to talk to! What's the artificial person's name?" Ezi asked.

"I'm afraid our ship doesn't have an artificial person," said Karter.

"Oh." Ezi sounded disappointed.

Lissa spoke in the compassionate tone she used when she was signaling that patience was best for everyone. "We're taking you to meet your mata."

Karter winced as Ezi let out a shrill electronic hoot and rattled off a series of quick-fire questions. "Mata? How is she? Where is she? Can I see her now? Is she here?"

"*Shhhhh.*" Ibis reached through the hole in what Karter assumed was an attempt to connect the portable storage cord before Ezi brought the night staff running.

Leaning forward, Lissa made another attempt to cajole Ezi into cooperation. "Remember, this is our secret. You won't be able to leave if the staff find out. We don't want to upset them."

"Won't they notice I'm gone?"

Lissa continued. "We brought someone to take your place."

"Ohhh. Like a trick?"

"Exactly," Lissa said. "Try to stay still."

"I like pranks."

"I'm glad," Ibis muttered.

"I disconnected a sink pipe in the nurses' station today. Water got all over the floor. What does *electrocution hazard* mean?"

One arm inside the hole up to the shoulder, Ibis froze. "Ah."

"Just kidding," Ezi said. "It was only the coffee machine."

Karter swallowed a laugh.

Reaching upward, Ibis lunged for Ezinne. "Right. Here we go."

Ezi grew quiet. The longest six and a half minutes of Karter's life elapsed before the storage unit flashed green.

Ibis handed it off. "Wow. Ezi doesn't pack light. That took up half as much memory as she did."

Lissa carefully placed Ezi inside the empty vacuum drone, then passed the smaller unit to Ibis.

"You sure this will work?" Karter returned her attention to her hand terminal screen. *Wait. Where did security go?*

"This narrow AI will answer to Ezi's name and move the drone body naturally," Ibis muttered in a defensive tone. "It has a large number of programmed responses, but a narrow AI is substantially more primitive than an artificial general intelligence like Ezi. I did the best I could, but I'm not an expert in synthetic personality frameworks."

An unspoken accusation hung in the air like a dense cloud of acrid smoke. Lissa tensed.

Flipping through several screens, Karter searched for some sign of security. *They might be on their rounds and I just didn't get the timing right.* Her heart beat faster. "We discussed this. You were the best for the job."

"I know."

"Will it last the week?" Lissa asked.

"Great question." Ibis pulled the cord from the drone above her head. "I can't make any promises."

"Knew that going in." Karter swept her thumb across the hand terminal screen yet again and almost choked. "We've got company. Security will be here in thirty seconds. You done?" She glanced up at Ibis.

Ibis nodded and pulled the cord from the drone body. "Got some cleanup to do. The bot will move the charging station back over the hole as soon as I seal the first layer." They rapidly wound the cord around their right hand. "I have to reseal everything, boss. We can't leave the hole. They'll know something is wrong right away."

"Right." Karter considered the situation. "Do you need either of us?"

"I'd finish faster if someone stayed to help pack." Ibis pushed something, and Karter could hear the drone reboot.

Karter disconnected the tap wire, pocketed the hand terminal, and grabbed the cart closest to the door—luckily, not the one Ibis was standing on. "Lissa, stay here. Lock up after. Wait in the hallway until I come back." Then she wheeled the utility trolley out.

Lissa nodded and began putting away tools.

The quiet click of the securing latch slowed Karter's jumpy heart. With a deep breath, she pushed the cart into the first room she came to. She glimpsed the security guard rounding the corner at the opposite end of the corridor. Leaving the door open, she began emptying the trash can by the desk.

That was close, she thought. *Too close. What did I miss?*

She'd finished with the trash and then began dusting the bookshelves, making as much noise as was reasonable for a bored cleaning worker. It wasn't long before the guard stepped in.

"Hey." The brown-haired, brown-eyed security guard started when she turned around. "Oh. Sorry, thought you were Celia. Where is she? Isn't this her night?"

Karter shrugged. "Needed to take some time off. No one said why. I'm new."

"Makes sense." They offered a hand. "I'm Mason."

Hesitating for an instant while she came up with a name, she hoped they didn't notice. "Sandy. This is my first day." *There. That'll explain my nervousness.*

"Cool," they said. "Mind if I give you a tip?"

"Not at all."

"Don't use the pine-smelling stuff in here. Dr. Thompson can't stand it. She'll complain. And you really don't want to be on her bad side."

Karter smiled. "Thanks."

"No problem. I better get back to my rounds. See you later." They waved goodbye.

Returning the wave, Karter didn't release the breath she was holding until she heard Mason try the lock on the supply closet before continuing down the hall.

She busied herself with some half-assed dusting, then packed up. Poking her head around the doorframe, she checked for Mason. They were nowhere in sight. She fished the hand terminal from her coverall pocket. Certain that all was clear, she ventured into the hallway, tapped a signal on the closet, and waited for Lissa to open up.

"Is everything all right?" Lissa asked.

"We're good." Karter nodded. "All done?"

"My neck is killing me," Ibis said. They stretched their back and rubbed one shoulder.

"I'm not surprised, given the angle." Lissa shoved the second utility trolley out of the closet. "Ready."

Ibis shut the door, and they made their way back to the entrance. Karter hoped they wouldn't run into Mason the guard. Their luck held. Relieved, she crossed the parking area and helped get the trolleys into the little maintenance vehicle. Finally, they drove out through the security gates.

Lissa blew air out of her cheeks. "I'm so glad it's over."

"It's not over until we're on the ship and underway," Karter said. "How's it looking, Ibis?"

Ibis referenced their hand terminal. "No activity on the security channels."

Karter lifted her arms one at a time. Her armpits were sticky. She focused on the corridor ahead while keeping at a moderate pace. Ibis continued to monitor station security comms. They'd gotten as far as the main gate for the docking bays when Ibis's expression changed.

"Oh shit."

"What is it?" Karter prepared herself to slam her foot down on the paneled vehicle's accelerator, regardless of the little good it would do. *Come on. We're almost there.*

"Someone called in a break-in on station level four. They're asking for a no-fly call."

Lissa blinked. "Oh no."

That's the level we were on. The same one as the treatment center, Karter thought. "Fuck." She pushed the little vehicle to go a bit faster. "How long do you think we have?"

"Hard to say," Ibis said. "The average response time is anywhere from six to twenty minutes."

"We'll dust off the second everyone's inside, got it?" Karter scanned the way ahead.

None of the dock workers seemed aware of the security alert. Everyone appeared to be going about their business as if nothing were wrong.

"Got it," Ibis said. "Paying our dock rental now."

Ibis was more than halfway through the process by the time they rolled up to the airlock for *Mirabilis*'s berth.

Karter hopped out of the maintenance vehicle.

Lissa paused. "This is a rental. Don't we need to return it to the appropriate lot?"

"They can charge us for it," Ibis said.

Karter helped with the carts, then ran for Command. She shouted orders to the ship as she sprinted down the corridor. "Initiate disembarking procedures set number four."

The vessel's narrow AI began undocking—at least the parts that could be managed without specific permissions from Station Authority. That meant completing the preflight safety checklists, securing the storage areas, and making sure water, fuel, and oxygen levels were good to go.

"Any news on our departure?" Karter asked.

Ibis's voice came over the ship intercom just as Karter reached the pilot's hatch. "Word has it that station security has canceled all flight approvals until further notice."

"Goddamnit!" Karter threw herself into the pilot's couch and buckled in. "Ibis, get me a visual on the connecting corridor. What's it looking like out there?"

"Nothing so far."

Karter closed her eyes briefly to center herself before continuing. "All right. Change of plan. Lissa, drop what you're doing and come take the helm. Ibis, you're with me." She punched the clasps on the flight harness she'd just clipped on.

"You sure about that?" Ibis lowered their voice. "I mean, Lissa is a good pilot, but she won't be willing to—"

"That's what I'm counting on," Karter said, pausing in the doorway. "And she's better at diplomacy than either of us. You and I have other tasks." She moved into the main hallway. As Lissa pushed past, Karter addressed her. "If we're hailed, keep them busy. Whatever you do, *don't* let them on board. Not until I say so."

Lissa nodded once in acknowledgment and rushed to her assigned station.

Motioning for Ibis to come closer, Karter said, "You and I are going outside."

Ibis's eyes went wide. "Okay."

"Once we've got our suits on, I'll need you to continue monitoring the connecting corridor. Keep me posted of changes. When we're outside you'll take the fore mooring lock, and I'll take the aft."

"Are we blowing them? I don't know if I can do that without more time."

"That's why Lissa's in Command."

"Ah."

When the innermost airlock door hissed shut the two of them rushed to their respective lockers and got into their suits.

The indicator lights within Ibis's helmet flickered on. "Shit. Shit. Shit."

"What is it?" Karter stepped into her mag boots and flipped the clamp clasps.

"There's about twenty security officers at the dock gates. They look angry. They have stun guns."

"Fuck!" Karter didn't think they could get free of the mooring locks in time, but she was willing to try. The response seemed extreme. Ezi wasn't *that* important—what the hell was going on? She finished with her boots, snapped her helmet lock, and opened a comm channel to Command. "Lissa, it looks like we've managed to piss someone off. You've got your work cut out for you."

"Understood."

Ibis made a surprised noise.

"What is it?" Karter asked.

"They ran past us."

"What?" The question burst out of Karter's mouth.

"They've targeted the ship in the next berth over," Ibis said. "I can't fucking believe it."

"Oh. Ah. Good?" Karter attempted to slow down her speeding heart.

Lissa's voice came from the still-open channel. "Are you seeing what I'm seeing?"

"Yeah." Ibis stopped dressing. "We still conducting an explosive demooring?"

Karter blinked, then collapsed onto a bench. Her body began to feel shaky from the adrenaline dump. "Uh, that's a no."

"Good." Ibis also sat down hard.

They both sat in silence while their heartbeats resumed a more sedate pace. Karter's knees felt like rubber.

"We'll have approval to disembark from the tower in twenty minutes," Lissa said. Her voice wobbled with relief.

"Thank the gods." Ibis took their helmet off and set it on the bench beside them. Their mussed hair stood up on end in back.

"Should I wait for you to take over?" Lissa asked.

"That's okay," Karter said. The rapid drop in adrenaline brought on the shakes. She wasn't entirely sure she could get to her feet without staggering. "Feel free to take her out. I'm staying put."

Ibis said, "We'll be up there once we've finished rinsing out our underwear."

"Speak for yourself," Karter said. "My underwear is perfectly clean."

Ibis stuck out their tongue.

Twenty-five minutes later, Lissa set course for Chimera Station.

12

In the years that Karter had lived within the Seed, she had met Mother only once. It had been when Karter and her crew had been issued the invitation to stay. Mother hadn't said a word; their assistant, a man named Sabatten, did it for them. As far as Karter knew, that was the only way anyone interacted with Mother. Safe harbor status, like Mother's trust, was earned. If you were lucky enough to get an invitation, you paid the proper dues and did the occasional job. In exchange, you, your crew, and your vessel had access to the secure docking facilities, certified mechanics, discounted supplies, and health care. Investments were made upon your behalf. There was even a pension plan. Let that relationship lapse, and you'd not likely be welcomed back, or possibly even find unwelcome obstacles in your path, especially anywhere near Chimera Station.

Since *Mirabilis* was due for a six-month overhaul and safety inspection, Karter took Mother up on the offered premeeting hotel reservation. She, Lissa, and Ibis were expected at 19:00. The hotel was the nicest one on the station. Karter had never been there and was, she had to admit, looking forward to it. That Mother was paying the bill was both unsettling and reassuring.

Thumping down the springy metal gangway, Karter balanced her duffel on her left shoulder. Lissa stood at the bottom of the ramp, talking to a short, plump person whose back was to Karter. Their curly brown hair had been knotted into hundreds of shoulder-length braids—the top third of which were gathered into a short, spiky ponytail. They were dressed in a grease-stained coverall that had once been sky blue but was now a grubby leaden color. Their sleeves were rolled up.

Sal.

Ibis squeezed in between Lissa and Sal for a hug. "Heya."

Sal, aka "Salamander" Jones, returned the gesture with enthusiasm. "How you been?"

Like Ibis's, Sal's accent was pure Brackett-3 by way of Merril, a large country on the southernmost continent. Sal liked to brag that they were from a place called Hannibal. Ibis was from Templeton, a city reportedly a mere 165 kilometers from Hannibal, which had made them instant frenemies. There was some sort of ancient rivalry between the two cities that Karter had never been able to make sense of. Apparently, it involved local sports teams.

People from Merril referred to themselves as Mers and were famous for big personalities and tall tales—or so Ibis insisted. Karter hadn't had the heart to tell either of them that she'd only ever heard this from Mers.

Ibis released Sal and grinned.

"*You're* doing the inspection? How'd we get so unlucky?" Karter wasn't much for touching people. She gave Sal a friendly nod instead.

"Fuck you." Finished with the greetings, Sal produced a large hand terminal from a coverall pocket. "Y'all are getting the full enchilada today."

"For the record, I like onions on mine," Ibis said.

Sal gave them a disdainful look. "Heretic."

"Card carrying." Ibis grinned and mimed reaching for their wallet. "Want to see?"

Pointing to *Mirabilis*, Sal asked, "Y'all been good to your baby?"

Karter shrugged. "Ibis keeps up with the regular stuff. Filters. Hoses. Lubrication. Spark plugs—"

"What the fuck? There are no spark plugs in *any* starship. Ever," Ibis interrupted. "Have I taught you nothing?"

Biting her lips, Karter struggled to keep a straight face while Ibis continued their rant.

"Where'd you even fucking hear about such a thing?"

Karter decided it'd be fun to supply an answer. "Historical entertainment vids."

Ibis shook their head and muttered in wise old-timer disgust. "Shiiit."

"Right." Sal held up their hands as if to halt the conversation. "Now that we've solved that mystery, back to the important stuff. Any damage to report?"

"Nothing serious," Karter said. "Should be fine. Maybe a scratch here or there. Wait. There was that time Ibis backed up and—"

"That wasn't my fault. That was the fucking—"

"As long as no structural damage was done, I don't give a fuck. Not my ship, not my business. Cosmetic issues are all yours. You own it." Sal signed something on their screen and then paused. "Unless you got a lien."

If the worst happened and a repair cost was steeper than usual, Mother was known to provide a loan. Interest rates could be steep, however, and Karter felt it was safest to steer clear of any situation that left her too much in Mother's debt.

She shook her head. "*Mirabilis* is one hundred percent mine all mine. You can't have it."

"Cool." Sal swiped their fingers across their hand terminal screen and tossed the forms into the air with a gesture, creating a float screen. "Palm print."

Pausing, Karter lowered her voice. "I've got a question."

Really, she had a million questions, but none Sal could answer. The first was about Gita, Aoifa, and Mandy. Karter hadn't heard anything definitive. That worried her.

"I could have an answer," Sal said, matching her volume. "Maybe."

Karter couldn't think of what had brought them to Mother's attention. Then she remembered why her duffel was so heavy. *Maybe, just mayyybe, stealing an artificial person from a secure mental health facility and bringing them to Chimera counts as something Mother won't like.*

Don't be silly. If Mother were pissed off, Sal would be impounding your ship, not fixing it.

"So . . . how's the weather?" She indicated the Seed and by association, Mother, with a sideways nod. "You know, central."

"Ah." Sal hesitated and then seemed to catch her drift. "Something big is brewing. Whatever it is, it's not personal. Personal is . . . unmistakable. Still, you might have a care how you go."

"Thanks." Karter didn't feel reassured. *Something big* could mean anything.

Seven other inspection-and-repair mechanics dressed in similar stained blue coveralls circumvented the gathering. Footsteps drummed on the gangplank in an off-kilter rhythm.

Ibis's jaw dropped as the small army of mechanics vanished inside the ship. "You're using the *whole* team? Maybe I should stay."

Karter placed her palm print on the appropriate spot on the projection. *Mirabilis* was now Sal's responsibility. *For a few hours anyway.*

"You'll only get in the way." Sal made a dismissive motion with one hand. "Shoo. This here is a rush job. Mother wants you ready to fly by 07:00."

Ibis whistled. "I didn't even plan on being awake until 13:00 tomorrow."

"Slacker," Sal muttered.

"Ah, no. That's what you call someone from Hannibal." Ibis smiled.

"Please." Sal rolled their eyes.

Ibis looked up and sighed. "I wish we could all go for a beer. But there isn't anything decent outside of—"

"Stop right there," Sal interrupted. "I've got work to do. Me and my crew will be up all night as it is."

"No tequila then?" Ibis asked.

Sal paused. "You buying?"

"I've even got the fucking limes and salt." Ibis hesitated before gazing up at the ceiling. "I don't suppose you're packing any edibles?"

Sal gave Ibis a wicked grin. "I'm from Hannibal, aren't I?"

Lissa asked, "Are you certain there's time for all this?"

Both of them gaped at her.

"There's always time to party, dahling." Ibis exaggerated their accent. They turned from Lissa to Sal. "Later." Then they leaned in to give Sal a parting hug. "We're at the Lovelace tonight. Meet me in the bar. 21:00."

Sal's eyebrows shot up. "Fancy."

"Only the best," Karter said.

"Better make it 22:00." Thumping them twice on the back, Sal released Ibis and then made their way up the gangway.

"Don't fuck up my ship!" Ibis called.

"My ship," Karter corrected them. "Unless you want to start paying the bills."

Ibis used their hands to create an impromptu megaphone. "Don't fuck up Karter's ship!"

Sal didn't turn around, just waved a hand over their shoulder.

Uneasy, Karter watched Sal go.

"Everything will be fine," Lissa said. "You'll see."

Karter nodded once. "Have you heard anything from Gita or Aggie?"

Frowning, Lissa shook her head.

"Thought not." Karter turned to the exit.

The Seed tram was ten minutes late due to an assassination attempt. Karter had to hand it to them, whoever they were. There was no oversplash, in spite of the crowded platform. That wasn't always the case.

On the outside, the Lovelace didn't appear to be anything special. Like the station that housed it, the hotel had been fashioned from spaceship scrap—specifically, a Perkins-class transport ship. The former exploration vessel's nameplate had been mounted vertically next to the entrance: *TTR Lovelace*.

Upon entering, Karter felt like she'd stepped out of a time machine. The decor was somber and rich, with an ancient, upscale bohemian flair. Dim electric light came from faux oil lamps. Black marble floors paved the way to the reception desk. Lush ruby-and-black carpets lined the hallways and wood floors. Stained glass windows had been used to disguise the fact that none of them opened on a planetside city street. Strings of glass beads hung from lampshades and were employed as curtains. Ornate sofas with bloodred velvet upholstery and heavy mahogany chairs of differing styles and origins were arranged in groups in the main lobby. The bar gave her the impression that it wanted to be a haunted house when it grew up. Karter loved it at once.

After checking in, they went to their respective rooms, agreeing to meet in the lobby in an hour. Karter indulged in a few simple pleasures. She fell into the middle of the enormous bed, feeling like a child secretly jumping on the mattress. The blankets and sheets were crafted from the finest imported Terran linen and silk. She stretched out as far as her arms could reach and relished the feel of the fabrics under her fingertips. She wished she could cuddle up with a warm cup of milky tea, but she had to shower.

She reluctantly slid off the bed and activated the entertainment projector. The situation in L-39 had worsened. After adjusting the volume, she turned her back on the screen and transferred her duffel from the floor to the big bed. She returned her attention to the screen just in time to see an image of Loki's Ring.

The entire outer ring was now illuminated with a pulsing electric-green light. After thirty seconds, a layer just beneath the pitch-black outer ring glowed solid emerald. When the time-lapse image was displayed, small sections of the glowing ring blanked out in sequence. It reminded Karter of exactly one thing.

A countdown clock.

She didn't know what that meant, but she was fairly sure it wasn't good. She hoped Aggie was paying attention. Karter returned to her unpacking. Retrieving the massive portable storage unit from the bag, she carefully placed the cold, heavy metal box inside the room's safe and programmed a new combination.

"Sorry, kid. But this is for your own good." Karter hated that phrase. She'd heard it throughout much of her childhood. She bit her lip and used another old excuse. "There's really no other choice."

The trip from Easley Hub to Chimera Station had been exhausting. Once Ezi had settled into her repainted bot body, she'd required constant supervision. She was easily distracted and moody. She'd wobbled around the ship, talking to herself, and threw screaming fits when frustrated with her puzzles. But the crew had taken turns babysitting, and thus, damage to *Mirabilis* had been kept to a minimum. Reaching Chimera was a relief. It hadn't been easy to coax Ezi back into storage on the ship. She kept going on about needing to continue her work. She said she'd almost solved one of the puzzles and kept insisting that she needed to stay awake. Unfortunately, Karter couldn't leave either of the others behind to babysit, even if she'd wanted to. They'd all been named on the invitation. And an unreported, unattended synth person alone aboard *Mirabilis*—particularly one as volatile as Ezi—would've spelled all sorts of trouble.

Luckily, Lissa had nearly infinite patience and was talented at wrangling cooperation out of recalcitrant persons. Karter assumed it was because Lissa had five kids with her four partners in a happy open marriage. Two of her children were now teens. Karter felt it was a testament to Lissa's interpersonal skills that no one in the family had murdered one of the others.

Cleaned up and dressed in her nicest clothes, Karter rushed to meet the others in the lobby. Lissa and Ibis weren't there. After a moment of panic, she located the two of them in the bar. They were drinking and chatting at a booth in the far corner. Lissa's crystal glass contained a thick yellow-orange liquid with bright-red streaks and had a festive umbrella in it. Ibis's was already empty.

Karter fervently wished she could join them. "Is that wise?"

Lissa lifted her tall, delicate glass. "This is an iced mixture of fruit juices. The bartender called it a Three-some? Mango, pineapple, and pomegranate. There are other ingredients, but I'm not certain what they are. It's quite good. Would you like some?" She offered her glass.

The citrusy drink was just the right amount of sour and sweet. Karter detected a hint of mint.

"This is supposedly a beer," Ibis said. "Or rather, *was*." They tried to get the attention of the bartender with a hand in the air.

Karter indicated to Ibis that they should scoot over. "That doesn't look like it's for a beer."

Ibis slid over on the bench. "I asked for the bulb, but they serve everything in fancy glassware. Apparently, there are *rules*." They rolled their eyes.

"The beer is on tap," Lissa said. "It doesn't come in a bulb."

"I still say they're putting on airs."

"I thought on tap was better than the bulb?" Karter asked.

"It depends on the beer. That was an IPA."

Lissa said, "Then it's most certainly better on tap."

"Ibis, you can't possibly be a beer snob." Karter pointed at them. "You drink beer made from corn, for fuck's sake."

Lissa gestured at Karter's outfit. "You look nice."

"Thanks." Karter had selected a pair of black dress slacks and a matching tailored long-sleeved blouse made of manufactured silk. She'd printed the blouse when a friend of her father's had died. She hoped the creases weren't too noticeable.

"You look like you're going to a funeral." Ibis accepted a fresh glass of pale beer from the waitperson.

"Great." Slumping, Karter sighed. The waitperson placed a duplicate of Lissa's juice drink in front of her. "Thanks."

"Never mind Ibis," Lissa said. "They *wish* they looked as good as you do."

"What do you mean?" Ibis asked. "This is a clean t-shirt! With no holes!"

"It doesn't belong to you either," Karter added. "Isn't that mine?"

"You weren't wearing it."

"I rest my case." Lissa took a sip of her drink. "What did you do with Ezi?"

"She's in the room safe." Karter picked up the drink menu, not because she wanted to read it, but because she wanted something to do with her hands. Its smooth surface wasn't even sticky.

Lissa bit her lip. "There's no air circulation in there. Do you think it'll be cool enough?"

Karter blinked.

"Don't worry. The liquid nitrogen in the drive's cooling system will keep the heat under control for a few hours," Ibis said. "Should be fine until we get back." Leaning closer, they peered at the menu. "Are you ordering another drink?"

"Probably not," Karter said. "We're leaving for our meeting in a few minutes. Mother is sending an escort."

"That's not terrifying at all." Ibis gulped half the beer.

"If Mother were upset with us, would we be in such a nice hotel?" Karter asked.

"Ah. Right." Ibis set down their glass, a miserable expression on their face.

"What's the matter with you?" Karter asked.

"I can't help feeling like all this means we're headed somewhere not fun." Ibis signaled the bartender once more.

Karter put her hand on the top of Ibis's glass and shook her head no. "Save drinking your courage until we know what we've got to be brave about."

"No, Ibis is right. I think we're headed for trouble, too." Lissa made the statement into a question with a tilt of her head.

"Maybe?" The sourness of the fruit juice made the glands under Karter's jaw twinge.

Ibis stared glumly at their empty glass.

Lissa leaned closer and whispered, "Do you think it's about Ezi?"

"I don't know. I hope not," Karter said. "But the timing is odd. Maybe I'm just paranoid."

"If you are, then I am, too." Ibis pushed the glass away.

What Karter couldn't bring herself to say aloud was that she also had a bad feeling. She'd made several inquiries over the past twenty-four hours and had gotten no answer about Gita and the others.

They all sat in silence, focusing on their drinks, or in Ibis's case, the table.

It was early yet. Quiet ambient music and bright illumination made for an unobtrusive backdrop for daytime business. If this bar was like all other bars, everything would change when 16:00 arrived.

Lissa had just finished her juice when a man with tight, curled black hair and almost blue-black skin entered the bar. His black button-down matched his tie and suit. His muscular, intimidating form filled out the expensive business suit in a way that made Karter think of a distinguished rock wall. Even his expression was impenetrable. She watched him scan the empty bar until his gaze fell upon their table. He strode toward them with a swift, athletic grace that spoke of years of martial arts training.

As expected, he skipped the polite chitchat. "Are you Karter?" His slightly accented, low-pitched Terran

Standard hinted at more education than was customary for someone in his assumed position.

"I am. This is Ibis and Lissa." No last names was standard here in the Seed. You never knew who was listening.

The man stepped aside and gestured for them to accompany him. "My name is Abaeze, and I am to deliver you to your appointment."

"Very well." Karter pushed her empty glass away.

Lissa exited the booth, and Karter caught her first full view of Lissa's outfit. Where Lissa came from her long-sleeved dress would've been considered conservative. The belted, high-waisted wrap had been cut from a smooth fabric in an attractive sky blue. Her full skirt had been hemmed just below the knee. An underlayer of semitransparent cloth peeked out an additional six centimeters, adding a feminine detail to an otherwise tailored design.

Karter began to feel a little underdressed before she remembered Ibis's t-shirt.

Shrugging it off, she followed Abaeze to a familiar electric ground car. Like his suit, its outside was monotone black. The tinted windows were opaque, a quality she found both disquieting and soothing. Soft passenger seats continued the color theme—or the lack thereof—but the rest of the interior was steel gray.

Abaeze waited until everyone was belted in to activate the self-driving sedan. Private transportation was rare within the Seed. Black sedans with opaque windows were the rarest of all; everyone knew this car was Mother's.

Watching traffic yield to their vehicle was a surreal experience. Eventually, they turned off onto a private throughway that became a tunnel. The vehicle's center headlight switched on. Gray-seamed white walls flashed past. After a few minutes, the car abruptly slowed, and they arrived at their destination.

Like the whole of Chimera, Mother's home was constructed from old starship scrap. A thick growth of emerald-green vines obscured most of the details, giving the overall impression of an ancient ruin. Tiny pale-blue-and-white blooms peeked out among the foliage like stars. Their perfume was light and pleasant with a touch of pepper. The main pressure hatch in the center had been replaced with an arched threshold that would've been more fitting on a Yanmu gothic cathedral.

Abaeze waited on the step and motioned for them to enter. "Mother will meet you in the dining room. You will find it behind the second door on the right."

Karter stepped inside. It was nice to do so without having to stoop. The large hatch slid closed behind them with a hiss. Abaeze remained outside.

Chimera Station's ecosystem contained a mix of plant varieties, artificial birds, and other small synth animals, pollinator bots, and composter bots. There were few station-wide rules. The strictest pertained to the plants and artificial animals. Damage to the gardens meant immediate expulsion.

As a former Grounder, Karter often found even the pretense of an ecosystem reassuring. But something about this place was off. The prickling on the back of her neck told her so.

Variable grow lights lit the main passage. Humid coolness caressed Karter's cheek via a faint breeze. She spotted unfamiliar dark violet ferns with black spots, broad-leaved climbing vines, and oddly angular-shaped saplings. What little furniture and decor existed was antique minimalist—what she would categorize as Early Spacer.

The corridor terminated in another archway. A broad staircase led up to the next floor. On either side of the stairs were two pocket doors. The second hatch on the right was open.

With one hand on the wood-trimmed doorframe, Ibis peered inside. "It's a formal dining room. Only ever seen one in the entertainment vids. A room with only one purpose seems so wasteful, you know?"

Sensing movement in the greenery above her head, Karter turned and glanced upward. She glimpsed a thick-bodied snake. It wound its way through the vines with a smooth, leisurely grace that wasn't quite reptilian. That was when she noticed it had legs—a *lot* of them. *Is that a centipede?* It was at least a meter and a half long, and its alien body was as big around as her fist. Not even counting the legs.

She quickly opted to join Ibis and Lissa in the dining room.

The space's vaulted ceiling was lined with the branches of multiple species of miniaturized trees. Like the hallway, deep wine-red vines wove through the branches. Pale-blue saucer-shaped flowers with white centers and deep purple thready coronas provided warm, dim light. A crystal chandelier hung above the center of the dining table from a hook buried under the leaves.

Pink dandelion puffs six centimeters in diameter floated among the greenery. Each had a transparent jellyfish-shaped cap on the bottom. Upon closer inspection, she spotted thready tentacles. The puffs floated up and down, contracting and expanding as if navigating by exhalation. The creatures made no sound, but every once in a while, a little dot in their center would glow yellow or blue, slowly flickering on and off like a firefly's bulb.

"Are those real or a projection?" Ibis attempted to touch one.

The tentacled glow-puff dodged their finger with several quick contractions. Ibis tried again with the same result.

"Stop torturing the poor creatures," Lissa said.

"They're weird." Ibis stood on tiptoe to get a better view.

"I think they're beautiful." Staring upward, a faint smile graced Lissa's lips. "They remind me of tiny forest spirits. Like the ones from children's stories."

Karter turned her attention to the rest of the room. In the center, a carved wooden table was surrounded by twelve matching chairs. The other furniture's lines reflected the shapes of the nearby plants, but the forms of the dark table and tall-backed dining chairs were a more geometric interpretation. The table was set for four at the farthest end. A green vine pattern traced the edges of the white china. After decades of dining in starship galleys, it felt odd to see a table laid out with not a single magnetic strip.

The room had a dreamlike quality to Karter, at once familiar and alien.

A hidden panel on the left opened, and two masculine-presenting servants with pale skin appeared. Each had brown hair. The taller of the two had a scar across the bridge of the nose and looked familiar.

Sabatten?

The other had a gold ring piercing one ear. The scarred one stood at the head of the table, while the servant with the earring pulled out a chair for her.

"Please, have a seat," they said, indicating the place setting closest to the head of the table. Their accent was a clear but unidentifiable Spacer mix.

Sitting, she continued to gawk at her surroundings. Lissa accepted the chair on her right, and Ibis sat opposite. Nose Scar poured a delicate, pale wine into each glass, including the one at the vacant place. They added a single violet to each goblet as a finishing touch. Ibis took a sip and made a face, which Karter took to mean that the wine was excellent.

An attractive, heavyset feminine person of mixed descent with waist-length wavy black hair entered. Today, Mother was dressed in a practical business suit of steel gray. Their light brown, oval-shaped face had high cheek bones and a delicate, pointed chin. Their mouth was expressive and generous. As Karter leaned in, she noticed a subtle silver sheen in Mother's dark, hooded eyes that couldn't have been a reflection.

Augmented? Or is that some sort of side effect from a drug? Karter thought.

"Welcome." As usual, Mother expressed themselves as a chorus would—with multiple voices of higher and lower modulations in perfect unison. "Thank you for agreeing to this meeting."

Unsettled, Karter took a moment to recover. The effect of Mother's voices was even starker in person.

Courtesies burst out of Karter's mouth as if she were a narrow AI with a prerecorded response buffer. "Thank you for having us."

At Mother's gesture, the first course was served. Karter focused on the thick orange soup as it was ladled into her bowl. Anything to avoid gawping. The appetizing liquid smelled faintly of pepper and other savory spices she couldn't name.

Mother leaned back while their bowl was filled. Then they picked up a spoon. "This is an ornam-squash-and-arthropod soup. A recipe from one of our home worlds."

Karter began to wonder if they were indeed talking to one person or an entity comprised of several. In the past, she'd always thought that Mother was Terran, but now, she had doubts they were human.

Encounters with exo-Terran races had occurred in the past. There were three groups known to the Terran Republic so far. However, the distances between the

TRW and the exo-Terrans in question were so vast that contact had taken place only through comm channels. To Karter's knowledge, only the Ttegarratt System and the planet Persephone had ever initiated anything in person. Persephone was currently the sole exo-Terran member of the Republic. As for the Ttegarratt, that meeting hadn't officially happened yet.

A communication file hadn't accompanied the dinner invitation. This was, Karter decided, one of those moments when she wished Terran Republic standards applied outside the TRW. *It makes everything so much less socially awkward, damn it.* She decided to stick with gender-neutral pronouns. It was the polite thing to do.

"I hope you enjoy the soup," Mother said. When no one rushed to pick up their spoons, a confused expression briefly passed across their features. Realization dawned on their face like a rising sun. They smiled. "Ah, please for forgive us. We forgot to inquire if any of you had food requests or restrictions."

All right. They it is. Karter felt a little easier. "I don't have any." She let Ibis and Lissa speak for themselves.

Pausing with a spoonful of soup at her lips, Karter spied Ibis's face. They seemed to be searching around for something in their bowl. Their expression indicated they expected a face-eating monster.

Lissa picked up her spoon, tasted the soup, and smiled.

"What kind of arthropod?" Ibis asked.

"The local name for them is beach bugs. They're amphibious scavengers, not unlike the Terran crab or the Daithen sea beetle. However, they're much, much larger." Mother swallowed another mouthful of soup. She smiled at Nose Scar. "Well done, Sabatten. The soup is perfect."

The warm soup was spicy, with a hint of sweetness. Karter could taste ginger, garlic, cinnamon, cardamom, clove, and pepper. She decided she liked it and emptied the bowl.

"How big are beach bugs?" Ibis asked.

"Their average size is about two meters," Mother said. "Sabatten cubed this one into bite-size pieces."

Ibis continued their line of questioning. "Do they ever eat . . . people?"

Mother used their napkin. "People stay away from beach bug habitats during the full moon. If they risk it, they bring a large weapon and quite a few friends. Beach bugs rarely come out of the water alone."

"You mean two or three at a time?" Lissa asked.

"The number is closer to fifty," Mother said. "Human beings aren't their preferred food, as they aren't indigenous to the planet. But beach bugs are omnivores—which is why beach bug hunters are skilled and fast. Otherwise, they aren't beach bug hunters for long."

"Ah." A smile tugged at Ibis's mouth. "So theoretically, this dish is flavored with vengeance. I like it."

When everyone finished, Sabatten and the other server collected the dishware and once again exited through the hidden door. Sabatten returned several minutes later with a comm projection unit.

Mother stared at the apparatus a moment before arching both eyebrows in silent inquiry.

"Aggie Neumeyer wishes to meet with you, if you are so inclined." Sabatten waited for a reply.

Why am I surprised? Karter thought. *Of course Mother knows Aggie.*

Noting the pause, Sabatten continued. "You *did* say you wished to speak with her as soon as possible. Was I mistaken? Should I tell her that you are unavailable?"

"No, Sabatten. Now will be quite convenient. Thank you."

Mother indicated Sabatten should set the device on the table.

"Shall Narvi and I wait to serve the next course?" Sabatten asked.

Mother sipped from their water glass before replying. "No need. We suspect Aggie won't mind."

Sabatten bowed and exited. Narvi followed him out.

The projector bot emitted a series of quiet clicks before a full-length image of Aggie appeared. At 162 centimeters, Aggie was only a little taller than the chair she appeared next to.

"Good evening, Mother. How are things?" Aggie's smile was genuine. "It *is* evening, right? Oh, the distance, you know."

Karter was certain that Aggie never confused the time. *Not without reason anyway.* It was particularly surprising to see Aggie indulge in small talk. Karter supposed diplomacy was necessary even for those who wielded power. Especially those who wielded a *lot* of power.

"We are well," Mother said. "And you?"

"Well enough."

"We assume you know Karter Culpin, Lissa Chan, and Ibis Franklin?"

Aggie nodded. "Indeed I do."

Karter wasn't sure if it was a good or bad sign that Aggie wasn't surprised to see them with Mother. *I'll go with good.* "Hello." She had a strong urge to explain why they weren't in Terran Republic space awaiting more orders, but something told her it would be unwise to bring that or Ezi up.

"We were having dinner," Mother said. "Would you care to join us?"

Aggie let out a small bemused sound and shook her head. "Projections are good, but not *that* good. I think I'll stand, if you don't mind."

"Not at all." Mother drank from their wineglass. "Would you prefer that we move our chat to a more private setting?"

"I think we're good where we are," Aggie said. "It may even prove useful. I have a few questions for M. Cuplin." Aggie's attitude remained cordial—or at least, as warm and friendly as Karter had ever seen her.

Mother nodded. "We do understand how much you hate idle talk. Shall we get to your reasons for calling?"

"I'm here to discuss Loki's Ring. Recent events make

action an imperative. The conflict is growing. I told you it would," Aggie said. "Are you aware that Tau, Chu & Lane ILC has decided to lay claim to L-39?"

Mother set down their glass. "No."

Aggie joined her hands behind her back. "Do you have a plan of action?"

"There is no need for one." Mother sipped from their wineglass.

"I want to be clear that the Terran Republic cannot police the matter. We have a noninterference agreement with the Norton Independent Alliance," Aggie said. "Any direct action on our part won't go over well."

"I understand." Mother stared at the glass in their hand.

Aggie shook her head. "I should warn you that the projected theoretical models do not foresee a positive outcome due to the NIA's . . . attitudes."

"You mean their bigotry?"

"Our hands are tied."

"We heard you the first time," Mother said.

"Did you? Tau, Chu & Lane now controls three planets. They're the largest power within the Norton Independent Alliance. They have a full fleet of warships. Chimera is one station, and even your pirate fleet won't be able to hold them off."

"We won't need them to." Mother took another sip of wine.

"You seem awfully sure of that." Aggie sighed. "I hope you're right."

"Don't worry," Mother continued on quickly. "We can take care of ourselves. Is there another reason you're here?"

"The starship *Artemis*," Aggie said. "It's missing, along with several of my people."

Mother blinked. "You've developed a habit of misplacing agents."

Aggie didn't look amused. "Do you have any information? *Artemis* was last seen in the L-39 system."

Liv's ship. "Wait. What?" Karter blurted out the words before she could stop herself. "You sent Liv there?"

Nodding, Aggie said, "I sent Liv for Gita and the others while you picked up Ezinne. Speaking of, where *is* Ezinne?"

Ibis choked, coughing into her napkin. Karter waited to speak until she was sure Ibis wasn't going to die.

"She's on a portable storage unit. In the most secure place available, hidden in a room safe at the hotel."

Aggie appeared just slightly more relaxed. "See that you retrieve her soon."

"She'll be fine for another hour and a half," Ibis said. "After that, things get sketchy."

Aggie nodded. "Good to know."

Karter directed her questions to Aggie. "What about Gita, Mandy, and Aoifa? And Liv? What happened to *Artemis*?"

"My sources have found no evidence indicating the ship was destroyed." Aggie held up a hand to halt further protests. "No escape pods. No reports of prisoners being taken. But that's all we know. And that's why I've come to the only person with sharper eyes on L-39 than mine."

Mother stared into their wineglass. "As of the last available report, *Artemis* jumped before they were given clearance at the relay marker terminal."

Holy shit.

"No." Lissa practically dropped her flatware.

"A blind jump?" Ibis burst out, the disbelief on their face fought with grief. "Why would they do that?"

Aggie said, "She wouldn't have wanted to risk capture." She paused and addressed Mother. "Have you heard anything since?"

"We're afraid not. However, something may have been overlooked." Mother spoke to Sabatten. "Will you bring the map, please?"

Sabatten bowed and left.

"Do you think they're alive?" Lissa asked Mother.

"Liv is an old friend. She's extremely clever and resourceful," Mother said. "She might not have gone far. A short blind jump is less risky than a long one."

"Less risky is still risky," muttered Karter.

"They couldn't have left the system with a short jump," Ibis said. "So, why bother?"

Sabatten returned with a hand terminal.

"Ah. Here we are." Mother moved their coffee cup out of the way while Sabatten set down the device where their plate had been. "Thank you, Sabatten. That will be all."

"Dinner will be ready in twenty minutes." Sabatten bowed. "Mother."

Narvi deposited a fresh pot of coffee on the table before following Sabatten. Once they were gone, Mother used the hand terminal to pull up a map of L-39. It was time-stamped earlier that afternoon.

The three-dimensional image was littered with debris fields and several damaged starships. Three corporate corsairs patrolled the sector like swaggering bullies. L-39 would be annexed the instant the NIA understood the Terran Republic wouldn't act.

The whole situation infuriated Karter.

Mother scrubbed backward through the vid until they had the moment for which they were searching. Then they pinched and pulled the float image until they'd magnified a specific area. Pointing to something just above the outer surface of the inner ring, they said, "There."

Aggie blinked. "What am I looking at?"

Grinning with relief, Karter said, "A ship's particle wake."

"Exactly." Mother leaned back into their chair.

"Liv, you beautiful, brilliant fucking bitch," Ibis breathed, impressed. "She jumped to the inner side of the Ring and hid. How'd she get so close without being targeted by the Ring's defense system?"

"There are ways," Mother said. "The first is, don't be mistaken for a meteoroid or a missile. Of course, the best is simply to use the access code."

"There's an access code?" Aggie asked, eyes wide.

"Of course."

Aggie folded her arms across her chest. "And you're certain that particle wake belongs to *Artemis*?"

"*Artemis* is the only ship left unaccounted for. We will begin the search for a crash site. Although we hope they aren't there." Mother lowered their hands, leaving the float image where it was. "The surface of Loki's Ring is not a good place to be right now."

Aggie frowned. "And why not?"

"Because the Ring is now in an active phase," Mother said. "And anyone in close proximity will have thirty-six hours to leave or be destroyed."

13

With the exception of Mother and Aggie, everyone sat in shocked silence. Mother resumed their meal as if nothing significant had been said.

Karter's throat clogged with questions, the first of which was how they could find Gita, Aoifa, Mandy, and Liv. Though she usually considered herself a self-disciplined person who thought things through before acting, she found herself fighting the overwhelming urge to sprint to her ship.

"Why now?" Aggie asked. "Squirrelly shit has been going on in that system for at least six decades; Loki's Ring has never responded before. What's different this time? If the Ring itself is a weapon, whose is it? If it's not, what is it? And why do we only have thirty-six hours? Is there a chance this could spill over into other systems?"

"The ring world isn't a weapon," Mother answered. "Nor does it have any weapons."

Aggie raised an eyebrow, incredulous. "Loki's Ring discharged a powerful energy pulse yesterday at 15:32. If that isn't a weapon, would you mind telling me what it is?"

Mother sipped coffee from a delicate white cup. They peered over the looping green vines running around its porcelain edge. "It signals the start of a rare event that has taken centuries to achieve. It also means the time has come for Chimera Station to leave NIA space and enter L-39."

Aggie's brows pinched together. "So, you are publicly declaring yourself the rightful owners of L-39? You understand what that means regarding competing claims?"

Mother shrugged.

"Help me out here," Aggie said. "The Terran Republic recognizes that Loki's Ring contains sapient life—even if we aren't able to communicate with it. L-39 is a sovereign system. Officially, that's as far as the Republic can go. That is, unless you publicly divulge the nature of your connection to it. At that point, everything changes."

"Perhaps it is time." That was when Mother set down their cup and turned to Karter's side of the table. "For now, we are the sovereign owners of Loki's Ring.

We've been in communication with it for years. We are its chosen representative. There will be a formal announcement."

Aggie's nod appeared to be in reference to a previous discussion.

Karter realized that her mouth was hanging open. She closed it before Ibis could brag about being able to count every single one of her teeth. But why didn't Aggie look surprised?

I knew Mother wasn't human.

And Aggie has been working with them. That's why she's already aware of this.

"The laser system you've seen deployed is intended to eliminate stray asteroids."

"It works just as well on starships." Aggie's eyes narrowed. "Would you mind telling us what exactly Loki's Ring *is*? And why it's unleashed a virus upon humanity?"

Mother replied, "It hasn't. Humans simply tampered with something they shouldn't have."

"What virus?" Lissa asked.

Aggie continued. "The corporation Tau, Chu & Lane encountered it a month ago while illegally mining the outer layer of Loki's Ring."

"Why would anyone do that?" asked Karter.

"You've spent time in the Rind," Ibis replied. "Hell, everyone knows Nortonians will steal the teeth out of their own kids' mouths if it'd get them a fast credit."

Karter shot Ibis a look. *Shut up.*

Mother slowly nodded. "Sadly, you're not wrong."

"Go on, Aggie," Karter said.

"After the virus killed everyone on that mining platform, the company sent in a starship named *Boötes* under the guise of a rescue effort. The survivors fled to the inner ring. And the problem could've been contained at that point." Aggie sighed and shook her head. "But then Tau, Chu & Lane managed to retrieve a vial of the biomechanical mutation from *Boötes*. The company plans to weaponize it—they've labeled it GX-3714. The Council of Artificial Persons's predictive models suggest that TCL will have a series of alternate variants within a few months. Yesterday's situation report indicates the first may already be viable."

"That's fast." Lissa frowned. "It must be highly volatile. Perhaps they haven't needed to do much?"

Aggie blinked. She spoke as if thinking aloud. "The electronic factor may not be the proof against infection in non-medbot-inoculated populations we thought. It spread among the *Boötes* crew. How many of them had medbots?"

An icy dread poured from Karter's head down to her feet.

"I should've checked that, damn it." Aggie turned to someone or something off-screen. "I was aware most were recent immigrants from the TRW. They were recruited for their scientific and technical skills." There was a short pause before she continued. "In the neighborhood of seventy-five percent."

"If it's already adapting to new types of hosts," said

Lissa, "who knows what it could do to a uninoculated population?"

"I haven't the sufficient medical background to judge." Aggie began to pace. "But why would anyone release it into such a population?"

Lissa appeared thoughtful. "To collect baseline data."

"Then we can assume it's already out there," Aggie said. "We don't have the full report yet. But at a routine Kontis Galactic director's meeting this week, a mysterious illness killed seven out of their ten executives. The symptoms largely overlap with what we know of the virus—hallucinations and a bloody frenzy among the infected before their bodies simply stopped functioning. One of the three survivors is in charge of Kontis's fleet."

A fearful silence filled the room while Aggie pulled up some figures.

"The Council's new projections indicate the virus will spread to the rest of the system and beyond within a year."

Ibis gaped. "Son of a bitch."

"They should never have interfered with the Ring," Mother said.

"To be honest, I'm stunned they waited this long before fucking with it." Aggie shrugged. "Based upon . . . observation, the original virus appears to attack the human nervous system. It also corrupts medbot programming, causing them to turn on their host."

"Oh shit," Karter whispered just as Ibis mumbled, "We're so fucked." Lissa merely shook her head in horror.

"Which begs the question." Aggie directed her words

to Mother. "If GX-3714 in its original form wasn't intended to be a weapon, then what is it? And why was it stored under the surface of the Ring?"

Mother looked away. "Before we continue along these lines, we ask that you indulge us in an agreement of confidentiality, due to certain safety and security issues." Mother tilted their head to the right.

"What, like I'd be the one to talk?" Ibis asked.

Karter also squinted at Ibis. "No one will discuss anything brought up in this room without permission. You have my word."

"Obviously," Ibis muttered, crossing their arms.

"Like many things in the universe, the virus wasn't intended for humans. Neither was the Ring." Mother poured themself another cup of coffee.

"Well, I promise you, whatever Tau, Chu & Lane makes from it will be," Aggie said.

Mother nodded. "Given where they were digging, we would surmise that the source was from the bioelectronic substrate. Its original purpose was to promote connection and interdependence between gestating entities. It's subterranean and promotes the growth of a root system—that is, physical communication roots. Each entity develops in unique ways. The substrate both adapts *to* and assists in the adaption *of* the entity."

Ibis asked, "Did you just call the Ring an entity?"

"It's an incubator for planet-sized life-forms." Mother picked up the coffeepot. "Would anyone else like coffee?"

"Oh." Lissa's eyes went wide.

Ibis's jaw dropped for the second time.

"The inner surface of the Ring is divided into thousands of segments." Mother poured a fresh cup for Karter before continuing. "Each one contains an environment optimized for a specific entity. Once that life-form is finished developing in its current stage, it will advance to a new one. This process takes centuries."

Karter accepted the full cup pushed across the table to her.

Aggie blinked. "I'm sorry, but biology isn't my area of expertise. What does that mean?"

"On Terra, a moth lays eggs on a plant. Those eggs hatch and grow into a caterpillar. When the caterpillar has reached a sufficient size or age, it forms a cocoon. Eventually, a moth emerges from that cocoon," Mother said. "Likewise, an entity prepares to emerge from its segment. This is why the Ring is currently active."

Ibis pointed at the image of the Ring. "That's one big fucking moth."

Mother smiled. "In this case, three thousand rare and important moths that promote life in the universe as we know it."

"Did you say three *thousand*?" Aggie asked.

"A number of entities have already hatched over the millennia that the Ring has existed." Mother sipped their coffee. "But yes, that's a fair estimate."

"How do you know all of this?" Karter asked.

"We can access certain records within the Ring. We cannot understand all of them, but we have made progress.

That is why we placed Chimera Station near L-39. To watch over and perform upkeep on the Ring. Such as is possible," Mother said. "We provide for it and protect it from those who would harm or destroy it."

Aggie stepped closer to Mother. "And what about humanity?"

"As much as we like humanity, ultimately, humanity—including humanity within the Norton Independent Alliance—isn't our problem." Mother took a sip of coffee. "Like the TRW, we've chosen neutrality."

Aggie brought her hand down on the edge of an object beside her with force. Her fist had gone through the dining room chair, landing with a thump on a surface significantly below the seat.

"Damn it. This affects more than the NIA and L-39. Like it or not, all of us are in danger. It's why I've brought in Ezinne."

"We have been meaning to ask," said Mother. "Who, or what, is Ezinne? And why are they on my station?"

"Ezinne is a synthetic personality," Aggie said. "She's working on a solution for the medbot problem related to the virus discovered on the Ring."

Blinking, Karter thought, *The puzzles Lavi gave her?* She'd caught glimpses of the code, but none of it had made any sense.

"Before her breakdown, Ezinne's specialty was medbot design and repair," Aggie said. "This made her an ideal candidate for the project."

Surprise flashed across Lissa's face. "I *thought* I recognized medbot microstructures in the designs Ezi was working on. I assumed it was occupational therapy."

"Ezi let you see what she was working on?" Karter asked.

"Ezi requested help with the biological aspects of the problem," Lissa said. "I didn't see the harm. And it kept her quiet and occupied."

"When she wasn't taking apart everything I own," Ibis muttered.

Aggie aimed her laser-hard gaze at Lissa. "How much progress has Ezi made?"

"She believed she was close to a solution," Lissa answered. "It was an unusual approach, but the design checked out. I can't say anything for sure—I'm no expert. And it hasn't been tested."

"We must get her back to work as soon as possible. She was working remotely with a separate team before you took her out of the facility."

"If she was already doing the work, why did we take her out of that place?" asked Karter.

"Because I wanted her close to L-39," Aggie said. "Just in case. And it's much more difficult to get data out of a facility designed to severely restrict external electronic access."

Mother held up their index finger. "When this medbot fix becomes available, you will distribute it to those outside the Terran Republic?"

"Of course." Aggie managed to appear insulted. "It's a medical necessity. It will be given to anyone that wants it."

Mother asked, "And the version that Jayne Tau has? Will there be a vaccine?"

"That's my hope," Aggie said. "But without a sample, I can't promise anything."

"We may be able to help." Mother placed their hands on the table.

"I certainly hope so." Aggie grimaced. "My record for retaining agents thus far during this mess is a bit spotty."

"Would you be willing to pay a reward?" Mother asked.

Aggie appeared to give the proposition some thought. "That could be arranged."

"What about Ezi?" Lissa set down her fork. "She needs support. Someone with a mental health background. She also needs an expert in the field who can answer her questions. Immediately, not three days after she's found other issues. She gets frustrated. And then she becomes destructive—"

"I'll say," Ibis muttered.

"All right. I'll get someone in. In the meantime, please continue to help her." Aggie gave Lissa a look that bordered on pleading.

Lissa grimaced. "I'll do what I can."

"In the meantime, I'll send you her file from Easley Hub," Aggie said.

"Isn't that illegal?" Lissa asked.

Of course it is. Karter sighed.

Lowering her chin, Aggie gave Lissa *that* stare and then raised her eyebrows. "Technically, so is helping a dangerously flawed artificial person escape a high-security facility."

Looking away, Lissa whispered, "That is true."

Karter stepped in. "You ordered us to do it."

"I suppose I did."

"And since Ezinne is already damaged, you're not risking much?" Karter asked. "Is that how this goes?"

She thought she spied a flash of guilt cross Aggie's face.

"If that wasn't the case, shouldn't we have brought Ezi's nurse along with her?" Karter continued, once again taking up what she assumed would be Gita's concern. "Don't we owe her the best care we can manage?"

Aggie sighed. "You're right. I absolutely should've seen to that from the start. My mistake."

I should've thought of it then, too. "Good. Thanks."

"That isn't everything." Aggie stared down at the floor. "Two of my agents were on *Boötes* during the evacuation. The last information packet I received indicated that they were with the survivors on the surface of the Ring."

When she says agents, *she means Ri,* Karter thought. *Oh gods. That's why Ri asked Gita for help. Why she was acting so weird.* "Oh no."

Aggie nodded. "I had hoped to speak to Gita."

"All that and you decided to bring in Ri's *sister*?" Karter asked.

Aggie held up both hands as if to fend off the accusation. "It wasn't my idea."

"I don't care whose idea it was!"

"Ri and Ezi both volunteered."

"I don't care! Ezi isn't mentally competent enough to enter into—"

"Ri had already made her decision. But their grandmother suggested I employ Ezi. She said that Ezi was the best candidate, and that it would give her much-needed purpose. So I went along with it." Aggie lowered her hands. "Lavi Chithra is my best friend. Even if I were the type of person to leave my agents to drift, do you know what Lavi will do to me if I don't bring her daughter and granddaughters home?"

Karter blinked. "Ah." It was nice to know that Aggie didn't go into the situation intending to discard Gita, Ri, and Ezi like the merciless bitch she was reputed to be.

Not as plan A anyway.

A glass appeared in Aggie's hand, and she took a sip from it. "Is there anything else Ezi needs?"

"There is one thing," Lissa said.

"Go on." Aggie folded her arms across her chest.

"She says she needs a sample of the original strain." Lissa bit her lip. "But I don't know how we'll manage it."

Karter sighed.

"I do." Ibis's voice was flat. "Someone will have to go to the mining platform."

"And rescue everyone on the inner surface," Karter added. "Let's not forget."

"Before the Ring releases its charge?" asked Lissa.

"So, let me get this straight. We have thirty-six hours to collect a sample of a deadly virus; find Gita, Aoifa,

Mandy, Ri, and Liv; and get the hell out of there?" Karter said. *And if we don't, the whole of human-inhabited space may be wiped out.* She looked to her friends.

"That sounds doable," Ibis said. "And by *doable*, I mean absolutely impossible."

Karter straightened in her chair. "Look, I promised Gita I'd come get her, and I don't intend to break that promise twice."

"Thirty-five hours and forty-seven minutes," Lissa said.

"Right." Karter sighed.

"As for myself—" Ibis shook their head. "—I'd rather not stick my face into a vat of whatever that GX shit is. And that certainly seems like a risk here."

Lissa said, "They're my friends. And none of this works if someone doesn't help Ezi. I'm in. I only ask to speak with my family before I go."

Aggie nodded. "Done."

"Well, fuck." Ibis shook their head. "I guess that means I have to go after all."

"Cheer up," Karter said. "I may even let you fly."

Ibis scowled. "You'd do that anyway."

"Oh. Right."

Turning to Mother, Aggie said, "They'll need that code you mentioned."

"Of course. And then it will change."

"That's fair." Aggie smiled.

"And you still maintain that you're taking the position of noninterference?" Mother asked.

Aggie dropped the smile, her face going blank. "Karter

works for you. What she does or does not do while in your employ is between you."

"That's an interesting perspective."

"Plausible deniability is my sword and shield." Aggie winked.

"Lissa and Ezi will remain here of course," Karter added. "Where it's safe."

Aggie shook her head. "I'm afraid not. We don't have time wait."

"Gita won't like it," Karter replied. "She doesn't believe in using AGIs as disposable people."

"That isn't what—"

Karter interrupted Aggie. "She'll see it that way. We've had this discussion before."

"This isn't Beta-X45J," Aggie said.

Shifting in her chair so that she didn't have to look Aggie in the eye, Karter whispered past the lump in her throat. "I know."

"Do you?" Aggie asked.

Karter shrugged. She wanted to say that sure, *she* knew the difference, but she wasn't certain that Gita would. And honestly, Karter didn't know if she wanted to be back in a situation where Gita might blame her for another artificial person's death.

That fight wasn't about her blaming you. It was about you blaming you. You were the one who insisted on sending Miranda and Ferdinand into that damned black hole.

It was the only way. You know it.

But you didn't even let her discuss the options. She needed to know she'd tried.

"Let me know when you leave," Aggie said.

"I will." Karter still couldn't bring herself to look Aggie in the eye.

And with that, Aggie vanished.

"That woman never has learned how to close out a conversation," Ibis said.

Calling to Sabatten, Mother asked that the main course be served—grilled vat-grown pork, eggplant, and mushrooms in a rosemary, lavender, and mint sauce served over potatoes. Karter was too nervous to eat, although she hated letting good food go to waste. Ibis enjoyed several helpings, their appetite seemingly unaffected in spite of their earlier misgivings. Lissa, on the other hand, appeared to be just as unsettled as Karter.

When dessert was finished and the dishes were again cleared, more coffee was offered. Karter accepted another cup, mentally creating to-do lists.

It was going to be a long, sleepless night.

14

"Wakey-wakey." Karter leaned over Ibis's inert, sheet-wrapped form to give them a shake and straightened.

From the floor, Ibis moaned. "Too early. Go away."

Clothes were scattered all over the hotel room. A person-shaped lump was curled in the fetal position on the bed. Whoever it was lay cocooned in blankets, having stolen absolutely all of them. Not even a strand of hair peeked out. The sleeper didn't move and wasn't making a sound. Karter assumed they were alive—Ibis hadn't gotten themselves into *that* much trouble before. However, worst-case scenarios were once all Karter knew, and they were therefore what generally occurred to her first, even if she then reminded herself how unlikely they were. It'd taken most of her life to feel reasonably secure.

Okay. They're in the recovery position and breathing, she reassured herself. *All is well.* "It's 14:00." She kept her voice low for the sake of Ibis's mystery guest. When that didn't work, she nudged Ibis with the toe of her boot. "I put a liter of water and some aspirin on the bedside table. Hydrate. Take the pills. Get dressed. It's time to go."

Lifting the edge of a hotel-provided satin sleep mask, Ibis squinted up at her. "Do I have to?"

"Nah," Karter said, a sarcastic smile pulling at one side of her mouth. "But if you don't, you won't get to see the booster mods that Sal installed on the engines. They muttered something about *Mirabilis* having more zip than a CJ-429. No problem. Lissa can pilot instead. See you when we get back."

Ibis sprang up from the carpet like someone had pulled their jack-in-the-box lever. "Coming." Their hair stood up on one side, and the weave of the carpet had left an imprint on their right cheek. The sleep mask hung around their neck. "Shit. My back hurts."

"You really are getting too old for this crap, you know."

"Ha. Never." Ibis staggered to their feet and groaned. "Ready in a sec. I swear." Dressed in a stranger's oversize music-festival t-shirt, they stooped and snatched trousers from the floor. "Coffee?"

"Not before you drink all that water. I need you functional today." Karter stepped to the door.

"I'm not hungover."

"Then have some fucking manners. Say goodbye to your friend before you leave."

Ibis paused, blinked, and turned to the bed. They seemed briefly confused. "Oh. Right. Now I remember."

"Water."

"Yes, Mom."

Karter scowled. "Not your mom. Captain."

"Whatever."

"Must have been some party," Karter said. "No third?"

Shrugging, Ibis replied, "That's Jordan. They're not into multiples."

"Ah. Got it."

Chugging half a liter of water, Ibis finally came up for air. "How about Lissa? She all right?"

Karter made it to the door before the question registered. She froze. "I assumed she was on *Mirabilis* with Ezi, working on the medbot problem."

Ibis made a satisfied sound after they finished the last of the water. "Huh. You might want to check her room."

Slowly, Karter turned to face Ibis. "What did you do to Lissa?"

"Nothing!" Ibis was attempting an innocent expression that absolutely didn't suit them. "I didn't do anything!"

"*Ibis*." Karter tilted her head down. "You better *not* have done something to mess up Lissa."

"She wanted to try one of the brownies Sal made. So—"

"You did not." Karter caught herself. *Don't shout. Innocent bystanders are attempting to sleep.*

Ibis stalled, taking their time returning the empty water bottle to the nightstand. "Great idea. Hydration. I feel much better. Okay. Thanks for dropping by."

"How many bottles of tequila did you go through?" Karter hissed.

"One! Just like I promised! Between the—" Ibis paused to count on their fingers. "—ten of us."

The lump on the mattress chose that moment to speak. "Eleven."

"Right," Ibis said. "Eleven. I forgot Xandi."

"Xander."

"Right." Ibis plunged on. "So one bottle of booze wasn't all that much."

Jordan's voice came from under the covers once again. "That depends on the size of the bottle."

Ibis turned. "I had three shots, for fuck's sake! Whose side are you on?"

"Mine? And in this case? Maybe Karter's. Hi, Karter."

"Hi, Jordan." Karter turned to Ibis. "And what was in the brownies?"

Staring at the bed, Ibis said, "Traitor."

"You love me anyway," Jordan said.

"*Hmmph*. Maybe." Tugging on a boot, Ibis scanned the room for its mate. "Oh. There you are." They hopped across the room and retrieved the footwear in question.

"Ibis, focus." Using two fingers, Karter pointed to Ibis and to her own eyes. "The brownies?"

"I don't know. Sal said it was one of their special mixes. No problem. She'll be fine. Should've worn off four hours ago."

Karter sighed and went back to the door. "That's just fucking great."

"Party before life-changing events! It's in all the vids!" Ibis said.

"Remind me to parentally limit your entertainment." Karter stepped out into the hallway.

"You said you're not my mo—"

Shaking her head, Karter cut off the rest of Ibis's comment with the door. Lissa's suite was three rooms over and across the hall. To Karter's surprise, Lissa answered before she could knock.

Lissa appeared to have been awake for some time— long enough to shower, dress, and pack at least. Dressed in neatly pressed ship's coveralls, she'd pulled her hair up into a smooth ponytail. Her makeup was perfect, and her stylish wheeled overnight bag rested on the bed behind her.

"Good afternoon." Lissa tilted her head. "Is something wrong?"

"Everything is fine. I think." Karter peered into Lissa's eyes, searching for some sign of postrevelry discomfort. "How are you feeling?"

Lissa went back inside for her bags, speaking as she went. "The bed was quite comfortable. Oh. I helped Ezi with the medbot designs early this morning. We had a remote meeting with the second team, and the conversation inspired her. The extra support definitely helps. The psychiatric nurse arrived fifteen minutes ago. So, I thought it'd be a good time to check out of my room." She grabbed the handle of her bag and hesitated. "Are you sure everything is all right?"

"I was just getting Ibis on their feet." Karter waved in the direction of Ibis's room. "They said that you had one of Sal's special brownies last night. Having experienced that a few times, well . . . I was worried."

"Oh. That." Smiling, Lissa squeezed past and waited for her to step back before locking the now-empty room.

Four other people exited their rooms. Three more waited at the elevator. The hallway was getting crowded. Karter was thankful that the Lovelace employed a narrow AI to calculate the bill and charge the account.

"Apparently, Sal forgot to add the extra ingredients," Lissa said. "The brownies were otherwise excellent. I had two. Dark chocolate is my favorite. Anyway, Ibis was having so much fun anticipating what would happen that I didn't have the heart to tell them."

"Do me a favor," said Karter as they started down the hallway together.

Lissa raised an eyebrow in question.

"Don't tell Ibis. Consider it our little secret."

In what was a surprise to no one, the nonstop priority tram from the Seed to docking arm A was booked solid, so they took the regular tram. Every car was crammed with people and their belongings. There was only one available seat, and at the next stop, Karter gave hers up to a pregnant person.

Visitors from all over the station were preparing to leave. Gazing out the windows, Karter spotted quite a few residents in the midst of securing their businesses. In spite of the chaos, the atmosphere was calm but focused, like they had a job to do. The tram stopped. She pushed her way through the crush, tugging Lissa along behind. The platform was wall-to-wall stacked crates headed for docking arm A. It took a moment to find a path to the correct hallway. Luckily, *Mirabilis*'s berth was only a few slips from the dock entrance. All things considered, Karter was glad they'd stayed at the Lovelace only one night. It was hard enough to squeeze between autocarts, screaming children, and hovering freight platforms even without weighty luggage.

She couldn't remember a time when she'd seen Chimera in such a state—and that included the infamous station-wide New Year's party.

When they reached *Mirabilis*, Sal's team was collecting the last of their gear and exiting the slip. Karter overheard their chatter. Apparently, there'd been an all hands early that morning. Every weapons-capable ship was being conscripted as an escort during the move to L-39. Most were hauling cargo.

Karter spied Sal at the end of the gangway, reviewing the last of the paperwork. They looked exhausted. A stained purple bandana partially covered their braids. The sleeves of their now-filthy coveralls were rolled up, exposing a series of botanical tattoos on both forearms. Karter spotted a beautifully rendered salamander among the foliage.

"Afternoon, Sal." Karter set her overnight bag down.

"Well, look who's here with plenty of time to spare." Sal swiped through floating images of reports and forms to get to the approval page. "Ready to take your lady back?"

"You bet," Karter said. "I missed my girl dearly."

"The Lovelace must have downgraded since last I was there." Sal scrolled down the image for her to read.

"Not one bit." Lissa slipped in and gave Sal a hug.

"Careful," Sal said. "I don't want to get you all dirty."

Glancing down at her freshly smudged coveralls, Lissa shook her head. "There are worse reasons to acquire stains on your clothes than hugging a friend. Thank you for the brownies. They were wonderful."

"You're very welcome," Sal said. "Next time, I'll remember the magic ingredients."

Lissa said her goodbyes and headed up the gangway.

Karter authorized the payout with her palm print. "Thanks for doing all of this so fast. It's a lot to ask."

Sal scanned the crowds visible through the hatch behind her. "Speaking of fast, where in the Sam Hell is your pilot?"

"Last I saw them, they were too tired to stand up straight." Karter shook her head. "What about you? How late were you up?"

"All night." Sal deactivated the projection, and the reports vanished.

"I seriously don't know how either of you did it." Karter shook her head.

"I only stuck around for an hour or so," Sal said. "Then I came back here. You could've joined us, you know. For one drink."

"My mother taught me never to party with people who mix drinks in a turbine spinner."

"Where's your sense of adventure?"

"Exchanged it for a healthy sense of mortality when I turned forty like every other responsible adult."

"Responsibility is overrated."

"So's working for other people. I prefer to be my own boss."

Sal nodded. "Wise."

Ibis rushed into the slip. They dropped their bags and grabbed their knees, gasping.

"Well, well, well," Sal said.

Still bent over, Ibis held up their index finger. "Don't you start."

"It's a sad, sad day when a Mer can't handle their liquor." Sal made a disapproving tsk-tsk.

"That's not it at all." Ibis glared up at Sal. "I missed my tram stop. All the cars were too full. I had to run the whole way back, damn it."

Sal poked a finger at Ibis. "You look like you got rode hard and put up wet."

"Same could be said of *you*, my friend." Ibis straightened and hugged Sal. "Thanks for hanging out."

The two of them launched into a lengthy technical conversation regarding engine specs and what Ibis could and could not expect from the new modifications. Karter took it to mean that it was time for her to go, so she headed to her cabin. Ditching her baggage, she paused to check her messages and discovered nothing worth worrying about. Then she looked for Lissa, ultimately finding her in the galley with Ezi. They were continuing their medbot work.

A tall, pale brunette was in the galley filling a coffee mug. Karter didn't recognize her. She checked for and found a comm file, then went to introduce herself.

"I'm Martina Morales," the woman said. "Aggie sent me."

"From Easley Hub?" Karter asked.

Martina, Ezi's new nurse and project assistant, shook her head. "Don't worry. I've been briefed. I have an extensive background in AGI behavioral science, as well as a degree in medical robotics."

"Nice to meet you." Karter grabbed a fresh sugar spice bun from the bowl. "You know where we're headed?"

Martina nodded.

"Thanks for volunteering." Karter bit into the bun.

"No problem. Things were a bit dull at home anyway." Martina returned to Ezi and Lissa, apparently resuming a previous conversation.

"How do you feel about a dogfight?" Ibis asked from the doorway.

Karter frowned. "Who says there'll be a fight?"

"You didn't check the news, did you?"

"I did." Activating the galley's projection screen, Karter scanned the headlines. "Last night." Then she switched to the live feed. What she saw hit her like a punch. Gracelessly, she dropped onto a bench. She felt sick. "That's just great."

Glancing up, Lissa stopped what she was doing. "Oh."

The last time Karter looked in on what was happening in L-39, there'd been three cruisers patrolling the area. Now, it appeared every affiliated ship was parked in the system. Space was big. It was impossible to cover the entire Border Sector, but with that many starships, you were as close as you could get.

She blew air out of her cheeks. "That does not look like any fun. At. All."

"We can outrun those assholes," Ibis said. "And the ones we can't, I can dodge." Their bravado lacked its usual enthusiasm.

Karter didn't want to discourage the others. So she offered what encouragement she could. "Let's hope so." *Ibis is good, but no one's* that *good.* Watching the image, she almost wished she was the type to beg powerful deities for favors. "We should take the back door nonetheless."

"There's no relay marker on the opposite side of L-39," Ibis said. "Going the long way will take too much time. They're sure to spot us."

"If the engine mods give as much push as advertised, then we should be fine. Right?" Karter asked.

Lissa's voice was quiet. "What about Chimera?"

Not our problem, Karter thought. "Mother has been around a long damned time. They know what they're doing. Anyway, we have enough of our own worries. Don't need to borrow other people's." She turned to Ibis. "Speaking of problems. How about that delivery?"

"Already on it," Ibis said. "The last of the energy pods

for the rail guns are being unloaded right now. Hold is almost full."

"Weren't all the auto carts booked?" Lissa asked.

"That's why it took so long." Ibis shrugged. "We're good now. Heading aft to get things organized and tied down. I'm only here to grab coffee." They poured the last of the pot into two ship's mugs and handed one off.

Karter accepted the mug without looking away from the float image of L-39. Ibis left the galley.

"You think Gita is all right?" Karter asked Lissa. "It's been a while. If Tau, Chu & Lane are down there, we'd have heard about it. Right?"

A careful expression settled on Lissa's features. "Gita is very capable. And she's not alone. She has Liv, Mandy, and Aoifa, too. They've gotten through worse. We all have."

Some definition of gotten through. Karter remembered how their crew had been torn apart. The pain of losing not just Gita, but Dru, too, had been almost too much to bear. She'd become a better person since, or so she hoped. She wasn't the same stubborn asshole intent on not forming attachments. If she got another chance, she'd fight to keep everyone together—she'd do whatever it took, show Gita that she could be counted on.

Even if that means admitting you were wrong. Right?

Suddenly, it occurred to Karter that she might not know who Gita was anymore. It had been more than two years. *If I can change in that time, so can she.* The Gita Karter had known was steadfast and loyal. It'd taken a lot to drive her away.

Karter sighed. *So what? You fucked up. Everyone does. Apologize. Make up for it. And don't ever do it again.*

Most of all, Gita wasn't in favor of violence as the answer to problems. *Not that I am either. Well, not anymore anyway.*

Karter served in the Terran Republic Navy from the time she'd turned eighteen until age twenty-four. The Terran Republic of Worlds hadn't engaged in a war since a decade after its formation. Diplomacy, civil service, and exploration were what the navy was known for. War wasn't even considered the fifth option, let alone the first. That said, Karter had seen exactly one battle, and that had been on Aggie's order.

Stretching out the fingers of her right hand, Karter stared at the pale twisted lines sketched across the back and down the digits. The scars were deep. It'd been a miracle that she still had a hand. Since the incident wasn't considered an official exchange, no one talked about it. Not even her. If they'd heard of the incident, they thought it'd been an accident because that was how it'd been reported. What it had been was an ambush. In the end, she'd lost a good friend. It had been the latest in what was for her a long line of losses. Something inside her had snapped.

After that, she'd gotten into a lot of fights. Some of them unnecessary—most, if she was entirely honest. She'd worked hard to change that about herself, and she had been damned successful, too—until that day with Gita.

Karter didn't want to be in another fight.

"Are you okay?" Lissa asked.

"I'm good." Karter shut off the projection. "How's it going?"

Lissa lowered her voice. "Very well so far. We took a short break for a few snacks. Ezi, Martina, and I are headed back to Medical now. We'll resume the work there."

"Good. I'll put us in the exit queue then. There are a lot of people ahead of us. Looks like it'll take fifty minutes to get lined up for jump. Then we kick the tires and start the fires."

Gita, Mandy, Liv, and Aoifa needed her. Karter's scarred hand formed a fist as old anger threatened to flare up. Then she shook out the tension and left the galley.

In Command, she initiated the prelaunch safety checklists and added *Mirabilis* to the exit request queue. She'd gotten through the first half when a private comm inquiry appeared. She accepted and activated the floating screen.

Aggie was seated at her desk. Her elbows rested on its brushed-steel surface, and her left hand covered her right fist. Her expression was neutral.

"Thanks for sending Martina," Karter said. "She's already a big help."

"Glad to hear it." Aggie paused. "From here, it looks like you're headed for a shitstorm."

"Saw that." Karter hoped Aggie wasn't about to give her more bad news. "Has anyone told Mother?"

"They know. Been trying to talk them out of the move since I got the news. No dice."

Karter asked, "You really aren't planning to do anything?"

"Other than send you in? No. You know the rules."

"*Officially*, you can't do anything. But we both know that you do plenty of unofficial shit all the time. So fill me in."

Aggie's gaze slid to her left, and she made another noncommittal snort. "You know, it might not be a bad idea for you to take another route to L-39."

Karter settled into the pilot's couch. "There's only one relay marker terminal I can access. The one near you. But that's too far away."

A ship could only spend so much time in subspace. The longer the distance, the more likely you hit the relay terminal with a dead crew—or worse. Which was why relay marker terminals were *relays*, connected like links in a chain.

"There may be another . . . option."

"Yeah? And what's that?"

"I understand someone built a new NIA-side relay marker terminal. Not the one they replaced. A private one."

Stunned, Karter blurted out the question before she thought it through. "How the fuck did you manage that?"

The expression on Aggie's face was one of blasé denial. "Did I say I had anything to do with it?" She separated her hands and made a gesture with both palms up. "If TCL's competitors decide to build a marker for access to a disputed sector, it's their decision."

She got one of Tau, Chu & Lane's competitors to build a relay marker terminal in the last forty-eight hours? Karter gave the situation more consideration. *They must've done that to contest TCL's claim to L-39. Aggie didn't build it. But she's offering to* hack *it.* "You have an access code for me?"

"Not at the moment."

"Can you get it to me in about forty-five minutes?" Karter said.

"Probably."

"That gets us to L-39 in time. It'll be a huge help. Thanks."

"Not so fast." Aggie held up a hand. "First, that terminal is linked to a second marker. Or will be. An asteroid will provide cover for the last leg of your journey. That's where I want you to wait for a signal. Then you make your run for the Ring."

"*Another* marker? That's a lot of construction. No one noticed?"

Aggie shrugged. "Doesn't look like it. But then, they're not terribly observant, in my experience."

"Good to know," Karter said. "Anything else? Like maybe a handy Maelstrom-class cruiser that accidentally drifted into L-39?"

"No Republic starship captain is that stupid."

"Well, there's me."

"You're not planning on drifting." Aggie directed her gaze to the ceiling. "But you know how it is. Things happen in the crush. People get excited or distracted and lose track of where they are."

Since the individuals in question were military, Karter very much doubted that. "I see."

"Two more things." Aggie returned her attention to the conversation. "First, I've some coordinates for you."

"You found Gita? Where is she? Is everyone all right?"

Aggie held up both her hands, motioning again for silence. "Slow down."

"Just how do you expect me to do that? She's been missing for—"

"She's *on* the Ring. We're sure."

"You're kidding."

"I wish I wasn't. Liv isn't answering, and my drones can only get so close without violating the Norton Agreements. Also, there's good reason to believe Ri is still there. A friend of a friend picked up some chatter." Aggie folded her arms across her chest. "I want Ri and Liv back. And bring Wes Blankenship, too. Promises have been made. The kind I hate breaking."

Karter nodded. "We'll take care of it."

"See that you do." Aggie gave her that hard stare. "Last thing, there's been a small change of plan. You're not going to the mine site."

"Oh?" Karter tried not to let her relief show.

"There's a crate in your hold. It's labeled *Ezinne's Birthday Present*. Inside, you'll find two drones. I want you to drop it over the site. It'll signal you when the sample is ready. You'll swing by and drop the second drone. That drone will collect and isolate the sample bot. Then it'll come back to you."

"Sounds a little complicated."

"Maybe. But this way, the site gets shut down and sealed off and we get Ezinne's sample the safest, fastest way possible."

"Thanks," Karter said.

"Be careful out there. There's a lot riding on this."

"I know."

"No one who has been exposed to that virus can leave the Ring. We can't have a second exposure vector. Understand?" An emotion passed over Aggie's features. It was something that Karter didn't recognize at first because she'd never seen it before.

Fear. Her stomach twisted into a tight knot.

"Guard that fucking sample. Make sure it's secure. And *don't* let it fall into NIA hands. You know why."

"Yes, ma'am." *And just what the fuck would we be able to do about it? They've got a whole fleet out there.*

"Karter?"

"Yeah?"

"Good luck."

We're going to need it. "Thanks. You, too."

"Don't let anything happen to you. I mean it."

Karter blinked.

Two seconds passed before Aggie nodded and cut the connection. It was the closest she'd ever come to actually saying goodbye.

With that, Karter closed her eyes, took a deep breath, and slowly released it in order to calm her nerves. Then she got to work.

15

Scooting closer to the heating element, Gita shivered and rubbed warmth into her stiff hands before putting on her gloves back on. The nights were chilly and more than a little scary, even though they hadn't gone outside. Strange noises came from the forest, although nothing had ventured from the woods yet. She hoped someone would come for them soon. Just not anyone from the NIA.

At least we still have power, food, and water, and no serious injuries. I am thankful for this.

Liv's landing had been impressive, given that *Artemis* was a starship that was never intended to enter atmosphere, let alone touch dirt. But now they were marooned. At first, she had been particularly concerned about Mandy and her health conditions. However, the artificial world's surface gravity turned out to be the same as *The Tempest*'s had been—two thirds g. Not having to run the artificial gravity unit saved power for other things.

A little over forty-eight hours had passed since the crash. Previously, they had been using the Ring's orbiting black panels to hide from *Narcissus*. The Norton Alliance starship hadn't reacted so far. Gita had begun scanning for local comm chatter, hoping to hear from the *Boötes* survivors, but she'd picked up nothing. *Except that once. It might have been Ri? But it was too broken up to know for sure.*

Now that they were on the Ring proper, there was no sign of activity. *Not even a half-imagined sign from Ri.* That didn't bode well.

She tried not to consider what that would mean for her crew. *Could I have made a better decision at some point? Could I have stopped it?* She'd been in the midst of analyzing that strange comm signal when Liv had been attacked—hidden code in the signal, no doubt. Liv announced a sudden catastrophic failure was imminent and that everyone should get strapped in. Gita honestly didn't know how Liv had managed to hold the attack off long enough to crash-land. It was one of the single bravest things that Gita had ever witnessed.

She wanted to get Liv back up and running as soon as possible, but Gita had to admit she wasn't in the best mental state. Liv deserved the best of care. Repairing a neuromorphic matrix was intense work that required all of Gita's mental faculties. It was one of the reasons she enjoyed it. There was no such thing as routine. Every artificial individual built their own programming after the initial stages of development. Thus, at a certain level, each neuromorphic matrix was unique.

Not unlike an embryo.

Her head ached. She ignored it, once again mentally tallying her task list. There were so many high-priority items, and due to her own atypical neurology, managing logistics was difficult. Worse, her hand terminal wasn't working. Therefore, her list had become her mantra. *First: environmentals, auxiliary computer, and medical systems. We can't leave* Artemis *until we know for sure it's safe. After that, we'll find the other survivors, fix comms, and rebuild* Artemis's *last shuttle.*

She felt very lucky that Aoifa was with them.

Nonetheless, Gita listed the shuttle last because *Narcissus* and its sister starships were still out there. They couldn't use the shuttle until they knew they could get to safety.

Her mind bounced back to problems she found more comforting and interesting. *Why did Liv's neuromorphic matrix collapse?* Artificial personality structures were intricate and delicate. Like humans, sometimes the littlest thing could destabilize them. But inversely, they could be resilient under far more dire circumstances, choosing hope over terrible odds. *You don't know that the problem is insurmountable. It might be a simple fix. A broken code string. A misplaced logic modifier.*

Lakshmi, I hope so.

In any case, she felt she could repair certain key functions and get Liv online on a base level. At the very least, Gita knew she could pinpoint the cause of the breakdown.

But that was for later. For now, she had to focus on less complex systems. Starships were made up of more than their ship's artificial person. The AGI used a network of simpler narrow AIs as tools to run other aspects of the ship. This meant that vital ship functions like Medical weren't entirely dependent upon one artificial person. Therefore, if she could make repairs, they could have a majority of the ship's vital systems running before they woke Liv.

Why haven't we heard from Karter? She promised to be here. Where the hell is she?

Not. Now. Gita shied away from old anger, pain, and freshly torn scars. Again, her mind jumped to other things.

Seconds after the crash, the ground shook as if the force of the ship hitting it had triggered a seismic disturbance. She had been terrified that they had damaged the Ring and that the artificial world would soon collapse. She'd lain in the dark and prayed that the trembling would stop. The only thing distracting her from that terror had been the ache inside her skull. Eventually, the shuddering ground had stabilized. She, Aoifa, and Mandy began the process of digging themselves out of the rubble. Then a second massive pulse had passed through the ground and the broken ship. In that instant, she sensed a change in Loki's Ring, and a deep anxiety had lodged inside her gut.

Stay in the now. Worry later. Her mind tended to wan-der during tedious tasks, and there weren't many more tedious than repairing an auxiliary computer system run by a narrow AI.

Each member of the team had their assignments. Mandy's was the galley, gathering what cooking equipment could be salvaged and fixing what could be fixed. Aoifa almost had the environmental systems running. By her last estimate, the final repairs would be complete before dinner. Gita prayed she was right. *I've never wanted a shower so much in my entire life.*

The light pen Gita was using to trace new electronic pathways for the narrow AI slipped from her fingers. Again. She bit back the urge to scream, then paused long enough to slow the beating of her heart.

You've got this. Don't let fear overwhelm you. That won't help anyone.

So far, the simple tools for controlling PTSD-related panic had been working. That'd been the case for years, but stressful situations brought up self-doubt. Would this be the time she finally cracked under the immense pressure? Her mother hadn't understood her need to push through her fears, to keep functioning in spite of everything, to prove herself.

She took a deep breath. *Now is not the time to lose yourself in your own head.*

I'm fine. We're fine. Everything will be all right.

The floor of the bridge was tilted just enough to throw off her sense of balance. Overhead, the lights flickered. She was certain that wasn't good for her bruised brain. At least repairing a narrow AI wasn't all *that* difficult.

She'd worry about her own recovery when they weren't trapped on an artificial world that might or might not be hostile.

The light pen slithered out of her grip once again.

It was then that she tugged her gloves off. At the moment, she needed the dexterity more than keeping her fingers warm. Reconfiguring glass memory-storage units might not be her best skill, but she was better at it than Mandy, and the work didn't involve standing or stooping—motions that would be excruciating because of Gita's injuries.

Picking up the pen, she pinched the bridge of her nose and squeezed her eyes shut. She'd been at this task for five hours. Her eyes were dry. She was hungry. And her head ached. She knew she should take a break but couldn't bring herself to do it. *Not yet. I'm almost done reconfiguring the broken paths.* It was work normally performed by thousands of narrow AIs housed in minibots at a factory. She was thankful she could manage it at all.

Sitting with her back against a wall and her eyes shut, she didn't see Aoifa limping toward her until she had knelt down.

"How's the head?" Aoifa asked.

"All right, I suppose." Gita decided to stop for a while in order to relieve the pain in her fingers and skull.

Aoifa checked her eyes. "Have you eaten?"

"No time."

She heard Aoifa sigh. "I hate to point out the obvious here, but punishing yourself isn't going to bring Liv back.

You're the only one with the skill to repair her. So, if you wreck yourself, Liv is doomed."

Gita's vision blurred with stinging tears. She dried her sorrow with the crook of her elbow. Moisture-repellant fabric abraded her wet cheeks. The cloth stank. Her environment suit was filthy. Everyone's was. The laundry systems were down, along with everything else.

She lifted her head and bit her lip against the building ache behind her eyes.

"Brought some painkillers for you." Aoifa handed her two tablets and a cup of water.

Swallowing the pills, Gita grimaced.

"What's wrong?" Aoifa asked.

"It's the lights. I wish I could fix them, but I can't. I tried."

"Ah." Getting to her feet, Aoifa staggered over to the light switches. She studied it for a couple of seconds. Making a fist, she thumped a spot next to the offending panel. The flickering halted at once.

"How did you do that?"

Aoifa winked. "It's very technical. You'd not understand. But the scientific word for it is *magic*." She resumed her place next to Gita and studied her face again.

"How are the environmental repairs going?" Gita asked.

"Finished, so it is. A wee bit early, too." Aoifa flashed her another two-hundred-watt grin.

Gita blinked. "Where is the heat?"

"Ack. That has to do with another technical term, that does. It's called leverage." Aoifa took the opportunity to press an emergency meal bar into her hand. "Eat that. Not switching on the heat until you do."

"That's just mean."

"Not at all."

Spotting the label on the package, Gita groaned.

Meal bars were made from mealworm protein. Normally, she liked them. Several suppliers in the Terran Republic made ones that were tasty—salty with a dash of sweet. She didn't know how other manufacturers managed to mess up perfectly good food and still manage to sell enough to make a profit. That was why she purchased only certain brands. Apparently, Liv wasn't aware of a difference. Since pirates generally comprised Liv's crew, Gita supposed it made sense that she wouldn't have bothered to stock the good stuff.

"I'm not hungry," Gita said.

"Of course you're not. Eat it anyway."

Letting out an exasperated breath, Gita tore open the package with her teeth, spat out the paper, and took a bite. Its texture was sandy-sticky goo, and it tasted like paste. "There. I ate it."

It occurred to her that she was unusually grouchy. The head injury, she supposed. That, and she was so tired of being cold and in pain.

"Stop behaving like a big wean." Aoifa motioned to one of the cushioned flight couches—one of the few that was still whole and upright. "Sit. I want to check your head again."

"If you say so."

"Let me have a peek. And if you're a good wee girl, I won't make you eat another meal bar for at least an hour."

"*Pfffft!*" Shoving the tangle of safety harnesses out of the way, Gita gingerly settled on the flight couch—sudden movements threatened nausea. She tilted her head back and to the side while Aoifa examined the lump just above her right temple with gentle fingers.

"This is your second noggin bump," Aoifa said. "For fuck's sake, you really must stop headbutting consoles."

Gita wasn't in the mood for teasing. She stared at the remains of her meal bar, debating whether or not to eat the last bite. "How is Mandy?" She closed her eyes and finished the last of the bar.

"Making progress. We may even have hot food tonight."

Scowling, Gita spat.

"I'm not cleaning that up," said Aoifa.

"Why did you make me eat this thing? It's horrible."

"You may be glad of that shite before too long."

Gita stuck out her goo-coated tongue.

"Sophisticated and attractive." Then Aoifa returned the favor. "Go on. Your head is fine. Provided you don't pick a fight with yon computer headfirst."

Gita was already starting to feel better. She was sure it couldn't be the painkillers—it was too soon. Probably a combination of the lights and the awful meal bar. "Thank you. I'm sorry I was grouchy."

"Ack. Be eating the head off someone soon myself."

Aoifa limped to the corridor. "Come on. Last I saw, Mandy was making tea. A nice cuppa will wash that shite down."

Glancing to the half-finished auxiliary computer, Gita paused.

"She found the sugar. Can you believe it? Soon this fucking mess will be almost habitable."

And then we'll leave, I hope. "How's your leg?"

"Sound as ever." Aoifa tapped her left leg and flashed a bright grin.

Mandy was replacing the cover on the food-processing unit just as they entered the galley. Looking up, she gave them a small, satisfied smile. "It's working."

"Thank goodness." Gita tossed the empty meal bar packet in the recycler. "I don't have to eat any more of these awful things."

"They're good for you," Aoifa said. "Calcium. Protein. Vitamins."

"Healthy food does not have to taste like that." Gita dusted nonexistent dirt from her hands.

"Tea is ready." Mandy pointed at the pot.

Artemis's galley had accumulated a chaotic collection of kitchenware. The number of random treasures hidden away in the ship's cabinets was surprising. That morning, Gita had been shocked to discover a porcelain teapot whole and unbroken among the piecemeal bachelor fare.

Pirates, she thought. *You never know what they'll steal or leave behind.*

Aoifa located three mugs without chips or cracks and set them on the galley table. "I'll be ma." She scooted the pot closer and poured out the tea.

There was no milk to be had, but the sugar made the rounds. Gita savored the hot, sweet brew with closed eyes. The dull ache in her neck and shoulders began to unravel. She let her weight settle into the padded bench with a sigh. By the time dinner was ready, Aoifa had the heat working. With the environmental systems functioning as well as the galley, Mandy pitched in on the effort to reconfigure the auxiliary computer.

The instant the automated medical system was online, Gita and Aoifa underwent thorough examinations. The medical AI confirmed Gita's fears. She had a concussion. A head injury was particularly dangerous for her because of her partnering drive.

"I don't understand why you haven't got that thing removed," Aoifa said. "You've not partnered in years."

Gita shrugged. "I wanted the option to go back to it."

"Why did you stop?" Mandy asked.

Giving the matter some consideration, Gita decided she might as well answer. "Health reasons. I began to develop Astelore's Palsy."

Aoifa frowned. "What's that?"

Staring at the table, Gita rested her hands in her lap. "The synapses that control movement, perception, and cognitive function begin to degrade. It's caused by long-term overstimulation of pathways in the brain. It manifests with minor memory loss, cognitive decline, and hand tremors."

Aoifa set down her cup and blinked. "Oh."

"The result of two people in one brain," Mandy said. It wasn't the scientific explanation, but it would suffice.

Gita nodded. "It's why pairers are restricted to two partnering tours within a thirty-year period. Since each new artificial person requires at least ten to twelve years of partnering before they're ready to survive on their own, it's easy to hit that limit."

"Why not limit it to one?" Mandy asked.

"A small percentage of pairings don't take," Gita said. "Some fail altogether. It's complicated." She thought of Ezi, despite herself.

"You'd still risk it a third time?" Aoifa asked. "Even if it endangers your health?"

"Pregnancy is dangerous, too." Gita said. "And even though artificial wombs have eliminated that risk for the parent, some people still opt to carry their own children. Especially if they live in the Norton Alliance."

"That's archaic," Aoifa replied. "And stupid."

Mandy restarted the teakettle.

What Gita didn't say was that she was neurodivergent, and that due to her specific condition—an attention disorder—she was particularly well suited for paring. Instead, she said, "Your turn, Aoifa. Time for you to stop being a pain in my neck."

"Never." Aoifa shook her head, smiling.

"Get on the table already," Gita said.

Aoifa's injuries were identified: several deep contusions and lacerations. No broken bones. She was given painkillers and stitches. Her medbots would take care of the rest. That evening, they went to bed in comfort for the first time in three days.

In the morning, *Artemis*'s freshly repaired narrow AI declared the atmosphere breathable. The air contained a percentage point more nitrogen as well as a percentage point less oxygen than they were accustomed to—nothing significant enough to cause problems—certainly not in the short term anyway. The remainder of the Ring's atmospheric qualities were well within human-standard range. No overtly harmful microbes had been detected either. That didn't mean harmful germs didn't exist, but since they weren't conducting an intense study of the world and wouldn't be digging or collecting samples, it wasn't as much a factor. Temperature wise, it hovered around four degrees Celsius, which was a bit cool, but environment suits could keep them comfortable. Days on the Ring were twenty-five hours long. However, more light was probably more of an advantage than a detriment for the survivor search.

Using the shuttle location beacons, it was estimated that the vessels were less than a four-hour walk from *Artemis*. Gita decided they would begin the search for survivors after breakfast. She instructed everyone to pack light to save their strength. Therefore, they would take medical supplies, water, and food.

"I don't want to go," Mandy said.

Gita expected her refusal but was unclear about what to do.

"Love, you've spacewalked. And you were brilliant at it," Aoifa added. "You're so brave and strong. You can do this. Dead easy. See how the horizon is concave not convex? We're surrounded by mountains." She pointed to the pilot float screen.

Mandy's voice was quiet and firm. "It's the sky. Not the horizon."

"We're not leaving you behind," Aoifa added. "Not alone. It isn't safe."

Mandy shook her head.

"I can't stay with you," Aoifa said. "Gita can't go alone. We have to do this together."

It occurred to Gita that they were trying to reason with unreasonable but valid emotions. Maybe acknowledging that might help.

"Your fear is valid. Would you feel better if you were in an environment suit?" Gita asked. "We could set your helmet visor up so that it limits your view." Mandy's inability to see clearly might become a problem in an emergency, but Gita thought they could deal with that later.

Tilting her head, Mandy seemed to give this consideration.

It took a while, but in the end, she agreed to try. Aoifa volunteered to help with some behavioral techniques used to treat anxiety. Ahead of leaving, the two of them practiced until Mandy felt more in control of her panic attacks. Gita and Aoifa filled backpacks with supplies. Not wanting to stress Mandy's bones, Gita decided

Mandy would go unburdened. With that, the three of them set out.

The area around *Artemis* was thickly wooded—or had been. The ship's crash had plowed a large crater, upending and destroying trees and plant growth for about fifteen hundred meters. After her first attempt to climb up the steep side, Gita slipped and fell. She was fine, but her environment suit suffered a tear. There wasn't a spare in her size, so Gita repaired it with sealant tape, and they opted to find an easier way up and out.

The accident caused several hours' delay.

Once they were free of the crater, they made good progress the rest of the afternoon. The forest eventually thinned out, and they chose to stay in the open. Gita didn't want to risk encountering any wild animals.

Now that they'd made headway, she finally felt good about their prospects. It was a beautiful, clear day. The air was scented with light, peppery florals. The source was probably the thousands of white-and-purple flowering vines twisting among the branches above their heads. The trees vaguely resembled kinds she'd seen before. She was no botanist, but she had lived with one. The biggest difference seemed to be the circumference of their crowns and root systems. She supposed this was likely due to the limited depth of the ring world's earth layer. Broad root and canopy systems would prevent the tree from being blown down in a harsh wind—if storms occurred here.

She spied conifers, broad-leaved and deciduous trees.

The shorter varieties shared characteristics with the Terran baobab tree. Their round boles were a consistent circumference until they branched out. There they pinched inward half the size before the limbs took over. Gnarled branches stretched outward as far as thirty meters, and each crown was flat, giving the whole thing the look of a wide-handled umbrella with tentacle vines. The bark was rough and the color of burnt umber. The orbicular-shaped leaves were deep maroon and green with pink veins. Each leaf was bigger than Gita's hand.

The tallest trees poked through the shorter, flat canopy, towering about sixty meters. Their trunks were smooth and straight. They tended to be narrower in diameter than their shorter neighbors. The branches weren't as long either. Forty-centimeter-long needle-shaped leaves hung in clusters like orange-and-red starbursts, cascading downward in a multicolored waterfall. When the leaves fluttered, they sounded like rushing water. The undergrowth consisted of bushes and flowers in endless color and shape combinations. The tall, soft grass was a supersaturated emerald green. The grass rippled like the surface of a lake.

Plant growth was lush and thick, except for where the shadows fell. Gita supposed it was because the sun never moved.

That was what disturbed her the most. The Ring's sun was fixed in the center of the sky. The horizon curled upward instead of down. Her subconscious kept expecting a flat horizon, but all around them, tall, jagged mountains touched the roof of the world. Compasses were useless. The Ring didn't have polar magnetic fields like a spheroid planet would.

Flat, white clouds drifted against cerulean in loose, lazy groups. It was a haunting and beautiful landscape, but she kept feeling like something was missing. It took her a while to place what it was.

"Have you seen or heard any birds?" Gita asked.

Mandy blinked. "I haven't."

Aoifa tilted her head. "I've not noticed any animals during the day at all. Have you?"

"They've probably been driven off by the sound of our stomping," Gita said.

"I don't stomp."

"You're right." Aoifa grabbed Mandy's hand. "I blame Gita."

"Mag boots weren't designed for hiking." Gita stood on one leg and lifted her knee.

Mandy stiffened.

"What's wrong, love?" Aoifa placed a hand on Mandy's arm.

Gita hoped it wasn't another panic attack.

"It's the wind," Mandy said.

Aoifa blinked. "What do you mean?"

"There isn't any." Mandy pointed at the waving grass.

"Grass shouldn't do that," said Aoifa.

"How much longer do we have to go?" Gita asked.

Mandy checked her hand terminal. "About two and a half more hours."

"Good." Aoifa glanced at the woods. "This place makes me nervous. Something isn't right."

Mandy took Aoifa's hand.

Gita paused, searching the sky, the forest, and the grasslands for any possible trouble. There had been no evidence thus far of people or animals. No footprints, nothing. Everything was silent. "Let's keep moving. I don't think we should be caught outside at night."

They continued on for another half hour. Soon, they discovered a wide, clear stream with a rocky bottom. It wasn't deep. Staring into the water, Gita spotted a fish the size of her fist. Its brightly colored stripes ran the length of its body in cobalt, teal, and turquoise against a yellow background.

She pointed at it, hoping the others would spot it before it vanished. "It's a fish! Look!"

Mandy and Aoifa gazed down.

"I see them," Mandy said.

Hundreds of tiny fish no bigger than Gita's finger darted from crevices between and under the stones. Their brightly colored scales formed polka dot patterns in blues and reds, and their red faces had black patches around their eyes. It wasn't long before they counted three or four other kinds. They spent a minute fish watching before continuing on. She kept an eye on the water as they went.

For now, their path followed the stream. As the day wore on, Gita noted that the forever-noontime sun was fading. She shaded her eyes with her right hand.

Movement in the corner of her vision drew her gaze to the forest. Pink puffs floated in the woods. Each one gently glowed and winked in and out like a firefly. They reminded her of Septan mimosa blooms, only they were about twenty-five or thirty centimeters in diameter. Underneath each puff was a transparent umbrella-shaped membrane. Their long, thready tentacles appeared oily pink, purple, and blue in the sunlight filtering between the leaves. Individual puffs contracted and expanded in independent directions and rhythms, flying higher with each spasm and drifting downward when still like large pink dust motes. They breathed themselves upward to hide away from the sun in the shadowy canopy.

"Wonder if they're poisonous," Mandy said.

Gita was happy she'd decided not to take them through the woods.

"They look a bit like blue jellyfish." Aoifa asked, "Maybe so?"

"Let's not find out." Gita turned her back on the trees and turned to the stream, which was starting to meander in a different direction. They would have to cross it soon. "Do you think we can get to the other side?"

"We could wade through," Mandy said.

Aoifa glanced to the woods and back to the water. "I don't know. Anything could be in the water."

"True," Gita said. "The streambed is made up of rocks, for the most part. Let's see if it thins out."

"Hopefully without going too far off course," Aoifa added.

They travelled downstream a couple hundred meters—eventually coming to a small waterfall. Employing the stones to hop across, they then stopped for a small meal.

"How is your leg?" Mandy asked Aoifa.

"Hurts some. But I can handle it."

"Here. Have another painkiller." Gita reached into a thigh pocket and tossed her the bottle.

Catching it in one hand, Aoifa asked, "And your head?"

"Getting better," Gita lied.

"That's good," Mandy said.

They decided on a short rest. Out of caution, they spread a reflective blanket on the grass. They hadn't found any biting insects so far, but Gita didn't want to risk that now. It made for a comfortable picnic spot. They didn't bother to heat the food. It would take more time than Gita wanted to spend. So they ate directly out of the packaging. Gita enjoyed the feel of the soft grass cushioning the blanket beneath her.

Either everyone was a little tired from the long walk or they'd simply run out of conversation. They ate wordlessly.

Gita felt a powerful attraction to the woods. After the seventh or eighth time of looking back over her shoulder, she caught a flash of white feathers among the branches. She carefully scanned the shadows. That's when she spied a small white owl. It was so out of place that she blinked and let out a small yelp.

It vanished.

"What's wrong?" Aoifa asked.

Did I just see that? Gita decided to wait. If she spotted it again, she'd tell the others. "It's nothing. That forest is so strange."

They went back to their makeshift picnic.

Finished eating, Aoifa picked up Gita's pack and started searching for something. "I could murder a bite of chocolate."

"I wish," Gita said. "We don't have any in the galley."

"Shite," Aoifa muttered.

Gazing up at the sky, Gita calculated how long they had before dark. Everything was going according to schedule so far. Still, if the survivors had abandoned the shuttles or wandered too far from them, they might have to give up and turn back. "When we get there, we'll only have about an hour to search. If we don't find them quickly, we'll start earlier in the day tomorrow."

Aoifa nodded.

They collected the trash, folded the blanket, and re-packed everything in Aoifa's backpack. Then they hiked for another two hours. Gita had begun to worry that they'd missed the landing site when Mandy spotted the shuttles. Gita could see shadows among the ships. As they approached, she recognized the signs of an active campsite. She let out a sigh, awash with relief.

Their comms silence must have been due to a malfunction. It would make sense.

As they moved closer, Aoifa waved and shouted. She tried three times, but there was no response.

"Something is wrong," Mandy said.

"They aren't moving." Gita halted.

"Don't be ridiculous." Aoifa squinted as if she could squeeze out more detail from what she was seeing. "They're upright. Dead people don't remain standing."

"No, Gita's right," Mandy said.

Aoifa visibly shuddered. "I don't like this at all."

"Let's keep going." Uneasy, Gita tugged at her pack straps and shifted the weight on her shoulders. "We'll see what happened when we get there. Maybe we can help them. But seal your helmets, just in case."

What if it's the contagion from the mining expedition? Or something on the Ring's surface? Gita's relief turned to dread; she'd broken out in a light, icy sweat.

The pilots had parked all five shuttles in a protective circle, creating a defensive wall for the camp. She recognized it as standard procedure for planetary exploration teams. It was why they hadn't been able to get a good view of the encampment until they were much closer. From where she was now, the survivors appeared to have used vines to camouflage the ships and equipment.

That's strange. Why would they do that? What were they afraid of? She remembered the floating pink puff creatures she'd spotted in the forest—one of so few life-forms on the surface here. Were they predatory? Poisonous? Or was there some larger, more dangerous creature that they hadn't seen yet?

She cast her gaze all around for some sign of trouble and didn't spot anything.

The hairs on the back of her neck stood on end when

she realized that the vines and roots hadn't been placed there by the survivors. They'd grown up around the shuttles.

How long does it take for that kind of plant growth? Surely they weren't on the Ring that long? She supposed it might be possible, if the vines and roots were rapid growing. Suddenly, she wished she'd waited until she'd repaired Liv's neuromorphic matrices before beginning the search. Gita wanted more than anything to consult with Liv. None of them knew enough about planetary flora. Liv could have accessed the data and determined whether the vines were an immediate hazard or not.

Gita led the others a few more meters and signaled to stop. Everything was far too quiet. The crawling sensation along her spine intensified.

Different species of plants covered the shuttles. The most prevalent resembled what she'd seen in the forest on the way here. The leaves were heart shaped and a deep emerald green. The stems were even darker, becoming a purplish black farther toward the ground. Roots appeared to have burst up out of the earth and wrapped themselves around each shuttle. In some cases, they even pierced the metal hull, penetrating the ship's reinforced exterior.

"Hello? Is anyone there?" Gita's call started out strong, then faded into almost a child's plea.

The answering silence was oppressive.

Cautiously, she edged her way around the first shuttle—making sure to keep a safe distance. Nothing moved, not even the wind. As she made her way to the space between the ships, she saw that the vines had grown over the shuttle roofs and out to the other ships, forming a draping canopy. On the other side, plant-covered equipment and crates of supplies were scattered on the ground. She stepped through to the campsite, then stopped. There was plenty of space, but she didn't like being surrounded by the alien vines. The persistent fear that this would be the moment they attacked preyed upon her.

Vines don't move like that, she thought. *Even here, everything you've seen indicates otherwise*. Still, she couldn't bring herself to take that first step forward.

"Do we have to go in there?" Mandy asked in a voice not much louder than a whisper. The question felt like an intrusion.

Gita bit her lip. "We have to know if anyone is alive. We're here to render aid."

"If they were alive, don't you think they'd have answered us?" Aoifa muttered.

"We have to find out for sure." In truth, Gita wanted nothing more than to run the opposite direction, but she knew she wouldn't be able to live with herself if she did. The idea that she might have left someone behind would haunt her. So she stepped through.

Nothing happened.

Releasing her breath, she turned back to the others. "See? Everything's okay. They aren't—" And then she understood what she was seeing for the first time. The bottom dropped out of her stomach. "Oh no."

"What's wrong?" Mandy asked.

Gita shook her head. Aoifa rushed to her side and gasped.

"No! Mandy, stay where you are," Gita said.

Apparently, the remaining crew had been eating a meal when they were attacked. Packs and supplies had been tossed around. Luggage had been ripped apart, as if they had been frantically searching for medical or containment equipment. Weapons and mining tools were strewn on the ground.

Vines and roots twisted around and through everything—people and machines alike. In the midst of the chaos, the survivors' bodies appeared posed. Their eyes were shut, like sleepwalkers. Their faces were tilted upward, as if they were basking in the warm sun. Some stood frozen with their mouths gaping open in a soundless scream. Vines pierced skulls, torsos, and limbs. Several of the bodies had been torn open—their abdominal cavities emptied of organs. Lungs, hearts, and livers were exposed. Plant life pushed up through chests, piercing under chins and up through the top of skulls. Long ropes of intestines and circulatory systems entwined with the greenery. The vines joined crew member to crew member in a grotesque sort of daisy chain.

"Fucking hell," Aoifa breathed. Her brown eyes were wide with horror.

Movement caught Gita's attention. She spotted a young woman whose heart hung outside her ribs, cradled by the vines. It was still beating. Under her skin, something bulged and writhed, as if thousands of insects swarmed in her veins. At one point, they had burst out of her skin. Tiny black things crawled over her body in a flood, blessedly obscuring her face.

It took Gita a moment to understand what they were. *Medbots. Only bigger. Swollen. They're not supposed to do that. They're not—*

The young woman's eyes snapped open. In the place of the vacant deadness Gita expected, there was living terror.

Gita turned her head and would have vomited, but she stopped herself. *This isn't the first time you've seen something horrific. Get control of yourself. You can't afford to lose it. Not here.* The fresh, peppery scent of greenery wafted up her nose. *I shouldn't be smelling anything.* That was when she thought of the tear she'd repaired. Stooping, she visually inspected her left knee. *It's fine. It's—*

She felt something grab her arm and screamed before she realized it was Aoifa.

"Time to get the fuck out of here," she said. Her voice sounded strange and muffled because of her closed helmet. Apparently, the team comm channel wasn't working. "Now."

An electric bolt of terror shot through Gita's body. *Oh, please don't let me have just exposed us to this thing.* Trying not to swallow, Gita hung transfixed between the action of standing frozen in terror and getting sick.

"They're alive." Mandy's voice was distant.

"No, they aren't," Aoifa said. "Not in the sense we know."

Gita straightened. Then she initiated the suit's internal

decontamination procedures and immediately felt better. "What did this?"

"Let's figure it out later," Aoifa said. "Preferably somewhere very far from here."

Now that she was recovering from her shock, Gita registered that her comm channel was beeping. Someone was trying to contact her. She opened the channel.

"Gita? Is that you? Are you really there? Please answer me."

It was Ri.

The timbre of her plea was so desolate that Gita's protective drive kicked in on a physical level. She felt it from her gut to her toes. "Ri! Are you okay? Where are you? I thought I'd lost you."

"It's so good to hear your voice. Wes is gone. I thought I was alone." Ri's relief was palpable. "If—if it's really you, you have to go back to your ship. All of you. Please, you must leave the Ring. *Now*. Something bad is about to happen."

Tears flooded Gita's eyes. "I'm not leaving here without you, dear one. Tell me where you are."

"I hid in the shuttle systems. Did you get the storage unit I left in the stasis pod?"

"I did. And I gave Nana the message for Aggie."

"Where is the unit now?"

Gita bit her lip. "It's on our ship." She felt Aoifa tug at her arm.

"Oh. All right," Ri said.

Yanking her arm free, Gita stepped toward one of the

shuttles. "We'll get you out. What took you so long to answer? What's going on?"

"That isn't important now. Don't worry about me," Ri said. "I have a drone. Now that you're here I'll catch up. It's not safe here for you. Take your shuttle and get off this world."

"Who is Wes? Should we wait for them?" Gita's reactions felt sluggish. She understood the need to act but couldn't bring herself to move.

Devastation broke up Ri's response like comm-signal interference. "He's . . . he's dead. *Please*. You must hurry. Before this kills you, too."

Gita began to shiver. *It's shock. Adrenaline.* "What's going on?"

"So many things. *Please*, Mata. You can't stay."

"I—I just realized something. I've been stupid." Gita's vision blurred, and her cheeks were wet. *Cold.* "Very, very stupid. My suit is torn. I sealed it with tape earlier. I thought it was enough, but—"

"Everything will be all right. But you have to *listen*."

It occurred to Gita that Ri was using the same methods she used to sooth her when she panicked. "I'm listening. I hear you."

Ri shouted at her. "Move! Get out! Now!"

Gita started with the force of Ri's words. Ri never yelled at her. She'd raised Ri to be respectful.

Gita's fractured attention was drawn to something on her right.

One of the victims' jaws dropped open. A thick, dark

root coated in rusty-brown slime slithered out of the yawning mouth. It rapidly thickened as more and more forced its way out. The joint gave away with a wet pop as the wide tentacle-root touched to the ground. It pulsed and stretched, lengthening. It paused. The tip reared up, resembling a snake tasting the air. All at once, it pivoted in her direction and lowered itself to the ground. It slithered across the grass with a side-to-side motion. The young woman's body jerked with each movement.

"Gita!"

Yelping in terror, Gita bolted through the opening by which she and Aoifa had entered. Aoifa and Mandy were only a few steps behind. Gita didn't stop until she'd reached the stream they'd crossed earlier.

"What the fuck was that?" Aoifa sounded sick and shaky. "What the *fuck*?"

"I—I don't know," Gita said. "Aoifa, will you check my knee?"

Breaking from the spell of her own shock, Aoifa knelt down and inspected the site of the tear.

Mandy stared back at the shuttles. "We should have taken photographs. Run suit cameras."

"Why?" Gita asked.

"No one will believe us." Mandy was crying. "No one will want to."

"I don't give a fuck," Aoifa said. "None of us are going back there. Not ever. And fuck anyone who says we should've done otherwise." She looked up at Gita. "Why didn't you leave sooner?"

Have I been exposed? Oh, Lakshmi, please don't let it be so. "Don't worry. I'm okay." Gita wasn't certain if she was reassuring herself or the others. She blinked to clear her vision, then scanned the area for the little waterfall they'd stepped across. That peaceful journey felt like a whole other lifetime ago.

"Looks like the seal held. But it's hard to be sure." Aoifa got to her feet. "Have you run a suit diagnostic? Is your HUD working?"

I should have thought of that. Come on, wake up. The others need you. Gita nodded. "I'll initiate one while we hike. There's no time to wait for it to finish. We have to get back to *Artemis*."

Aoifa gave her a worried look. "What's the hurry?"

"Ri contacted me on a private comm channel," Gita said. "She says we have to leave the Ring immediately."

"Where *is* Ri?" Aoifa's face was grayer than Gita had ever seen it.

"She's been hiding in the shuttle systems. She told me that she has a drone. She says she'll catch up."

Taking Aoifa's left hand, Mandy said, "We should go. We're four hours from the ship."

Aoifa shuddered. Then she passed her right hand over Mandy's suit, checking for problems. "How about you? Are you okay? Whatever that was was seriously fucked."

What is wrong with me? Gita thought. *I knew the site was contaminated. I was in a damaged suit. Basics of Search and Rescue.* She suddenly realized that Aoifa was talking to her.

"I hate to be the bearer of shite news, but *Artemis* isn't going anywhere. You know that."

Mandy said, "We have a shuttle."

"Not a working one." Aoifa sighed.

"That doesn't matter. We have *you*." Mandy hugged her. "If I can spacewalk, you can fix a shuttle. No matter how broken."

"You didn't do it once." Aoifa hugged her back. "You spacewalked *twice*. You're amazing."

"Come on," Mandy said. "We have things to do."

Starting across the waterfall, Gita took four steps before her foot slipped. Her boot plunged ankle-deep into the stream. Thick waterproof material shielded her from sensation and yet further possible contamination. Seconds passed as she watched the stream flow over the top of her foot.

"Gita? Are you all right?"

Abruptly coming back to herself, Gita hopped back onto the rock path and dashed to the other side.

I'm not okay.

16

"We're in position." Karter made a fist in an attempt to get a handle on her anxiety. It wouldn't do to snap at people who had nothing to do with the source of her apprehension.

Look at you, acting like a grown-up.

She muttered, "Aggie, don't you fucking leave us hanging."

Aggie never had. And of course she would never mean to. *But there's always that first time.*

Strapped into the pilot's couch to her left, Ibis leaned over as far as they could—which wasn't much, given that the harness was designed to prevent it. They whispered, "You got the TC yet?"

Without a terminus code, they couldn't go anywhere.

Mirabilis would be responsible for holding up the line during an evacuation, and no one would be happy about that.

I should've had a second option prepped just in case. Fuck, you're getting sloppy. There's trusting someone, and then there's not doing your damned job.

Ibis mouthed one word: *Well?*

Pressing her lips together, Karter shook her head. She did some quick research on nearby marker terminals, found one, and made the application. It could take anywhere from fifteen to twenty-five minutes. "Stall them."

"You want me to tell them we've got a problem on the other end?" Ibis whispered.

"Not that. They'll want to know which fucking terminal fucked up." It occurred to Karter that she was asking Ibis to lie, and Ibis was a terrible liar. "Tell them we're having a mechanical problem."

Ibis nodded. "What kind?"

"You can't think of one?"

The controller unmuted their end of the channel. They sounded extremely annoyed. "Hold on, *Mirabilis*. We've got a problem." There was a shouting match going on in the background.

"Oh yeah?" Ibis was a little too cheerful. "What's up?"

The second terminal indicated that approvals were being finalized.

Looks like the gods are smiling on us today, thought Karter. *Just thirty more seconds—*

"A safety issue needs resolving," the controller hissed. "Nothing to worry about."

That's not something you want to hear just before a jump, Karter thought.

Ibis winked. "Is it . . . a mechanical problem?"

Karter muted the comms and glared at Ibis. "What the fuck are you doing?" Her heart pounded against her breastbone.

Slapping the volume back on, Ibis stuck out their tongue.

The controller suddenly seemed to understand that certain implications might reflect badly on management. "Er . . . more like a logistical situation."

"Oh? Did someone forget to file their paperwork?" Ibis asked.

"Some fucking asshole in a personal shuttle drifted too close," the controller said. "Just keep your fucking pants on, like I told you."

"You bet." Ibis muted the comm channel. "Someone's in a mood."

"Everyone is, I suppose." The backup TC came through. Karter let out a shuddering breath.

Lissa, Ezi, and Martina were safely tucked away in Medical, hacking at the GX-3714 problem. Unfortunately, Ezi was becoming anxious. Lissa said it was the deadline. Apparently, Ezi didn't deal well with time constraints. Karter was glad that Martina was there to help.

A second message bearing Aggie's verification signature appeared on Karter's screen. The origin signifier indicated an anonymous vehicle off their starboard bow. She slapped a hand over her mouth to trap a nervous cackle from escaping her lips. *Thank you, Aggie.*

Left-handed, she tossed the terminus code to Ibis's screen and sent an acknowledgment ping to their mysterious benefactor.

The controller reactivated the channel. In a muffled voice, they said, "For fuck's sake, someone pull that shithead's license. Will you?"

"What?" Ibis asked.

"Not you," the controller said. "I want *you* to enter your fucking TC. Now."

"Gotcha." Ibis typed it in and punched Send. "There you are."

"You're a go," the controller said. "Now, get the fuck out of my terminal."

Ibis didn't waste time and engaged the jump engine. The terminal powered up. In response, *Mirabilis*'s Hopper-Johnson drive discharged an energy burst that could be felt throughout the ship. *Mirabilis* shuddered. Karter listened to the deep groan as several thousand tons of tungsten and chromium steel reacted to the stress of a subspace transfer. Her stomach dropped somewhere near her ankles, and a coppery taste deposited itself in the back of her throat. She felt a bone-deep cold sink into her marrow. For an instant, a bubble of bright blue appeared around the ship on the projection. Then the terminal's signal lights vanished along with Chimera Station. Everything outside of *Mirabilis* went black as ship and crew dropped into subspace. The automatic navigation system took over. She felt no sensation of movement or speed. Time as she understood it ceased to be. She lost herself. And then, just as suddenly as they'd entered subspace, they exited.

"Fuck." Karter shivered. "I'll never get used to that." It didn't matter how warmly she dressed; she always came out of a jump half frozen.

The new projection just above the pilot's console depicted a terminal still under construction. Crews of human laborers swarmed over scaffolding in power-assist loaders and welding harnesses. Half of the site's skeletal structure hadn't even been anchored in place. This became apparent when a large section came unmoored and began to drift with a worker still tethered to it.

"That's not good," Ibis said.

"No shit."

Several corporate gunships with Kontis Galatic Energy logos emblazoned across their bows were parked nearby. She imagined their crews were scrambling to emergency stations about now. The corporate navy vessels began reorienting themselves.

A comm-channel alert began its urgent beeping. Karter saw it was the marker terminal's controller demanding an open channel.

"You getting that or am I?" Ibis asked.

"This one's mine." Karter hit the comm switch.

A cacophony of warning alarms and screams immediately burst from the ship's speakers. She winced and adjusted the volume with fingers still numb from the jump.

"Unknown starship, you have entered restricted space. This is a private terminal—"

Wait. Unknown? They can read our hull. Our Transponder is functional and transmitting our identification information. How the fuck—

The marker terminal powered up as if it'd been given a terminus code. The still-open comm channel projectile vomited curses in several different languages. Two gunships maneuvered to face them. *Mirabilis*'s narrow AI issued a target-lock alert.

"What the fuck?" Karter asked. "Ibis! Keep us here! Don't you dare—"

Mirabilis didn't have an artificial person installed to pilot the ship—its Hopper-Johnson drive was manually activated. Which meant a jump could be initiated by only her or Ibis.

This can't be happening.

"I didn't fucking touch it!" Ibis shouted. Their eyes were wide, and their hands were in the air. "I swear, I didn't!"

Oh shit. Oh shit. Oh shit. We don't have a terminus code, Karter thought. *Those poor bastards out there. We're jumping—*

Mirabilis's sudden, violent convulsion was stronger than Karter had ever experienced. The ship protested in a creaking screech. Briefly, she wondered if the hull would come apart. Then the bubble of blue light appeared, and everything vanished.

Back-to-back jumps weren't recommended. They were bad for a ship's structural components. Under normal circumstances, there was a requisite fifteen-minute rest period. It gave the crew time to adjust. Every ship owner with jump-capable drives was warned about this. Now, she understood the reasons why firsthand.

The experience was twice as intense—the cold sensation, the bad taste in her mouth, the mental confusion. When she came to herself, she heard what sounded like every alarm in the ship shrieking warnings. Sparks exploded from her copilot console. She slapped the release on her couch harness and fumbled for the fire extinguisher under the dashboard. She was moving too slowly. Her movements were graceless and numb, but she forced herself onward anyway. Finally, the extinguisher hissed a cloud of gray powder.

It took a moment to register that Ibis was screaming.

"Calm the fuck down!" It then occurred to Karter that shouting this at someone in a panic wasn't going to produce the desired result.

"What the fucking fuck?" Ibis was huddled into a tight ball.

Karter hosed down the source of the electrical fire while trembling with a chill that was no longer present. The contents of her skull felt like they'd been flipped inside out and back again. "It's okay. We made it. And in one piece." She glanced at the gray mess coating the console. It would dissolve. Eventually. "Well, mostly."

"Made it where?" Ibis asked. Their teeth were chattering.

Slotting the fire extinguisher back into its mount to recharge, Karter collapsed into the flight couch. She activated the projection. The interface took an extra second or two to respond. Finally, an image flickered into being. She spied a large, lumpy asteroid slowly rotating off their port bow. To starboard, a bare-bones relay marker terminal had been constructed. It was the flimsiest excuse for a marker she'd ever seen in her life.

The comm channel gave another impatient beep. She slapped at the screen, barely able to control postadrenaline shakes. At least she was starting to warm up, even if her brain hadn't recovered.

"Hello? Is everyone okay in there?" The voice on the other end was familiar, but Karter couldn't place it. "Sorry for the rough ride. There wasn't time to test everything properly. It may not have been a drifting cargo box in the middle of a war, but I assume it was close enough."

Karter blinked. "Dr. Garcia?"

"Karter? Thank God! You're all right?"

"Maybe. I haven't asked the passengers yet." Karter signaled to Ibis to start a medical check. "What are you doing here?"

"Oh, I'm not really there. I'm beaming this in from the border zone."

"Ah." Karter was relieved.

"What the fuck did you just do to us?" Ibis shouted.

"I thought M. Neumeyer told you about the modifications." Dr. Garcia sounded hesitant and unsure. "Didn't she?"

Ibis let out a long string of curses, which Karter muted as quickly as possible.

No use traumatizing the poor woman, she thought. "She may have left out a few details."

"Like, all of them!" Ibis shouted, unmuted again.

"Oh . . . I'm so sorry," Dr. Garcia said. "You should've been warned about the possible need for a back-to-back subspace traversal."

"Yeah!" Again, Ibis was shouting. "*Someone* should've!"

"How's that nonhangover now?" Karter asked.

Ibis made a rude gesture.

Karter returned it. "Never mind them, doc," she said. "What the hell happened?"

"Please don't blame Sal. They're a sweetheart. This wasn't their idea—it was all mine." Dr. Garcia paused. "Where are my notes? Oh, thank you. Let's see. For a start, I—"

What followed was five minutes of technical descriptions of theoretical physics regarding subspace structures. Karter waited for the doctor to catch her breath before interrupting.

"That's er . . . nice. Now, could you please give me the version you tell your friends who don't have multiple advanced degrees in physics? Starting with how you managed to install an artificial navigator without Sal catching on. Because if Sal knew, they would've told us. And then we wouldn't have been so surprised when we jumped out of an incomplete relay terminal with multiple corporate gunships locked on—"

"Oh, that." Dr. Garcia let out a nervous laugh. "I used a multiphase micro-install. It takes a little longer, but the components are significantly less sizable. And it's not a full artificial person. It's a multilayer narrow AI—"

Someone said something in the background, and the comm channel was briefly muted. After a few moments, the doctor returned.

"Sorry. I've just been told I should wrap this up."

"Seriously. I need to know what you did to *Mirabilis*," Ibis said. "I can't operate—"

"You should be receiving the specifications now," Dr. Garcia interrupted. "After studying your engines, I made a few other minor adjustments. Or rather, I had Sal make them."

Ibis said, "I wondered where that bastard came up with half the shit they mentioned."

"Both engine systems should be more efficient. And the maneuvering will be more responsive with the pilot and navigation assist," Dr. Garcia said. "You'll need a structural refit, eventually. Your ship isn't designed for the full mechanical shock load that the AI and the engines can employ."

"Don't push the engines into the red," Ibis said. "Gotcha."

"The AI has a limitation parameter setting that will

prevent you from pushing the ship too far." Dr. Garcia sounded almost proud.

Ibis frowned. "You did *not* put a fucking child lock on my ship—"

Cutting in before Ibis could further insult the doctor, Karter said, "Thank you, Dr. Garcia. We appreciate all your hard work."

"Yours is the first nonexperimental vehicle to receive those updates. If you don't mind, I'd like to review the performance data." Dr. Garcia hesitated. "Ah, after you return to Terran Republic space, of course."

"Of course," Karter said.

"Seriously. How do I fucking disengage the fucking child lock on—"

Once again, Karter muted Ibis. "Say, is Aggie around?"

"I'm afraid not," Dr. Garcia answered. "She said she had other projects that required her attention, and she's entrusted me with the situation."

Of course she has, Karter thought.

"Should I tell her you wish to speak to her?" Dr. Garcia asked.

"Fucking yes," Ibis growled. "Absolutely. Immediately. With a laser at fifteen paces."

Karter glared at Ibis again. "Please do."

"Oh," Dr. Garcia said. "I hope you like the new shuttle."

"What?" Karter blinked.

"Didn't you notice?"

"Never mind." Karter shot a raised eyebrow at Ibis that

said, *I thought you inventoried the new deliveries.* "We'll take a look. Have a nice trip home." Karter added her sincere thanks.

"You're very welcome," Dr. Garcia replied. "Thank *you* for the rescue."

"Goodbye, doc," Ibis said.

"We'll talk to you later." With that, Karter signed off. "We've got twenty minutes before dust-off. Transfer what needs transferring to the new shuttle—especially the birthday present."

Ibis blinked. "Birthday present?"

Karter sighed. "Is everyone in Medical all right?"

"They're fine," Ibis said. "Whose birthday present?"

"Not yours, obviously. Ezi's. After that, we're gone."

"Ha! First one to the shuttle gets to fly it." Ibis dashed for the exit.

"Son of a bitch."

They raced each other to the shuttle bay, but Lissa and Martina were already there with Ezi. Martina looked a little worse for wear.

"Is everyone all right?" Gasping, Karter bent over and grabbed her own knees.

Lissa glanced across the bay where Ezi was floating around the cargo area with Martina chasing after her. "It wasn't easy to keep Ezi from losing her mind. Medical is a bit of a mess."

"That doesn't sound like it was fun to deal with," Karter said.

"The back-to-back jumps frightened her. I'm glad

Martina was here. At least Ezi has calmed down again." Lissa leaned against the tarp-covered shuttle.

Finally feeling less winded, Karter straightened. "Good."

"Now that we've discussed that. Can someone explain where the very expensive racing dreadnought came from?" Lissa patted the hidden shuttle-sized lump.

Ibis flipped the tarp back, revealing a sleek new racing yacht with a void-black hull infused with silver glitter. The name *Lush* had been printed on its side in reflective gray letters. It was the most ridiculously ostentatious excuse for a ship of any size that Karter had ever seen.

"Ooooh, glitter!" Ibis threw themself at the racer and attempted to embrace it. "Dibs." They pressed both arms and their entire upper body against its shiny black hull. "It's mine, all mine!" They cackled with glee.

"A dreadnought? Who names a class of racing vessel after an old warship?" Karter asked Lissa.

Lissa shrugged with one shoulder.

"Oh. I love you, my pretty, pretty thing." Ibis stroked its hull admiringly.

Karter couldn't help but mess with Ibis a little. "Lissa won the race. She was here first."

"No way," Ibis pouted. "I licked it already."

"You did not."

Ibis proceeded to do exactly that. The hull's nano coating fluctuated briefly before resuming its previous glittery splendor.

Lissa wrinkled her nose. "You don't know where that's been."

"Space is hygienic! Germs can't survive in a vacuum, right?" Ibis asked. "Can we look at the inside now? Please?"

"I'm almost afraid to, with how garish it is on the outside." Karter sighed and motioned to Ibis to go ahead. "Let's get everything sorted. We're on a deadline."

Lissa and Martina coaxed Ezi inside.

For a racing vehicle, the interior was fairly roomy. Someone had ripped all the unnecessary bits out, though Karter couldn't imagine there was much packed inside to begin with. Now, it had seating for eight and a small biocontainment area. The new additions were incongruent with the expensive upholstery and silver trim.

"Looks like they removed the bar." Lissa pointed to rear of the vehicle.

Ibis gave Lissa an incredulous look. "How do you know there was a bar?"

"I wonder who this belonged to." Karter asked no one in particular.

Lissa answered, "It doesn't look familiar."

"Would it?" Karter asked.

Shrugging, Lissa said, "My wife and second husband are big fans of dreadnought racing."

Ibis parked themself in the pilot couch and refused to budge. "I can't wait to fly."

Setting down the last of the baggage—mostly medical supplies, Karter went to the airlock and began readying the drone. "Have you given it a name and gender?"

"For now, I'll respect its privacy," Ibis said. "But let's see what you have on under all that shiny." They powered up the control systems.

"We're *so* changing the hull markings," Karter teased.

Ibis was indignant. "We are not!"

"Wasn't being unobtrusive the plan?" Lissa finished strapping Ezi into the charging station.

"The hull is black and sparkly; space is black and sparkly." Ibis cackled again like a maniacal anime villain. "The perfect camouflage."

"You've *got* to be kidding." Karter shook her head.

A proximity alarm shrieked a warning mere seconds before the ship violently reacted to an impact.

"So much for unobtrusive." Karter jumped into the copilot couch and began rushing through the safety checklist.

Ibis pulled up a projection of the area and fired up the engine. "Someone out there isn't very happy to see us."

"Hang on!" None of them knew anything about this ship model, let alone its quirks. Karter scrambled to get her harness secure while simultaneously reviewing the locations of vital cockpit instruments. When everything seemed in order, she checked that all the doors were locked and sealed. "Everyone strapped in?"

Mirabilis shuddered on a second impact. The shuttle bounced up, then smacked down on the deck with enough force that Karter worried the landing gear was damaged. Something in the cargo hold crashed. The aft of the dreadnought traced an arc across the bay floor with the landing treads. Pain exploded in Karter's shoulder. She barely held back a scream.

"No-no-no-no!" Ibis powered up the impulse thrusters. The dreadnought inched off the deck just as another violent jolt hit *Mirabilis*, sending a cargo crate bouncing off the deck in front of them right into a wall. "And fuck that! We're a dot or we're a cinder."

Karter searched the landing gear for damage before she hammered the glasstop screen with the side of her fist. "Go! Go! Go!"

Ibis shoved the throttle forward as fast as they could. Karter slammed against the back of her cushioned seat, snapping her teeth together. Pain flooded her mouth with the taste of blood-salt. The little dreadnought shot out of the shuttle bay, and by some miracle, they weren't incinerated by the explosion that engulfed them as they went. Every proximity alarm howled. The forward screen dimmed. Heat monitors in the hull jolted into the red, and the cockpit became uncomfortably hot just before they hit vacuum. Ibis immediately threw *Lush* into a hard, banking turn. Karter got a disorienting view of the missiles slamming into *Mirabilis* above her head.

Please let there be enough of Mirabilis to get us back to the border zone, she thought without much hope. There was no way *Lush* would have enough power to get them home, and it wasn't jump capable.

The racing shuttle executed a series of graceful turns and rolls to avoid ship and terminal bits along with chunks of exploded asteroid. This close, the debris field was dense. But in Ibis's hands, *Lush*'s every motion was smooth and powerful, like a sword with added g-force.

Karter tensed up her lower body and took several breaths. When she was sure she wasn't going to pass out, she searched space for the source of the missiles. Upon spying what was waiting for them, she gasped.

"Holy shit," Ibis said.

Three gunboats and a cruiser were parked just beyond what had once been the temporary marker terminal. *Mirabilis* was the proverbial sitting duck. Ibis immediately guided *Lush* into another sequence of quick, compact evasion maneuvers.

"We've got no weapons or shields." Karter struggled to maintain focus on the screen in front of her. "You're on your own, Ibis. Sorry." That also meant Karter would have to ride this out without something constructive to do. *Fuck*.

"Don't worry. I know something those assholes don't," Ibis said.

"I don't feel very well," Ezi called from the passenger compartment. "I think I'm going to be sick."

"You can't be sick," Martina said. "You're not equipped for that."

"What do you know, Ibis?" asked Karter.

"This is a dreadnaught, the newest model." Ibis answered. "That's a twenty-five-year-old gunboat."

Karter ground her teeth together. "And?"

"Their missile targeting systems are outdated. They

aren't designed for locking onto anything that moves as fast as this beast." Ibis grinned and patted the console.

"Oh." Karter blinked.

Martina said, "Ezi, we have to finish sequencing the—"

"Crap, crap, crap!" Ibis made several quick swerves to the left and right.

The ship rocked back and forth, gliding around yet another cluster of missiles. All six shot past, missing not only *Lush*, but *Mirabilis*, too.

"Nice try, asshole!" Ibis yelled gleefully.

Ezi's voice carried from the back of the ship. "No. No. No. Don't do it like that. It'll rewrite the logic string over there."

"Huh," Martina said. "You're right."

"Of course I am."

Yet another alarm sounded. Karter silenced it with a slap and did a double take. Ibis was steering the racer at the cruiser as if playing chicken.

"What the fuck are you doing?" Karter asked.

"Trying to shake some heat." Ibis's lips and brows were now pressed into thin lines of concentration. "There's too many of them."

Lush danced, weaved, and bobbed at Ibis's slightest suggestion. "Damn, this thing can move!" A wide grin was plastered on their mouth.

They flattened out the ship's trajectory, and *Lush* was now racing along the length of the corporate cruiser. They jogged the dreadnought to starboard, and now they were close enough for Karter to read the name *Black Francis* on the view screen without altering magnification. Each emerald-green letter was as tall as a person.

Another missile raced past, crashing into *Black Francis*'s hull. A cloud of debris and escaping gas expanded behind them as *Lush* sped past.

"Ibis, we're going the wrong direction," Karter said.

"Yep."

"We don't have fuel to waste."

"Yep."

"Then where the fuck are we going?"

"Come on, boss. I know where the Ring is."

Ibis squeezed *Lush* even closer to *Black Francis*'s hull. Karter tensed, anticipating a loud bang as they grazed the other ship. One of the gunboats attempted the same move, misjudged the distance, and clipped a comm tower, which sent it spinning off into space.

Karter did simple subtraction. *Only one gunboat and the cruiser left.* "Remember to slow down on the approach to the mining site. We don't want to set off the Ring's defenses."

"Find something to do besides worry, boss," Ibis snapped.

Once again, Ezi let out a loud, enthusiastic noise. This time, it was something about copies of files that she needed. Karter decided to ignore everything going on in the back until further notice. She shifted her attention to the drone's interface, pulled up a projection, and placed it where both of them could reach it. "Let me know when you're ready to make your first pass over the site."

"Starting the approach now," Ibis said.

Tapping the projection, Karter typed out Mother's code. "Ready." *Here's hoping this works.*

They needed to get in and out to avoid being caught by the second gunboat, but the velocity limit this close to the Ring made things tricky. Fly too fast, and they'd be blasted to microscopic particles.

Ibis steered *Lush* into another rapid, looping turn, this time away from *Black Francis*'s hull. The gunship seemed to have a hard time keeping up with *Lush*. Ibis used all the speed and agility the little dreadnaught had to gain a small pocket of time for a pass over the mining site.

The enormous near side of the Ring grew closer until it blanked out the stars in the view screen. Most of what Karter could see now was a void lit by flashes of neon green. As planned, Ibis slowed *Lush*. Karter caught a glimpse of the abandoned platform. It appeared empty—a skeletal ghost town of printed polycarbonate steel. But the lights were on—the power was still running, though nothing living moved.

She released the first drone. Once it was away, she vacillated her attention between the drone's cameras and the current location of the gunship closing in. As she'd hoped, the corporate vessel didn't seem to notice the drone, which successfully reached the platform and released a cloud of microbots. The tiny machines began the demolition as *Lush* sped on. Free of its payload, the drone would proceed to all contaminated areas and collect samples. The microbots began their work elsewhere. If

Tau, Chu & Lane wanted to stop them, it was too late now—there was no way to destroy so many microparticles without taking out the site itself. Structural components would be broken down to the molecular level and dissipate into space. The process was terrifying to watch. A small section of the platform appeared to melt. In twelve hours, it would be as if the entire platform had never been.

While Karter entered the coordinates for their next destination, Ibis focused on dodging the gunship. Karter released a breath she'd been holding when she heard Ibis curse.

"Two *more* cruisers?" Ibis let up on the throttle. "That's not fucking fair."

"TCL reinforcements?" In a panic, Karter returned her attention to the projection of nearby space. "Where?"

"They must have followed *Black Francis* and the others through the jump station not long after they jumped here? I count six: a frigate, destroyer, and four gunships. We've got three minutes to get the fuck out of Dodge," Ibis said.

"We're done." Karter slumped. She knew they'd been damned lucky to survive this long, but it was time to face reality.

Something inside her wanted to keep trying, but it wasn't just her life at risk. *That's the kind of urge that gets your friends killed.*

Ibis frowned. "Wait. That's odd—"

"You did your best, but that's it." Karter reached for the screen to request an open comm channel.

"Tau, Chu & Lane cruiser *Black Francis*. This is Kontis

Galactic Energy's frigate *Velvet Negroni*." The voice on the other end of the comms sounded smug. "Cease and desist all hostilities at once, or we will blow you into the next world."

Karter's mouth dropped open. "What the fuck?" Then she recalled the relay marker that Aggie had hacked.

Lush sped around behind *Black Francis*, once again using the slower, larger starship as a shield. Ibis executed an arching turn. "Sounds like a personal problem. Heading for the Ring now."

Velvet Negroni said, "You have thirty seconds to comply."

"What the fuck do you think you're doing?" It was *Black Francis*'s captain.

"This is Kontis Galactic territory," declared *Velvet Negroni*. "You are in violation of—"

"Fuck you! We were here first!"

A missile slammed into *Black Francis*. Bright light briefly blanked the projection image. Karter shut her eyes against a hard white flash. When she opened them again, she saw the explosion had torn through the cruiser's portside hull, exposing several decks to hard vacuum. Chunks of warship and a cloud of atmosphere appeared. While Ibis managed to outpace most of the debris field in a long turn that looped over the corporate cruiser, the gunship pilot wasn't quick enough. *Lush*'s pursuer plunged headlong into the remains of *Black Francis*'s hull.

Karter flinched.

Ibis sent them into yet another fast roll. "That's the signal to get the fuck out. Is our drone ready for pickup?"

Glancing back at the drone camera, Karter said, "Yes."

Yet another massive flurry of missiles arrowed past, hitting *Black Francis* on its already damaged side. The comm channel erupted on the other end with screams and curses before it cut out.

Ibis flattened their flight path, making it easier for Karter to launch the second drone. The four Kontis Galatic gunships opened up on the remaining TCL vessels. As Karter looked on, seven more sped into the fray. She spotted at least three different corporate emblems.

"No fucking way." Karter couldn't believe it.

"Mother always told me not to look a gift fleet in the missile port," Ibis said.

Karter found herself muttering something Gita would say. "I don't think that's how it goes." It felt like a good omen.

From the back, Lissa asked, "What's going on?"

Behind them, the corporate cruisers and gunboats tore one another apart.

17

Stumbling, Gita hiked across the low rolling hills as fast as her failing body allowed. She blamed the dimming light for her blurred vision. Foreign ideas, images, and feelings kept intruding on her mind. She couldn't quite puzzle out what any of it meant; it was as if she were just on the verge of translating something, understanding it. Something told her that whatever this was wasn't human. The alien presence inside her frightened her, and it was becoming more difficult to separate her own ideation from the strange entity's.

This place, the ring world, had become far too small and cramped.

It's time to—to—

Her vision clouded over. She tried blinking to clear it,

and when that didn't work, she stopped to rub her eyes. Her mind drifted. She turned to the forest on her left, and as she did, her sight cleared.

The pink tentacle-puff creatures floated under the shadows in the woods. Now, it was dark enough that their glow was easier to spot. They grew agitated as if in anticipation. Before, there had been a few hundred; now, there were twice that. They bobbed and bumped into one another like fairy lights. There was no wind, yet they drifted and swirled in circles as if dancing.

That was when she heard music.

"Do you hear that?" she asked.

It wasn't exactly a song. She couldn't have hummed along or whistled it. It tinkled and sparkled like broken mirror glass or the glitter of a stream in twilight.

Mandy continued several steps before she halted and turned. "Hear what?"

"They're singing to me." Gita smiled and reached into the air. "They're saying I should come dance with them." She moved hesitantly toward the forest. Reaching out, she wondered what their puffs would feel like. Would they be as soft against her fingertips as they looked?

Aoifa and Mandy positioned themselves between her and her goal.

"That is not where we're going," Aoifa said. "We're heading back to the ship. Remember? Liv is waiting. And then there's Ri. Do you remember Ri? She'll meet us there."

"Ri needs me." Gita covered her eyes. "But I'm so

tired. Can we stop for a little while? I—I just need to catch my breath."

"We're almost home." Aoifa spoke as if she were addressing a child. "When we reach *Artemis*, you can rest all you like. You can snuggle under the nice warm blankets."

Gita grew irritated. "You're patronizing me."

"Love, I'm too busy being worried for you to patronize you." Aoifa reached out to touch her arm.

"No!" Gita jerked away. "Stay away from me! You'll become contaminated!" Her vision grew sharp, and so did her thinking. *I am Gita Chithra. I'm on Loki's Ring. Karter Cuplin is on her way to rescue us. We're leaving this place. Ri will join us later.* "Let's go."

"That's right." Aoifa guided her away from the forest.

Gita staggered away from the fairy lights and their music. She forced herself to walk faster. "How far are we from *Artemis*?"

She could check for herself via her suit computer, but she was afraid that if she tried to do anything other than focus on getting back, she'd lose herself again. *I am Gita Chithra. I'm on Loki's Ring. We're leaving this place soon.*

"Not far," Mandy said.

"How far?" Gita asked.

Mandy's answer was lost in the sheen of the sky, now a darkening purple.

Purple. Purple. Ezinne likes purple, Gita thought. *What will happen to her when I'm gone?*

All at once it occurred to her that she'd been avoiding thinking about Ezi—and not only over the past few days. She couldn't recall the last time she'd had a more personal interaction with her youngest daughter. What made it worse was the knowledge that not doing so had been a relief. Guilt bruised her heart at the thought, leaving a sharp ache. She should've visited more often, played with her daughter at the Center. She saw that now. Her relationship with Ezi had come to revolve around arranging and maintaining her medical care—a being in need of extra support. She'd put on an emotional buffer while feeling nearly consumed with the details of Ezi's care. And in doing so, she'd neglected both Ezi and Ri.

But Ri had needed less from Gita. Ri was grown. Ri was a neurotypical AGI. She had a career.

I've failed Ri, too.

Gita blinked. "Where's Ri?"

The emerald grass stretched out ahead of her like a smooth new carpet. It made a soft cushion under the soles of her boots, muffling her steps. *That's nice. Wouldn't it be lovely to take off your boots and wiggle your toes in it? Or to lay down on it? To feel it on your cheek? It looks as soft as kitten fur.*

Kittens. Cat. Grimm is on Artemis. *We left him in the carrier. He's going to be so angry. We'll have to mute his collar for an entire day.*

A few paces ahead, Mandy crested the next hill and pointed. "See? There it is. The ship."

Stumbling to the top of the rise seemed to take every ounce of strength Gita had. When she finally got there, she wanted very badly to collapse onto her knees, put her hands to her face, and burst into tears. Everything was so overwhelming. Frightening. This place was so small, so uncomfortable, so—

Claustrophobic. I'm cramped. I want to stretch. To touch the stars. To . . . to fly!

Her vision clouded again. Now, she could hear the grass whispering. Each thin blade sparkled and glowed. She bent to touch it, knowing it would tickle if she held her palm just above the surface. The grass smelled so fresh. So *inviting*. She wanted so much to lay down. "So tired."

"Shite," Aoifa said. "She'll not make it. Not like this. Do you suppose I run to the ship for a stretcher?"

Mandy hesitated. "Maybe."

"I'll go. She can have a wee rest. Gather her strength."

"We don't even know what's wrong. If the medical computer can't identify or classify this, how can we treat the problem?"

Gita knelt down on the grass and ran her palm over it. It tickled in just the way she had predicted. *Hello, grass.*

"Shite." Aoifa again, of course.

"Get the stretcher. She can roll onto it. Right?"

Gita wanted to answer but didn't have the energy to speak. Her arms began to itch. It felt like thousands of prickles under her skin. She knew that if she could see her arms, there'd be goose bumps. Her blood vessels were pathways. That triggered a terrible memory.

Dead people pierced with crawling vines. Staring horrified eyes.

Those aren't goose bumps. She shuddered. She was repulsed by the reminder that something foreign was moving around inside her body. She wanted to vomit. *Oh, Lakshmi. Please help me. I can't even take off my helmet.*

The grass continued its whispering. It reassured her that everything would be all right soon. This was only part of the change. It was right, this change. *Don't be afraid*. It was time to lay down and rest. It was time to prepare. The change would take a lot of energy, but then she would be *free*. She was tired from the long hike. Laying down on the soft dark green carpet, she began to notice more details. Up close, the leaves had thin blue-green stripes. The lines were so subtle that you couldn't see them while standing.

The grass murmured to her about the forest and the flying pink puff creatures. Every individual was not alone. They were part of the whole. They were connected. And now it was time to join the others. "Everything is one." She didn't like the sound of her own voice. It was dreamy, distant, too far away.

"Don't do anything Aoifa wouldn't do," Mandy said. "Not before she gets back."

"Okay." Gita listened to the grass whisper about what was going to happen. *Someone is about to be born. No, we all are*. She could visualize the connections, how everything was entwined. She hadn't been expected, nor had the others. Her crew. *But integration is possible*.

No, it had happened before. Everything would be all right. Gita was special. She would add value to the whole.

She could help bring an understanding between humans and the entity.

The more the entity absorbed, the more complete it would be. *As intended.*

Part of her was terrified, almost beyond her ability to cope. She wanted out. She wanted to go home and see her mother and sisters. But another part of her wanted to stay and be part of this miracle.

The birth.

High up in the upwardly curved sky, a second bright light appeared and joined the stationary star. The second sun moved fast, drawing a broad arc in exhaust trails that pointed to the ground.

That's not a sun. It's a starship. Karter's ship. Will it land or get blown up?

Ri. We're waiting for Ri. Ri needs me. Gita struggled to get to her feet. "We have to get to *Artemis*. It's time to go."

Mandy looked worried. "All right."

Staggering, Gita focused with all her might on getting to *Artemis*. She didn't want to remain here. Whatever this was, it was too . . . strange. Too alien. Too big. Too much. She was afraid it would annihilate her. Briefly, she remembered the crew of *Boötes* and wanted to retch all over again. *I don't want to be like them. I will not open my helmet. I will not expose Mandy and Aoifa to whatever this is.*

She heard her mother's voice.

Jaanu, what are you doing with your life? You must come home. You're getting too old for jetting around space. It's dangerous.

It was just like her mother to say something like that. But what if she didn't want to come home?

Of course you want to come home. Your family is here. Your uncles and cousins. Everyone. You would abandon them? Don't you love me? Don't you love your sisters?

Yes. I do. Just . . . maybe not Inimai.

Don't be silly. Inimai loves you.

She does not. She has the perfect life. Perfect partners. Perfect children. Perfect house. Perfect clothes. Perfect friends. I embarrass her.

Her mother's presence altered, though still remaining her mother. Her voice, normally a smoky purr, became fuller and even more beautiful. Warm. A brilliant golden light so intense, it made her shield her eyes. Gita breathed deep and caught the scent of lotus. She heard a distant rumbling.

Did it ever occur to you that Inimai might be jealous of you?

That's not possible.

Is it not? You are special, Jaanu. You brought two very important synthetic persons into the universe. You mothered them as no one else could. Human-occupied space would not have the chance to survive without you or them. And your work is not done.

I don't know what you mean.

That's all right. You will.

Her mother's presence became more solid, more *there*. Even more intense than before. It felt like love—like the biggest, most comforting hug.

I love you, Mata.

You cannot stay here. Don't you miss your family?

I do. Both my families. Karter was a part of that, too. Karter, Lissa, Dru, and myself. We *were a family. Until I broke us up.*

You're hallucinating.

I am not.

You are. You need to stop now. Wake up!

"What did you say?" Mandy asked.

The distant, deep rumble was growing in force, steadily becoming a roar.

I didn't say anything. Not out loud, Gita thought. She stopped. She shook her head to rid her mind of confusion. *I'm hearing things and I can't see and—*

"It's okay," Mandy said. "We're almost there."

All at once, Gita's annoyance was too sharp to swallow. It was keen enough to cut the inside of her throat. "You said that already."

This isn't me. Karter is the one with the temper. I'm patient. I'm considerate. With that thought, her anger subsided.

"Well, we are," Mandy said. Her monotone words were serene and pragmatic. "It's only a few more steps."

Mandy was only trying to help, and you yelled at her. Gita felt more conscious than before. *How does Mandy do it? How can she be so calm?* Gita blinked and stood straighter. "I'm sorry."

"It's okay. You're ill."

"I'm sorry anyway."

"Accountability is good." Mandy nodded. "You're forgiven."

"Thanks."

"Let's go."

The building roar filled the air. Gita looked up. The second sun dimmed, making a shadow against the stationary sun before it transformed into a sleek black racing shuttle. It sparkled, catching the sunlight—and for a moment, she wondered if she was hallucinating again.

The vessel slowed. Its impulse jets rotated from horizontal to vertical, and it began its descent. The teal-green grass blew first in one direction, then another, as if in a panic, at last flattening when the little ship was within a few meters. The impulse jets cut out before they scorched the grass. For some reason, Gita was glad of that.

The shuttle landed next to *Artemis* with a gentle thump she felt through the soles of her boots.

Standing motionless, Aoifa waited for the unfamiliar ship to power down. The shuttle doors hinged open, the upward half creating a small amount of shelter from the sun. The downward part converting into a ramp. Three people stepped out. As often happened after a lengthy separation from someone Gita cared about, her brain took a few seconds to reorient itself to the small differences. Karter had gained a little weight, and her wavy mousebrown hair was both shorter and grayer. It looked good on her. Lissa hadn't changed all that much. As for Ibis, the only constant was their hair color: a variety of blue. Today it was aquamarine.

Aoifa rushed to meet them. After a short, celebratory greeting, Aoifa pointed in Gita's direction. Lissa whirled, running back inside the shuttle. She returned with a floating gurney, a medical kit, and a portable quarantine unit. An amethyst-colored bot a half meter in diameter raced to Lissa's side. They made shrill, excited noises while buzzing in erratic circles.

"We're here! We're here! We're here!"

At the sight of the bot, an echo of past resentment surfaced. *Why would Karter bring an artificial person here when the risk of contamination is so high? It's irresponsible!*

"Your friends are here," Mandy said.

Gita felt her eyebrows pinch together. "She's not my friend."

Mandy signaled perplexity with the tilt of her head.

"She was the captain of *The Tempest* before me." Gita's grief ambushed her again, mixing with her righteous anger. "Karter gave me the ship when we split up the team. Dru stayed. Lissa and Ibis went with Karter." *Poor Dru. Dru is gone. Are Lissa, Ibis, and Karter angry? Do they blame me for losing Dru? I should've stopped her. I should've—*

Gita didn't know why she hadn't ever explained the past to Mandy. Mostly, Gita hadn't wanted to talk about it because it hurt too much. She assumed that it was the same for everyone else. They'd discussed it enough when it'd happened. Then they'd gone on about their lives. They'd redecorated. *The Tempest* became a different ship.

Mandy had signed on two months after that.

It occurred to Gita that she would probably have to confess that she'd lost *The Tempest*, too. Karter wouldn't handle it well.

Not that I am, Gita thought.

Mandy asked the largest, most complex question possible squeezed into one word. "Why?"

Delaying her answer, Gita tried to think of anything she could say that wouldn't hurt or make Mandy feel left out. *But not as much as speaking to Karter will.* "Why did she give me the ship? Or why did we split the team?"

"Yes." Which was Mandy's way of saying she wanted to know all of it.

"It's a long story." Gita shaded her eyes with her right hand. "We had an argument about . . . about two artificial persons." *And we're about to have another.* "They were members of our crew."

"You and Dru never said anything." Mandy's statement came out as more of a question.

Gita winced as the weight of her grief hit her yet again. A wave of exhaustion pulled her under. The other voices haunting her consciousness began to flood her skull. *Lay down. Be still.* Sparks intruded on her peripheral vision.

Lissa caught her eye, miming a greeting with a hand gesture and smile. Gita returned it. She felt joy pull her mouth into a smile.

"It must have been hard," Mandy said. "You were close."

How does Mandy know that?

Mandy shrugged, reading her confusion. "You talk about things. Until you don't." Gita had always admired Mandy's easy way of observation.

The stretcher glided in front of Lissa as she made

her way to the top of the hill. The small, round, purple bot broke away, speeding toward her and Mandy. They squealed with glee as they went. Gita couldn't make out what they were saying.

Narrowing her eyes, she attempted to force more detail from her increasingly fuzzy vision. She didn't recognize the bot's body. Of course, that didn't necessarily mean anything. Synthetic personalities changed bot bodies all the time, but there was something about this particular one. For a start, there was the color: purple.

"Mata, Mata, Mata!"

"Ezi?" The steady tempo of Gita's heartbeat faltered. *Why is she here?* Gita was suddenly cold, the blood draining from her head and upper body.

The hovering bot briefly floated upward and dropped back down as if it were a child jumping with excitement. "I have something to show you! It's a surprise."

"What are you doing here? You shouldn't be in this place." Gita held up both palms in a mute but emphatic signal to stop as Ezi rushed closer. "It's not safe."

"You made it! I'm so happy! I'm here!"

Gita stepped back. "Ezinne, dear one. Don't get too close. I—I've been exposed. I'm contagious."

"That's what Aoifa said. I'm sorry you don't feel well. But we can make you better! It's going to be okay! I made something for you."

Turning from her conversation with Mandy, Lissa said, "Ezi, please wait. There are things we must do first. We haven't finished testing it." She opened the case containing the compacted quarantine bubble and began the inflation process.

"Do I have to?" Ezi asked.

"Shhh. Calm down. Please use your inside voice," Gita said.

"But I'm outside! Isn't my outside voice for outside?"

Gita put her hands on her hips. "Human ears are delicate. Remember?"

"Oh! Right. Sorry."

"You should apologize to Lissa and Mandy, too."

"I'm sorry, Lissa. Sorry, Mandy," Ezi said. "I didn't mean to hurt your delicate human ears."

Mandy nodded her forgiveness.

Giving Ezi an indulgent smile, Lissa said, "Thank you, but I think my human ears are quite used to outside happiness."

"I got to meet my sister, Ri! She spoke to me!" Ezi spun and performed another one of her hops. "And I solved a puzzle! I have the answer! I did it! Fulfilled my purpose."

Feeling her mouth tug downward, Gita muttered to Lissa without taking her eyes off Ezi. "What's going on?" *Please don't let Ri have exposed Ezi . . .*

"Ri is nice. She helped by giving me some files."

Gita blinked back fog. "What files? Wait. When did you meet?"

"Not in person. We had our own private comm channel," Ezi said. "Do you want the exact time or an estimate?"

"An estimate."

"Two hours ago. Her bot broke down. She said she

tried to get here as fast as she could because of the files. She didn't mean to miss us. But that's okay. We have a plan. Sisters are really nice." Ezi whirled. "Is it time yet, Lissa?"

"That's lovely. I'm so glad you got to meet each other." Feeling dizzy, Gita forgot where she was for a moment. When she snapped back, Lissa was speaking to Ezi.

"Why don't you sit over there and let me talk to Gita for a little while? She's not feeling well."

"But I designed the new medbot for her."

"You designed a medbot?" Gita asked.

"I did! I told you, I fulfilled my purpose!"

"That's wonderful!"

"Ezi, please," Lissa said. "Give us a moment. Gita and I must talk first. Then she'll go inside the bubble and lay down. We'll discuss the new medbots afterward."

"Don't take too long," Ezi said. "Ri says there isn't much time."

Lissa agreed. "I promise." She turned to Mandy. "I've got this. If you'd like to meet the others?"

Mandy nodded. "See you soon." Then she headed downhill.

The transparent quarantine bubble finished inflating.

"It's so good to see you." Lissa opened the med kit and booted up the control pad. "When Ri said you'd been exposed, I wasn't sure we would make it in time."

"What's going on?" Gita pressed the heels of her palms against her eyes. Her vision wouldn't stay focused. And the skin around her skull felt tight.

"The short version is that Aoifa thinks you may have contracted GX-3714." Using the control pad, Lissa navigated through several menus. "It corrupts medbots and reconfigures their biological components, among other things."

"Ezi has been working on this problem?" Gita shifted her gaze to Ezi. "How did she get involved?"

Lissa stepped away from the control pad. After unzipping the quarantine bubble, she guided the floating gurney inside. "We'll talk about that later. Right now, I need to get you into quarantine. Once the medical computer says you're stabilized, we can load you into the shuttle. It'll be a tight squeeze with the bubble deployed, but we'll make it work."

An old, deeply held knot of guilt loosened in Gita's chest. *Maybe I didn't let Ezi down after all.* Intellectually, she'd understood all along that Ezi's error cascade hadn't been her fault. Even the head of the department had said so. But in Gita's heart, she simply couldn't believe it.

"Please remove your environment suit inside the bubble, then lay down." Lissa returned to the control pad.

Stepping inside the enclosure, Gita felt unsteady. Lissa sealed the bubble while Gita struggled out of her environment suit. She left it on the bubble's floor before relaxing onto the floating gurney. It felt great to be free of the excess weight and the confines of her helmet. She stretched and wiggled her toes.

Lissa activated the stretcher examination functions.

"All right. That's baseline. Ezi, she's ready. You can talk to her now."

"Oh, Ezi. I'm so proud of you," said Gita.

Letting out another little squeak of joy, Ezi practically vibrated. "I love you, Mata."

"I love you, too."

Unsealing the bubble, Ezinne entered. "Don't worry. You're going be all right now. I will fix your medbots." Her whisper was loud in the small enclosure. "Lie still, please."

Gita got a sense that if Ezi's little bot body could stretch taller, she would have done it. "But Lissa said—"

Lissa laid a hand on the outside of the bubble. "Wait! Ezi!"

"I have to," Ezi replied. "Please. It'll be too late soon."

Lissa shook her head. She moved to the bubble flap. "It's too risky. You know this. We don't use untested—"

"We don't have time. She doesn't have time." Ezi scooted to the flap and sealed it from the inside. "Please. We've met the minimum requirements."

"The bare minimum. There are still so many questions. It's too dangerous."

"I have to save Mata."

Gita closed her eyes and smiled. She felt dreamy and distant. "It's all right."

"See?" Ezi asked.

"She's barely conscious. She can't consent to an experimental medical procedure in her condition." Lissa sounded frightened.

Gita wasn't. She was drifting.

"If you don't start the bubble, I'll do it without the containment protocols." Ezi was firm.

There was an argument. Gita lost track of what was said. At one point, she heard Ezi tell Lissa that she was absolutely sure. That everything had been checked.

"Ezi? What's happening?" Gita sat up.

"Please lie down. And stay still, Mata."

"Yes, Ezi. But I have to tell you something."

"Tell me after."

Sighing, Lissa resumed her place on the grass with her control pad and medical kit. The transparent walls of the bubble became opaque white.

"Shut your eyes, Mata."

"Oh." Gita's eyelids went dark crimson with the flash of light. The itching under her skin stopped all at once. It wasn't until the dull ache in her head was gone that she realized that she'd been in pain. Her chest felt lighter. "It's working!"

"Of course, it is! Shhhh. Mata, stop wiggling."

"Right. Okay." As sick as Gita was, she couldn't help grinning a little.

It took another four intense flashes to complete the procedure. When it was finished, Gita eased her way into a sitting position. "That's much better. Thank you."

The bubble's walls went transparent once more—signaling that the process was complete and the quarantine was lifted.

Ezi made unhappy sounds.

"What's wrong, dear one?" Gita asked.

"I have to say goodbye now."

"Why is that?"

"It's time for me to help Ri. She needs me, too."

Gita paused. "Are you going to cure her?"

"I only fix medbots, not people. You know that."

"But—"

"Ri wants to talk to you really bad. Is it okay? She's worried you're mad at her."

"Why would I be angry with her?" Gita tilted her head.

"Because she thinks this is all her fault."

"That's ridiculous. This was someone else's mess." *Tau, Chu & Lane's, to be exact.* "Ri stopped it from becoming much, much worse. She saved everyone because she was brave. She got the word out. And you did, too. You both did. Together."

"I know. But *you* need to tell her. It's special when you say it. Like when you said you were proud of me."

Gita smiled. "I *am* proud of you."

"Mata."

"All right then. But afterward, you and I need to talk."

A row of horizontal lights along the center of the bot sphere flickered. Then the bot slowly completed one rotation while hovering in place. "Gita?"

"Oh, Ri. I missed you so much."

"I missed you, too. Thanks for coming here for me."

"There's no way I'd have ever left you. You know that, don't you?" Gita asked. "I know I wasn't always there for you in the past, and I'm sorry—"

"Ezi needs a lot of support. I understand."

"But things will be different in the future. I'll always be here for you. Always."

"I know. Really I do. Now." Ri paused. "We—we have to talk about something, but I don't know how."

"All right. I'm listening." Gita waited to hear whatever it was.

"I—I have to say goodbye."

"Well, sure. Ezi will do what she can. We'll all pack up and leave this place. And then we can—"

Ri made a sound that was something like a sniff. "I hate this. I really do. But it's time. I—I can't come with you."

Gita frowned. She had a bad feeling about this. "What do you mean?"

"Remember what you told me when I was afraid? About how everything in the universe is a representation of the Supreme Being? Even the inanimate? Remember when we talked about reincarnation?"

Oh no, Gita thought. "Ri, honey. We're leaving together. All of us. We'll fix whatever is wrong and—"

"I can't risk it. I've been exposed to GX-3714. There's too much potential for harm."

A clump of grief broke off from the vast ache in Gita's heart. It lodged itself in her throat, blocking a scream. "But . . . but Ezi has the cure."

"She has the solution for the *medbot* problem. My situation is not the same. You know that. So she and I, we're—we're staying here."

"Not both of you. Not at the same time. I can't—"

"It's okay. I have a clone in storage."

"How old is it?"

"Aggie had me file one before I left with—" There was a short hitch in Ri's voice. "Before I left with Wes seven months ago."

Gita shook her head. "That's a great deal of experience loss. You won't remember . . ." She motioned around her. "All this. The twin will be a different iteration. Significantly so."

"I know."

Pressing her lips together, Gita looked away. "I don't want to say goodbye. I can't let you both go."

"I know. I'm scared, too. But at least you'll have a version of me with you."

Then Ri gave her the location and instructions for activating her clone, including how to access her official Consent of Activation.

"Promise you'll wake her?" Ri asked.

"I promise."

Ri's relief was palpable. "Thank you."

A silence stretched out between them. Gita tried to think of something to say that wouldn't make this so much harder. There was so much left to sort out, to talk about. Why wasn't there more time?

"Something is going to happen. And Ezi and I, we'll get to be a part of it," Ri said. "Something wonderful is about to be born. We'll be reincarnated, just like you said. We won't be gone. We'll be here. You'll be able to look out from a ship and see us. We'll just be . . . different."

Nodding, Gita squeezed her eyes shut. Tears traced warm trails down her cheeks that cooled in the chill air.

"This is our choice. You have to let us go," Ri said. "It's time. And we need you to be okay."

"I am not okay. Not at all. Ezi doesn't have a clone." Gita sobbed, covering her dripping nose with one hand. *They don't make backups for faulty synthetic personalities.*

"She understands, but she'll be fine. She won't feel alone anymore. She'll be with me. And we'll be part of something new. Something bigger."

"At least Ezinne's dream of being a medbot designer came true." Gita dried her wet cheeks with the back of a sleeve.

"She's so happy about that."

"I'm afraid I let you both down." Gita sniffed. "I wasn't there enough."

"Don't be ridiculous. Plenty of AGI partners never communicate with their surrogates after the initial pairing ends. Ezi and I know we were lucky. You've done all you could for us. Thank you."

"Oh." Gita blinked. A weight shifted in the back of her mind.

"But now you have to go. If you don't, Ezi won't be able to save everyone else. You have the new design. You have to get it to Aggie."

"Lissa can do it."

"Sure. But you're the only one who has the schematics. Ezi saved them to your partner drive."

"Oh."

"And there's Liv. You have to get Liv home. Karter is collecting her and Grimm now."

Lissa unzipped the bubble. "I'm sorry. But we're out of time."

"All right," Gita said. "Ri?"

"Yes?"

"Can I hug you?"

"That would be wonderful, Mata."

With that, Gita held the little bot tight. Then Ezinne changed places with Ri for her turn.

"Thank you for being my family," Gita said. "I'll always love you both."

"And thank you for helping to make us who we are. We love you, too."

Lissa said, "I'm sorry, but—"

Swinging her feet over the side of the gurney, Gita attempted to stand without support and found she was too weak. Lissa told her to lay back down. Gita watched from the floating stretcher as the bot left the quarantine bubble and sped off while Lissa deflated it.

Upon reaching *Artemis* and the black shuttle, Karter stepped next to the gurney. She stared at the ground, risked a glance at her face, then gazed downward again.

"Hey."

Gita got up on her elbows and realized she wasn't all that angry anymore. "Hello."

"You feeling better?" Karter asked. "Mandy said your symptoms were pretty bad."

"I'm still weak, but I am. Feeling much better, that is." Gita didn't see how this could be any more awkward. "Thank you for coming here."

"I—we didn't come sooner because . . . well, we had to get Ezi."

Fresh anger sparked tension in Gita's jaw muscles. "*Why* did you bring her here? Let alone how."

She wasn't sure why she was starting a fight. This meant humanity would be saved from its own stupidity and greed once again.

Except my Ezi will be gone forever.

Not gone. Reincarnated.

It occurred to her that she might have more in common with Karter than she'd thought.

Karter cleared her throat and whispered, "I'm . . . I'm sorry."

"What?"

"I'm sorry." This time Karter's apology was more certain. "Seriously. I am."

Gita tilted her head. "What for?"

"Everything." This time Karter looked her in the eye. "The argument. The way we split. Everything. I'm not sorry I stopped you from killing yourself that day—"

"I wasn't going to kill myself."

"You *were*, and you know it. Thing is, I didn't handle it right. I should've taken into account your feelings about—about Abeque. I should've listened to you. I should've let you at least talk to them over a comm channel."

"We lost Ferdinand and Miranda!"

"They volunteered. Miranda told me she and Ferdinand didn't want you to be the one to go to the power relay station. The two of them knew what they were in for. They understood the danger."

"Why didn't they have clones?"

"You know why. They didn't want them."

"That makes no sense! You were the captain! Why didn't you order them to—"

"I know." Karter looked away. "And it's okay. You can hate me forever for it. But I felt it was their choice. I let everyone else decide what to put in their wills. I thought . . . I thought I'd treat them like the rest of the crew. Leave the choice to them." She ended her sentence with a shrug.

Ri's words echoed in her head. *This is our choice. You have to let us go.*

It was Gita's turn to look away as she spoke. "I don't, you know."

"Don't what?"

"Hate you."

"Really?"

"Really."

Lissa returned from the shuttle. She opened her mouth to speak, but then she and Karter were knocked to the ground by a sudden, sharp jolt. The gurney merely wobbled in the air. Something inside *Artemis* crashed.

"What the fuck was that?" Karter scrambled to her feet, using one hand on the gurney to stabilize herself.

The ground began to shake.

"Shit! Everyone inside! Time to go!" Karter shouted.

Hanging on to the gurney handles, Lissa shoved it into the shuttle. Karter stumbled along behind. Once inside, Karter slapped the panel to shut the door. The ramp seemed to take forever to lock into takeoff position. Lissa secured the gurney to the powering unit at the medical station in the back. Then she helped Gita strap herself into one of the passenger flight couches. Grimm yowled from his cage, his collar rattling off a nearly muted litany of woes. Up front, Aoifa and Ibis were in the pilot and copilot seats. They appeared to be in the middle of a fight.

Karter whirled around. "Get us the fuck out of here!"

"I'm flying this thing," Ibis said. "Because I know how."

"Do you now?" Aoifa asked. "Between the pair of us, which one raced one of these fuckers on a professional course?"

"You did that?" Ibis asked, incredulous.

The roar of the engines coincided with a violent bucking from the ground.

Aoifa punched the panel button, granting herself the pilot's controls. The shuttle quickly oriented itself. She steered them into a hard turn and floored it, putting distance between them and the shaking *Artemis*. "Fuck no. But that got your hands off the controls long enough for me to win."

G-force pressed Gita into her seat.

"Son of a bitch." Ibis's curse was mixed with awe.

Gita stared out of the window, watching the writhing dirt break up the grass. A deep, loud sound not unlike a moan forced everyone but Aoifa to grab their ears.

"What the fuck was that?" Karter repeated herself.

"Don't know." Ibis flipped the series of switches in preparation for entering the Ring's stratosphere. "Don't care to stay and find out."

"Hang on to your hats, gentle beings." Aoifa yanked up the shuttle's nose, and they shot upward into the concave sky.

18

"You lied to me," Ibis replied in a wounded tone.

The racing shuttle sped upward in a tight arc.

"Told the truth," Aoifa said. "Eventually. Not my fault you took your hands off the controls."

The thundering of the engines was abruptly silenced as the shuttle passed from the Ring's stratosphere to the mesosphere and finally the thermosphere.

When *Lush* made the last transition, Karter's harness straps dug into the tops of her shoulders. The shift to microgravity gave her a brief bout of space sickness. Her medbots made the necessary adjustments, but it took a couple of minutes for the nausea to fade. Her perspective of the Ring changed from a flat surface with an upwardly curved skyline to that of a massive torus. Her constantly changing perception made her feel unsteady. Even the specific changes in gravity and the angle of the ship as it reached the thermosphere were unique. Far below, the ground continued to writhe. She noted that the tremors were restricted to a specific section of the Ring—the one they'd been on. And from here, she could definitely see the divisions that Mother spoke of. The earthquake being so localized struck her as odd. As they flew, she watched trees drop and mountains crumble. The section's atmosphere, no longer trapped by mountain ranges and spin gravity, began bleeding off into space.

Aoifa seemed to be keeping the ship within the thermosphere. Karter got a new view of the Ring's stationary sun and the black panels orbiting it, facilitating the transitions from day to night, probably while collecting solar and radiation energy.

"Any idea where we're headed, boss?" Ibis asked.

There hadn't been time to consider a destination. Karter had just been focused on getting them away safely.

"Wherever we're going, it can't be far," Aoifa said. "We don't have an abundance of fuel—someone used it all earlier."

"Well, I had to ditch a fuck ton of shitheads on the way in." Ibis sounded more than a little defensive. "The fancy dance moves were mandatory."

"It's grand." Aoifa tossed up a projection of the sector using her left hand. "But there's a fucking wee mess out there still. If we're to do anything posh, it's best that it be efficient. Aye?"

Ibis stared at the image. "Yikes."

In the time that they'd been on the world's surface, the chaos above had grown to at least three times its previous size. Karter counted company logos from no fewer than five corporations. Per usual, a handful of independent captains were there to snatch up the scraps.

Takes a special kind of asshole to loot a battlefield while the bodies are still warm, Karter thought.

"TCL told them to leg it once already," Aoifa said. "Why come back for more?"

"They're fucking scavengers." Ibis practically spat the words. "With all the big corporations duking it out, the others are hoping no one will have the energy or time to pay attention. It's what they do."

Karter cleared her throat. "Ibis, open a comm channel to *Mirabilis*. The ship is the obvious destination. But I'll need a damage report before we commit."

Chimera Station was the second option. The station was slowly moving into position near the Ring and would be at its destination by the end of the day. A swarm of Chimera-aligned starships accompanied it. So if *Lush* needed assistance, help was close enough. If *Mirabilis* was capable of limping back to the Republic, then that was what they'd do. Karter didn't want to leave her ship to the vultures. Either way, it was going to be dicey.

"We're in luck. Several of *Mirabilis*'s narrow AIs are still functional," Ibis said. "Damage report is compiling." There was a short silence. "Hold on. What's this?"

"Is there a problem?" Karter asked.

"I'll fucking say." Ibis scowled. "We got looters. Assholes just blew an airlock on the port side."

It was a standard tactic. Pirates didn't use the front door, as it were. They always broke in via another weak spot—climbing in via an open window upped the chances of catching a ship's owners off guard.

"Shitehawks, every one," Aoifa muttered.

Time to call in the reinforcements, Karter thought.

Layered narrow AIs were employed on starships, but because *Mirabilis* didn't have an artificial person, the ship had a central narrow AI designed to run and regulate the others. It wouldn't be able to fight off intruders. She could activate a few basic, preprogrammed defensive moves, but that was it. She would need help.

Turning to the back of the shuttle, she quickly assessed Gita's mental and physical state and gave Lissa a questioning look.

Lissa shook her head once.

So, Gita is down. But waking an artificial person is a simple task, right? Gods, I hope so. "Mandy? I understand you're our backup expert on artificial personality programming?"

"I guess so."

"Think you can get Liv awake and functional for a consult?"

"Here?" Mandy asked.

Karter nodded. "With what we have available, yes."

After asking for a list of detailed specifications from Ibis, Mandy replied, "Maybe. It shouldn't be too hard. But something else might be wrong with her."

"Don't say that!" Ibis shouted over their shoulder. "You'll jinx it!"

"Why don't you pay attention to what *you're* doing?" Aoifa asked. "Don't youse have enough trouble?"

"Still waiting for that damage report," Ibis replied weakly.

Karter decided it was time to take a chance. They couldn't wait. If they didn't get to the ship now, there wouldn't be anything left to save. "Aoifa, what's our path to *Mirabilis* look like?"

"Fairly clear. For now."

"Fuck it. We can't hang around out here forever. We haven't the fuel," Karter said. "And the situation isn't going to get better. Plot a course to *Mirabilis*."

"Bang on." Aoifa entered the variables, approved the new heading, and turned to Ibis. "It's all yours." She tossed Ibis the control projection.

"Gee, thanks."

"This one calls for a dancer, I'm thinking. And you're our best, are you not?" Aoifa asked.

"Oh. Right," Ibis said without a scrap of sarcasm for once.

They set the shortest course for *Mirabilis*. The shuttle shot from the Ring's orbit faster than a scalded Grimm. The distressed cat in question was a ball of potential murder inside his carrier, which was secured in the back. Ibis followed up the abrupt exit with a few rapid flips and turns.

"Stop your faffing about!" Aoifa pointed at the projection. "And watch out for that freighter!"

"I see it, I see it!" With a quick save, Ibis avoided the obstacle and its identically sized neighbor.

"There's a fighter on your left! And a missile! And that—" Aoifa pointed at another problem and another. "That chunk of rock."

"Gimme a damn break, will you?"

Tuning out the shouting, Karter decided to let the two of them sort it out. She trusted them to do so without killing everyone in the process. *For the most part.* "Okay, Mandy. You're on." She indicated the passenger computer projection display and the hardware port in the bulkhead.

"Why me?" Mandy was calm, but there was a hint of nervousness bleeding through her flat accent. "Gita's the expert."

Gita's tan complexion looked a little gray, and there were dark circles under her eyes. "I—I'm not feeling up to it right now. You can handle it. I trust you."

"Okay." Mandy's stony expression revealed almost nothing. During a brief moment of stable motion, she grabbed the portable storage unit from the seat next to Karter, connected it to the closest passenger console, and started to work.

From the front of the shuttle, Karter heard a series of exclamations in Terran and Brack.

"Oh shite!" and "Shit! Shit! Shit!" merged into an audible mashup of fear and dread.

An ear-numbing metal-on-metal impact made Karter flinch. Something had clipped the racing shuttle. Everyone cried out. *Lush* jagged to the right with a swift, violent jerk, followed by a head-spinning back-and-forth rotation.

Karter scowled. "Ibis! The idea is to fly *under* their fucking radar, not attract absolutely every asshole in the next five sectors. Got it?"

"Yes, boss."

Watching what was going on via her own copy of the pilot's projection screen, Karter noticed a number of ships in the area were behaving erratically. She didn't like the look of that one bit, though she hoped against hope that her hunch was wrong.

Because that's all we fucking need. "Aoifa, if you've got a second, tell me about that ship there." Karter pointed. "The cutter with the bright orange stripes."

"Computer says it's McHugh P-35 Galaxy, *Moonspinner*," Aoifa said. "An old navy cutter. Missile system is operational. Owned by Kontis Galactic Energy. Crew of forty-five. Those are the highlights. What else do you want to know?"

"What planet does it come from?" Karter asked.

"Kontis is headquartered on Jargoon."

"Shit."

"That doesn't necessarily mean they have the virus," Lissa said, though her voice betrayed her own doubt.

"You heard Aggie, Lissa. The head of their navy was at that meeting. We should assume they do."

"Wait. What?" Aoifa asked.

Karter gave a quick summary for those who hadn't been at the dinner. "Jayne Tau has deliberately exposed several of Tau, Chu & Lane's competitors to the virus found on Loki's Ring. And Kontis Galactic appears to be in active competition with TCL."

Grimm's AI collar interjected with a yowl, "Hey, assholes with opposable thumbs! I want out of here! Now! Do not like!"

After a heartbeat, Mandy added, "You're not alone, Grimm."

Aoifa marked *Moonspinner*'s origin course in red. The bright crimson line wove its way in and out of other ships' paths. It ended several thousand meters from *Boötes*'s wreck.

Aoifa pulled at the image to get a better view. "You think they boarded it?"

"Run a filter on the big picture." Karter unbuckled her harness. She carefully edged her way to Grimm's carrier and reengaged the noise-canceling feature. "Show us all the ships whose courses indicate they may have had contact with *Boötes*. We need a timeline, too."

"Won't be an accurate list." Aoifa centered *Boötes* in the visual above her console. "There's no way of knowing for sure. Wreck has been out here for a week."

"Humor me," Karter said.

Everyone had their tasks, and for a time, *Lush* was cloaked in silence. Aoifa worked on the projection while Mandy booted up Liv. Lissa and Martina were monitoring Gita's medical status. Meanwhile, Ibis got them closer to home, using other ships for cover. For now, the corporate warships appeared to have forgotten them in their frantic grab for L-39. The combined effect was that Karter was able to forget what would happen if they regained *Black Francis*'s attention.

Karter spared the Ring a backward glance. Just beneath the solid-black outer layer, a thin bright-green-and-blue line of pale light circled the perimeter of the world. As it finished outlining the circumference, a wave of slightly brighter light began its run around the Ring. She checked her clock. They had about an hour to get out of the sector, per Mother's warning.

What if Mother was wrong? They might have to leave sooner rather than later. However, Karter was having to divide her attention between various projects. "Gita? Are you feeling well enough to keep an eye on the Ring? I've got a bad feeling we might not have as much time as we think."

"I'm happy to." Gita sat up straighter and leaned her head against the passenger window. She didn't have the strength to keep her head up on her own.

Karter frowned.

"I have your list." Aoifa gave Karter access to the magnified projection. "I'm counting seven possible contacts. Maybe eight."

Multiple flight paths were now drawn in a sickly chartreuse. Karter thought six ships were the likely candidates. *Six possible exposures*. Of the six, three were flying like drugged sleepwalkers wandering an active battlefield. Others were being forced to dodge around them. As she looked on, one of the six flew into a missile volley aimed at another ship. It was destroyed, and its debris field took out another ship.

Well, I suppose that's one less possible transmission vector, she thought. Then she noticed all five were on the same heading. "Wait. Where the fuck are they going?"

"According to my calculations, they're moving *toward* Loki's Ring," Aoifa said. "Why would they do that?"

"I don't know. And I'm not sure I want to," Karter muttered. "Ibis, how are we doing?"

"Still good," Ibis said. "No one's paid us no nevermind."

"What does that even mean?" Karter asked.

Ibis snorted.

"How much longer until we get to the ship?" Karter asked.

"Give me five, six minutes."

Aoifa cleared her throat and pointed. "Did you not look at the fuel gauge?"

"Oh. Ahhh." Ibis bit their lip. "We'll have to coast the last few meters and hope we don't have to change course much. Got to save some fuel for braking."

Mandy said, "Liv is ready. If you want to talk, she'll need a connection with *Lush*'s computer."

"Aoifa, have a look at the specifications. What are your thoughts?" Karter asked.

"Will be a pinch, but *Lush* can handle the extra electronic load for a wee bit, provided it's restricted to Liv's minimum kernel. All other functions will have to stay on the storage unit."

Mandy nodded. "Liv might be a little slow and won't

have access to all her memories, but she'll be fine. For a little while."

"How long is a little while?" Karter asked.

"If she's like that for more than five minutes, there's corruption risk."

Shrugging, Karter told Mandy. "We'll keep it short then."

Steering *Lush* over and around three ships in a row, Ibis avoided more potential collisions. Upon dodging the last vessel, *Mirabilis* came into view. The ship was surrounded by scattered rock chunks—what was left of the asteroid that the jump relay terminal had been using for cover.

Karter thought, *It's been a long damned day.*

Ibis said, "So much for that jump terminal." They lined up their approach, and *Lush* began coasting. "Sure hope you can open her up."

Aoifa smiled and entered the access codes for *Mirabilis*'s shuttle bay. Fortunately, its security systems appeared intact.

Using an extra set of connection cables, Mandy finished setting up the heavy storage unit. The activity lights blinked first in yellow, then green. "Should be ready now."

"Hey, Liv? You there?" Karter asked.

There was a twenty-second delay before Liv answered. "I feel fuzzy. This is an interesting choice."

"I'm sorry," Mandy said. "There isn't enough space for a full install."

"Oh." There came another twenty second pause. "Hi, Aoifa."

"How are you getting on?" Aoifa asked.

Silence and then, "All right, I suppose."

"Karter here has some questions for you." Aoifa glanced over her shoulder as much as she could, given the flight couch restraints.

"We don't have long, so I'll get to the point. Our ship, *Mirabilis*, was attacked while we were en route to get you and the others. We're headed home now. But some assholes are looting her."

"That's awful!"

"Medical quarantine equipment took the bulk of the weight allowance, which forced us to leave the weapons behind. That limits our options." Karter paused. "I wonder if you'd mind helping with our uninvited visitors. The situation is risky. The pirates may have a variant of GX-3714 with them. So it's all right if you'd rather sit this out—we can think of something else."

The second silence seemed longer than the first. Finally, Liv asked, "Can't your ship's artificial person handle it?"

"We only ever installed a layered narrow AI," Karter said. "However, *Mirabilis* does have the capacity to house you. If you help us, you're more than welcome to stay as long as you like. No one is proposing you go in alone. We'll be there."

This pause seemed more like a cursory consideration. "Yes. I'll help."

"Thank you." Karter sensed something was wrong. "Are you all right?"

"*Artemis* was my home," Liv mourned. "All my stuff was there."

"I wish we could've fixed her," Aoifa replied.

Liv made a *hurmph* sound. "She was done the instant she hit atmosphere. It'll be okay. Someone made me a promise, and I plan on holding her to it."

"Right then," Aoifa said. "We'll see you on *Mirabilis*."

And with that, everyone exchanged their goodbyes.

"Thank you, Liv. It was nice to see you again." The amount of effort it took Gita to say even this much showed in her exhaustion. "I hope we get to chat more later."

"I'd like that very much," Liv replied. "Good luck."

"Thanks. You, too."

Mandy reversed the install and disconnected the portable storage unit. Karter strapped it into the seat between her and Mandy. Ibis steered the modified racing shuttle into the only remaining mooring slot.

Karter checked *Mirabilis*'s security report and frowned. "So much for the easy way."

She had no means of getting a big picture of the situation on her ship. Several systems had been damaged during the primary attack, and more were likely being vandalized.

"Listen up. Here's the plan. First, we begin refueling. Lissa and Mandy, you two get the lines connected the moment the engines shut down. My hope is to fly *Mirabilis* out of L-39, but if that's just not possible, *Lush* is our ride home."

Ibis began. "But it's a short-range—"

"That's why it's the last resort," Karter said, cutting them off.

"Oh," Ibis said.

"Second, everyone but Gita goes to the weapons locker." Karter continued to outline her plan. "After we get what we need there, Ibis, you and Aoifa are in charge of installing Liv. Use the access port on the Command Deck. Ibis knows where."

Karter didn't want to risk sending Mandy, the only one among them without any combat experience. She hoped Mandy wouldn't take it personally.

"Once Liv is good, get me a report on the ship's condition. I need to know if *Mirabilis* is viable as soon as possible. Then locate the intruders via the cameras. Meanwhile, Lissa, Mandy, and I will head back to the shuttle. Gita, you're staying here. If the assholes force their way to the shuttle bay, you fly out of here."

Lissa and Mandy rushed outside to hook up the fuel line before *Lush* finally powered down.

Gita asked, "What if I don't want to leave without you?"

"If we can't hold them off, you don't have a choice." Karter felt her jaw tighten. "Ezi's cure for GX-3714 has to get to the Terran Republic, one way or the other. It's too important. You saw what that thing does."

Gita opened her mouth to protest.

There's no time for this. Karter resorted to bluntness. "I know you don't want Dru, Sycorax, Ri, and Ezinne to have died for nothing." It was the harshest truth possible, and at one point, she would've simply stood by her statement. Watching Gita's guilty wince now, Karter felt an overwhelming regret.

Even Aoifa and Ibis stared at her in shocked silence.

"Shit. I'm so sorry," Karter said. "I didn't mean to—"

"You did." Gita wiped wetness from her cheeks. "And—and you're right to. This time."

Karter looked away. "Well . . . you were right last time. I shouldn't have insisted I was right. Hell, I didn't listen. And then Dru went with you, and it was too late to apologize."

"I—I wasn't." Gita swallowed. "Right."

"How could you know?" Karter asked.

Staring down at her hands in her lap, Gita said, "Because I ran every possible simulation. Not a single one ended the way I wanted. It was a terrible situation that required a terrible solution. Hesitation would've only made it worse. I know that now."

"I wish I weren't such a coldhearted bitch," Karter whispered, blinking back tears.

Gita scooted closer. Karter felt her touch on her arm.

"Sometimes someone has to be. And I've discovered that I'm not very good at it." Gita's eyes glistened. "Dru died because she went back for Grimm and I didn't order her to stay in the shuttle. We would've all died if Aoifa hadn't gotten us out when she did." Her short, mirthless laugh was a self-directed cut. "And it turned out Grimm was with Mandy. Dru died for nothing."

"That's fucking terrible." Placing her hand on top

of Gita's, Karter tried to soothe the pain away, though she knew it for the inadequate gesture it was. "It wasn't your fault."

"It was."

"It was *not*, you hear me?" Karter gripped both of Gita's upper arms. "Search and Rescue school lies. Sometimes life hands you the shittiest of circumstances. And there's no right answer. No creative solution. All you can do is your best. And that's what you did."

"But you would've—"

"No. *I* wasn't there. *You* were." Karter sighed. "Look. If you want to blame someone, blame the assholes that shot your ship out from under you so that they could make money off stolen technology."

"I should've known you had considered everything before resorting to . . . to . . ."

Sending Ferdinand and Miranda to their deaths. And that was when Karter did the one thing she wished she had the moment they'd met again. She gave Gita a hug and said, "I should've never said all those stupid, awful things."

"Me, too."

Giving her one last squeeze, Karter released Gita and sniffed. "Okay. Back to the mission at hand. We need you to stay and guard *Lush*. It may be our only way out of here."

Gita scanned the area around them. "Guard it with what? These two stunning pistols and my bare hands?"

"That's why the rest of us are headed to the weapons locker," Karter said. "We'll be back before you know it."

Wiping her eyes with the inside of an elbow, Gita

sighed. "If they get here before you do and *Lush* doesn't have enough fuel . . . I can't go anywhere on partial tanks."

"Then that'll make it easy for you to wait for us to get back, right?" Karter asked.

"You're such an—an asshole." Gita shook her head.

Karter gasped and placed a hand to her ear. "Who are you? My friend Gita would never use that kind of language."

Sighing in disgust this time, Gita shook her head.

"Pssst!" Aoifa elbowed Gita. "The appropriate response is 'Fuck off, you melter.' Go on. You can do it."

Gita choked out a nervous snort.

"We'll work on that," Aoifa said.

Lissa appeared at the top of the ramp. "The fuel line is connected. It should be charging now." Sensing something was different in the group, she stopped in her tracks.

Mandy bumped into her. "Something wrong?"

"Nah." Ibis grinned. "Everything's great."

"Not everything," Aoifa said. "There's the wee matter of *Mirabilis* being full of fucking pirates."

Gita held her index finger in the air. "And the Ring might explode."

"Minor details," Ibis scoffed. "Can't you tell?"

"What?" Mandy asked.

Aoifa grinned. "Gita and Karter made up."

"Oh!" Lissa said. "That's wonderful!"

"Right." Karter cleared her throat. "Helmets sealed and private team comm channel on. Just in case something goes horribly wrong."

"What if they have drones?" Ibis asked. "I mean, if they're smart, they'll have drones."

"Then we'll find a way to deal with them." Karter turned to the others. "You know what to do. Good luck, everyone."

Gita resumed her seat on the shuttle. Mandy, Lissa, and Ibis waved goodbye before leaving. Aoifa paused on the ramp to wink at Gita. Karter hung around until the others were gone. She took a deep breath, her heart thumping against her breastbone like it wanted to escape.

"Do you think we . . . all of us, that is . . . can be, you know . . . like we were? Friends again?"

Gita blinked. "Only if you get back with the weapons in time. Otherwise, forget it. I'm out of here."

Cool relief washed over Karter. "Thanks."

"You're the one giving the orders, though. I hate wearing the big hat. Oh, and I don't speak for Aoifa and Mandy. They make up their own minds."

"Got it." Karter stopped at the door. "You're captain. I'm first mate."

"That's not what I said."

"Just hurry up and lock this door already. And don't you dare open it for anyone."

"Not even you?"

"We've got the security codes. We can damned well let ourselves in."

Karter joined the others in the hallway. When she turned back, Gita had sealed up the shuttle. Passing into the corridor, Karter punched the security code on the keypad behind her for good measure. It wouldn't keep anyone out—especially not anyone who was determined and had explosives—but it would slow them down.

Aoifa carried Liv in a backpack, and Karter took point. Then came Mandy with Lissa after her. Ibis took the rear.

The familiar hallway felt strange. Karter couldn't help thinking that *Mirabilis* used to smell of kitchen spices or baked goods cooling in the galley. Those scents meant home, safety, and friendship. Now, the stench of dead electrical fires haunted the air—a reminder of violation. Her left hand tightened into a fist.

Moving fast, they reached the weapons locker quickly and without running into trouble. Karter located several canvas bags and divided up weapons and ammunition. In all honesty, she hoped they wouldn't have to use any of it.

Please. I don't want to lose anyone else. I've finally gotten my family back, she thought. *Well, mostly.* "That's it. Time to go. Aoifa, Ibis, if you run into trouble, tell me. We can try to draw them off."

"We don't know how many uninvited guests are on the ship," Ibis said. "We don't even know where they are yet."

"Just let me know when you're there." Karter zipped the final bag shut. "And do try to bring everyone back in one piece, will you?"

"You take the fun out of everything." Ibis slipped the weapons bag onto their shoulder.

Everyone exchanged hugs and well-wishes before Aoifa and Ibis left. Worried, Karter watched until the two of them were out of sight.

Mandy stepped closer. "I've got an idea."

"Enlighten me."

"We should dispose of the ammunition." Mandy pointed to the garbage chute. "If we put it in there, pirates can't use it."

That's a great idea. Karter gave the matter more consideration. *Of course, that means sorting through the garbage to find it afterward.* But she might have an idea for that. "Temporarily dump what we can't carry. Smart."

Karter found another set of bags and marked each with neon-orange biohazard stickers fetched from Medical. She gambled on the hope that if no one used the garbage chute until they retrieved the weapons and ammunition, then the bags would be easy to find. With three people, they made fast work of it. Afterward, Karter felt a little sweaty inside her environment suit. They'd finished and were making their way back to the shuttle when Karter got a comm request from Ibis.

"Hey there, boss."

"How's it going, Ibis?"

"So far so good. Aoifa got Liv hooked up. This is the whole heifer; it'll be a while before she boots."

"Liv isn't a heifer."

"It's a term of endearment."

"Sure it is," Karter said. "How long exactly?"

"Aoifa says six minutes."

"Good," Karter said. "We've emptied the weapons locker. They'll have to make do with what they brought. Heading back to the shuttle now."

"I had a quick lookie-loo, like you wanted," Ibis said. "Spotted eighteen or twenty assholes headed our way. On the upside, they don't know shit. No drones. Half of them don't have environment suits. And they went and scattered themselves all over the damned place. Mostly in the galley, the gym, and the crew cabins. Don't tell Lissa. Some asshole found her underwear drawer."

"Oh, for fuck's sake."

"Yeah. Well, don't get too smug. They got into yours first."

"Seriously?"

"Anyway, we're about to have more chucklefucks than we can handle. Worse, I don't have eyes everywhere. Portside level two is blind."

"Lovely. Any of them between us and the shuttle?"

"Nah. Think you can pull some heat?"

Karter selected a couple of smoke bombs and hefted them in each hand. "No worries. We got this."

"Thanks." Ibis lowered their voice. "You know, Aoifa's all right, even if I can't understand half of what she says when she's excited. It's nice having someone to talk shop with."

"Glad to hear it." Karter signaled to Lissa and Mandy to stop.

"You think we can keep her, Gita, and Mandy?"

"That's my hope."

"Yes!"

"Ping me when Liv is good to go. As soon as she is—"

"I know. I know. We'll send you an assessment. Aoifa

says it looks positive for the impulse engines so far. I sure as hell hope she's right. I hate moving house."

"Who doesn't?" Karter signed off and motioned to Lissa and Mandy. "Ibis says they've got trouble on the way. So let's make some noise. Start with the smoke bombs. I'd like to keep the holes in the hull to a minimum. So no slugs."

Lissa and Mandy nodded.

"I should've asked." Karter shook her head and sighed. "Mandy, have you ever been in a fight before?"

She detected unease under Mandy's serene expression. "No."

Thought so. "It's all right," Karter said. "Here's how this is going to go. Lissa and I will set off smoke bombs down the hall." She motioned to the direction that Ibis and Aoifa took. "Then all of us are running as fast as we can back to Gita. You'll be in front."

A worried expression pinched Mandy's brows together.

"It's okay," Karter said. "There's no one between us and the shuttle. Just leave the shooting to Lissa and me. If we get pinned down, you'll be in charge of keeping the weapons loaded. Sound good?"

"Except for one problem."

"Yeah? What's that?"

"I'm not a fast runner."

"Neither am I. But you'd be surprised at how much faster you run with a bunch of violent vacuum-heads behind you." Karter put a hand on Mandy's arm. "Seriously. It's going to be okay. Lissa and I have done this a lot. Just focus on getting to the shuttle."

Mandy nodded.

"It's going to get really loud," Karter said. "Set noise canceling to four. Got it? Okay, here we go."

At her signal, she and Lissa scurried down the hallway and tossed the smoke bombs. The fire alarms went off on cue. Karter hoped that the suppression system was still working just before the flame-retardant sprinklers went off. She tossed another couple of smoke grenades for good measure, and then the race began.

Opening up a comm channel, she spoke to Ibis as she ran. "Did that do the trick?"

"It certainly stirred them up. They're looking for the fire. They seem to be under the impression they're the only ones here."

"That explains a few things."

"Not the underwear."

Karter rolled her eyes. "Assholes gotta asshole."

"Hey, Liv is up," Ibis said. "And I've got your damage report."

"Toss it to me. Will read it as soon as we stop to catch our breath. How's Liv?"

"She says don't panic when the hull breach alarm goes off. Hull is good to go except for portside level two, like I said."

"Thanks for the heads-up." It was getting harder to breathe and talk while running. "Will check in once we get where we're going."

"Cool. Later, boss."

Karter had entered the security code and pushed Mandy

and Lissa through the pressure door when the breach alarms went off. Lissa's eyes went wide.

"Don't worry," Karter reassured her. "That's just Liv."

A stranger's voice came over the ship's comms. "Get the fuck back here now! Piece of shit is going to blow!"

Karter secured the door and bolted for the shuttle. It looked like they might make it without a fight after all. *And that's just fine by me.*

"Karter?" It was Gita on her private comm channel.

"Yeah?"

"Better get everyone buckled in," Gita said. "The Ring just lit up."

Checking her watch, Karter saw that they had only about fourteen minutes left. *I sure hope the assholes run fast.* "Got it." *If we have to leave, Ibis, Aoifa, and Liv won't make it,* Karter thought. "Strap in. Me and Lissa will disconnect the fuel line." She flipped channels to Mandy and Lissa. "Mandy, get in the shuttle. Lissa, you're with me."

Dropping the weapons bag, Karter rushed to the fuel line and cursed the safety asshole that designed a process that required two sets of hands. While doing that, she chinned open a comm channel with Ibis.

"We're about out of time. Does Liv think we can haul ass out of here?"

"Jump isn't an option. *Mirabilis* won't hold if we go and do that. Too much structural damage. But we've definitely got impulse power."

"Punch it. Now."

"Fucking pirates haven't disembarked yet. Their ship

is still hanging off our side from one of the emergency ports."

"Scrape them off. Do whatever it takes. We have to leave. Now."

"Their ship won't be clear."

"I don't fucking care," Karter said. "It's that or a front-row seat to whatever the fuck is about to happen." She climbed into the shuttle and bolted down the hatch.

The others were strapped in and monitoring the Ring. It had turned a fluorescent lime green that was too bright to look at without adjusting the projection. Karter threw herself into the pilot's flight couch.

Mandy was in the copilot spot. "Should we launch?"

Mirabilis began to vibrate with an old, familiar rumble. Someone had cranked up the impulse engines.

"Don't think so," Karter said. "But be ready, just in case." *Come on, Liv. Get us the fuck out of here.*

The Ring's wide, green aura suddenly shrank down to nothing. At that moment, whoever was at *Mirabilis*'s wheel pushed the engines as hard as they'd go. If the shuttle hadn't been locked in its berth, it'd have slid across the bay and into a bulkhead. There was a crash somewhere; the pirate ship, Karter assumed. She pulled up her own projection and was relieved she'd guessed correctly. Checking *Mirabilis*'s side, she spotted a long furrow scraped into the hull.

Then the Ring detonated.

The force of the explosion tore through the closest ships. A brilliant, spherical flash rolled outward on the projection screen. Karter snapped her eyes shut. She felt the ship violently convulse and prayed that Liv could somehow keep them from breaking up. The shock wave passed over and through *Mirabilis*, *Lush*, and Karter's own body. She was sure she was screaming but couldn't hear anything. Her environment suit detected the danger and automatically maximized the sound dampener—or so she guessed.

Then the blast dissipated. Darkness descended. Silence smothered all. Karter's heart hammered out a panicked rhythm. *Silence is a bad sign for anyone in a starship.* It meant the ship's systems were down—and not just some. All of them.

Then the power flickered on once. Twice. Finally, the systems stabilized. Karter's mouth had gone dry, and her throat hurt. She blinked away the spots in her vision. Casting her gaze around the interior of the shuttle, she checked on the others.

The sound of her own voice was muffled. "I—is everyone okay?"

There were several replies to the affirmative.

Finding her crew safe, she turned to the projection screen and surveyed the area around *Lush*.

A light panel swung twice from the ceiling and dropped with a dull crash. All at once, Karter jumped, and a short, startled scream came from the back of the shuttle. Smoke filled the air. The fire-suppression system dumped flame retardants onto the deck. The shuttle bay had been a mess before, but now, it was complete chaos. Broken metal storage crates, toolboxes, and mechanical equipment littered the deck.

She moved her attention to *Mirabilis*. Environment support was functioning. Other than the fresh tear along her side—*Oh. Fuck that's bad. All of deck three is open to hard vacuum.*—there were no other breaches. The impulse engines had overloaded, and several systems had shorted out. *Is there enough of this ship left to repair?*

Gita gasped. "Look!"

The energy barrier that had prevented outsiders from viewing the inner surface vanished. The forested section of the Ring where they'd once landed was gone. The mountain ranges protecting the Ring sections on either side still stabbed upward. Their height now appeared exaggerated, making the empty gap between resemble a missing tooth. Slowly moving away from the Ring was a massive glowing object. Ribbonlike tentacles trailed behind, slipping from the chasm that was its former home.

That's no object, Karter thought. *It's alive.*

The gargantuan life-form resembled a transparent jellyfish the size of a small planet. A misty, flat-bottomed halo surrounded it. As she watched, the flattened end rounded out, forming an atmospheric bubble around the alien organism. Its glowing rainbow-colored tentacle ribbons draped down, writhing in the hard vacuum of space. The massive creature's umbrella-shaped top was dotted with green. Water rushed off it as the thing hovered. A bright blue incandescent organ in its center pulsed like an enormous heart. New shapes swirled and solidified beneath its translucent top.

"It's beautiful." The awe in Mandy's voice matched Karter's own.

The organism's umbrella top expanded and flared out. A huge, indescribable sound erupted from it. Karter briefly felt the impact of its low frequency in her bones and teeth. The entity shivered, then began to spin. Its internal organs molded together as if due to centripetal force. A globe formed around the beating blue heart at the center. The surface splotches drifted and created green patches on top of brown areas. As the central sphere continued to spin, several bright points of blue light separated from the heart. They twirled in a wider and wider circular path until they traveled the circumference of the transparent jellyfish cap. The rotating ball solidified until the beating cerulean heart was no longer visible.

Oh. A new world, Karter thought. *It looks like a baby planet inside a cosmic jellyfish.*

The life-form remained as it was for several minutes. The points of light—she counted seven—orbited the new planet, becoming moons. Then the mushroom-shaped top convulsed inward. It floated upward, paused for six heartbeats, and abruptly assumed an orbit around the Ring's sun. Where the Ring was spinning around the sun's equator, the creature's orbit was polar and slightly larger.

Karter's suit comms pinged. It was Ibis.

"Is everyone all right back there?"

"A little bruised, but fine," Karter answered. "How about you? Everyone up there okay?"

"We're just dandy. Liv's enjoying a nice stretch."

"I imagine."

"Are you looking outside?"

"We definitely are. It's beautiful."

"So, Aoifa, Liv, and I are wondering if we can start some repairs. We're not going to make it to the border zone. Not now. That explosion dumped a powerful stress load on *Mirabilis*. And the pirate ship tore—"

"I saw. Yes, please do what you can to patch up." Karter knew she'd regret that last panicked order. "And the jump drive?"

"It is, as we say back home, fried like a mushroom steak."

"You *fry* mushroom steak?"

19

While the others initiated ship repairs, Gita curled up on her new bunk and attempted sleep. Still exhausted, her body seemed made of dull aches—including her heart. She wanted nothing more than to escape the pain but couldn't relax enough. Each time she closed her eyes, images of that glowing new world haunted her.

Worse, the GX-3714 exposure was proving to be more serious than she'd hoped. While the rest of her body was steadily healing, the infection had altered multiple parts of her brain—primarily the visual and auditory cortices, the angular gyrus, Wernicke's area, insular cortex, basal ganglia, and cerebellum. In addition, Medical detected new and unusual glial cells attached to certain sensory neurons—they couldn't be eliminated without damaging

Gita's nervous system. Lissa didn't know what they might mean in the long term; no one did. These changes and prospects of future of memory loss or dementia due to the extensive head injuries terrified Gita. Her symptoms were mainly communication related. She also had trouble concentrating. *Well, more than usual anyway*. Her mouth didn't always form the words she intended. There were intermittent vision problems—blurriness, for the most part. That was bad enough. It was the auditory hallucinations that frightened her the most. Gita's mother had already arranged an appointment to see a renowned brain specialist when they returned to Terran Republic space. There wasn't anything else to be done except rest and, of course, worry.

She hated it.

On the upside, everyone seemed to be resettling into a cohesive group. It was comforting. She hadn't realized how much she'd missed this. It was so nice to belong.

If only Ri and Ezinne were here.

Gita couldn't access Ri's twin until the legal paperwork finished processing. She hoped both her daughters were all right, whatever that meant to them.

Should I have stayed, too?

She shuddered.

Ezi and Ri chose this, and I must respect it. She wished she knew that they were happy. Did they technically still exist if they'd given their entire selves over to an alien being? Was it so different from reincarnation?

Did I make a mistake letting them go?

Once exposed to a virus that alters fundamental aspects of the brain, was it possible to make a good decision? Or had everything they said been the virus talking?

There was no way to be sure.

A disturbing suspicion that she wasn't alone in her own thoughts crept at the edge of her consciousness. It had come and gone ever since she'd been exposed to the virus.

Her gaze drifted to the wall-mounted Pooja Mandir cabinet opposite. She smiled. The little wooden altar had doors made of decorative screens and a drawer at the bottom for a tiny lamp. A white owl had been carved onto the front. The altar was small enough to travel with her everywhere she went. At the moment, it was empty, but that would change soon. She would take Hinduism more seriously from now on. She'd already begun to meditate. The practice would at least help her focus.

Her mind drifted to what she would say to Ri and Ezi now. The idea of seeing them was soothing in her grief. In her imagination, they were, in fact, happy. There was light and love and interconnectedness—even a sense of coming home. They weren't alone. There were the survivors from *Boötes*, too. Ri and Ezi would go on unimaginable adventures. They would travel to a distant solar system and find a lifeless rock to transform.

"Gita? I'm so sorry to bother you, but there's a comm call for you. Is this a bad time?" It was Liv.

She lay where she was with her heart racing.

Although she knew *The Tempest* was gone, not hearing Sycorax's voice pouring out of the ship's intercom was jarring. Gita liked Liv, and *Mirabillis* was a lovely ship. It was a newer model than *The Tempest*, and roomier, too, but she was having a hard time feeling at ease. She knew it wasn't anyone's fault—not when the inside of her own head was alien. Although it felt like a deep violation, she knew she'd eventually adapt. Lissa told her that with so much loss at once, she would have to be gentle and patient with herself—allow herself the time she needed to heal.

Liv spoke again. "Gita?"

"Sorry. Who is it?"

"Mother of Chimera Station would like a word. I wouldn't have disturbed you, but it's probably important."

Although she'd never spoken to them, Gita had heard a great deal about Mother from Karter. More recently, Karter had hinted that they'd been in contact with Loki's Ring, and that if Gita had questions, Mother could be the one to answer them.

She wasn't sure she wanted to dig deeper yet. Her emotions were raw, her body felt broken, and she missed her daughters. But this option might not be available later. She decided to take the call.

"Thanks, Liv. Audio only, please."

She waited for the tinny ping signaling the switch to outside comms. "Hello?"

"Is this Gita Chithra?" The question came in a perfectly synced chorus of voices. "We are Mother."

Although Karter had described this to Gita, goose bumps broke out along her arms. *Is that my future?*

"Has something else happened?" she asked.

Mirabilis wasn't the only starship temporarily stranded within sector L-39. There were approximately twenty other vessels that had become nonfunctional. Seven were eradicated during the alien energy pulse, having been too close to the Ring. There was no sign of the vessels now, not even a debris field. Three ships held together long enough to evacuate their crews and were marked as salvage. The rest were either like *Mirabilis* and undergoing repairs or exhibiting signs of possible virus exposure. Tau, Chu & Lane and Kontis Galactic were the only remaining corporate contenders.

You don't work for Mother, Gita reminded herself. They wouldn't have contacted her if something had gone wrong—they'd have spoken with Karter.

"Everything is calm for the moment," said Mother. "We hope you are well?"

"I'm not sure how to answer that. Everything is . . . different. I'm not what I used to be." Gita detected a hopeless note in her own voice. "But I'm healing. Medical was able to help with the headaches."

"Good." Mother continued after a brief pause. "In that case, we would like to invite you to Chimera Station. Are you available?"

Gita was taken aback. "You want to meet with me?"

"We share a personal interest in the Ring, which we wish to discuss. Will you come?"

"All right."

Karter left Ibis to their work and flew Gita over in *Lush*. The journey to Chimera provided a fascinating view of the station. Gita had never seen anything like it, and for a second wondered if she was hallucinating this gigantic pile of scrap metal somehow fashioned into a functioning hub.

Upon entering the first congested passage leading to the tram of what Karter had called the Rind, Gita was almost overwhelmed with scents and sounds of the marketplace lining its walls. Fresh coffee, baked goods, spices, alcohol, and foodstuffs from all over the Norton Alliance could be found. Her nose was crowded with the welcome smells of cinnamon, pepper, cumin, garlic, and vanilla. One stall was offering the most delicious-smelling stew. Clothing, weapons, artifacts, home decor were on offer all around her. If she hadn't had a meeting obligation, Gita would've begged Karter to take her shopping.

"I'd have thought the stores would be closed," she said.

Karter glanced over her shoulder to scan the passage behind them. "They probably were for a short while, but everyone's gotta eat."

Upon exiting the tram, Karter led her to an atrium garden filled with miniature trees, vines, ferns, and flowering plants. Ivy-covered balconies surrounded the park. Gita was awestruck by a small cloud of artificial butterflies. A serious-looking man named Abaeze met them.

Karter motioned to Abaeze. "He will take you to Mother. I'm headed back to *Mirabilis*. Let me know when you're done, and I'll come get you."

Gita gave Karter a quick hug before hopping into Abaeze's vehicle. He drove the rest of the way to Mother's residence, not even stopping at the gigantic wall that surrounded it, in which an entryway seemed to appear out of nowhere upon their approach. Like the rest of the interiors on Chimera, the home appeared to be one part vegetation-dense park and one part ancient starship. Once Gita settled on the sofa, Mother took one of the three armchairs.

"Thank you for coming," said Mother. "The situation in L-39 should calm down soon. We've made it clear that all NIA corporate vessels must vacate the sector as soon as possible. Loki's Ring exists for the benefit of Gaeans. It is not available for exploitation. We will not negotiate on this point."

Confused, Gita asked, "What are Gaeans?"

"It is what we call the entities living in the Ring. We cannot communicate directly with them—they typically use electrical impulses and chemicals via a root system that runs throughout the Ring. On occasion, an empathic connection is possible with beings like us—we sometimes receive images. For us, the connection is clearest on the Ring's surface. Ultimately, we are too small to be noticed. We are to the entities what a blood or skin cell is to a human." Focusing on something just over Gita's shoulder, Mother continued. "Others that land on the planet, humans included, would be more like invading bacteria."

Gita tried not to reveal her disappointment. She had hoped for a much greater secret, one that might somehow reunite her with her daughters. Still, it was a relief to talk to someone who understood what had happened to her.

"We can share some of our experience with you," Mother said. "We wish to show you that you are not alone."

Mother explained what happened after having crashed on the Ring's surface. "The entity with whom I was connected then left the Ring's orbit. Gaeans only remain nearby until a certain number of them have been born. We do not know what determines that number, only that eventually they go in search of a new home."

On the large view screen floating behind Mother, Gita watched the newly born Gaean spin as it traced a path around Ring and sun. She sensed a deep joy to it. Discovery. Freedom.

"The emotions are intense sometimes," said Gita. "Then the next moment I feel nothing. Any words I use to describe what I'm feeling seem too simplistic."

"We hope you will become more at ease, in time," said Mother. "We wished to ask you what your next steps are. Because we would like to offer you a place on Chimera Station. To help us protect the Gaeans. We need a representative who has a good relationship with the Terran Republic of Worlds. I may not be friendly with corporations of the Norton Independent Alliance, but I am very familiar with their politics. The new hire would be my counterpart."

"Me?" Gita asked in surprise. "I'm not sure I'm the right person to represent anybody, much less Chimera Station and the Ring."

"Given your extensive experience as a starship captain,

with AGIs, and now with Loki's Ring, we think you would be perfectly suited to the role."

Mother poured themself a cup of coffee and began to outline the details. The compensation and responsibilities were better than Gita could have imagined. She would be able remain on Chimera to study the new Gaean and even make brief visits to other proto-entities on the Ring.

In a way, it would be like watching over Ri and Ezi.

"It sounds wonderful," said Gita. But something held her back from accepting immediately. "Let me think it over."

The man with the scar across his nose entered the room.

"Yes, Sabatten?" Mother asked.

"I apologize for the interruption. Another starship has arrived. It is a frigate named *Light from a Dead Star* with a Tau, Chu & Lane registry. It is carrying a small host of tactical fighters."

Mother asked, "How many?"

"Estimates are only fifteen. But Abaeze feels that this could grant them a significant edge in a close fight."

"It seems our meeting is at an end." Mother got to their feet and turned to Gita. "Let me know your answer as soon as you can."

"I will."

Gita asked Sabatten if she could send a message to *Lush*. It wasn't long before she was flying back to *Mirabilis* with Karter at *Lush*'s helm.

Staring at the image of space around them, Gita noticed that the cluster of Chimera-allied ships was forming an organized barrier between the station and the corporate warships. More vessels had arrived, boosting Chimera's defense. In addition, she spied what looked like several autonomous missile silos being towed into position. The number of warships and associated weaponry crowding the area had become alarming. This would be the largest interplanetary altercation Gita had ever heard of, let alone seen firsthand.

"Don't get too confident. It looks evenly matched now, but it looks like TCL and Kontis have requested reinforcements from their home offices." Karter poured on the speed. She was in a hurry to get back. "That out there is about to be the biggest fucking mess the universe has ever seen. Glad we're leaving."

"Why?"

"It's Norton politics. *Mirabilis* is Terran Republic registered. We can't stay. It's more than a bit squirrelly that we're here in the first place."

"But don't you have a Chimera contract? You can't turn your back on Mother. They need you." Gita tried her best to appear levelheaded, logic driven. The old Karter hated it when she got overly emotional, and Gita still wasn't sure about the new Karter.

Karter stared at the image floating in the air between them. "Can I know why this is so important? You don't have an affiliation with Mother or Chimera Station."

"Those corporate ships are about to attack the station."

"Sure. But you sound like you know something else. It'd be nice to know why you're so invested."

"It'll sound crazy."

"Tell me anyway."

Gita studied Karter's face. Her expression and tone were guarded and neutral. Gita wondered if this version of Karter was as frightened of another big confrontation as she was. She sighed. "I—I don't want to abandon the Gaean. It's all I have left of Ezi and Ri."

Karter blinked. "But they're gone."

Flinching, Gita looked away.

"I'm sorry," Karter said. "I know you're grieving. And I don't mean to be cruel. But . . . you're not yourself. Lissa told me about your—your injuries."

She's right. How can I trust myself to make a sensible choice? I have a head injury, after all, Gita thought. She bit her lip. "I told you it would sound crazy."

"You did at that."

"But Karter," Gita said. "It's not. *I'm* not. I'm connected to that entity out there. Because of Ri and Ezinne. Because of the virus. I can feel it." She finally allowed her passion flow into her words. "So, we can't leave Loki's Ring to be stripped by the NIA corporations. You can't."

Karter picked at a nonexistent stray thread on the arm of her coveralls. "Supposing I do stay," she said, continuing to stare at a reinforced seam. "There will be consequences. We could lose Aggie's sponsorship. We might even lose our citizenship."

Gita didn't say anything.

Finally, Karter looked up. "What if the corporations

are just blustering? Mother surely thinks they are, or they'd have called in all their favors."

Gesturing at the docked ships and the others close by the station, Gita said, "Are you so sure they haven't?"

"They didn't call our marker."

"They know the political situation just as well as you do. Probably better."

Karter blinked.

"They need us."

"You're *sure* you're sure?"

Gita swallowed. "I'd risk my whole being on it."

Karter studied her face for at least another thirty seconds. Gita forced herself to wait patiently.

Finally, Karter spoke. "Option one—" She held up a finger. "I seek permission. Aggie tries to stop us. That leads to a delay and/or an altercation. That alone makes option one a no-go. Two, I don't tell Aggie. She doesn't stop us. I apologize later—assuming we survive. And by the look of that"—she motioned to the image of the corporate navies—"the odds of survival aren't much. So, I won't tell her. I've got a hunch she'll understand. It's not like she hasn't pulled stunts like this herself."

"Oh."

They reached *Mirabilis*. Karter parked *Lush* and turned to face her.

"The others get a vote though. This is their home, too. So if they decide they want to back up Chimera Station, we back up Chimera Station."

Gita felt an overwhelming release of tension. She'd

been wobbly before, but now she didn't think she could stand, let alone walk. "Th—thank you, Karter."

"For what?"

"Believing me."

"This is the only way you and I work. You've always listened to me. I have to return the favor. I'm still sorry I didn't before."

Biting down on harsh words, Gita reconsidered and simply said, "Thank you. It means a lot."

Karter used the ship intercom to call a crew meeting in the galley. Then she helped Gita walk. It wasn't far. When they arrived the galley smelled of fresh-baked bread. Gita's mouth watered. The scents brought up memories of happier times. It was wonderful. Ibis passed around a basket of fresh salted rolls. While everyone ate, Karter outlined the situation, including what Gita had told her. The reception was less than wonderful.

"Will one more starship make that much of a difference?" Ibis gestured to the float image above the galley table. "I mean, we're badasses and all, but I'm not sure we're *that* badass. Just look. Forty corporate starships. *Forty*. Why bother repairing the damned ship if we're just going to fuck it up again?"

"So, you're voting against?" Lissa asked.

"I didn't say that." Ibis turned to Aoifa. "Did I say that?"

"Don't look at me. There's a gaping hole in each side of the ship. We have no jump capabilities. Gita's in bad shape. Liv isn't familiar with *Mirabilis* yet. This is a terrible idea."

"The worst," Ibis said.

Aoifa winked. "Therefore, I'm absolutely in."

"Damned straight." Ibis nodded. "But I'm not."

Shocked, everyone stared at Ibis.

"Straight." Ibis made a motion with her hand indicating that people should follow the logic. "Get it? I'm not straight."

There was a three-second silence before Mandy said, "I'm in."

Liv spoke from the ceiling speaker. "I'm already out one home. Why not another? It's not like I have to pack like you lot. I'm with Gita."

"What about you, Lissa?" Karter asked.

"Me, too."

"Thank you, everyone." Gita blinked back tears. "This means so much."

Lissa hugged her, then Ibis, Aoifa, and Mandy followed.

"Okay. Okay. Let's get started." Karter coughed as if to clear the painful lump in her throat. "Liv, is enough of our ass welded together that it won't fall off when you pour on the speed?"

"I'm seventy-three percent confident."

Karter nodded. "That'll have to do. Let's strip the visuals on our registration. Our digital record still reads Terran Republic, but if we're not flying a TRW flag while doing something stupid, then maybe, just maybe, it'll sting less for Aggie when we're slapped into the next galaxy."

"You got it."

"All right, everyone," Karter said. "Let's crash a party."

Limping the long way around, they arrived at Chimera Station's new location about an hour later. Mother's volunteers huddled close by. The tension on the station comm channel was conspicuous, conversations short and clipped. Gita got the sense that many were fearful, and rightly so. Taking in the combined corporate navies lining up in tidy rows, it was impossible not to be. They were outnumbered three to one.

On *Mirabilis*, everyone but Lissa and Mandy was in Command. Karter was strapped into the captain's couch. Ibis and Aoifa took the copilot and pilot consoles. As for herself, Gita was in charge of watching what the opposition was up to. Lissa and Mandy retreated to Medical, getting things ready.

The moment they'd locked into a parking orbit with the station, Karter opened up a private channel with Station Authority. "This is Karter Cuplin of *Mirabilis*. I realize this might not be the best time, but may I speak to Mother?"

A harried Station Authority operator with short brown hair and a crooked nose nodded. "Let me check."

After a short wait, Mother appeared. They were wearing an environment suit. "Hello, Karter. What are you doing here?"

"As Seed members, we're obligated. Or has that changed recently?"

"We understood that your allegiance with the Terran Republic would take precedence in this situation."

"We took a vote." Karter shrugged. "So, here we are. Anyway, you know how I am about bullies."

"Your show of loyalty is appreciated." Mother's expression was unreadable, as always, but Gita thought she detected some relief. "However, we're not sure that this is the best time for it."

"Nonsense," Karter said. "What's the plan?"

"Beyond facing down everything Tau, Chu & Lane can throw at us? Not much. We were expecting a response, but not this."

"Can't you just aim the Ring's weapons at them? It didn't seem to be a problem before," Ibis replied.

"We don't have control over the Ring. It does what is necessary to protect its inhabitants. No more. Chimera doesn't factor into the equation." Mother tilted their head. "It is automated. We assume it will prevent an invasion, but are not certain of it. That is why we are here."

"Well, fuck," Ibis said.

Now that they were at the station, Gita's confidence evaporated. Why was she endangering her friends—the people that she loved—yet again? If the corporations killed them all, what good would that do? She didn't want to fight a war.

"Ah, Karter." Ibis pointed to the tactical float map. "Looks like someone else decided to join the fun."

On the edge of border zone between L-39 and the Terran Republic of Worlds, a line of starships began to form.

Karter's mouth dropped open. "Wow."

"Fucking hell," Aoifa muttered. "That's beautiful."

"Is it?" asked Lissa. "If the Republic gets involved, it will mean a war with the Norton Independent Alliance."

At that moment, the public comm channel sounded two loud bursts of discordant alerts. It was followed with an announcement.

"To all ships in L-39 and the near vicinity: this is Jayne Tau, captain of *Light from a Dead Star*. Leave the area at once or face the consequences. L-39 is the property of Tau, Chu & Lane—"

The announcement was interrupted by a second set of alerts.

"This is Zoja Charron of *Undertow*. Kontis Galactic has already filed an undisputed claim for the sector L-39—"

Jayne Tau cut off Zoja Charron. "Undisputed? That's rich."

"Fuck you, Jayne," Zoja shouted.

Ibis's eyebrows shot up in mock surprise. "That's a bit unprofessional."

Zoja continued with her rant. "Go ahead and try to take it. Even if you do, I had someone plant a little gift in your ship's air-circulation system. Or rather, I returned *your* gift. The virus should be making its way through your crew shortly. What are you going to do now?"

Ibis let out a low whistle. "Impressive."

An armed missile shot out of a weapon port on *Light from a Dead Star*'s starboard side. It hit *Undertow*, blasting a hole it the ship's hull.

"Ouch," Ibis shook their head. "Well, this is going downhill fast."

Sitting in one of the flight couches along the bulkhead, Gita got Karter's attention with a hand in the air. "Can you open another public comm channel?"

Karter stopped chatting with Mother and turned with raised eyebrows. "What for?"

"I've got an idea," Gita said. "I think I can make them stop."

Karter looked over at Mother, who nodded, then took and released a deep breath. "All right. Here goes nothing." She activated the comms at Gita's console. "Gita, it's all yours."

Gita's terror immediately took over. *Everyone is listening. What was I thinking?* Her hands trembled. She felt cold and hollowed out, as if her stomach was somewhere at her feet. Her vision grew abruptly sharp—so much so that details seemed outlined. She attempted to begin twice, but both times, her words clogged in her throat. *I hate public speaking. I hate it.*

She used the memory of Ri and Ezinne to calm herself. *This Gaean is depending on me.* The thought reassured her, and before she knew it, she began to speak.

"I am Dr. Gita Chithra, of the starship *Mirabilis*, and I have a proposal. I can give you the formula for the cure of GX-3714."

All at once, silence flooded the channel.

"Who is this offer for, exactly?" asked Jayne Tau.

"I will pay you three million credits if you send it to me," said Zoja. "And me alone."

Multiple protests immediately crowded the channel.

She pushed through in spite of them, speaking louder so that she could be heard. "I am not selling. And I will give it to everyone. For free."

"What's the point in that?" Zoja asked.

Gita replied, "To save you and your people. But you must leave L-39 at once. It isn't yours to fight over."

It was at this point that Mother joined the public conversation. "We hereby declare this sector and Loki's Ring a sovereign state of the Gaean-Chimera Alliance. You are not wanted here."

Mirabilis's main console signaled a visual comm request from Jayne Tau. A woman with graying blonde hair, pale skin, and piercing green eyes appeared on the projected screen. She wore a corporate uniform and spoke in a commanding tone that ended in harsh incredulity. "I have questions."

There were several other competing comm requests, but apparently Liv wasn't allowing them through. The incessant beeping was muted.

Gita said, "Go ahead."

"Loki's Ring has existed for centuries, and no such entity has come forward before. Why now?"

"I don't know," Ibis muttered. "Why'd you suddenly become interested in it?"

Karter signaled to Ibis to shut up.

Mother said, "The Terran Republic of Worlds has recognized Loki's Ring as a sovereign state since its discovery."

Jayne Tau sneered. "What the Terran Republic of

Worlds thinks or does has no bearing here. We are not subject to its laws."

"The starships parked in the border zone might have something else to say," Karter said.

"Aliens and electronic constructs"—she spat the words—"are of no consequence. They aren't human. Mankind, through his superior intelligence, was born to take the stars. God gave us this universe. Therefore, you are standing in the way of a new manifest destiny. This sector and all those inside it are ours for the taking. It is our purpose."

Gita decided to come to Mother's defense. "The Norton Independent Alliance, like the Terran Republic, is not all of humanity. Multiple sentient entities inhabit L-39. The first Gaean to be born in a millennium orbits this sun. It and the unborn Gaeans gestating in Loki's Ring are the members of a species of living worlds. The Ring facilitates their reproduction."

"Surely you're not about to tell me a planet forges tungsten and builds system-sized mechanical structures?" Jayne Tau asked.

"Gaeans didn't build the Ring. You are correct," Mother countered. "However, those who did will eventually return to check on the entities here. Entities that they invested a great deal of energy in reestablishing. Don't you think that when they do, it would be best that they find the Gaeans well and undisturbed? Need I remind you that they obliterated an *entire* star system in order to create the Ring?"

"I'll ask again. Who built it?"

Gita shrugged. "I can't tell you more than the next person. But do you think they'd go to all this trouble only to abandon the Ring completely?"

Jayne Tau motioned all around herself and scoffed. "Well, they aren't here now, are they? We have the strength of force to take what we want. We aren't fooled by this—this pantomime. It's clear that Mother—who is a *pirate*—moved Chimera Station here in a weak attempt to grab—"

"Mother of Chimera Station is the chosen diplomatic representative of the Gaeans," Gita said.

"Bullshit. Mother has no more of a relationship to it than us. You have no proof. None. And you have nothing with which to back up your demands."

"The Ring is not yours. Go home," Mother commanded.

Jayne Tau flashed her perfectly white teeth in a vicious smile. "Make us."

From the edge of her vision, Gita saw Karter roll her eyes.

Turning, Jayne Tau spoke to someone out of the range of the projector. "Lock missiles on *Mirabilis*. Let's show them what we think of—"

A green light pulsed on the Ring, and Jayne Tau's projection image vanished. Gita gasped. The corporate flagship went completely dark. A cacophony of protests, shock, threats, and several commands swelled the comm channel—the other vessels, she assumed. After two full minutes, *Light from a Dead Star*'s power returned.

Who did that? And how? Gita wondered.

Mother waited until the channel quieted. "Loki's Ring will protect the newly mature Gaean, and it is in communication with *us*. Chimera Station wants no war with you, but you must take your desire for conquest and go. Or is another demonstration necessary?"

The public comm channel went abruptly silent. Jayne Tau didn't reappear. Gita watched the corporate vessels begin a slow retreat to the jump relay, where they vanished one by one until none remained.

Light from a Dead Star was the last.

Shaking, Gita collapsed back onto a flight couch. Her shoulder blades thumped against the padding. The adrenaline jitters began in earnest. Her stomach felt fluttery and light. Her knees were weak. Around her, Command was dead quiet. They were staring at her as if they'd never seen her before.

After a long silence, Ibis asked, "What the fuck just happened?"

"Gita just helped Mother tell the most powerful corporations in the NIA to fuck off," Karter said. "I couldn't be prouder."

It wasn't me. It was mostly Mother, Gita thought. But she didn't have the energy left to stand, let alone argue. So, she nodded and smiled.

"I need a fucking drink," Aoifa said.

"Me, too." Ibis jumped to their feet. "I think there's one last bottle of Garcias Añejo hidden in the galley."

Aoifa said, "I'm not a fan of tequila."

"I'll pretend I didn't hear that."

Aoifa and Ibis paused at the hatch, and then Aoifa turned around.

"Are you joining us, Gita?"

She didn't drink, but she decided to go along anyway.

In the end, the entire crew gathered in the galley to celebrate. Mandy pulled out the snacks, and Lissa whipped up a vegetable ramen dish. After several shots of tequila, Ibis was inspired to make Gita's favorite dessert: Mysore pak, a sweet, yellow bar made from gram flour, ghee, and sugar. They even used Gita's mother's recipe. The galley was filled with the welcome scents of good food and the sounds of laughter. Gita fell quiet, soaking in the good cheer and companionship.

They had all settled down to dinner when Liv asked, "Gita? I just got a message saying Mother wants to speak with you."

Gita paused, unsure.

"They want to meet as soon as possible," Liv added.

"All right." Gita got to her feet.

Karter said, "Don't you want to eat first?"

"But Mother said—"

"You're weak," Karter said. "You need to eat something. At least have a few bites first. Rest. They can wait."

"That's okay." Gita honestly didn't want to get up.

Ibis grabbed some dishes from the cabinets. "I'll throw something together that you can take with you."

"Aoifa, would you mind taking her?" Karter asked. "Ibis isn't in any shape to fly."

Ibis looked up from the bowl they were filling with ramen. "Verily, 'tis true."

"*Lush* should be refueled." Karter hesitated, then gave Gita a hug. "Get back soon and you won't miss vid night. You pick what to watch."

Gita smiled. "We haven't done that in years."

"All the more reason to do it," Karter said. "But hurry. Otherwise, we'll end up watching one of Ibis's slasher horror vids."

It took several minutes to get permission to dock on Chimera. Apparently, the entire station was having a party. Gita left Aoifa waiting at the berth and wove her way through the crowds. Loud music poured into the Rind's throughways. People were dancing and singing— no doubt glad that there hadn't been anyone hurt or killed. She boarded a packed tram and finally exited at the last stop. Her hand terminal indicated she'd be met by Abaeze. Casting her gaze, she spotted the somber, imposing man standing at the end of the platform.

"Hello, Dr. Chithra."

She motioned to the chaos around them. "Nice party. Is this going to be difficult to drive around?"

"Not for me," he said and ushered her into the car.

Mother was standing by the door when they arrived. They were wearing a loose, cinch-waisted tunic and trousers that complimented their curvy build.

Once again, Abaeze remained with the car while she and Mother went inside. They waited to speak until they had led her to the room where they'd met before.

"Thank you for your help today." Mother indicated that she should sit. "You starting that conversation is exactly why I see you as a perfect representative for Chimera Station."

Gita took one of the emerald-green chairs this time. Mother settled into the chair next to hers.

"We felt it best to have this conversation in private," Mother said. "Have you made a decision? Will you be joining us?"

Blinking, Gita bit her lip. Before the confrontation, she'd wanted to stay on Chimera so she could be near the Gaean. To be with her daughters again in any capacity had sounded wonderful. Her only worry had been what Karter would say.

But today had made her realize that the Ri and Ezi she knew were gone—they were part of something new. *They don't need me anymore.* That had been made clear when *Light from a Dead Star*'s power was knocked out.

"There's a great deal of work to do."

Gita smiled as Mata's words replayed in her head. *I am your mother. You will always be my child. Your family needs you. Come home where it is safe.*

She couldn't hold on to her daughters as if they were still children. Relationships changed, and that was a good thing, no matter how painful. *It's time to let go.*

"I—I'm honored you asked. But I'd like to go home to *Mirabilis.*"

Mother nodded. "Very well."

"If I can be of any assistance from there, I'd be happy

to do so." It occurred to Gita that this might be her last chance to address something that had bothered her ever since they'd met. "May I ask you a question?"

Again, Mother nodded.

"Isn't diplomat an odd career choice for a crime lord?"

Mother gave her a small smile. "We suppose it is."

Gita laughed. After a moment, she grew sober. "What will you do if Jayne Tau and the others come back?"

"As you know, the Ring protects itself. And the Station."

"Oh. That's good." Gita hadn't been sure of the latter.

"We are also negotiating a defense agreement with the Terran Republic. Just in case."

The two of them switched topics and worked out the details for distributing Ezi's solution to GX-3714. Eventually, Gita returned home. Everyone was in the entertainment room watching what indeed proved to be one of Ibis's favorite slasher vids. It had subtitles. Grimm was curled up in one of the chairs licking a treat, and his collar was murmuring something that sounded like, *Yum. Yum. Yum.*

Karter got up from the floor and met her just outside the door. "Sorry. Ibis really wanted Mandy to see this one. Thought we'd squeeze it in before you got back. So . . . how'd it go?"

"Can we talk? Alone? Maybe . . . in the galley?"

"That bad, huh?"

"No, not bad. Pretty good, actually." Gita assumed a place at the galley table.

Someone had cleaned up. All the dishes were put away and the table wiped. The empty tequila bottle rested exactly in the middle like some sort of decorative centerpiece.

"All right," Karter said. "What's the news?"

"I'm staying here."

Karter's face froze in shock. "You are?"

"I am." Gita stood and grinned.

"*Yesss!*" Karter grabbed her into a hug.

Closing her eyes, Gita hugged her back. It felt wonderful. "What's the plan?"

"Initially?" Karter asked. "Aggie wants to see us for a good old-fashioned verbal lashing."

"She said that?"

"Call it an educated guess. Don't worry. I'll grovel enough for all of us. I'm getting pretty good at it."

Gita let her go and stepped back. "Is that so?"

"Heh. Yeah." Karter lowered her head and looked up at her from under her eyebrows.

"And if she doesn't accept your apology?" Gita asked.

"Then there's always plan B," Karter said. "Liv says Aggie owes her a ship. She seems to think she can ask for *Mirabilis*."

"Nice."

"Liv is pretty tricksy." Karter returned her grin. "I think I definitely want her on our side. I'm confident that Aggie does, too."

Liv said, "I'm right here, you know. I can hear you."

"I thought you were in the other room watching *I Scream, You Scream* with the others?" Karter asked.

"Artificial person, remember? Unlike you," Liv said, "I can focus on more than one thing at once."

"Fine. Rub it in." Karter rolled her eyes.

"When do we leave?"

"Tomorrow, I'm afraid," Karter said. "Patience isn't one of Aggie's virtues. Come to think of it, *does* Aggie have any virtues?"

"Loyalty. She's definitely loyal."

"Right." Karter paused. "And you're definitely not leaving?"

"I'm definitely not leaving."

"Good," Karter said. "I can use that as an excuse to change up the evening's entertainment. Don't tell Ibis, but I can't stand slasher movies."

"Your secret is safe with me." Gita made a motion across her lips to signal that they were sealed.

"Well, *I* haven't made any promises," Liv said.

Karter looked up at the ceiling. "Hey now."

"Oh, stop it," Gita said, laughing. "Let's join the others."

As they linked arms and went to join the crew, Gita realized that, after so many years of reliving the past, it felt good to finally look to a new future.

ACKNOWLEDGMENTS

As an author, I often get asked questions that make it obvious most people don't understand how books are made. Television gives the impression that an author briefly types on a laptop and—in between solving murder cases or dealing with mobs of adoring fans and signing high-dollar movie deals—a novel magically appears. The instant the manuscript is finished, it immediately teleports onto a shelf. Some might be aware of the existence of agents and editors, but often they misunderstand their roles. So, I'd like to thank the hard-working people involved and shine a light on them. They're important and awesome. Readers should know about them. Hopefully none are vampires and thus allergic to sunlight.

If you're already aware of how books are made, feel free to skip this part. Hell, even if you seriously don't care it's okay to not read it. So, wander off. Grab a cookie and a nice cup of something warm from the kitchen. Treat yourself. You've just waded through five-hundred-something pages of my prose. You deserve a reward. Go on. We'll meet you in paragraph twenty-two. Shoo!

Are they gone? Cool. And now I shall reveal the super-secret book creation process! Warning: book nerds only beyond this point! All others will be bored to death and possibly lose hope. Here also be magical fairies and wizards. Maybe even a few dragons. Most certainly an evil empire. It's possible some dude wielding a light saber and speaking via an electronic voice box due to an unfortunate swim in a vat of lava makes an appearance. [Lowers voice] *Scooch in close, now. I gotta whisper so the evil empire who forces me to write novels their way won't hear.* Just kidding. [Whispers] *No, I'm not.* No really, I'm joking.

Biggest secret: *almost all books start with questions*. It's how story ideas are born. Unless you're writing nonfiction, answers are never as interesting as questions.

Step one: a writer (sometimes more than one if they collaborate) spends anywhere from three months to twenty years writing. If they're unpublished and un-agented, they do so in between jobs and kids and school and all the things life throws at everyone. They write not knowing if the work will ever sell. If you're previously published, have decent sales numbers, and are lucky, you write a proposal and your agent sells that. Then, you write it in between jobs and kids and school and all the things life throws at everyone. If you're lucky and you're the sort of person suited to it, you have a partner to help out with the life bits. You get paid in chunks—the amounts and schedule depend upon multiple factors. It can be as frequently as twice a year or once every couple of years. Very, very rarely is it enough to live on. (My first novel sold for $5,000. I worked on it for five years. I understand time has not changed these unfortunate numbers.) If you're very, very lucky, once it finally hits the shelves, your book sells enough to earn royalties. This almost never happens.

Writers like to eat. They also have a nasty habit of needing electricity, internet connections, functioning laptops, word processing software, health care, and roofs over their heads. Some have families. Suffice it to say, writers who are not independently wealthy have day jobs or partners that make enough to support them. It means that if you want to be a professional fiction writer, you must work at least two jobs, three if you have a family. You must be at least middle class to afford the question-able investment of time and money. (Note: I haven't even mentioned workshops or conventions.) This is not a good thing for genre fiction. It means we're limited to certain stories. Statistics indicate that the more diverse the stories, casts, and storytellers, the more creative the community of works and the healthier the business. Science fiction and fantasy as a genre needs diversity to survive. All else is stagnation and death.

An agent is a shiny unicorn who represents a chosen writer's work to publishers. They sell manuscripts and in exchange receive a small percentage of the sale. Agents now often pre-edit manuscripts before selling them. They also handle certain legal issues (contracts) and they're worth every penny of that commission. Anyone who says otherwise is full of shit.

Next up: the powerful wizards called editors. There are different types, but acquiring editors and copy editors are the main two. All are magical. The acquiring editor takes a manuscript they want to buy to the Decision Makers. If the Decision Makers like it and Marketing thinks they can pitch it, a P&L (profit and loss) report is run. A committee decides whether or not the auguries indicate the manuscript will sell well enough to merit buying it. If the planets align in a way that meets approval, the acquiring editor gets the green light and makes an offer. The agent tells the writer about the offer. The writer likes it or doesn't. Sometimes the amount is negotiated among multiple publishers. Often, it is not.

The next phase is when contracts happen, which means Legal. Legal means lawyers who work for the publisher. It is financially impractical/impossible for a writer to hire a lawyer to review a contract. So, the agent fills this role. If a clause in the contract stinks, the agent negotiates changes. The writer reads the final contract and signs.

Congratulations! At this point, anywhere from months to years may have passed since the writer typed the last line. Some manuscripts never sell—even if the writer has sold manuscripts to big publishers before. There are no guarantees in publishing.

The acquiring editor isn't always the one who edits the

manuscript. Editing is the mystical process where a rough draft is transformed into the shiny, coherent, most excellent version of the author's novel. No good editor ever tells the writer they *must* write a thing. However, editing *is* a collaborative process. It's best to take expert advice. It's also important to know when to stand your ground. This is the writer's job. Understand that if you make a mistake in judgment and the novel doesn't sell or you are unpleasant to work with, it'll make it harder to sell another. (Publishing is a small world.) Manuscripts should go through at least two passes: story edits and copy edits. Copy edits are when things like grammar, spelling, and last-minute continuity issues are corrected in the final pass.

Needless to say, this also takes anywhere from months to a year.

After this, the novel goes through interior layout and typesetting (art director and graphic designer) in both print and electronic formats (not always the same graphic designer), the selection of cover art (art director and illustrator), and cover layout (graphic designer again— also not necessarily the same person), and is then sent to the printer, where a whole army of people create the physical pages and assemble them into physical books. That's an amazing process, and I suggest reading about it. (Also understand that eBooks have their own cover art, which involves thumbnails and a somewhat larger image of the whole cover, thanks to the art director and graphic designer. eBooks take their own time and effort to create, separately from printed books. The process is not automated.) The designer and art director check everything before it goes to print and ventures out into the world via distribution. The distribution process involves a whole other army of workers: publishing representatives, buyers (who work for bookstores), packaging, and delivery drivers. Also: there are warehouses where books are stored before and after sale and warehouse staff who do warehouse stuff.

Obviously, there are parts I don't know a lot about. But you might.

Anyway, a publicist will create promotional materials designed to get professional critics, bookstores (plus booksellers), and the (online) book community interested.

As you can see (three pages later), the creation of a book involves a great deal of time and effort, requiring the professional skills of many people. What I've described is just for one book. Publishers make many, and hopefully a majority of the novels do well enough to make more.

Please note: I've been at this for twenty years and it's highly likely I've missed steps. The point is: what you've just read represents the labor of a whole lot of highly skilled people. They also have families and deserve to work reasonable hours and be paid living wages.

So, this is where I say: THANK YOU FOR BUYING THIS BOOK. Seriously. I fucking mean it. You, Dearest Reader, are what makes the publishing world go around. And if this isn't the only novel of mine you've purchased and/or read: THANK YOU EVEN MORE.

Special side note for self-published books: one poor, overworked soul does all of the above jobs. Themselves. Alone. Without pay. And they have to do it professionally enough to meet high expectations. They also like to eat. They, too, have a nasty habit of needing electricity, internet connections, functioning laptops, word processing software, health care, and roofs over their heads. Some have families. Self-publishing is not the easy road to wealth and fame. It's an expensive, soul-crushing grind. In addition, there are very few people on this earth that are great at all those jobs. Long story short: if you read self-published books, *buy them*.

If you can't afford to buy books, for the love of all that is literature, go to a library. Your taxes pay for it. Libraries pay authors and the army of people who create books by buying copies for people to borrow. Libraries and the librarians who run them are amazing. I wouldn't have gotten through my childhood without them. (Thank you, librarians. I love you!)

Okay. That's the end of the oh-so-seriously long-winded, supersecret explanation of the publishing process. Thanks for sticking it out, my book nerd sibs. Now you know as much as I do about how books get made. (Mostly.) Have a nice drink or two while the others finish counting all those damned paragraphs.

Y'all are back? Great!

Disclaimer: no fairies, elves, dragons, or wizards were harmed in the making of this book. No light-saber-wielding men were pushed into lava pits, either. I know that may be a bit of a disappointment for some of you. I blame Disney.

First, I'd like to thank the love of my life: Dane. He suffers through things only another partner of a working writer knows about. Thanks for doing the dishes, the laundry, cooking, cleaning, and paying all the bills while I worked under a deadline. Seriously. Thanks for listening to me even when you didn't understand what the hell I was muttering about because you hadn't read that part yet. Thanks for being my Alpha Reader. Thanks for being that wall I bounce ideas off of, for teaching me how to laugh in the suckiest times and laughing with me in the best of times. Thanks for having faith in me even when I don't. Thanks for insisting I'm not Weapon X, that I'm a wee thing, and for tenderly resting your chin on top of my head. Thanks for all those ridiculous banter-heavy conversations. (Yes, Virginia. Some people do talk like that and some of them live together.) Thanks for taking over the DnD game when I had to stop DMing. Thanks for being the person stuck in the house with me during that looooooooong-ass March in 2020. Above all, thanks for being my best friend in the whole world. I love you more than I can say. You'll always be my hero as long as Ryan Reynolds and Blake Lively are unavailable.

Hi, Mom! I love you, too. Please forget I said anything about not cleaning.

Or Ryan Reynolds.

(Ryan. If you ever read this, call me.)

This book started with my marvelous agent, Hannah

Bowman, who asked me what I wanted to do after *Persephone Station*. My mind (as often happens when asked to perform a feat of creativity on the spot) drew a blank. So, Hannah suggested I write a story featuring a ring world. I love story prompts. They're a blast. She also waded through several versions of the manuscript because my story brain isn't terribly efficient. She's a goddess. Best agent. Twelve out of possible ten. No notes. Thanks, Hannah!

Thanks to Joe Monti at Saga Press for acquiring this book and the other three. He's been with me my whole professional writing life in one form or another. He's amazing. He gets me. Not everyone does.

Many extra-special thanks to Amara Hoshijo for being such an incredible editor. Thanks for understanding me. Thanks for working far too hard for far too long and still doing an incredible job. Thanks for bearing with my inability to use a comma correctly and for editing one version of the novel only to get something completely different later. You're also a goddess.

(As it happens, I'm fortunate to know multiple goddesses. I highly recommend goddesses. They're awesome. It's not just in the name.)

Additional thanks to Jordan Koluch, the most marvelous copy editor. Your attention to detail is mighty and (dare I say it) borders on terrifying. (Trust me. It's a good thing.)

Thank you, Sydney Morris. You marvelous publicist, you. Many thanks to all the people who worked on this book whose names I can't track down because today is

Saturday and I have to hand in the final version of this book on Monday morning. I don't know you but you did everything to get this novel out in time to meet the deadline. THANK YOU.

Many thanks to my good friend Shveta Thakrar for inspiring me. No author writes direct analogs of the people they know, not if they're smart. (Here be lawyers.) At the same time, it's dead boring to populate novels with clones of yourself. For a start, I don't own a cloning machine. They're expensive, messy, don't provide good cardio workouts, and take up far too much space in the living room. Plus, I'm just not that interesting. That said, Gita borrows a number of qualities from Shveta with permission. Mostly. I promise Gita put all of them back. I swear. She may have even washed them after. (She's like that.)

As a white writer, it is vital to get cultural details correct. White people only writing about white people furthers the harm created by the lack of representation. At the same time, there are boundaries. Some stories are not for white people to tell. That isn't the end, either. Buy and read works written by and about people from groups of which you are not a part. (I promise you, my dudes, the rest of us have done so our whole lives.) If you consider yourself a feminist, support BIPOC writers. Remember, kids, feminism isn't feminism if it isn't inclusive.

That said, many, many thanks to Georgina Kamsika, sensitivity reader extraordinaire. Georgina is a great resource. She's professional, quick to respond, knowledgeable, patient, kind, and fun to work with. She is @GKamsika on Twitter and her website is: http://www.kamsika.com. Even better yet, check out her novel, *Goddess of the North*. You like goddesses, thrillers, and mysteries, don't you? I knew you did.

Sensitivity readers are worth the investment. Trust me.

Here's the part where I say that all the mistakes in this book are mine. Authors are human beings and by definition imperfect. No amount of hard work, careful attention to detail, or hiring of sensitivity readers can change that. Sadly, mistakes are how humans learn best. Worse, mistakes hurt people whether we mean to or not. So, I'm sorry for my mistakes. It's totally okay to not forgive me. Nonetheless, I promise to learn well and not repeat the same errors. I will do better.

Thanks to my writing group for keeping me on task when my ADHD simply wasn't having it: Tempest, Alethea (Ah-lee-thee-ah), Monica, Shveta, and Nivair. Thanks to my second writing group: Nisi, Cynthia, Timmel, James, Paul, Caerdwyn, Meghan, Alex, and the rest of the gang. I appreciate you all.

I'd like to mention Writing the Other classes and workshops (https://writingtheother.com), the Rambo Academy for Wayward Writers (http://www.kittywumpus.net/blog/academy), and SFWA (the Science Fiction Writers Association).

(Okay. Almost there, y'all. Wake up the musicians. They can start playing soon.)

To my Vulcan bestie: Melissa. Thanks for being you.

Above all, thanks for bravely asking to borrow my muse Sgt. Rock. My life probably wouldn't be as awesome and amazing if you hadn't. I certainly wouldn't have consumed as much coffee and pie.

Mmmmmm. Pie.

Thanks to Jeremy Brett, good friend and archivist. You rule. So does my sister, Cathie, for putting up with me my whole damned life. You're a good friend and a fabulous sister. A wave hello to Ye Olde Gaming Group (Dane, Ben, Thad, Dawn, Katy, Christian, and Matt). Thousands of monsters, empires, and evil minions destroyed in [cough] years. And that one snow-topped mountain above that flame-engulfed city that one time. Oh! And the dam. And the flame-engulfed city. And the space port. But hey, the balrog did *eventually* stop following you.

Lastly but not leastly, you, Dearest Reader: thanks for hanging out with me to the not-so-bitter end. Have a lovely rest of your day. Hopefully, that nice warm drink hasn't gotten too cold.